MW01116178

Z-RISEN

BOOKS 1 - 3

TIMOTHY W. LONG

This is the first through third installment in the Z-RISEN zombie thriller series by author Timothy W. Long.

Join Tim's mailing list for news, upcoming releases, deals, and appearances.

TimothyWLong.com

SERIES BY TIMOTHY W. LONG

Z-Risen

Z-Risen 1: Outbreak

Z-Risen 2: Outcasts

Z-Risen 3: Poisoned Earth

Z-Risen 4: Reavers

Z-Risen 5: Barriers

Z-Risen 6: Outsiders

Z-Risen 7: Survivors (Forthcoming)

Z-Risen 8: Fortress (Forthcoming)

Beyond the Barriers (From the Z-Risen Universe)

Day of the Rage Apocalypse (From the Z-Risen Universe)

Bradley Adams

Drums of War

March to War

Casualties of War

Among the Living

Among the Living

Among the Dead

OUTBREAK

Z-RISEN BOOK 1

PREFACE

In the event this log is found with my corpse, I'm Machinist Mate First Class Jackson Creed and it's been a a few weeks since we arrived in San Diego following the event. With me is Marine Sergeant Joel "Cruze" Kelly.

We were both stationed on the USS McClusky, an Oliver Hazard Perry-class frigate out of San Diego. Our ship was overrun by the dead and we barely escaped with our lives.

Now we live in the middle of Undead Central.

BEER RUN

The fuckening has become more bearable even though we almost joined the crawlers today.

Supplies:

- A pound and a half of Jasmine rice
- A half pound of dried beans
- Two pounds of that tofu-jerky shit that gives me gas
- Seven cans of tuna
- Two cans of cat food that I'm saving for Butch in case he returns
- A case of canned spinach that I eat even though every bite makes me want to puke my guts up

I want to go on record as saying that this whole stupid day was Joel's fault.

18:25 hours approximate
Location: San Diego, CA

"Look at all of those crawlers. Everyone wants a piece of us," Joel whispered. "Must be my good looks."

I snorted.

Joel wore tactical gear with a New York Fire Department ball cap pulled down low to keep the sun off his face. Beneath the hat, his face bore a pair of Tom Cruise-style Ray-Bans we'd found in an overturned car a few days ago.

Joel lay prone and stared down the barrel of his Rock River Arms AR-15. He switched on the EOTech holographic sight and shifted his barrel left and right.

We'd found the assault rifle the day after we'd founded Fortress, not far from our area of operations. Some civilian had purchased the piece and stored it for a rainy day, or the end of the world. Yeah, I see the irony. It was so new that it still had the manual and price tag. Even the magazines hadn't been unpacked. The second bonus had been a green canister filled with 400 rounds of 5.56.

Joel was probably sweating his ass off in all that gear. The one thing he managed to escape the ship with was most of an IMTV - Improved Modular Tactical Vest.

"Let's make sure they don't get a piece. I like all my limbs," I whispered. "How many are there?"

"Six, and there's one of those weird shufflers."

I popped up and did a quick scan. Five of them were moving around the freaky creeper. The shuffler was down on all fours like a retarded crab missing a few legs. The other Z's were your garden-variety dead. They moaned and cast milky white gazes on nothing in particular while they shambled.

We were perched behind an abandoned house about a mile from the naval base. Our area of operations had spread out over the last weeks as we ranged farther and farther away from the fortress. It had to be done; our search for food and supplies was getting harder every day.

This had been a residential neighborhood with an elementary school and apartments along a large main road that led to Interstate 5. There a number of houses, but most had already been ransacked. Some sported graffiti and broken windows. Most had furniture and belongings dragged out onto front yards and dumped next to corpses that, thank God, did not move.

We'd learned the hard way not to bother with the houses. Walk in an open door and it could become a deathtrap. Open a bedroom and it could be filled with the fucking Z's. When panic hits and you're in an unfamiliar location, suddenly you don't know which way to exit.

"Your call. I'm good and didn't need a beer run in the first place," I lied.

I needed a beer run bad. I'd kill for a cold one but would settle for a six-pack of warm. But this mission was more than about getting a few brews. If his friend was still alive we might find food and a more secure location to call home.

My gut rumbled, thanks to our light breakfast of dried tofu and some leftover beans and rice. God, what if he had potato chips and Little Debbie Cakes? What if Kelly's friend had boxes of crackers and Cheez Whiz? My mouth flooded with saliva and I feared the creepers would hear my stomach rumble. This wasn't just about beer. We needed anything we could scavenge.

It was getting close to dusk. A bead of sweat formed on my shaved head and ran down my forehead. I wiped it with the ridiculous orange sweatband around my wrist. Joel had been sick of me bitching and dug it out of an overturned bin in a Walmart we'd raided a few days ago. The rest of the store had been a bust. By the time we arrived, it'd been picked over ten times. We also found out the hard way that it was filled with about a hundred snarling Z's. When we got out, I wore the sweatband to remind myself to never enter a big department store again.

"Go distract them. See that dumpster at three o'clock? Just poke your head around it and say hi. I'll pop a couple in the head. When they come toward the sound of my shots, you finish off the rest with your club." He nodded toward my wrench.

I shaded my eyes and studied the battlefield. A green dumpster sat next to a low wall. There was a break right next to it that

would provide me with an easy way to get on the party's "six."
I bet Joel thought it was funny as hell, sending me out with my
ass exposed while he shot from a distance.

"I don't like it."

"Roger that. Let's pack up and go home."

"Well, hold up there a second, Professor," I said. We might
not have a chance to explore this area again. "If we leave now,
your friend's place will be picked over. Might already be
empty."

"I told you. He's a security nut. His front door is solid metal,
plus he'd have left it bolted."

"I still don't know how we're going to get in."

"If he's not there, I have a plan." Joel didn't turn but he had
that cocksure sound in his voice that I no longer questioned.

"What if he is there and tells us to fuck off?"

"He won't. He owes me." I didn't ask about Joel's time in Iraq
because it pissed him off.

After a few seconds of cursing, I hefted my wrench. At
twenty-four inches and eight pounds, this was a devastating
weapon when applied to Z's heads. Joel chambered a round but
didn't look back to make sure I'd left. After a week of this shit,
we were like goddamn mind readers.

"Stupid fucking idea," I said under my breath, and moved
around a dying hedge.

I dropped low and hoped there weren't another dozen
hiding behind us. You could lose them if you moved fast or
stuck to shoot-and-scoot tactics, but try to make a stand and it
was a quick trip to Undeadville.

I rounded the block and cut back toward Joel's position,
sticking to a sidewalk that was already overgrown with grass. I
constantly scanned my surroundings, looking for the slightest
hint of additional Z's.

The red wrench wasn't my only weapon. I also wore one of
the newer Colt M45A1 pistols on my hip that I'd taken from a
corpse back on the base. I had one extra mag and a pocketful of
rounds in case things got real hairy. What concerned me was the
noise a booming gun could draw. I might as well attract a horde

with all six-feet, three-inches of me bouncing up and down while singing the national anthem.

The thirty or so rounds did make me feel better. As long as I kept an extra one in the little coin pocket at my right hip, I felt like I was safe. I'd take as many of them as I could, but that last bullet had my name on it.

Literally.

Sun glistened on my arm to reveal that I was still losing muscle mass. I needed protein, not beer, but I'd settle for a buzz after the last shitty weeks I thought back to the day when our ship, filled with undead sailors, plowed into the pier. Joel and I had been tearing through the passageways, firing into the mass that had previously lived on the USS McClusky.

I ducked again as one of the creepers looked my way. Milky eyes brushed over my position as I hit the ground. Even at a mere twenty feet away, I still marveled at their ability to actually see or hear a damn thing. As the days rolled by and they rotted a little more, they had to slow down and lose some of their senses. At least, that was my logic. It's one of those things you tell yourself over and over. It's not that bad, it's not so crazy out there. Things will get better in a few days, just wait it out. But that didn't happen.

One thing that did grow was their hunger and, as that got stronger, so did their need to eat. Us.

I used to read zombie books and think Z's would be about as scary as drunken senior citizens. These weren't. They had started mad and gotten madder. The shufflers were the worst. When they changed, so did their disposition. Not content to wander around mindlessly, they were driven by a need to rise and attack, and they'd go psychotic whenever they spotted the living.

The slow ones weren't so bad, but get twenty or thirty of those relentless fucking monsters on your case, and they'd run you right into the ground.

I scanned my entry point and crouched again, then brushed past another dying hedge. I rounded the corner near the dumpster and the pack came into view.

I slid next to the giant green monstrosity and plugged my nose with my fingertips. Foul, very foul. I stood and waved a hand in the air, hoping to hell Joel wasn't currently getting swarmed. Then I stopped. What use was it? He wasn't about to announce his hiding place.

"You ugly godless fucks come here often?" I lowered the wrench, letting all 8.4 pounds of the weapon become an extension of my arm.

The creeper that had fixed his milky gaze on me earlier turned his head on his creaking neck and drew back desiccated lips over rotted teeth. The others swiveled to take me in. A chill raced over my body at the thought of one of those assholes sinking their teeth into me.

One shot and the creeper's head popped to the side, followed by his body. Brain matter splattered and blood sprayed. Two Z's moved toward the noise, leaving three for me. Terrific.

"Hey assholes," called Joel.

I risked a glance at my watch. The action had already occupied five seconds of the thirty we allotted any battle. If we couldn't wrap things up in that time frame, we'd bug out.

I swung the wrench up and took the nearest right under the chin. I hit him so hard I thought his head was going to come off. Poor kid. Couldn't have been more than fifteen when he turned. Dressed in shorts and a gaudy t-shirt, he wore only one knee pad. He did have pads on both elbows, though. Probably some skate punk that was now a dead punk.

The second Z closed in. I gave ground, lifted my size fourteen US Navy-issued boot, and kicked him in the groin. That didn't put him down but it bought me a moment. As far as I knew, they didn't have functioning nads, but a swift kick could still put them in their place.

Another pair of shots, but I had things to worry about other than Joel's body-count.

I didn't have time to beat these things to death, so I drew the M45 with my left hand, aimed just as I'd practiced a hundred times over the last couple of weeks, and shot one through the neck. It sounds cool but I was actually aiming for its forehead. I'd lowered the gun just a fraction at the last second.

The Z fell away, gurgling blood from its neck. I aimed and fired at the shuffler but it was already on the move. It'd been caressing the ground on all fours, doing that shuffle step that freaks me the fuck out. The man had long wisps of hair hanging from his scalp and, somehow, a pair of glasses perched on the remains of his face. His mouth was full of blood, drool, and something that looked a lot like human flesh.

I fired again. The bullet punched through his gut just before he smashed into me.

I hit the dumpster hard enough to knock my breath out and staggered to the side. He fell away but was on his feet in a flash. His eyes had the same milky white look but they somehow fixed on me. He howled a wordless scream of fury and launched himself. I swung the pipe but there wasn't a lot of strength behind it. The glancing blow barely kept him from biting my arm.

I staggered back again and bullets whizzed through the air, taking the creepers out with extreme prejudice.

I fired again, but the shot went wide because I'd panicked. The shuffler didn't cower, it didn't hide, and it didn't turn and run. It was completely unreasonable—and its only desire was to rip into my flesh.

I gave ground, fighting for breath, and when he attacked again, I punched him. I didn't get a lot behind the strike but it was enough to knock the Z down. I lifted the gun, took a half breath, and blew his fucking brains all over the pavement.

Joel moved in on my position, Ray-Bans looking everywhere as he ran. He had the assault rifle across his chest, finger on the trigger guard. We didn't stop to admire our handiwork. Instead, we moved out at a fast clip because we were well over our thirty seconds and that was bad news. Another half minute and we'd be overrun.

18:45 hours approximate
Location: San Diego, CA

WE EXITED THE BLOCK AND RAN INTO THE PARKING LOT OF AN apartment complex. Joel and I had dodged behind cars and concrete dividers at every opportunity. Our sprint had carried us nearly a hundred and fifty yards away from the dumpster and I, for one, had begun to feel it.

I panted, hunched next to a car; Joel did the same. He swept his ball cap off his black head and wiped sweat from his brow with his sleeve. San Diego might be a comfortable seventy degrees but running for your life has a tendency to make you sweat like a pig.

I pointed at my orange wristband and he gave me the finger. While we took a breather, I ejected the magazine from the M45 and filled the five rounds I'd emptied into Z's. Joel took a moment to do the same with his AR. We waited and looked toward the area we'd just left, only to find that luck was on our side and we'd avoided a larger confrontation.

I eyed car interiors while Joel stayed on point. I actually found an old beat-up Ford that hadn't been broken into and pressed the end of the wrench against the closed window. I looked around quickly, then pulled back and hit it just hard enough to break glass. It imploded with a soft pop and tinkle. I opened the door and felt around under the seat and came up with a small paper bag. The glove box had some mints and papers. I slid the items over my shoulder and into my Swiss Army backpack as I moved out.

"What's in the bag?" Joel whispered.

"Not sure. It's not very heavy; check it when we're clear?"

"Sounds good." He moved out in a semi-crouch, rifle stock pressed to his cheek.

We advanced on the apartment complex and came to a cross-street that had been a battlefield. Police cars overturned next to military vehicles. Blood splatters everywhere. Broken bodies, both civilian and military, lay on the pavement or over car hoods. Some hung out of broken windows, faces torn away or necks gnawed to the bone.

"Fuck me," Joel said, and moved to a body. We did a quick check but only came up with a few stray rounds. Someone had stripped this place clean.

Joel eyed a map and then we were on the move again. A few minutes later, we had the condo in sight.

No Z's in the immediate vicinity. Luck was on our side, for a change.

We dashed across what was once a very expensive plot of grass but was now a dry and yellowed bed of tinder. If a stray spark caught, this whole block would go up in flames.

We reached the stairway without challenge. At the top of the second flight, Joel advanced down a hallway on the outside of the building while I followed. Doors had already been ripped open and goods tossed on the balcony. Joel didn't bother with the residences and kept moving with me right behind.

"This is it," Joel said.

We'd reached something different, a solid door with no marks around the door jamb. Someone had tossed a car jack to the ground in frustration.

Joel knocked gently.

"Ty. You there, Ty? It's Joel Kelly from the base. Come on buddy, at least let me know you're on the other side of that door."

He knocked a few more times then shook his head in frustration.

"What's the plan?"

"Watch my back."

Joel glanced left and right, dropped the backpack, and went to one knee. He rummaged around in the bag until he came up with a MacGyver-looking complement of tools and wires. He'd split a large coffee can in half and lined the concave surface with grey packs of something that looked dangerous. He yanked out a double wrapped freezer bag of water and added it to the package.

"The fuck?" I whispered.

Joel shook his head and held the can up against the door. He broke out duct tape and applied a few strips until the device was held in place. He stood back and tugged a wire out of the side of the can, then looked around again.

"Shit."

"What?"

"Be right back."

He dashed to the condo next to us and came out twenty seconds later dragging a mattress. I moved to help but he pointed at his eyes then forked his fingers, indicating that I needed to stay sharp.

Joel tugged the mattress over and draped it against the door. He pulled the wire out of the can while shielding himself with the mattress, then ran it down the hallway, gesturing for me to follow. We crouched around the corner while he plugged the wire into a detonator.

"Holy fuck balls," I whispered. "Don't. It'll wake up the whole city."

"In and out, buddy. In and out." Joel smiled, then held the device up.

"Dude. How many will that bring?" But it was too late. He already had his finger on the trigger.

I covered my ears; he tried to do the same by using one hand and an elbow. Even with the mattress in place, the explosion was immense. The building shook and dust and debris showered the floor. Joel was level-headed and didn't rattle easily, but when it came to fuck ups, this was a big one.

I looked at my watch and marked the time. Thirty seconds were going to come to an end very quickly. In fact, I doubted we even had fifteen seconds. Shaking my head, I followed him into his friend's condo.

I waved smoke out of my face as we entered. Joel had his assault rifle at the ready, so I followed suit and pulled out my M45.

The door had been blown off its hinges. Joel walked over it in a half-crouch. He had the AR level with his shoulder and aimed into the smoky interior. I followed closely but kept my eyes on the entrance. Just as I cleared the entryway I got a look over the railing.

I gasped and reached for Joel to get his attention but he wasn't there.

Out on the brown grass, the dead were gathering. Not a few, not even a dozen. It seemed like they were coming out of their undead comas from every corner of the city.

I swore and walked into the haze left by the explosion.

The entryway was a mess. The door had been blown into the small space and smashed whatever furniture had been there. The smell of smoke and explosives burned my nose. There was a mirror on one wall but it had been shattered, and when I looked into it, I saw my face splintered into five pieces.

"Ty, don't shoot us, man!" Joel called. "It's me, Joel. I told you I'd come."

Hey Ty, we just broke into your house but it's cool because you and Joel go way back, so don't, you know, blow us away. If someone broke into my castle I'd be pissed whether I knew them or not, and would probably shoot them out of pure spite.

"Joel!" I whispered as loud as I dared. "A shitload of dead are on the way. We don't have thirty seconds."

Joel came back into the hallway and gestured. I followed him into the living room and found it filled with tech gadgets. A huge flat-screen TV sat dead on the wall, surrounded by speakers and stereo equipment. There were cables and wires everywhere, some attached to a huge car battery. Whatever the occupant had been trying to do had gone to the grave with him.

In front of a gorgeous tan leather couch lay an unmoving figure. He was a black guy in his twenties, as far as I could tell. He couldn't have been dead all that long because his face wasn't a rotted mess. He had a series of bite marks on his arm, the same arm that held a handgun which had been applied to his forehead before a bullet had torn his brains out of the other side of his head.

"Goddamn," I said.

Joel dropped to one knee and said a prayer. He took the handgun from his dead friend's grip, hit the safety, and slipped it into the band of one of his tactical vest's many straps. He touched his friend's eyes below the bullet hole and tried to close them, but they were frozen open.

"I wish you would have held out, buddy."

I pointed out the bite marks. Joel stood up and moved away.

Joel and I advanced on the kitchen like the starving heroes we were. I raided the fridge and found Nirvana. A couple of six-packs of cheap PBR. An unopened package of store-bought pepperoni. No power, but that was okay. The fridge wasn't that hot and pepperoni could sit for days. Joel and I devoured a half-pound of the thin slices like it was fucking filet mignon.

"We. Need. To. Go!" I said as I swallowed.

He tore open cabinets while I inspected the pantry. Ty had left a lot of goods. There were boxes and bags of pasta, jars of sauces, and canned fruits and vegetables. I practically fainted at the bounty. The problem was that we couldn't carry all of it. I had my backpack and Joel had his, but if we weighed ourselves down, we'd be moving targets.

I grabbed the pasta and a few cans of fruit and jammed them into my backpack. I added one precious jar of spaghetti sauce and then tested the weight. I added a few cans of veggies, saw spinach and avoided it like the plague.

Joel moved beside me and packed his backpack as well. We'd been inside for a few minutes, and with every beat of my palpitating heart, I knew the dead fucks were getting closer.

"You pack the heavy stuff," he said, and handed me his backpack. "We're going out there and you're not letting go of my shoulder. We move as one until we're free of the mess."

"Why do I have to be the fucking pack mule?"

"Because you're built like one and I need to shoot shit."

He made all kinds of sense but I didn't have to be happy about it. Before we headed out, I grabbed a six-pack, jammed it into my backpack and tried to close the bag, but the beer stuck out of the top.

"Drop your wrench and use your Colt. It's going to get hairy."

"The fuck you say. I ain't leaving my weapon."

Joel wanted to argue - he gets like that - but we didn't have time. I jammed the tool into my belt and fought to keep my overalls straight as it tugged them down toward my knees. I shrugged and pointed at the door.

19:05 hours approximate
Location: San Diego, CA

WE HIT THE LANDING AND TORE TO THE RIGHT. I GRIPPED JOEL'S shoulder while he moved (once again) in a crouch. I drew my M45 and switched it to my dominant right hand. On the grass, an army of the dead had congregated. Joel leaned over the railing, aimed...and fired at a car of all things. What the hell? He'd picked a high-end BMW; when the bullets punched into the hood, they set off an alarm.

"Jesus fucking Christ!" I cried.

The dead turned toward the sound and I realized Joel was smarter than he looked. Give a Marine a gun and they suddenly turn into a fucking brain surgeon.

"Let's go."

We rounded the corner we'd hidden behind when Joel had blown the door off. I wished we could have stayed, but this place was going to be swarmed. Once the dead moved on, scavengers would surely pick the place over before we could make another trip. Dammit! The condo had been a treasure trove of goods.

We moved to the other side of the building and took the stairs. I'd been sweating before, but now the last few minutes of activity hit me. I was carrying about forty pounds on my back and we were rushing down hallways and stairs.

Luck was still on our side when we hit the ground level – it wasn't swarming with Z's. The car alarm continued to howl behind us, but that just drew away any that were on the other side of the building.

A small pack wandered away at nine o'clock. Joel motioned

to stop and stay still. The pack didn't see us, so we moved toward the street. Making our way north, we skirted the block that hosted the swarm and kept on jogging. The pack beat at my back with each step and I had no doubt the wrench would leave bruises.

We came to a house and stopped for a breath. As I stood there gasping, Joel, with no respect for my lack of stamina, moved on. We rounded a corner, found a trampoline, a pool, and four Z's. I broke right and fired as soon as I had a bead. Joel followed suit and pumped two rounds into the lead crawler's head. The old man fell down but another, even older guy in a tropical-print shirt stumbled over him. Joel put that one down, as well, while I took out their wives. It must have been the world's worst pool party even before the shit had hit the fan. One of the women had to be in her sixties and was dressed in a one-piece swimsuit. I shot her out of pity.

We had to skirt a tall chain-link fence before the area started to look familiar.

Joel and I moved at a fast pace, again taking out stragglers as quickly as we could. A few more minutes of hiding behind houses, ducking behind cars, and then Fortress came into view.

The house we occupied was set behind a few tall trees. We'd boarded up everything on the first floor and had left no easy way to the second. We had a ladder, but it was buried under a pile of old leaves and branches, and when we were inside, we just pulled the ladder up. Even if Z's surrounded us, we'd be able to wait them out.

I still worried about determined human scavengers.

Joel moved out on point and I was left behind a hedge to catch my breath. I wiped sweat off my head again and studied the area. No zombies stumbling around made me smile. It had been a bitch of a mission but at least we'd made it with food and a six-pack of beer intact.

Then my day went downhill.

The first crawler broke free from a cluster of dying hedges and was followed by six or seven other equally ugly, rotting souls. White eyes swiveled to find me, and like an army, they advanced.

"Oh fuck-knuckle!" I swore, falling back and drawing my M45A1 as I went. I drew a bead, fired, and missed the head zombie—a guy dressed in a sanitation outfit. It was on me before I could scream for help and, just like that, I was fighting for my life.

I slammed it to the side, my forearm working like a hammer, but it just kept on coming. A shot rang out and I swore again. One thing we tried to avoid at all cost was the sound of gunfire near our home base. We'd already broken that rule twice in the last fifteen seconds.

Another shot and one of the Z's dropped. I punched my attacker again. His head cocked to the side, but then he snarled and I got a look at broken teeth. There wasn't time to make a smart-ass quip. I tried to avoid a bite but screamed in horror as his mouth closed on my arm.

Thank god for my jumpsuit. It was hot as hell but the zombie's mouth closed on fabric, and when he tore, he got a piece of that instead of my skin. I pushed him away, raised my Colt .45 and blew off the back of his head.

A shuffler took notice and was in the air before I could take aim. I emptied the magazine but didn't have a chance to reach for a fresh one because the shuffler came in with flailing arms and a screaming mouth. I kicked his legs out from under him and shrugged out of my backpacks so I could maneuver. When the shuffler hit the ground, I ducked away from his wild grasping, got behind him, and kicked him in the ass.

He went down but was back on his feet in a heartbeat.

I reached down and grabbed my wrench. When he leapt at me again, his mouth a snarling howl of hate, I swung the wrench around and caught his jaw, ripping it loose.

But that was the problem with shufflers. They were so psychotic that even a massive amount of damage couldn't put them down. Headshot or enough damage to squish the brain had to be applied.

Joel's AR jammed. He dropped it and drew the pistol his

friend had used to kill himself, then moved on the last couple of Z's. He put one down and fired a few more times until the gun was dry.

The shuffler, minus a jaw and part of his face, was on me again. I stepped on the body of the sanitation worker I'd shot and went down on my ass. The shuffler, arms still flailing, hit me hard enough to knock the breath out of my body for the second time.

I got a foot up and caught him in the chest as he bent down for me. Joel barreled into the shuffler, allowing me to roll to the side. I came up slowly because my body was all beat to hell. Another Z was on Joel, so he drew his Ontario 498 combat knife and slashed the creature across the gut, spilling intestines in a wet pile of gore. He reversed his grip and drove the blade into the dead woman's head.

He faded back as the shuffler looked between us.

He must have made up his mind because he went for Joel, the remnants of his mouth producing gurgles in place of a howl of fury.

I grabbed the wrench and closed in on the shuffler. Joel saw me coming and pushed the psychotic Z back. I hefted my weapon and let him have it, crushing his skull like it was a soft egg. The corpse dropped to the ground; Joel nodded at me and then the wrench with a half grin.

We dragged the corpses away from Fortress, retrieved the ladder, and scurried up as soon as we were sure no one was watching. Inside, we unpacked our treasure. I was not a happy camper to learn that a couple of our beer cans had exploded in one of my falls. At least we survived another expedition and came back with food and a new weapon.

"Sorry about your friend," I said.

Joel nodded. "Thanks, man. We saw some action in Iraq. He always had my back and I had his. Like you and me."

"Are you going to look that sad when it's my turn to bite it?"

"Depends on if I have to put you down myself, motherfucker." He grinned.

I grinned back and we toasted the day with warm PBRs.

"Oh yeah, what was in the paper bag?"

I dug out the bag I'd pulled from under the front seat of the old Ford pickup and looked inside.

"Shit yeah," I said, and pulled out an ounce of weed with a California medical dispensary logo on the bag.

"Stay sharp and don't smoke that shit. You white boys get all sad-eyed when you're high."

"Only on special occasions. Besides, I bet we can trade it if we run into other survivors."

"Good call. I'm gonna go use a few baby wipes to take a bath." Joel rose to his feet and headed toward his room. "Good work out there, Creed. And thanks for saving my ass."

Joel nodded again and left.

I sat back and drained my beer, then eyed the weed. Special occasion, eh? How about still being alive.

THE BOAT

Nothing to do except hang out and try not to kill each other. We're flush with supplies for a day or two but no reason to start stroking each other's egos after yesterday's mess. Frankly, I'm surprised we're still alive. And with all of these supplies I'm really missing Tylenol. My body feels like I worked out until I puked.

So the day we boarded up the place, Joel had the bright idea to fill the tubs with water. We drank until our eyeballs were floating and then we drank some more. Joel kept telling me what it would be like in a week when the water stopped running and he was right. Now the water tastes foul and I'm worried about mosquitoes. I run a vegetable strainer over the surface every few hours. Tomorrow I'll use cheesecloth but that won't kill parasites. So do we burn through the few remaining Sterno cans boiling water or just put up with a bad case of the shits?

Joel said we can treat the water with a little bleach but I'll be damned if I can find a bottle in the house. I guess we'll have to find some on our next run.

Supplies:

- 1 pound of Jasmine rice
- ¼ pound of dried beans

- 1 ½ pounds of tofu-jerky
- 7 cans of tuna
- 2 cans of cat food - where the hell is Butch?
- 6 boxes of pasta
- 1 beautiful jar of spaghetti sauce
- 5 cans of various veggies
- 2 cans of mixed
- 1 case of canned spinach

"WHEN YOU GONNA TALK ABOUT HOW WE MET?" JOEL POINTED AT my logbook. I had the pen ready to start recounting our day – and that was going to be boring.

Day X: Sat on ass. Stared at empty beer bottles. Pissed in a bucket.

"Like the day you bought me flowers and a drink?" I looked across the Sterno flame and batted my eyelashes at Joel. "Fucking Marines. Always trying to get into a lady's panties."

We had a can of water boiling up some rice so we could put it aside and let the grain set. It was the quickest way to accomplish two tasks. Boil water and have a little food in an hour. I'd probably toss in some tofu jerky just to add to the blandness.

Fortress was hot. It might be October out there, but this house hadn't had a breath of fresh air in days. No fans, no central air. That meant we sat in a room and fanned ourselves with a collection of Playboys I'd found stashed under a kid's bed.

"Yours were pretty fucking frigid," Joel chuckled, "and it took a whole bottle, but just like a Navy puke, you put out on the first date."

I stifled laughter.

"Too bad you couldn't get it up. You know they make little blue pills for that?"

Joel had his assault rifle stripped and was quizzing me on parts while rubbing them down with motor oil. His towel had been white a few days ago. Now it looked as grimy as gopher guts.

"Marines are giant blue pills. Just being in the Corps gets me hard," he said. "That's what my old Drill Sergeant used to say just before he quarter-decked the shit out of us."

"Drill Sergeants are like that. Dicks."

"He was just doin' his job. Gunny made me the man I am today."

"Hooah!" I said.

"They only say that in movies," Joel retorted.

"Imagine I'm Brad Pitt when I say it."

Joel held out a long piece of metal that looked like a tube. "What's this called?"

"The bolt thing."

He sighed and tossed it to me. "It's not called 'the bolt thing,' it's called a bolt carrier assembly and even Brad Pitt would know, because I bet he pays more attention than you whether he's stripping a gun or that hot wife of his. Now take this part." Joel gave me the charging handle, something I actually remembered the name of. I took the pieces and slid the handle into the bolt carrier assembly, locking it in place before giving it back.

"There."

"You ain't as useless as I thought."

"Guess not."

"Too fucking hot for this. Go write about the ship," Joel grumbled.

I'd avoided writing that chapter for a lot of reasons, but after the last few days of scrambling for survival I knew it was time to get it out of my system. If I waited much longer I was going to start forgetting important facts.

"Not yet. Man, I really want to say it."

"Don't. We made it and I don't need thanks. We wouldn't be here if we weren't a team, even if you are a stupid fucking hole snipe."

"Words hurt, Joel. Words hurt." I leaned over my friend. Even seated I towered over him, but he didn't back down.

"Why all that writing anyway? Never heard of a hole snipe fond of jotting things down besides readings."

"I always wanted to be a writer. Sue me."

"What-the-fuck-ever. Just do it. Write about the boat; we ain't getting any younger and we might be dead and eaten tomorrow."

"Ship, it's called a ship. A boat has oars - and what a morbid fuck you are today!"

"Like I said. What-the-fuck-ever. Just write it."

So I did.

05:45 hours approximate
Location: USS McClusky, San Diego CA

I HAD THE WORST FUCKING HANGOVER OF MY LIFE THE DAY THE world went to shit. I lay in my bunk, hand over my eyes, and dreaded going on watch. My head pounded and my mouth felt like someone shit in it. We ain't supposed to drink at sea but I'm a classic Navy alcoholic and I keep a stash of booze you wouldn't believe. Last night I dumped a third of a 2-liter Pepsi down the drain and topped it off with some Thai whiskey I picked up in Pattaya Beach.

That was only two hours ago. I barely got enough sleep as it was. Emergency flight ops had blown me out of my bunk, and that shit went on until dawn.

There were rumors that something big was happening back at base, and that's why we were recalled. Then flight ops had started and never ended. Helos arrived and departed every fifteen minutes – that should have been my first clue that something was really wrong.

I had about fifteen minutes to shit, shower, and shave. Smitty got to be an angry little bitch when I was late even though he'd never been on time for watch a day in his life.

Then the alarm sounded and I thought my head was literally going to explode.

"General quarters, general quarters, all hands man your battlesta..."

The first line wasn't even finished, unless you counted the screaming. I sprang up and jumped out of my top bunk. Why a top bunk after this many years in the Navy? Because I fucking like it, that's why.

I stared up at the speakers and wondered whose idea of a joke that had been.

"The fuck was that shit?" Feely asked.

He wore a pair of South Park boxers and socks that smelled like death. Feely had a weird OCD thing with socks and only changed them once a week. One time I bought him a bag of socks at the ship commissary and left them on his bunk. Gratis. He tossed them in the trash.

I dug out a pair of dark blue overalls and gave them the sniff test. Yeah, they'd get me through one more day. They weren't as bad as Feely's socks. Those fuckers were probably going to get up and walk around on their own.

Wanglund fell out of his bunk and looked ready to punch anyone that got in his way. His mustache was turning into a biker's handlebar, but with shore in sight today he'd be shaving it. CHENG might put up with that shit on deployment but not when we were headed for port. The thing about Wanglund was that he was bigger than me and I'm a big dude. He was a boiler tech and looked like a gorilla, with hairy arms and enough fur on his back to let him fill in for the next Planet of the Apes movie.

Wanglund also owed me a hundred bucks from our last game of spades. I'd mention it later when it wasn't so early in the morning and he didn't look like punching someone.

I TRUDGED TOWARD THE ENGINE ROOM, ALREADY DREADING THE heat and noise. The ship hummed around me. That's the kind of environment you live in when you are stationed on a Naval vessel. It's never quiet, not ever. From the grind of machinery to the sound of forced air in nearly every compartment, all you get is noise. Then there are the smells: the oil, the fuel, the cleaning chemicals. It's an assault when you first board ship, but then you get back on land and suddenly you forget how to walk straight because the ground is no longer rocking and rolling under your feet.

I moved along the same bulkheads I'd passed every day for the last twelve months. Boring, white, yellow emergency lights in every corner. I didn't see any other crewmen and that was weird. Maybe everyone was up early for mess. Was there an inspection I'd forgotten about?

Earplugs inserted, I descended a pair of ladders and stopped for a cup of shitty coffee before heading to main control. The whine of the turbines would be deafening without earplugs. As it was, the tone was slightly less annoying that having a tooth drilled. The engine was insulated and taller than a greyhound bus. I glanced at a couple of dials. Everything nominal.

The Chief Engineer was sitting at the console while newly-minted Chief Harmikle stood watch over the room. I was surprised he didn't have his nose up CHENG's ass. I tossed him a quick salute but he didn't bother responding. Petty Officer Mahan had the helm. He was spinning the giant steam valve to slow the ship. It looked like we'd just come down from Flank 1.

"How long we been at Flank?" I asked him.

"Too long if you ask me. Some crazy stuff is going on back home, man. You're my relief, right?"

"Nah, I got Smitty."

"Damn, he's ill too. They took him to sick bay an hour ago."

"What happened?"

"No clue, man. I've been stuck here all damn night."

"Say again?" CHENG barked into the phone. Then he banged it on the desk a few times. "Say again! Don't make me come the fuck up there!"

"S'going on?" I asked Chief Harmikle.

"Some fucking bullshit on the bridge. Sent Keen up to take a look."

"Does he even know where the bridge is, Sir?" Keen was so new he hadn't washed the creases out of his BDU's.

"Doubt it." The Chief Engineer said, hanging up the phone and hitting me with that "officer look" that's supposed to intimidate. I towered over him by a good seven inches and had arms the size of his neck, but somehow he always made me feel like he could take me in a fight. Maybe because he never wilted or looked away from one of my "pissed off" looks that sent other guys scurrying.

"You go look for Keen, Creed," he ordered.

I almost smiled. Just a few minutes on watch and I was already on my first errand. Looked like some coffee in mess would be my first stop.

"And Creed, don't get lost up there."

I nodded, took my pounding head out of main, and started back the way I'd come. Well, fuck me six ways from Sunday. This watch was off to a shitty start, but at least I was out of the hot engine room.

I headed starboard hoping I'd run into Keen's skinny ass. Instead, I ran into a riot.

Something was happening, something big. The passageways on a ship are already small and when a bunch of screaming guys are occupying the one ahead of you it's not like you can find a way around. I'd have to walk back until I could cut across the center of the ship.

I assessed my options. Walk all the way back on a mission to find Keen? Nah. I decided I'd rather get into some trouble. My last Captain's Mast was six months ago.

Fuck it. I was due.

I passed berths and came to a cross-section filled with a riotous crowd. I hung back but didn't see any engineers to rescue and couldn't figure out who to hit first. Getting into a fight wasn't the best cure for a hangover but I'd settle for it today.

I didn't personally know most of these guys but they were still familiar. You spend a few months at sea with a hundred and seventy-five or so guys and pretty soon you know a lot of names. They looked like electricians with their pressed shirts.

"Can someone let me through before I start breaking stuff?" I bellowed.

That got attention, but the wrong kind. A Lieutenant with fresh bars turned on me and looked at my stenciled name.

"Creed. Get some security here, now. And don't yell on my ship again. Got it, Sailor?"

"Yes Sir," I muttered, wanting to punch his fucking lights out. Then I saw blood on his hands.

"Sir?"

"It's...I don't know. One of the radio techs bit one of my men and then both of them went nuts. Go wake up the Marines."

That was all I needed. Crazy-ass nerds biting each other? That wasn't my problem. I was going to continue my search for Keen but then remembered that the LT knew my name. He also knew my size and it'd take about three seconds to find me.

I knew where the Marines bunked but never ventured down there. Why should I? They never came to my side of the ship.

I huffed it down their ladder and found myself in near-darkness. It was still the middle of the damn night, so that made sense, but a couple of black guys in tank tops were throwing cards at a table. One of the men jumped up on his chair and threw the little Joker.

"Suck it!" He yelled.

I cleared my throat. "Sorry to interrupt, fellas, but some LT sent me. Some guys are biting each other and the LT wants security."

"See my shirt?" asked little Joker. "Do you see 'babysitter' stenciled on it?"

I looked. I squinted. I peered.

"Huh. Nope. Umm...what's your name, man? I need to know for the LT; you know how it is."

"GENERAL QUARTERS, GENERAL QUARTERS, ALL HANDS MAN YOUR BATTLE STATIONS. THIS IS NOT A DRILL. GENERAL QUARTERS..." The voice trailed off this time without screams, but screams or not I was really starting to get a very bad feeling about today.

"Thought it was a joke before." The Marine nodded toward the speaker in the ceiling.

"That sounded legit," one of the other guys said.

They looked at each other and then back toward their bunks.

Then I heard a sound I'd never heard on a ship before. Gunfire.

The Marines went into some turbo mode, moving around each other like they had a secret language. Before I could scratch my balls more than once, the black guy that had given me a ration of shit was back and half-dressed. He buttoned up a shirt and stared at me like I was a stranger. His stenciled name read 'Kelly.' He wore an oversized vest of some sort and slapped it over his body, securing straps and Velcro here and there as he patted down pouches and pockets.

"Weapons locker!" One of the other Marines yelled and suddenly there were guns everywhere. Kelly strapped a belt around his waist with a holster and pistol. My fists were the only weapon I'd ever been even halfway shitty with.

"Secure yourself, Sailor! Stay or go - just keep out of our way."

"Fine man, whatever. Just don't shoot anyone by mistake. Especially me." I rattled off the coordinates I'd marked in my head when I'd left the LT. As soon as the men were assembled, Kelly nodded. He pulled his sidearm and racked the bolt back, did an inspection, and let it slam home. He slid it back into his holster and then was up the stairs as fast as Spiderman.

I followed them and hit the passageway while they moved out. I wasn't more than a few steps from the ladder when a guy screamed and bore down on me. I knew his name but not much else. Bauman was a skinny little guy that wore his pants too high on his hips. He was covered in blood from a wound on his skull. The blood streamed down his head and into another wound on his face. Christ! Most of his cheek was ripped away! He howled, creating a weird hissing sound.

"The fuck?"

"Move!" one of the Marines ordered.

I ignored him and stood my ground. Come on Bauman, if you got the guts.

In a heartbeat, the bloodied, howling sailor was on me. I lashed my arm out and punched him square in the middle of the face. His nose erupted around my knuckles and he went down like a bag of potatoes.

My hand hurt like a bitch but I wore my poker face for the Marines. See? I can be a badass too.

"Dude!" One of the Marines brushed past me and leaned over to check on the sailor I'd decked. I wiped blood on my pants.

"Hey man, he attacked me," I said.

Skinny Bauman should have been out for the day after the punch I'd landed, but his eyes snapped open as he howled and leapt up, landing on his knees with a crack of bone.

He spun and attacked the Marine. The sailor bit in and yanked flesh from the other man's arm until blood flowed. The guy screamed in pain, pulled his gun, and hit Bauman hard enough to knock out teeth.

"What the shit!" I backed up in horror.

Kelly moved to my side and watched with his mouth wide open as the Marine dropped to the ground and thrashed his body up and down. It looked like he was having an epileptic fit. My Aunt used to get those and they were not pretty. The downed Marine screamed, but then something quickly changed as his wails of pain became those of rage.

Bauman should have been completely knocked the fuck out - or even dead - but he staggered to his feet and raised his hands, which were twisted and splayed like tight little claws. He howled again, that awful hissing sound now bubbling with blood, and then he was on us.

Me and Kelly beat the shit out of the guy, but every time he went down he just got back on his feet and came at us. Then Kelly's marine buddy went bat shit insane.

What the fucking hell!

First he was staring at his arm in horror. Then he was trying to stop the flow of blood with his hand. Next he gasped and flopped over on his back. He thrashed and held his arm as more and more blood squirted. It spread over his shirt and pressed pants. You could have split a grapefruit on those seams a few minutes ago, but now they just soaked up the crimson.

"Angel, man, Angel!" Kelly yelled.

Behind me, a riot had broken out.

Two of the Marines had advanced down the hallway to confront a new foe. Only this wasn't an argument. The same shit that was going on here was happening over there. Blood flowed, and lots of it. I had the stupid thought that it was going to take hours for someone to clean it all up. Screams, howls, some in pain, some in anger. Fists on skin, striking and ripping. It was worse than a riot. It was worse than any concert mosh pit I'd ever seen.

"Okay, fuck this," I said to no one in particular. I'd had enough. If anyone needed me, I'd be in main control with my people, safely locked up behind a properly dogged hatch.

Kelly took out a radio and barked orders into it. He listened to a muffled voice and then stared at the device in confusion. I paused to see if he had news.

"Say again?"

"Don't let anyone bite you. You got me, Marine? If that happens, you are dead, and then you aren't any use to anyone."

Kelly looked at me. I shook my head because it sounded crazy.

Then Angel gasped, foamed at the mouth and flopped around three or four times before his body went completely still. Kelly stared in horror as his friend died. I tried to look away from the riot that was occurring down the passageway, because it felt less real than what was happening right in front of me.

"Sir, Corporal Angel is down, Sir. He...he got bit. What do I do?"

"Shoot him in the fucking head. He isn't your buddy anymore. If you don't have a gun, then find something to bash his skull."

"Sir?"

"That's an order, Marine. You do it or I'll come down there and personally rip your head off and shit down your neck!" Kelly stared at the radio in horror. "We need to contain this before it goes any farther."

Kelly drew his sidearm and aimed it at his friend.

"Oh fuck this," I said and backed away. A riot behind or an execution ahead.

"I can't do it." Kelly put his sidearm away. The mob that had been behind us shifted momentum and was now coming toward us. One of Kelly's Marine buddies was being chased.

"Go!" the Marine yelled, then turned and opened fire. The explosions were deafening as he fired into the chaotic mass of people. Sailors and another Marine fell, but the mob kept coming. The narrow passageway created a natural bottleneck.

We fell back, Kelly pushing me while he swept his gun back and forth.

Angel picked that moment to groan and sit up. He bubbled up a putrid load of blood, his lips pulled back from his teeth in a rictus grin of pure horror. He snarled and struggled to his feet. I knocked him down but he reached for my leg and tried to bite me. Bite me! Son of a bitch! I kicked him but pulled the blow at the last second, fearing the Marines wouldn't take too kindly to me stomping one of their own.

A snarling group came at us from the port side of the ship. They bumped into each other as they tried to maneuver the small passageway. When they got a look at us a pair moaned. Moaned! One of them howled and staggered toward me with arms raised, his hands like claws.

"Up, we need to go up!" I yelled.

Kelly looked at his friend and then back at the other Marine who had been firing. He couldn't even speak. He just shot while backing up along the passageway.

Kelly pointed his gun at Angel as the unfortunate Marine crawled toward us. Kelly aimed, but he couldn't do it. I wished I had the guts.

As our window of opportunity to escape narrowed to tens of feet, I decided that I wasn't going out screaming. I knocked Angel back to the ground and reached for his sidearm, fighting with a damn snap that secured it. Blood and drool bubbled out of Angel's mouth. Every hair on my body came to attention as he let loose with a keening noise that grew into a sound from nightmares.

"GENERAL QUARTERS GENERAL QUARTERS. THIS IS CAPTAIN MCGLASSON AND THIS IS NOT A DRILL. ABANDON SHIP. ABANDON SHIP!"

Someone howled in horror over the PA system. It might have been the captain, or maybe one of the yeomen. Either way, I was done with this shit.

"That's enough for me," I said and pointed the gun down the passageway, waving it around like I knew the first thing about weapons. Sure, I'd sunk hundreds of hours into Call of Duty but that didn't mean I knew the first damn thing about real guns.

I pulled the trigger and nothing happened.

"Come on, squid!" Kelly said and grabbed my arm. He pulled at the gun but I slapped his hand away. He looked pissed, but he'd have to put that shit on hold or we were going to get into a scuffle just before we were devoured.

"I can't leave a man behind!" the other Marine resolutely exclaimed. His name tag was covered in blood.

"Does he look like Angel? Look, man!" Kelly yelled.

Enough of this. I dove for the first ladder leading up and ran right into another mass of crazies. I aimed again, then realized there was something I'd forgotten to do and looked at the side of the gun. Sure enough, there was a safety. I flipped it, aimed again, and fired.

One of the sailors folded over as my bullet punched into him, but he quickly straightened, moving toward me and streaming blood.

Kelly moved up the ladder behind me, his buddy behind him. Great, blocked from all sides. I leapt up and barreled past the freaks, undogging the hatch leading outside. Kelly and his friend were directly on my tail as we were thrust into pre-dawn light.

"Land!" Kelly said.

I looked fore-ward and saw that the city of San Diego was coming up on us fast. What was CHENG doing down there? Had everyone decided to leave their station? Christ, the ship didn't have a chance of slowing.

"We need to get off this ship now!" I yelled over the noise of the waves.

Kelly nodded. He reached to close the hatch, but a body slipped through. Kelly lashed out and punched the moaning creeper in the face. That didn't do much more than piss him off. Kelly drew his gun again, pointed it at the man, and then shot him in the head.

"Oh shit oh shit oh shit," was all I could manage as I monkeyed with a life raft.

We had the newer MK-7s that could seat 25 but right now I couldn't even get it loose. My head pounded and I had the desire to puke up everything I'd eaten over the last 24 hours. Then I remembered the hydraulic release and hit it. The canister shot over the side but I wasn't as fast, probably because I was frozen in terror at the idea of following it.

"Are we going over?" Kelly asked.

A pair of former sailors pushed through the hatch, trailing half the crew behind them.

"Fucking zombies!" I yelled out loud, and that seemed to give me power over them. Admitting what my mind had been screaming and denying finally woke me up.

I ran to the next life raft capsule and called to Kelly and his friend.

"When I let this one rip, you guys be ready to follow it. We won't have a lot of time because that water is gonna suck. Just stick with it and follow me. Got it?" I triggered the release.

The second capsule sailed over the side and I was right behind it. The minute the capsule hit the water it exploded into a bright yellow raft. My stomach leapt into my throat as I fell toward the waves below. I crossed my arms over my chest, pinched my nose with my fingers, and clenched my asshole so I didn't get a seawater enema.

Hitting the water was like being dropped onto soggy concrete. Even with my body straight, toes pointed, I felt the impact in my chest. Cold water sucked at me. I stayed in the same position and waited to become buoyant. When "up" became apparent I kicked my legs a few times, saw light, and broke the surface with a gasp. I struck toward the raft with long strokes.

Behind me, my two Marine friends were doing their best to not drown. Kelly was the worst in his heavy vest. He tried to keep his weapon out of the water but it was already soaked.

"Come on, you pussy!" I challenged him.

Kelly did his best to give me the finger. His buddy swam up beside him and gave an assist. Together, they made it to the raft, though it was a genuine struggle with Kelly wearing that heavy combat gear. I helped haul them both in but couldn't take my eyes off of what was happening on the ship. As it sped away, sailors were jumping overboard.

Waves tossed us up and down like a yoyo. My hangover had evaporated during the chaos. I guess having a bunch of friends trying to kill you does something to the body. As we bobbed on the water, the hangover came back with a vengeance.

Kelly was still lying on his back taking in deep breaths. The other Marine stared with me toward port.

"What's your name, man?" I asked him.

"Joey Reynolds." We did introductions but neither of us looked each other in the eyes; our attention was devoted to watching our base.

"I hate the water!" Kelly sat up and followed our gaze. "Fuck me," he said.

Out of the pre-dawn chill, a layer of fog rose. After a few seconds, I realized it was smoke; San Diego was in flames. Columns rose into the air as fires grew. We were still a few miles out, but it was apparent that some kind of massive riot or catastrophic event was occurring.

The McClusky continued to steam straight toward a dock. A

transport of some kind did its best to move out of the way while other ships sat silent. The white ship, whose name I couldn't make out for the life of me, must have kicked the engines into high gear. She quickly maneuvered around, front end swinging away from the dock, as the fast frigate I'd just occupied sped home.

At least the white ship managed to make it.

Men poured over the side, some following lifeboats but many with only life jackets. Others came after them: the snarling masses that had chased us right off the ship. Some of the zombies jumped, landing on sailors, while others managed to get hung up in the railing.

"There were life vests?" Kelly muttered.

A smaller ship struggled to get out of the way of the McClusky but ended up getting clipped. The sound of the two metal beasts screeching against each other was like the world's longest train wreck. But the McClusky wasn't done on her journey. She was nudged to the side; her giant propellers carried her straight past the pier to impact with the dock behind it.

"Oh my god," Reynolds said.

As if pounded by a behemoth pile-driver, the ship crumpled when her mass abruptly shifted from rear to front. Her ass-end swung around after impact and carried the rest of the ship into the dock. It took two full minutes before the McClusky was lifted into the air by a massive explosion. As the sound reached us, I hunkered down and wrapped my arms around my head, then I risked a glance over the side of the raft. The McClusky was briefly suspended on a ball of fire that destroyed the ship like it had been a tin can.

"This can't be happening," Kelly said. He reached into his pocket to pull out a cell phone, but after studying the display for a few minutes he tossed the dead device into the middle of the raft.

"Shit. I don't even have my phone," I said.

"Where is it?" Reynolds asked.

I pointed at the remnants of the ship.

THAT'S ENOUGH FOR TODAY. NEXT CHANCE I GET I'LL WRITE ABOUT Reynolds and how we established Fortress. Now I'm just sick of sitting around. Joel crashed earlier and has been snoring ever since.

I'm going to use a couple of cups of water to take a bath.

Noises outside, but not the typical crawling dead we hear wandering around out there most nights. I'll guess I'll go downstairs and check it out before I call it a night.

REAL MONSTERS

10:30 hours approximate
Location: Undead Central, San Diego CA – Fortress

S upplies:

- ¾ pound of Jasmine rice
- ¼ pound of dried beans
- 1 pound of that tofu-jerky
- 5 cans of tuna
- 2 cans of cat food - where the hell is Butch?
- 5 boxes of pasta
- ½ beautiful jar of spaghetti sauce
- 3 cans of various veggies
- 2 cans of mixed fruit
- 1 case of canned spinach that neither one of us had touched since we got here.

There wasn't much to do but sit around and glare at each other. Joel and I exchanged very few words.

No girls to chase. No football games to stare at. No beer to toss back. No smokes to smoke. No Xbox to play and no hot wings. Man I miss hot wings. I saw a whole bunch of seagulls the other day and all I could thing about was shooting them out of the sky so we could cook up some hot wings. I'd eat the shit out of some spicy seagull right about now.

Instead we cleaned weapons with a can of old motor oil. It wasn't pretty but it got the job done. It made me smell like a mechanic which was just like being back at home on the USS McClusky.

Just a few days ago we'd gone out and tried to raid a few houses but had little to show for it. One place had yielded a few cans of baby formula. Another had provided some aspirin and a full bottle of Tums, found buried in the back of the upstairs bathroom cabinet. We feasted on a few of those for the calcium. We dared each other to drink the baby formula. I ended up liking it but didn't tell Joel.

We went out empty-handed and that was how we came back to Fortress.

We aren't the only survivors, that's for damn sure.

Some of the homes we hit already had doors kicked open and pantries cleared. We found a bunch of empty bags one day that had contained dried beans. Next to those I found a can of condensed soup someone had punctured with a knife and drained. That had to be fun, sucking warm congealed soup without even a straw, but it beat the hell out of going hungry. Probably tasted amazing on seagull.

"Think we can shoot a few birds?"

"Are you crazy? Bring half the damn city to this location just so we can eat one of those scrawny things."

"I said a few. One scrawny bird for you and one scrawny bird for me. Probably good with the spinach."

"I'd rather eat dirt."

"Don't be so fucking morbid," I said.

Joel didn't smile.

JOEL WAS BEING A JERK. HE KEPT YELLING AT ME ABOUT WHAT A pain in the ass it was to watch after me when we went out. Like

I knew the first goddamn thing about surviving the first goddamn zombie apocalypse.

"Fuck you, Joel Kelly. I'm good out there and you know it. Just because I don't know all the Marine hand signals like when to jerk one off doesn't mean I don't pay attention."

"Just stay low. You're big and you stick out like a sore thumb," he lectured me. "We always go in the back and we always keep an eye out for each other."

"I'm pretty sure that's what I did yesterday when I saved your ass at Ty's place." I shot back.

Joel relented with a shake of his head and went back to dour Marine looks.

I left and went upstairs to dig around in a closet again. The kid's room was filled with toys and small clothes but I figured that if I looked around long enough I'd find his stash of candy bars or Twinkies. So far I'd had no luck. He did have a toolbox filled with action figures from some super hero movie I hadn't even seen - and never would see.

Fortress was a fucking pit. An hour later, I opened the windows on the top floor but the air didn't even stir. I sat by the open portal and sucked a light breeze but then it was gone and I was miserable again.

You'd think the silence would be comforting, but it's not. All those sounds you get used to like a television or radio. Heat or running air conditioning. We had none of that. The only sound was an occasional moan, scream, or gunshot in the distance.

We'd been here for a couple of days but it felt weird living in someone else's home. I had to be careful when opening any cabinets or doors. No telling what in the hell would happen. One wrong move and a bunch of crap would be falling on the floor and all that noise would bring *them*.

Later, Joel apologized for being a dick. I nodded but didn't give in so easily.

"All you do is preach about caution but you're the first one to raise your voice out there, or worse, blow a door off its hinges. No one likes a fucking hypocrite, Joel."

"Just blowing off steam. Nothing to shoot at today so I guess words are my ammo."

"Oh that's real deep, Joel. Words as ammo. You should write a rap album."

"Are you going to go racist on me?"

"Yeah. Cause I want the only guy with a clue to think I'm a racist. Brilliant. Just shoot me in the head now."

"Like I haven't thought about it. Damn engineer. Bullets probably bounce off that thick skull."

LATER, JOEL ATTEMPTED TO BE PATIENT WHILE TEACHING ME survival skills. I was too pissed off to pay attention. Firing mechanism this and charging lever that. Blah blah blah.

Butch kept circling us. He whined his skinny cat ass off while we bickered. Every time I tried to reach down and scratch his scruffy head, he moved toward Joel.

Cat only had one eye and it was the evil kind and that was all he offered me.

Joel and I were both hungry and that meant one thing.

"You're the sailor. Don't you eat that shit up like Popeye?"

"You and spinach—the fuck is wrong with you? Popeye's a cartoon. What you're doing is called stereotyping."

"My black ass knows all about stereotyping." Joel shot back.

Shit. He had me there.

"I don't eat spinach. Period."

"A few days without food and I think you'll change your mind."

"Won't you?" I asked Joel.

"Nah. I'd rather starve. That shit is nasty."

We both laughed at that and the tension left the room. Funny how that happens from time to time. Other times we strut around and act like we want to kill each other.

We both knew the truth. We were rationing our supplies. If we ate our fill we'd be out of food in two days.

Butch meowed that long and forlorn mewl of his—I guess

he's a he. I didn't really stop to think about checking to see if he had balls. I shushed him, so he did it again.

"If that cat brings a horde of zombies our way I'm feeding his furry butt to the first shuffler I see."

"Fucking shufflers. What are those things?"

"Dude. Do not get me started." I said.

"So many of the slow ones. Bunch of drunk bastards that can't chase worth a shit."

"Yeah but get enough of them together…I remember the base," I said and thought, with sadness, of Reynolds.

"Anyway. The shufflers."

"They don't move like people and they don't move like your garden variety Z. They got that weird step and how the hell do they creep along on their hands and feet?"

Joel got on all fours and tried to duplicate the move. It was hilarious. He tried to stay on his hands and feet and move but he kept straining to stay low to the ground. After ten or fifteen seconds he gave up and rolled over on his back.

"That shit is insane," he said, panting.

"Thanks for making my day." I laughed and clapped him on the shoulder.

"Five minutes. Let's get in the war."

"A war indicates there's an enemy out there that is shooting back. So far it's been pretty one-sided, Joel."

"Should be an easy one to win," Joel said and got up to strap on his tactical gear.

I nodded and went to gather up my stuff. I couldn't help but wonder what we'd do if we won.

THE FIRST TIME WE WENT OUT WAS AT NIGHT. IT DIDN'T MATTER that we snuck around like a couple of special-needs ninjas. The thing about the Z's was that it was easier to see them than worry about them seeing us. Besides, we only had the one NVG and Joel wore that because he was the goddamn action hero, leaving me stumbling into stuff.

The next time we went out it was early morning. We left just as dawn was burning away and there was that low mist that hung around. It was creepy under normal circumstances but add in a bunch of Z's and it's like some nightmare movie. You just don't walk around in that soup, see a dude missing half his fucking face, and act like it's a normal day.

I'd already shrugged into my BDU's, wearing them over a thick flannel shirt left by the owners of the house. The material was hot but I felt a little bit safer having it cover my arms. One bite was all it took, and if this kept me from losing some skin, I could put up with it. I'd feel even better if I had duct tape wrapped around each sleeve but then I'd have to cut my way out. Besides, I'd worked in an engine room for years and the thick layer was just shy of uncomfortable. See that, grunge rockers? This shit is functional.

We went over the side and then stashed the ladder. The front was locked up and hammered shut. I straightened our "looters will be shot dead" sign, and then we moved out.

We crept around a few houses we'd already searched. Others had boarded up windows and barred doors so we didn't bother. As much as I'd like to say we talked with other survivors that just wasn't the case.

In the movies everyone goes into hyper survival mode and shoots, rapes, or pillages with glee. In reality, we'd found that most survivors just wanted to be left alone. Everyone was distrustful and that was fine with me. I didn't want to worry about feeding any more mouths.

We moved onto a new section of town about half a mile from our current location. Joel wore his combat gear and had the NYFD ball cap on backwards. His AR-15 swept in every direction. We had a map back at Fortress and Joel kept marking off sections we'd explored. This wasn't one of them. Virgin territory to us. Probably Z-infested and picked over but we had to get lucky eventually.

There were older homes here and we were far enough from the Naval base that I hoped we weren't busting into other sailor's houses and stealing their shit. Yeah, I realize that most of them were probably dead but it still felt like the wrong thing to do.

We came across the home at the end of a cul-de-sac. The place was newer or remodeled and really out of place in the ghetto that made up most of this neighborhood. That's what Joel called it, but it was a lot nicer than where I grew up in Detroit. My school was so rough, the only things that kept me from getting my ass kicked, consistently, were my fists and my size. I'd been a bully then, because it was expected, but I never liked it. Much.

"How about this place?" I whispered near Joel's ear.

He was crouched behind a beat up sedan and going over his rifle. When he wasn't shooting at Z's, Joel was inspecting his weapon. I had my .45 M45A1 holstered but my pipe wrench was at hand. Bring on the Z's. I was ready to bash some heads. I was the silent partner, as Joel liked to put it. Point me in the direction of a few of the dead and I'd take them down with a swing or two.

A group of Z's moved one block west of our location. They were a nasty bunch that probably turned during the first few days of the outbreak. Dressed in rags, they had that starved look with sunken cheeks and hollow eye sockets. The leader had a steady but slow gait, thanks to a broken foot. His face was caved in and one eye socket was covered in dried blood and a fuck load of maggots.

"I'm gonna puke," Joel whispered.

"Don't start cause I'll be right behind you. Hard to shoot Z's when you're tossing your lunch."

"Good Christ in heaven. How is something like that even on its feet?

Every time he staggered forward, a couple of bugs fell off his face and he nearly lost his footing. Then this decayed dude would right himself, swing his good leg again and stumble forward. The four behind him weren't in much better shape. A woman in a jogging suit was missing most of her face but at least it wasn't filled with maggots. Just gore and stuff that might have been bone.

Another group followed and this bunch was much fresher. When I write about fresh Z's you have to understand that there's a whole host of the dead out there. Sure, the first bunch were old and rotted. We saw a lot of those. When the body dies, or comes down with whatever shit virus had killed the world, the body rots. Then stuff starts to fall off. The parts that are left reek like the worst rancid meat you ever smelled. Man, I just can't describe it. Go to a dump in the summer and walk right to the center. I guarantee it won't be as bad as these things.

So the second batch were a lot fresher. The rot was setting in but they were walking and jawing. That is, their mouths kind of unhinged and their tongues stuck out. If one of these Z's fell, odds were good that a hunk of meat was hitting the ground, maybe a piece of a kneecap or an elbow. The biggest problem was how fast they were. Take a week-old rotted Z. They can't chase worth a shit. A day-old slugger? They're almost as fast as a live person. Get ten of those together and it's a hell of a bad day.

They moved around the first group, seemingly oblivious to the rotters. Then they pressed on toward the end of the block, but not before one whipped its head around and stared right at our hiding spot. It shuffled around in a circle then looked toward the sky and let out a moan. Milky white eyes settled on us again, but they weren't aware we were in the bushes.

It was a long five minutes while we waited for the second batch to round the corner and move out of eyesight. One of the rotters, however, picked a spot on the ground and stared at it. That's when I saw the figure dart around a house next to the one we were trying to raid. They were dressed in black and wore a ski mask. They had a bunch of knives strapped to their chest and a handgun of some sort. They took up a position in the shadow of the green rambler and froze in place.

Joel didn't move, either, and that meant I was a statue. After a few minutes the figure moved off. He or she did not even look in our direction. Joel and I sighed at about the same time and then shot each other disapproving looks.

We moved around the house and checked the windows. Locked.

The house's front door was closed and that was a good sign. Too often we came across front doors and windows smashed in, and that meant someone had already picked the place clean.

"This place looks deserted but it might be like fortress. Guy in there with a shotgun would take us down pretty easily," Joel whispered.

"Should we knock?" I asked.

"Yeah. You go knock and if you get shot I'll know to go back to Fortress."

"Let's scout the back."

Joel clapped my back. "See, I'll make a warrior out of you yet."

"Be better if you could make some damn hot wings," I said.

The house had an older pine fence with most of a finish. Looks like the apocalypse put a stop to that. A can of wood stain lay off to one side. It was kicked over and empty. I moved to peek over the top and didn't see a dog waiting to chase us toward our recently departed zombie horde.

Joel pushed at the gate but it didn't budge. I slipped my hand over the top and felt around until I found a release, then slid the gate open. We crept into the back yard with Joel Kelly in the lead. He dashed to the edge of the home and then crouched with his AR covering the backyard. He didn't move for a full fifteen seconds and then slipped around the back.

I had to wonder what I'd do if I was, say, lounging around in my back yard in a pair of boxers and someone crept along the side of my house dressed in tactical gear and carrying an assault rifle. I'd probably shit myself and then offer them everything in my wallet.

Joel moved into the yard and I followed. Then he stopped, dropped to a crouch, and gestured for me to get down. I complied with his instructions and faded toward a small maple. It was one of the healthiest trees I'd seen and that worried me. Did someone live here? Someone with the means to take care of their shrubs? I shook my head. It was probably just the unseasonably warm autumn we were experiencing. It really looked healthy. It was garnet and willowy but didn't provide a lot of cover, especially for my BDU's

Joel motioned and I followed his hands. There was a pile of something near the sliding glass door. I shook my head because I couldn't believe it.

There had to be fifteen or twenty bodies in various states of decay. Flies buzzed around in a swarm of black. The sound was enough to drive me nuts.

The smell was horrendous.

All of the bodies were female and all were nude. Clothing was lain on top of them but arranged in a garish way, like they were some kind of clowns. The woman on top was probably in her fifties when she died and not exactly the spitting image of a super model. She was a mom, or had been, but now she was dead and her face was covered in someone's crude attempt at makeup. Bright red hooker lipstick rode her dry lips. Her mouth was open and she didn't have any teeth, just a bunch of bloody holes.

"The fuck?" Joel said exactly what I was thinking, except I was thinking it over and over in my head.

Another woman was much younger but most of her face was smashed in. Her neck was cocked at an impossible angle and I feared that if I touched her the head would loll toward me and her eyes would snap open.

"Were they all Z's before they were killed?"

"I don't know, man. I don't know." Joel shook his head.

I wondered if he was thinking what I was thinking. That some sick fuck needed to die for this. Take a Z down, man. Don't be a fucking asshole.

I pointed at the house and Joel followed my finger and stared for a full half minute.

"We should go somewhere else."

"Yeah. We should. Stay here and back me up."

"Dammit. We should leave," I whispered.

"I want to know what's up," Joel said. His eyes didn't look inquisitive. They looked pissed.

"Going in blazing?" I asked.

"I'm not stupid."

"Yeah, okay, Mr. Marine."

Joel puckered his lips like he was preparing to blow me a Marine kiss and then shot me the finger. He crept to the edge of the house and lowered himself next to the sliding glass door. He took a quick peek and then dropped back a few feet. No one blasted. Good enough start.

Joel took another look and this time lingered. He stared and stared and then he motioned for me to join him.

"Break it. Break the fucking door." He nodded at my giant wrench.

"Really?"

"Dude. Just do it." His eyes burned so I shrugged and took a swing.

Just before the wrench shattered the window, I saw why.

When the glass hit the patio and floor, I stood in place while my brain tried to make sense of the scene.

Then my face flushed and my blood boiled.

Joel went in yelling.

"Down, get the fuck down! I am not messing around! If you make one wrong move I'll erase you!"

The man with his pants around his ankles looked at us and then slowly raised his arms.

I took a step toward him with the wrench raised and murder in my blood. I wanted to beat this guy until he was pulp and then toss him on the pile outside.

His living room was a mess of old clothes and empty food containers. There were so many empty packs of crackers and candy bars I wouldn't be able to take a step without something crackling under foot.

Someone had spray-painted the words "MONSTER KEN" on one of the walls in blood red paint.

The house was dark and warm. It reeked of garbage and blood. It smelled like the dead. On top of that, the guy before us smelled like he hadn't showered in a month.

The worst part was the girl. She was bent over the arm of a

light brown leather couch that was stained with blood. Her naked legs moved but that was all. Her arms were tied at the wrist, behind her back. She moaned but couldn't move her head because a rope had been tied around her neck and stretched to the other side of the couch and then tied to something.

"Notmenotmenotmenotme! It's Ken. He's the monstermonster monsterman! Ken's coming back. Not me not me not fucking me."

"Shut up or I'll end you." Joel's voice was full of barely-controlled rage.

I didn't say anything because every fiber of my being wanted to crush in his skull. I clenched the wrench so hard my hand trembled.

"Ken did Ken did Ken did," the guy rambled on and on under his breath.

"Let her go," I said.

"Can't. Can't do it. Can't until Ken gets here but he said I could take a turn. See? He said it was cool so it's cool and everything's cool. So cool." He touched the girl's back and ran his hands over her waist, then gave her butt a squeeze.

"Rapist." Joel pronounced it like a death sentence and raised his weapon.

"Can't rape the dead." The man cackled.

I backed up a step and tried to keep my lunch down.

"What the fuck!" Joel said and centered the man in his sights.

Then something crashed down the hallway and we both froze.

'Ken!" the guy screeched, and that was enough for me.

I hit him so hard he probably didn't even feel it, just saw a blast of light.

A figure dashed across the hallway into the kitchen. Joel dropped and fired a few rounds.

I dropped behind the couch and tried to pick a spot to crawl toward. The woman's eyes settled on mine and she snarled even though she was gagged. She couldn't have been more than eighteen years old. She wore the same shade of lipstick as the bodies outside.

Another figure appeared in the hallway but it moved slowly. Joel didn't stop to ask questions; he just shot the person in the chest. Then another shape appeared.

"Out!" Joel said and rose to cover me.

A pair of shots came from the direction of the first figure, now in the kitchen, and struck the wall. The bullets were high but they were enough to tell me that I didn't like being shot at.

I went flat as Joel backed up and fired a few more rounds.

This was beyond our thirty-second battle drill. We should be hauling ass. I tried to shimmy along the floor but realized it would leave my big ass exposed and stayed low.

"When I fire, you move. Got it?" Joel didn't waste any time and ripped half a dozen rounds at the indistinct shape in the kitchen. Then he dropped the creeper coming up the hallway, but there was one more behind them.

At least we hit whoever was shooting at us. The person grunted and then fell. Joel aimed in his direction but was stopped because of the fresh hell that was about to enter my living nightmare.

The shuffler moved faster than anything alive. It didn't even pause to check out the naked girl bent over the couch, it just came at us like a rabid dog. It snarled and sputtered with a sound that was like coughing. It ran at Joel, took a bullet to the shoulder and didn't stop.

The guy in the kitchen must have figured this was his chance. He peeked around the corner and for the first time I got a look at him. It was the same person I'd seen earlier wearing a ski mask.

I dropped my wrench and tugged the big .45 out of my holster, checked the safety, raised it, and shot at the guy.

He ducked back around the corner. His handgun came out and he emptied a magazine into the room. We tried to duck, but the shuffler was on us.

He went for Joel with a leap that barely cleared the couch. I risked grabbing my wrench and then swung it around. I missed, but it was better than accidentally shooting Joel.

They both crashed through the remains of the glass door and went down in a heap. Joel abandoned his assault rifle and went for his side arm but his hand was batted aside. He tried to throw a punch while getting up and was tackled. Then he was out of sight.

I lifted the handgun and fired back at the man in black out of fear and panic. I had to rescue Joel. He was a tough and fast son of a bitch, but he was facing a shuffler all alone. I fired wildly and made for the screen door but bullets zipped over my head.

"Ken. That's a shuffler. Let me kill it or we're both done."

Another form appeared in the shadows of the hallway.

"I know. I brought them for you." A man's voice cackled. "Think you can sneak into my house? My house? I brought them."

Boom! The shot ripped through the space over my head.

"For you!"

Then he fired several more times while I hugged the floor. Made it my best friend.

I curled up in a ball and wondered if I was going to be Z-chow in a minute.

A grunt from the outside made me snap my head in that direction. Was Joel dead? Did the shuffler get him? I had to get out there and I had to get out there now.

The form that had appeared in the doorway staggered toward me. Ken laughed. Monster Ken – what a perfect name for this asshole.

The fresh Z was a large woman in her thirties. Her face was a mess of bite marks but her guts hung around her waist. I lifted the gun to shoot at her but it clicked empty. Great. I'd forgotten Joel Kelly's rules. I rolled against the side of the couch, put my hand on the cushion to steady myself, and was almost bitten by the girl strapped there.

Reloading was a cinch thanks to hundreds of practice runs. I silently vowed to thank my Marine friend.

I fired four rounds in Ken's direction while he fired back.

The space between us had to be less than fifteen feet, but I was the lucky one. Ken grunted and then screamed. The Z in the hallway turned her head and moaned in his direction, then moved toward him.

I rushed out the door, expecting the worse.

The shuffler was on his back in the pile of the dead. He twitched, then rolled over and cackled. His hand went to his mouth while he considered me. The man's hair hung in clumps over his forehead. His face was covered in blood and gore. His clothing was just as soaked in crimson.

He bit off one of his fingers while he stared from milky eyes that had the oddest hint of green. It was like they glowed with some otherworldly intelligence.

Joel staggered to his feet and for a moment I feared he'd been bitten and was already turning, but he pulled his Marine combat knife. Then he took a step toward the shuffler. Oh, I get it. This was one of those Marine things that I should stay out of. Joel was only interested in finishing the monster.

The shuffler leapt. Sure, I could have let Joel Kelly, Marine superman take the shuffler, and with any luck Joel would come out the victor. But I'd had enough of this entire scouting mission. I swung hard and caught the shuffler in the side, changing his reality in mid leap from forward momentum to crushed bones and flailing limbs. The creature howled and fell into an awkward tangle.

Joel advanced but I lifted the .45 and shot the son of a bitch in the head. Twice.

Fuck that guy.

Joel staggered into me and got an arm around my shoulder.

"If you bite me I'm going to be really fucking disappointed, Joel Kelly."

"He didn't get me. He just hit me hard enough to make me see stars. Thanks, man. I didn't think I'd be able to take him."

"So what, you just judo-threw him or something?"

"Got my gun around and cracked him upside the head. He fell back on the pile, but goddamn – that thing was fast. And strong."

"So this is my reward? A Marine hug. If you kiss me I'm going to hit you with my really big wrench."

Joel laughed and punched me in the shoulder hard enough to leave a bruise. Such a kidder, that guy.

"I think Monster Ken is still alive in there."

"Yeah?"

I grinned and went in but kept low in case Ken'd gotten lucky with the dead lady.

The only sounds were his calls for help.

I advanced quietly on the kitchen and poked my head in to see even more squalor. There were wrappers everywhere. Empty water bottles. Rotting meat in the sink. What kind of meat, I had no interest in discovering.

The rapist twitched. Shit, didn't I kill that son of a bitch?

Joel came in and covered me. He pointed his assault rifle at the woman on the couch but I shook my head.

"Enough shooting for one day. We gotta move, buddy. Our thirty seconds ended about five minutes ago."

"What about dickless in there?"

I poked my head around the corner and saw that the Z was on top of Ken. She had knocked him down and he must have hit something hard because his right arm was at a bad angle. I ducked in and snagged his gun. It was a Sig Sauer P229 and that seemed like a hell of a sexy gun.

"How's it going, Ken?" I asked.

He turned blazing eyes on me as he tried to fight off the woman. She got her mouth into his shoulder and ripped up. Ken screamed.

"Don't be such a fucking pansy," I said and went back to the living room.

The guy I hit twitched and one eye opened. The other had been crushed in by my wrench.

Joel grabbed the rapist and dragged him while I untied the woman and led her into the kitchen by the rope. She was covered in wounds and barely put up a struggle. She didn't have any clothing on, but the last thing I wanted to do was look at the twin horrors that were her tits.

"Hey Joel. It's an orgy," I said and pushed her toward Ken.

Joel dragged the other rapist in and tossed him onto the pile. The naked girl went at him. She ripped up his shirt and dug her mouth into his soft belly. Even with his head half bashed in, the man managed to open his eyes and start muttering "no no no" over and over again.

"Hansi," Ken yelled and reached for his friend.

Movement at the front of the house. I risked a look to confirm it was the faster pack we'd seen a few minutes ago right outside the house. So Ken really had led a bunch of Z's here just to protect his home. Did he think he'd be able to over-power them and us when it was all over? Was Ken really enough of a Z survivor to take us all down?

Joel pointed at the back door and I nodded. We hustled and slipped out, hurrying past the pile of dead. We found the side of the house and hid next to the fence. A minute later the street cleared, so we moved out.

Behind me, the screams went on for a long time.

I couldn't stop smiling.

WE CROUCHED NEAR FORTRESS AND WATCHED FOR A FULL TEN minutes. Joel kept his eye on the house while I watched out back. The backyard we'd picked for our reconnaissance had a kid's playground. There was a trampoline with a body on it. The sides were covered in mesh so no one would fall out. Now it was a weird grave for the man that had blown his brains out while lying on it.

The yard also had a bunch of tall bushes we frequently used for cover.

A few days ago we'd gone into this home to look for supplies. We'd only turned up a few small bags of dried beans on the top shelf of the pantry. Someone had beaten us to this place.

We'd found the family in one room. A woman, presumably the mother, had been lain out on the bed with a pair of small bodies. The covers were pulled up and cloths placed over their faces. Someone had shot all three of them. My money was on the guy on the trampoline. After that, we never went into the house again. It was a mausoleum now.

Satisfied that no one was raiding Fortress, we went home.

"Empty-handed," I muttered as we used a few precious baby wipes to clean up back at Fortress.

I lit a Sterno can and contemplated the spinach.

"I'll eat one if you eat one," Joel challenged.

"Christ. I guess it's come to this."

The cans took a few minutes to warm up but not so long to devour. Tasted like shit but it was better than being belly up at Ken's house. Joel was smart and suggested adding a little bit of our precious supply of rice to the containers for the carbs. My gut rolled over but I was hungry enough to ignore the taste. The house hadn't had a lot of food when we claimed it, but we'd found a box of chicken bouillon cubes and they'd gone in just about everything we attempted to cook.

"What the hell, man?" I finally spoke after we sat in silence for a few moments.

"Don't even get me started."

"Who does that shit? Who?"

"Monster Ken."

"Yeah. Well, Monster Ken is a real monster now. I hope that jerk is wandering around tomorrow so we can kill him again."

"We didn't actually finish our sweep yesterday. Head back?" Joel grinned.

"I like how you think, buddy," I smiled and hit Joel in the arm hard enough to leave a bruise.

He choked back a gasp and then looked stoic.

I went to bed with a smile on my face for the first time in days.

I guess the fucking zombie apocalypse could be worse.

NIGHT TERRORS

19:40 hours approximate
Location: San Diego CA - Fortress

Why in the hell did we ever leave? There is a reason I named this place Fortress and leaving it was never a good idea. Unfortunately, Joel made a very convincing argument that we needed to return to the San Diego Naval base for supplies. He used small words like "we need food and ammo, you dumb squid."

Joel never listened to my ideas. I'd made a few but I was sick and tired of the Marine giving me a ration of shit for every single one of them.

"Let's go raid cars."

"Bad idea," he'd say. "Could be the wrong car is full of dead."

Could be? Sure, but we're good at killing them. Real good. If there was an Olympics held today for how to kill Z's, we'd at least win the bronze.

"Let's go find a house with an abandoned hot tub so we can take a bath."

"Then we'd be caught with our pants down." Jesus, he could be such a drag.

"Let's go find other survivors."

"They'll just steal our stuff or maybe try to eat us." On second thought, that one actually made sense.

"Christ, Joel. No one's going to eat us."

"Not yet. Wait until they haven't eaten for a few days," he said ominously. I dropped it.

Anyway, I would do my usual list of food supplies but I'm too pissed off right now so I'll do it tomorrow. There'll be less to write about by then if Roz has her say.

Yeah – Roz.

24 October, 20:08 hours approximate
Location: San Diego CA

Weapons:

- 1 AR-15
- 3 30 round mags
- 97 Rounds of 5.56 ammo
- 1 Colt M45A1 Handgun
- 42 Rounds of .45 ammo
- 1 Sig Sauer P229
- 14 rounds of 9mm ammo
- 1 very large fucking wrench
- 1 12 gauge Remington pump action shotgun
- 4 12 gauge shells

The other night I finished up my entry regarding how Joel, Reynolds, and I escaped from the USS McClusky. As best as I could tell, of the 178 souls on board, only three of us managed to get off the ship before it smashed into the pier and exploded.

It was late and I was about to blow out my candle for the night when I heard something below. Night gets real quiet except for the occasional helicopter in the distance or an airplane too high to see. Every time I heard those I wondered if it was our time to die. I was surprised they hadn't already nuked this dead fucking cesspool.

The noise was different than the Z's that sometimes shamble by. This was more like someone on the move. Someone that has a purpose. But it was gone as soon as I'd convinced myself to get up and check it out.

Eventually I fell asleep but had my wrench within reach and the pistol tucked under my pillow. I may be one paranoid mother fucker but I'm also one very alive mother fucker.

Today we did the same thing as yesterday—broke down our weapons and cleaned them. I even took a cloth to my wrench head and got most of the blood, hair, and brain matter off of it.

After we'd bitched and bickered and then managed not to kill each other, I went to bed and considered rolling a joint. I didn't, though, because as much as I love to give the Marine shit, I didn't really want to let him down. And if I got high and some of those things got in here I might just giggle my ass off while I looked for something to kill them with.

I was dozing when I heard it again.

I was sure I'd heard voices and then something got knocked over. Shit! Now I knew I wasn't crazy. I heard more voices and decided that if we had looters alerted to our location I should just go out there and scare them away. Now how fucking stupid is that? What was I going to do? Go out there dressed like a horrible monster? Those are a dime a dozen now. I'd be like "BOO!" And they'd be like "SHOOT IT!"

I felt around in the dark until I located my lighter, struck a flame, then fumbled around for my shirt. Joel had left his pair of NVG's hanging on the wall so I grabbed those and slid them over my head. He'd be pissed if he found me wearing his toys. Joel always worried about how much juice the batteries had remaining. I worried about being killed by those fucking things out there, so I guess that made us kind of even.

Switching on the NVG's brought the world into shades of green. I moved to a window and scanned the ground below. There were a few trees out there but most were so dry from the heat, they didn't even have leaves. Bushes were easy to pick out. I could look out without the goggles and see a dozen things that scared the shit out of me.

I hovered for a few minutes just watching the ground a story below. When nothing materialized, I moved to the other side of the house. Joel was still snoring away behind his cracked door. I looked in and found him sprawled out on the mattress. The first thing Joel did when we took over the house was drag the mattress off the bed. I asked him why and he said he felt safer.

"A Marine scared of things under the bed?" I'd asked.

"Hey man. There are a lot of things out there to be scared about. This is one less."

With the Night Vision Goggle over my eye I was able to move around the dark house with ease. I checked the other side of the house but didn't see anything. I hovered by a window and listened for a good fifteen minutes but there was nothing.

Maybe I was just going stir crazy.

It took a half-second to wake up Joel. He was on his feet and reaching for his assault rifle so fast it was like he had a giant spring built in his ass. His room smelled like sweat and oil. That would be Joel and his best friend, an assault rifle.

"Shh," I whispered. "I think someone's outside."

"Just leave the dead fucks be. They'll wander away. Now let a brother get some shut eye."

"I don't know. It's so quiet, maybe I was just hearing things, but these things sounded like voices."

"Shit," Joel said. "Lemme grab the NVGs."

I handed them over. Good thing it was dark so I didn't have to put up with a dirty look.

Joel grumped around doing Marine shit while I waited. I did a check of my side arm and ran through ammo, slide, and safety positioning. I had a full mag of 7 rounds and one in the chamber. One more mag went into a pocket and I dropped a handful of shells into my other. My lucky .45 round was still in its place right next to my hip. All I needed was my wrench and I was ready to bash some heads.

GOING OUTSIDE MEANT NAVIGATING OFF THE DECK. THERE'S NO other way in unless someone has a tool that can bust the front door off. We picked this place because it had one main entrance. We filled the entryway with crap like a sofa and then piled a few bodies on top. It made for a gruesome entry.

Next chapter I'll write about Fortress, promise. That way, if my corpse is found, readers will understand what a pain in the ass this place was to secure and appreciate all the effort we went through.

You're welcome.

The only dead that stopped by were ignored. If they got persistent Joel and I would drop cinder blocks on their heads. The blocks were attached to ropes so we could pull them back up. We had a pool going on weekly kills and I was up by three. The best part was trying to get their attention just before the block struck. They'd look up with that blank face, those white eyes, and then SPLAT!

Joel went out and stared into the dark for so long I thought he'd fallen asleep standing up. I waited and went over my gun again and again.

Joel had taught me to treat it like a girl with a rocking body. You want to know every inch of her because you can't dream about her later unless you've been hands-on for hours.

"There's no one out here."

"Yeah. Now. There was a few minutes ago."

"You been hitting the ganja?" Joel asked.

"Not today. I swear, man, I heard something."

"They're gone now. Get some sleep. We need to leave in a couple of hours."

"Yeah. I'll do my best."

When Joel left I dragged my mattress next to the sliding glass door and left it cracked open so the breeze rolled over me, but also so I could hear anyone approaching. The thin bit of breeze helped, but I was a long way from anything resembling sleep. I tossed and turned as I strained to hear anything besides the occasional moan of one of the Z's wandering around in the dark.

Finally I closed my eyes and drifted off, dreaming that I was back on the McClusky and the crew had been replaced by a team of bikini models all named Helen. Every one of them.

Joel's hand on my shoulder tore me out of sleep.

"Ugh," I muttered.

"Mission time," he said and moved away.

I was tempted to just go back to sleep. Fuck exploration, it was the middle of the goddamn night. I sat up and rubbed what felt like sand out of my eyes.

While I suited up in my engineer overalls, Joel stood to the side of the deck entrance and scanned the area. He was already dressed in his combat gear. He checked his pockets one more time, pulling magazines out to do a visual inspection by the light of the moon. Satisfied, he stuffed them back into pouches at his chest and side, then secured them by pressing flaps in. Early on, we'd learned the hard way that the crackle of a Velcro pocket could bring a pack in seconds.

Joel dragged the ladder out and lowered it to the ground, moving it around until he was satisfied it had a good hold on the ground. He slung his AR-15 over his shoulder and then went down the ladder while I trained the .45 around the area. When he was on the ground, he covered for me.

We hid the ladder under a pile of brush and dragged a pair of rotting corpses on top to keep prying eyes on other things.

Our destination was the naval base. Joel had wanted to return for the past week, but the Z's in the area had been too heavy. After some scouting earlier today we determined that it might be safe to slip in, find some warehouse he knew about, commandeer a car, and get the fuck back to dodge, all before the night was over. We really needed to load up on ammo and maybe another weapon or two. If we got stuck with our current weapon pool, I doubted we'd be able to shoot our way out of a wet paper bag before we ran out of rounds.

Fucking zombies. I hate them.

Joel scouted ahead while I brought up the rear. I grumbled but a look from the Marine reminded me that it was time to get serious. One misstep out in this world and we'd be dead meat.

I did find that with night came something amazing. Cold air. It rolled off the water and reminded me of what it was like before we ended up stuck in Fortress. Going out like this was familiar. We'd already done it half a dozen times and we were still alive. The other thing that I found was the smell of decay. It was everywhere. Trash and bodies rotting in the sun made for a disgusting reek that clung to everything.

The idea was to remain quiet. As quiet as a sleeping baby. Any loud noises and you were likely to call in a pack of the dead. Not that they actually traveled together, because they had no thoughts in their heads. They reacted to some bizarre need to find live flesh. I liked my flesh right where it was – on my bones.

Joel stopped alongside a house and then faded against the wall. He moved around the corner with me right behind. Joel held up a hand and I stopped in my tracks. He did something with his NVG's and then motioned for me to advance.

I crept around the corner and stopped as well.

Joel signaled for me to creep forward, then stopped me when I was a few feet away. He turned and put his fingers to his lips. Joel slipped the NVG's off his head and handed them to me. I slid my handgun into the holster, took the glasses and slipped them over my head. He had his eyes closed but pointed at the garage. Curious about what the hell he wanted to show me, I moved toward it in the half crouch I'd seen him pull off many times. He made it look easy but I was a lot bigger. Shit was not easy.

The world jumped to life in hues and shades of green. The house was a single story rambler with the remains of a broken fence scattered all over the lawn. The front door hung off its hinges and a corpse lay on the small concrete patio. Even in the pale light of the moon, I could tell that his form had been torn to shreds. A rifle lay next to him. Other bodies littered the patio. It appeared the guy had done his best to fend for his home, but in the end, the Z's got him.

The garage door was stuck half-open but that wasn't what made me freeze in my tracks. It was the sounds.

If I didn't know any better I'd have guessed there was some kind of feast underway in the garage. Maybe a barbecue in San Diego. Just another night for some civilian (or more likely, military) family.

What I saw was anything but.

I lowered myself to a crouch and moved my head around the corner of the house. The walls were stacked with boxes and some old furniture had been pushed into corners. A bike hung from the ceiling. That's where "normal" ended.

In the center of the room sat four figures. They were dressed in rags and slicked with something wet; even with the NVG's, I knew it was blood. One gazed up at the wall from its meal. I stifled a gasp when I realized the Z had been chewing on his own fingers. One of the four was an overweight woman missing most of her clothes. She sat and gibbered to herself while also chewing on the ends of her fingers. I don't mean nibbled, either. She had literally devoured them. A couple of teens rounded out the family from hell.

It was so absurd that all I wanted to do was go in and shoot each one in the damn head.

I ducked back around the corner and shrugged my shoulders at Joel. He leaned in close.

"That shit is fucked up," he whispered.

I dragged my finger across my neck and shrugged again. Joel shook his head.

He motioned toward my head so I took the NVG's off and handed them over. As Joel grasped them, I heard someone approach from the other side of the house. I dropped to a crouch while Joel fumbled with the glasses.

A figure entered the yard from the west side and was doing nothing to mask his sounds. With the glasses off it took a few seconds to adjust to the natural light of the moon. I drew the Colt M45A1 as quietly as possible, lifted it with two hands, and aimed.

The person went to the corpse in the middle of the yard and picked up the rifle. They looked it over then felt around in the corpse's pockets and came up with shells. The sound of them being loaded into the shotgun was like firecrackers popping in the still of night.

Joel crouched next to the side of the house and aimed the assault rifle. Shit! Shit! Shit! If we got into a firefight with someone, the Z's would be here in a heartbeat.

I moved to his side and looked around the corner. The person lifted the gun and came toward us. Before we could react, the person walked into the garage and the shotgun sounded like a cannon blast. The gun was pumped and boomed again. Feet scrambled on concrete and the form backed out in a hurry. There were three of them on the person, who got off one more shot.

"Fuckers! You killed my family!" she screamed. Yeah – she.

She backed up a few more steps and racked another shell into the gun. She fired but ended up clipping one of the Z's arms. Part of the arm disappeared, leaving shreds of clothing and flesh.

They advanced on her.

She backed up, pumping the shot gun over and over again, but she must have been empty. When she cleared the garage with the three Z's nearly on her, I broke from cover. I slid my handgun back into its holster and hefted my wrench. The last Z stumbled out of the garage and I was horrified to see it was one of the kids. She staggered and moaned but didn't have a lot of momentum. Then I saw why. She was dragging one of her feet at an angle that was impossible for a normal person. It was definitely broken, a gruesome fracture with the bone sticking out, but little Miss Sunshine didn't care.

I moved behind her in a couple of steps and brought the wrench around in an arc that ended with her head. She dropped like a rock and I was rewarded with a pile of brain matter on the end of wrench head.

Then I hit something on the ground, a rock or broken piece of crap from the house, and stumbled. My ankle twisted under me and I almost went down.

One of the Z's turned on me and it was all I could do to fend him off. The guy was almost as big as me and dressed in khaki shorts with the remains of a black t-shirt clinging to his body. I took his attack and tried to turn him away by using his own momentum to toss him aside, but my foot screamed in agony and I ended up in a heap.

Fucker was fresh dead. He wasn't like the slower corpses that had been hanging out for a few days. This guy was quick and his teeth gnashed in toward my shoulder like a viper. I got the wrench in the way and smacked him aside. I managed to get an elbow in and hit him hard enough to roll the fucker off me. Jesus Christ! He smelled horrible – and I've worked around sailors for most of my life, so that should tell you something.

I swung the wrench again, but I panicked and it crashed into his chest. Any normal man would have been crushed. It barely fazed this dead fuck.

The girl must have figured out how to get her shot gun functioning because it boomed again. I swore, hoping she didn't mistake me for one of the dead. I rolled to my side and almost got my hands on the ground to pick myself up. Then I felt a claw on my shirt as the guy pulled me back down. I rolled and got a boot up. I lifted it high in the air and hit the Z again, but just in the chest, and all that did was knock him flat.

Where the hell was Joel?

"Get out of the fucking way!" Joel kept his voice low.

"About time!" I tried to echo his tone but panic rode my voice and I may have sounded like a scared six-year-old girl.

The Z grabbed my leg but I kicked free and rolled again. Joel's boots came into view and then the AR-15 fired. The Z was blown onto his back. One more shot to the head and the guy didn't move again.

I got to my feet and limped after Joel, ankle aching with every step.

"Are they dead?" The girl with the shotgun approached. She didn't even look us in the face; she just studied the corpses on the ground.

"Yeah, all dead - need to clear this area before more arrive." Joel said.

"I'll stay here and hold them back. Thanks for the assist." She said. Her voice had a slight Latino accent.

"Come with us," I said impulsively. Or was it impulsive? Were we just supposed to leave another survivor behind while we made an escape?

Joel grabbed my shirt sleeve and tugged.

"We can't leave her."

"If she wants to stay, let her," he said near my ear, but she was probably able to hear him.

"We can't leave someone behind like that."

"Since when did you grow a fucking sense of morality? We ain't got the supplies for another survivor."

"Just go," the girl said. "That's my dad on the lawn. The eaters in the garage killed everyone. There's nothing left."

"Oh, for fucks sake." Joel said and stared at both of us.

The sound of something shuffling down the street sent a chill down my neck. I looked for shapes.

I grabbed the girl's hand and tugged her close. "Just until we get free; then you can do whatever you want."

"I don't care. I just don't care anymore. I got nothing," she repeated.

"I need help, okay? I can't run because I sprained my ankle."

"Fine. Fuck! You helped me, so I'll help you." She lifted my arm and put it around her shoulders.

Joel swore a few more times and then took point. I gimped along behind him, holding the girl close.

"I'm Jackson," I told her as I trained the gun all over the place.

"I'm Roz. Jackson your first or last name?"

"First. Jackson Creed."

"Okay, man. Now that we got introductions out of the way, why don't you shut the fuck up so we don't get swarmed?"

"Me? You're the one that came in with guns blazing. If it weren't for my wrench you'd be one of them by now."

"Keep your wrench in your pants and keep that gun aimed. Where we going anyway?"

"Fortress, I guess."

"Fortress?"

"It's just what we call home. Do you have any food?"

"Lots in my house. Before we were overrun we had a big stash."

"How'd you get overrun?"

"They were making a lot of noise. Dad snuck out to see what it was. One of them saw him and that was all it took. They killed my sister and a kid we'd taken in. Dad made me go. He made me leave them, but I couldn't just go without knowing, so I came back a few hours later. Eyes front so we don't get killed out here."

"Eyes front? Play a lot of video games?"

"I'm in the Army, dumbass. I was home on leave when this shit went down."

"Would you two kindly shut the fuck up?" Joel whispered.

We'd covered a few blocks when Joel stuck his hand up, fist closed. I stopped and fought my twisted foot. We were in the backyard of a house with a dead lawn and a small fence. I staggered to the fence and lowered myself to my knees, then covered Joel as he advanced on the house. He paused in the middle of the yard and didn't move for a few seconds, then ran toward the side of the house and planted himself in a deep shadow.

The back of the home had a shattered sliding glass door; the accompanying screen door was in shreds on the ground. There was a body sticking its legs out of the doorway. They didn't move.

Noises near the street in front of the home.

Roz turned her gun to the side and examined it, then slid a few shells into the breech. Then there was movement out front; Joel faded from sight, but he wasn't gone long. Like someone had set his ass on fire, he came running back.

"Thirty or forty of them on my three o'clock."

"We're cut off?"

"Worse, there's lights in Fortress. We're blown."

I swore like the sailor I am for a few seconds.

"Back to my house. We have supplies and it used to be boarded up before Dad got himself killed," Roz said.

"The house we just left? Could have told us that before we walked half the fucking city," Joel said we moved around a fence keeping low.

"You asked for my help, man. You didn't ask me for a place to stay, so secure that fucking attitude."

"Well, yes ma'am," Joel said. I could almost hear his eye-roll.

"It's safe for the night, then we can try your place again."

"No reason to go back there. It'll be picked clean." Joel said.

I wanted to punch someone.

"I don't think we have a choice," I said between clenched teeth.

Something shambled near us in the dark. I glanced up, almost too late.

A figure stumbled upon us, moaning, white eyes searching. Its mouth was stretched into a jagged grin of glee. Joel didn't hesitate. He shot the fucker, but missed a head-shot in his haste. The shot nicked its throat, though, and spun it to the side. I hopped up on my bad foot and almost screamed in pain. I covered by swinging the wrench into the Z's jaw. The blow arced upward as I stood, so it had the force of a fucking car wreck and lifted the Z off the ground. It flopped backward and didn't move.

Joel shot another shape and then Roz fired her shotgun, blowing a hole in the middle of a Z.

"Shit! Zulu's everywhere! Go go go!" Joel said, and we did just that.

We hauled ass, Joel weaving between fences and houses as we tried to keep up. My twisted foot was a constant shriek of pain, but it was better than the alternative.

We broke through a bunch of dried up shrubs and were on the other side of the house we'd just left. Roz tapped Joel and pointed at a single story home right next to it. The place was darker than fortress and as we drew closer I realized why.

Boards had been nailed to the inside of the windows. The door was shut but writing was spray-painted onto it.

"Looters will be shot by well-armed occupants."

Well, hell. That had been our trick at Fortress. I guess advertising wasn't such a good idea. Someone must have waited for us to leave and then moved in on our territory. Voices. Now I knew I'd heard them. Now they were in our home. I had a brief fantasy of Joel using his assault rifle with some kind of scope that can see through walls to take out the sons of bitches.

We moved into the open, but a shaped drifted near the front of the house and then stopped to stare at the moon. The figure swayed back and forth. Joel lifted his AR but I waved him off.

Another shape came into view and stood next to the first. The man wore a ripped t-shirt and nothing else. His legs hung with grey slack skin. The girl wore what was once a white dress. She was tiny and one arm flopped against her side when she lurched.

I lifted my wrench and pointed. Roz got the idea and produced a huge knife with a serrated edge.

I leaned over and whispered to Joel, "Cover us."

Joel nodded, pointed, and drew his finger across his neck. He then put his finger to his lip and blew gently.

Roz headed straight toward the man, leaving me the girl. I would have cut Roz off but I couldn't walk fast enough. I 'hmphed' and advanced with her.

We were a few feet away when the guy turned. Roz had the knife raised and was about to drive it into his skull. The girl didn't see me, so when the man surprised us I changed tactics and hit him across the head. Roz turned on me and I thought she was going to drive the knife into me.

The guy fell to the side but his foot spasmodically kicked out and tangled with Roz's legs. They both went down, and the girl in the white dress, seeing her opportunity, leaped on top of Roz. Roz pushed her up by the neck, but when I swung, the girl rolled to the side and my blow sailed over both of them. The girl snarled as she tried to get back on top of Roz, but Roz was having none of that. She came up in a crouch and drove the blade into the girl's chest.

Blood gushed from the Z's mouth. The knife got stuck, so I leaned over, aiming carefully this time, and crushed the girl's head with the wrench.

Together we staggered into the house and Roz quietly closed the door behind us. There was a thick metal bar in the hallway. She and Joel picked it up and dropped it into slots on either side of the entry way. Then she showed us a huge dresser that she and Joel pushed against the door.

Roz held up a hand, so we waited. She marched down the hallway and looked into rooms. She came back and moved into the kitchen and then the living room, training the shotgun on every corner. She finally came back and ushered us in.

We staggered into what had been the living room and Roz collapsed on a couch.

"Don't you ever fucking do that to me again, asshole," she said.

I looked around in confusion. Me?

"What?"

"I had that shit, man. You didn't have to get in my way."

"Yeah, Creed. Fucking jerk," Joel added from a dark corner.

"I'm going to bed. You fuckers try anything and I got a shotgun shell with your name on it."

The room was too dark to show Roz clearly, but I couldn't help noticing that she had a knockout figure.

"We aren't animals," Joel said.

"Whatever, man. Just keep your dicks out here and no one gets killed."

A door closed down the hallway.

We were left in a strange place and it was pitch black. Joel slipped on his NVG's and moved around the house.

I laid back on a lazy-boy, propped my feet up, and tried not to think of how miserable I felt. Damn leg hurt. I was thirsty, fucking exhausted, and so hungry I could eat about six meals.

After some rustling around, Joel came back and put something in my lap. I almost broke into tears when I realized it was bottled water and a pair of food bars in plastic wrappers.

It's late and I can't write any more. It was hard enough getting used to sleeping in Fortress; now we have this temporary home around us and a new friend.

THE BASE

9:15 hours approximate
Location: San Diego CA – Roz's Place

After losing Fortress last night, we crashed with our new friend Roz. She's about five-foot-five and Latino. She's got dark brown hair and she'd probably clean up pretty nice. Roz is cute, I won't lie, and she's got some killer bod, at least the little I noticed while I had my arm draped over her shoulder last night. She also looks like she will kill me if I look at her that way again.

My leg is a mess. I hurt my ankle last night and now it's swollen, but I don't think it's a full sprain. I can walk on it, even though it's more of a hobble than an actual steady stride. Joel Kelly just looked at me like I was a puss. Fuck you, Marine-boy. I did it protecting you and Roz.

Roz tossed me an ace bandage so I could wrap it tight. I wish I had ice. I also wish a Burger King drive-through worked by hot strippers would suddenly appear where the front window is boarded up. I wish I had a way to go back in time a few years and tell Jenny Collins that I liked her. Not love, just liked. We did some shit over her clothes, but I know I could have gotten her with a little more skill. Might as well wish for a tropical get-away while I'm at it.

Joel was nothing but unhappy smiles and pissy Marine attitude. He stormed around all morning. Stripped his gun, put it back together, counted rounds, swore a lot, and snapped at either one of us if we asked him what the plan was.

I asked about eight times.

We had water and food, but mostly some kind of emergency rations Roz's father had collected over the last couple of years. They'd started the end of the world out with a three-month supply of food and clean drinking water for four, but after inviting in a few family members and a kid from the neighborhood, they'd used up a decent chunk. We drank sparingly, but it was hard not to guzzle. The last time I had clean water was about a week ago.

Joel finally got cabin fever and said he was going to check on Fortress.

"I'll go with you."

"Rest your foot. We may need to get mobile soon. I'll be right back."

"Dude. I'll go. You can't make it without me."

"Believe it or not, I'm a Marine and I don't need a gimp squid tagging along, asking me to wipe his nose."

"Whatever. If you run into trouble what are you going to do?"

"At the first sign of a real threat I'll come back. Get some sleep and don't give Roz any shit."

Like I wanted a knife in my chest.

"Your idea of trouble and my idea are different. You think a pack of Z's is a challenge. I think they're a death squad."

"Whatever. Just chill. I'll be back. Here – write about Reynolds, because he deserves it." Joel dropped the log book in my lap.

He'd already strapped on his combat gear and filled his pouches with magazines and a couple of energy bars from Roz's stash. He downed a bottle of water in three gulps and slid the blinds aside to take a look.

Shit. That was one day I wanted to erase from my memory.

But he had a point. If we were to honor Reynolds' sacrifice, it needed to start with his story. I can't say that his story will ever be more important than those of the millions that have already died, but to us, he was a hero. The kind you hear about on the nightly news.

Jesus. The media, TV, newspapers, and cell towers. None of that shit works anymore. None of it. And that is just the start of the hell we now live in.

Joel shot me the finger and then closed the front door quietly behind him.

08:15 hours approximate
Location: A little yellow life raft, near San Diego CA

WEAPONS:

- 1 Colt 1911 .45
- 22 Rounds of .45 ammo
- 1 Heckler and Koch MP5-N sub machine gun
- 14 Rounds 9X19 Parabellum
- 1 large knife

Near distance - a massive fire. Gunships. Jets rocketing overhead. Explosions. Fire. Smoke and chaos.

Ahead was the biggest disaster—the USS McClusky. My home for the last year. She crashed into the pier at close to full speed and that was all she wrote. But that wasn't the only thing burning. The rest of the base was a crazy mess of flames, smoke, and gunfire. Even from this distance, we heard the guns, and they were not being kind to whoever they were aimed at.

A haze settled in as the morning sun rose, further obscuring our view of the naval base. The view snapped quickly back, however, thanks to a plane that roared close to the surface of the water.

"The fuck was that?" I yelled over the noise.

"That was an A-10 warthog. They fly low and blow up tanks and stuff."

"Do you think the same shit that went down on the ship is happening there?" Reynolds pointed.

"It's some shit. That's for sure," Kelly said.

The Marines went over their gear as we closed in. We had to angle around the piers because there didn't appear to be a way to climb up. A ship rides up about twenty feet in the air, so that means the piers are a long way up and I wasn't sure we'd be able to Bruce Willis our asses up some rope.

Luckily, a smaller pier cut to the south of us, so we followed land until we could angle in. Planes continued to rocket over head. To my horror, the fuckers were shooting at people on the ground. Machine guns rattled and spent munitions fell.

"Fucking hell!" Reynolds said exactly what I was thinking.

Another jet started firing from directly overhead. A building bloomed into flame in the distance and then an explosion from another section of the base roared into the air.

"Jesus! Are we at war?" Reynolds was once again thinking my thoughts.

"I don't know. Should we even try to make it to land? Maybe we can paddle toward the city," I said.

"It's the base. We gotta help." Kelly made a lot of sense – unfortunately.

A couple of helicopters shook the raft as they flew by. They settled over the eastern part of the base and opened fire on something. More flames rose into the air. The shots weren't confined to just the aircraft. From the distance we picked up on plenty of small arms fire.

"It's the same stuff from the boat. The same goddamn stuff but its spread all over the base," Reynolds said.

"What if it's more widespread than just the base? What then?" I felt like I was whining but Kelly got a faraway look in his eye.

We came alongside a small tender and I used the railing to pull us along until we were flush with a pier. Reynolds crawled over first with his MP-5 pointing ahead. Kelly covered him and then I was next. I didn't have a weapon but I spotted a large toolbox near a small ship and lifted the lid. Inside were a number of screw drivers, nuts, bolts, and assorted tools, but the prize was a pipe wrench nearly two feet long. I lifted it and found the heft to my liking.

Kelly shot me a questioning look so I mimed bashing in a head.

"Too heavy."

"Maybe for you, ya scrawny Marine," I said.

He smirked and nodded toward Reynolds, who was taking up position next to a building with corrugated metal siding. I was surprised they hadn't left my sorry ass yet. I didn't have a fancy gun and hadn't fired one in years with the exception of video games. In virtual life I'd probably killed an entire nation of people; in real life I had no desire to shoot at another person for as long as I lived.

I followed because I didn't know what else to do. I knew the base, which meant I knew where the commissary and bars were. I knew how to get off the base for the same reason. Food, beer, and occasionally to find a date, even if it had to be paid for in Tijuana.

I could always desert these guys and just find the barracks I'd stayed in a few times, but what if that was also under attack? What a clusterfuck my day was turning into.

Gunfire to the west drew my attention. I snapped my wrench up like I was going to bat bullets out to the air. Reynolds had extended the stock of the little machine gun and moved ahead of us in a quick, steady manner. He slipped to the side of a building, slid along it to a corner and then peeked around. He motioned and Kelly followed while I brought up the rear.

Something roared nearby, causing me to spin in fear. I hit the side of the metal building with the wrench and immediately regretted it. The sound was like a Chinese game-show gong in the morning air.

A column of smoke rose from the direction of the noise that

has startled me, and then an unholy explosion shook the ground. A building went up in flames, the roof disintegrating as it exploded.

A HUMVEE overflowing with people zipped past us. A guy hung onto the roof while someone else batted at the figure from the hatch. Then it was gone, careening behind another building. It grew silent for a few seconds before the vehicle crashed.

"Let's check it out," Joel said.

"Let's not and say we did," I muttered. "Fuck this, dude. We need to find someone in charge and report in. We have to tell them about the McClusky."

"I hear ya, but something is going on. Something bad. Caution is what we need right now," Reynolds said.

"And that caution means investigating crashed HUMVEES? That's what just passed, right?" I asked.

"It was, and it had Marine insignia, so it's our duty."

"Oh Christ. At least give me a gun."

"As soon as I have a spare," Joel Kelly said and clapped me on the shoulder.

Joel nodded and moved toward the sound of the crash with his handgun ready. Reynolds moved behind me and covered us as I followed the Marine.

Then someone staggered around the side of the building, but stopped when he saw us. The guy was dressed in BDU's. His head, face, and mustache were all covered in blood. It dribbled from a wound on his forehead that wasn't going to stop bleeding anytime soon, unless he put a bandage on it.

"Damn, man," I said. "You okay?"

"I don't think he's okay," Reynolds said.

Joel grabbed my shirtsleeve and shook his head.

"But he looks hurt and he's a squid—so there. You guys and your 'always going back for your own'."

"Dude ain't normal. Look at him," Reynolds said.

He was right.

The sailor advanced on us with an unsteady walk, like he was drunk off his ass. He snarled and moaned as he stumbled over his own two feet. One arm came up and that's when I noticed that his other arm was hanging at a weird angle. Not only that, but some of his fingers were completely gone.

"Is he like one of the guys on the ship?"

"Looks like it," Reynolds said.

"Sir. Sir!" Joel yelled and advanced.

Goddamn Marine. I moved ahead to block his aim because I wasn't going to watch him gun down another squid. If this guy was in shock from the accident, I didn't want these trigger-happy gun jocks shooting him just because he couldn't walk right.

Then the sailor attacked me.

I batted his arms aside and wished to hell I'd never gotten in Joel's way. The blood-splattered guy was crazy and he reeked of shit! He grabbed for me, but his hands didn't have enough fingers to get a hold on my shirt. He swung his other arm like a club and caught me across the temple. I briefly saw stars, but I'd been hit harder by one of my brothers and brushed it off.

I pushed him back but he swung his arms up again and opened his trap. Oh, fuck me, but that was some horror. His mouth was filled with broken teeth and blood. His tongue dangled out on a strip of muscle and flopped against his chin. He snarled and groaned but couldn't get his tongue back in. It would have been funny as shit if he hadn't been attempting to eat me.

I staggered backward and almost fell, but Joel really did have my back.

Joel used his body to keep me from falling and then pushed me off. That was all I needed.

I swung because I was scared. Of course, at that point I'd only seen the things on the ship and they'd frightened me, but I was also in denial, like the whole event wasn't really happening. Yet here was another of the crazy things and he wanted to kill me, not talk.

He drooled red saliva. When he tried to snarl again, blood bubbled out and something pink fell out of his mouth. It smacked the ground and I was left to stare at a piece of partially chewed human skin.

That's when I lost it. I swung the wrench with a cry and hit the bastard across the side of his head. The tool weighed about eight pounds, so it was practically a battering ram.

He dropped and didn't move again.

"Nice work," Joel said.

I wanted to puke. I'll never forget that sound, man. I'll never forget what it felt like to hit a human like that. I was horrified and I was disgusted.

More gunfire all around us and then another series of jets roared overhead. I ducked but looked up as they departed. A few seconds later, the sounds of explosions reverberated in the direction of the city.

Joel looked troubled, gestured for me to follow, and moved out.

They were hitting the city? Good Christ, how far had this spread?

We came across the crash a few minutes later. The Humvee had struck the side of a building filled with ship parts. Whoever had been on top of the military truck was smashed against the wall in a smear of blood and gore that would haunt my nightmares for days to come. Shit! This whole damn day was going to necessitate a hell of a lot of therapy.

A soldier rolled out of a rear door and fell onto the ground. He didn't move for a few seconds. We stared at each other and then back at him. From the angle he lay in, it seemed obvious that his hips had to be broken. Legs just couldn't be in that position. He twitched and I was afraid he was one of them, but he got one hand under his body and lifted himself up a few inches so he could look at us. Joel moved in, gun trained on the guy.

"Help," the man said. He was dressed in camo and had a host of magazines and bulging pockets on his upper body.

"Damn. What happened, brother?" Joel moved in and helped the guy roll over.

"Everything. I'm hurt bad. Can you get someone to help? Please? Take me to medical or get a chopper."

"Hold on. We'll do our best. I promise," Reynolds said. He dropped beside Joel Kelly and me and took the hurt man's hand in his.

Blood spread across the fallen Marine's tactical vest. Reynolds leaned over and opened it to reveal that something had penetrated his chest. He took a gurgling breath and then sighed.

"This is not good," Reynolds said.

"It's bad, man. I can't even feel my legs."

"Help's on the way," Joel said.

Was it? I didn't hear the sound of sirens or see the flash of red lights.

"It's worse than that. Ah, shit. Just gimme a gun and one shot, then go. Get the fuck out of here and don't look back."

That's when I saw it. The sleeve of his other arm was ripped open and blood, fresh and crimson, coated the fabric. He'd removed his belt and cinched it just below his elbow. The man had been bitten, and assuming that what had happened on the ship was "the new normal," this guy was so screwed.

"What happened?"

"It's all messed up. So royally messed up. Were you here when it started?"

"No brother. We were on a ship. Just got here."

"Shit. Lucky you. It's a virus of some kind. Whole city's gone crazy. We heard the same stuff hit other bases."

"What's your name?"

"Norvell, Mike Norvell. Guys used to call me Big Papa." Mike choked on a glob of blood and spat it out.

"Tell me about the base, Norvell."

"You guys need to go," Norvell gasped and then frowned. His body stiffened and he looked about as miserable as anyone I'd ever seen in my life.

"You're going to be alright."

"The tourniquet slows it down but I can feel it. It's like my blood's filled with sand."

"Sorry we can't do better by you, man. But please. What happened?"

"It happened so fast. Something docked that wasn't supposed to, some ship from overseas. They quarantined it, but something happened. A few days later the first cases showed up. Then rumors. Rumors of the virus at other seaports and military bases."

"What? Like an attack?"

I unholstered the gun at Norvell's side, held it up and ejected the magazine. I took out all but one bullet, pocketed what I was pretty sure were 9 mm rounds, put the magazine back in and racked a shell into the chamber. I held the gun out to Reynolds. He took it, stared at it for a few seconds and then put it in the guy's hand.

Norvell coughed up another blast of blood and that seemed to be enough for Reynolds. The Marine got to his feet and moved back. Mike "Big Papa" Norvell thrashed on the ground. His eyes bulged so much I thought they were going to explode. He shook as he lifted his hand and just barely managed to put the barrel of the gun under his chin.

We all looked away when the shot snapped across the area.

Joel got up and went to the vehicle. He rummaged around and then came out with a rifle and a small backpack. He put the items on the ground and hunted around again. He came out with a pair of handguns, then placed four magazines on the ground.

Joel had a crap load of gear laid out. The guys, still soaking wet from the dip in the ocean, strapped on as much as they could, to a soundtrack of squishing noises. Reynolds slung his little machine gun behind his back, picked up one of the rifles and checked it. They tossed me a handgun. I did as I'd done with Norvell's gun because I wasn't a complete idiot when it came to weapons. I did a quick inspection, counted how many rounds I had in the Smith and Wesson, then added a pair of magazines to my pockets.

We moved out toward the center of base. Why? I had no idea; I was just along for the walk in hell. Before we departed, Joel looked over the HUMVEE just to make sure it was toast. Didn't take a fucking mechanic to see the damage was beyond any of us or a shop, a week, and a hell of a repair bill. The front end was completely destroyed from hitting the corner of the building, but the seats were also covered in blood, and that was reason enough for me to stay out.

Two buildings later, we ran into a shit storm.

Someone had set up a barricade of cars, trucks, and fences to block at least one cross-street. Joel jogged the perimeter and then dashed back a minute later. He shook his head, so we looked back the way we'd come.

Joel was in the process of hauling ass around the corner of a barracks when he ran smack into one of the creatures. It was missing part of a foot and toppled over when Joel struck him. The Marine didn't hesitate; he splattered its brains all over the road with two quick shots.

"Oh, fuck me running!" Reynolds said.

I echoed his sentiment in my head.

There had to be fifty of them massed around the remains of the barricade. Bodies were pressing against the corners and they weren't interested in the fence, because they were eating – Fucking eating – the soldiers.

"Oh no you don't!" Reynolds yelled.

He started shooting. The booming of his assault rifle was ridiculously loud. Joel Kelly took a wide stance and also started popping guys in the head, neck, and body. He practically ripped a guy's arm off with a couple of shots, then a beauty of a blast took the guy right through the temple as he tried to turn on us.

I raised my own gun to take aim, and then I couldn't pull the trigger. The uniformed person that fell under my aim was a woman about my age. She was slight and had a head of blonde hair. I would have given her a second and third look if we passed each other on the street.

Now she was covered in her own blood—or someone else's. Her shirt was ripped away, revealing lots of pale flesh, but I was not interested in the slightest. One of her breasts was practically torn away. Talk about the opposite of a little blue pill.

I turned to gag. Kelly, seeing me in distress, shot her twice.

The first shot was off to her shoulder but he snapped the gun up and put one through her nose. She collapsed without a sound.

"Fuck this!" That was it for me. I shuddered in revulsion and considered jumping back into the ocean.

"Get it together, man!" Joel Kelly said, and I thought he was going to hit me.

Reynolds stayed in the fight and fired as quickly as he could focus in on targets. Joel moved to assist, so I decided it was time to man the fuck up.

I put an advancing soldier that slobbered and drooled blood between my cross hairs and shot him three times. The first two went to his chest; those just backed him up. I knew how this shit worked, so I shot him in the head as my brain caught up with the rest of my body.

Then a tide of them came at us. It was like the flood gates had opened. Holy shit, there were a lot of the undead bastards. They poured out of buildings, side roads, out of stopped vehicles, and God knew where else. I said a prayer, but Joel had a better idea.

"Fall back. Let's head for the barracks."

Reynolds followed him but I took a few seconds to shoot the lead Z a couple of times, and then my gun ran empty. I pulled the trigger on the Smith and Wesson but it just clicked. Kelly was the one to break me out of my daze by smacking me upside the head.

"Don't touch me!" I screamed.

"Get your head in the game, man. Let's go!"

He was right. There were ten or fifteen of them for each one of us and more coming. The only thing stopping them from overrunning our position were the remains of the barricade. We could make a valiant stand and take a shit load of them with us.

Or we could do something else. We could haul ass.

We did the latter.

12:25 hours approximate
Location: San Diego CA – Roz's Place

IT'S BEEN A WEEK SINCE THAT DAY, AND I STILL THINK ABOUT IT maybe more than everything else that's happened since. But I'll have to get to that later.

Joel's back from his little trip to Fortress and he isn't alone. He brought a couple of teenagers with him. Were these the little shits that broke into our house?

Joel had knocked on the door three times and then once. He'd paused and done it again, so Roz opened the door. She took one look at him and at the two dirty faced behind him, and she didn't seem annoyed or put out at all. She just motioned for them to come inside.

Roz took one look at them and motioned for them to join us.

"Fortress?" I asked.

"Gone, but we got bigger problems."

"Bigger? What's bigger than losing our home?"

"Losing everything. That's a hell of a lot bigger."

"What do you mean?"

Joel turned to the kids – a boy and girl – and nodded. The girl was fifteen at the most. She tried to look brave but she was a mess. Her hair was a pale bird's nest that pointed in every direction. The boy was older by a few years and he was well armed. He had a small bat slung over his back. The strap was a piece of rope but I noticed right away it would be easy to swing it under his arm and have it at the ready.

He had a pair of knives tucked into his belt and a snub nose revolver in a holster at his waist. Call this kid Dirty Harry.

"I'm Christie and this is Craig."

"Hey." Craig nodded.

He had a deep voice for such a skinny kid. If he weighed a buck ten I'd be surprised. But he was gangly and I bet he could swing that little baseball bat with devastating force. They were both dressed in clothes that had seen better days a week ago. Now they were practically rags and covered in dirt. Neither one smelled all that great, but who was I to judge? Joel and I had lived in our own sweat for ten or eleven days now.

"So you took over our home?"

"Wasn't us. Someone came before and searched it. We just moved in after they left. Thought you guys were gone."

"Was that you I heard rummaging around the night before?"

"Yeah. Sorry about that. We were so hungry but we waited until you were gone. We were just going to eat some food and leave, but the other guys got there first. Not us. We went in later. Got a few scraps."

Roz went to the kitchen and cracked open some packages. She brought them both bottled water and a "meal ready to eat" apiece. They tore into it like it was a number 3 at McDonalds.

"So who took our shit?"

"Some dudes that looked like they were ready for war. Looked tougher than you guys."

Joel burst into laughter.

"We do alright," I protested.

Craig looked us over but clearly wasn't impressed.

I stared at the kid for a minute while that processed. A helicopter overhead rattled the windows, giving me a scare and a half.

Joel moved to the window and cracked open the blinds to look up. He craned his neck around but shook his head after a few seconds.

"We're saved?" I asked Joel.

"Can't tell, man, but it can't be worse than a city full of fucking zombies."

Roz 'hmphed' and looked toward the kids.

"Sorry. Gosh darned zombies."

Both of the young ones snickered.

"What else could it be?" I asked.

The answer to that question would come soon because Joel was gearing up, and that meant we were going to reconnoiter. I thought about my swollen ankle and decided that if he was going out, I was going along as well. Enough of this sitting around.

I'd have to wrap it tight and take my chances, because I was not letting the Marine go out there without me. I'll finish up the story of how we got off the base and founded Fortress later.

FIGHT AND FLIGHT

19:45 hours approximate
Location: San Diego CA – Roz's Roof

S upplies

- Food: a few protein bars
- Weapons: almost zip
- Worst. Day. Ever.

My dad was a big guy who didn't talk much. He was in the Army and told me that the military wasn't the best place for a kid like me. He said I'd be better suited for a blue-collar job like construction or sanitation where I didn't have someone constantly telling me when to wipe my ass. I said that would be funny if I was in sanitation. He smacked me upside the head.

Why didn't I listen to him? He was a goddamn genius.

Don't get me wrong, I got nothing against blue-collar workers or the job I ended up with in the Navy. Someone's gotta keep the fires on a ship lit. Gotta keep that engine turning. I just wanted to do something different, like get into journalism, but that required money. I joined the Navy so I could see the world, fuck a lot of girls, and then have my college paid for.

I got one of those wishes.

One wish I didn't make was for my very own Marine Sergeant Joel "Cruze" Kelly. One night I asked Joel what the "Cruze" was all about. He smiled and deflected the question. Jerk. I kept bugging him about it, because what the hell else did we have to talk about? I asked if it was some kind of Marine secret handshake. After a few minutes of my good-natured ribbing, he finally told me it was something his Mom had called him as a kid and it just stuck around. I didn't bother him about it after that.

My own mother didn't have an opinion either way about me joining up. On one hand, I'm sure she didn't want her youngest son leaving the house. On the other hand, it was probably a relief. My three older bothers weren't amounting to much and continued to mooch off our folks while I had dreams of going to college. Money I wasn't going to make working at Burger King.

I was going to join the Army, like Dad, but then I watched some videos of boot camp and decided a ship would be a much more interesting place to hang out instead of in the sand while some asshole shot at me.

Joel did not have a similar story. His dad was in the Marines, and his dad's dad was in the Corps, so that meant that Joel Kelly was destined to hold an assault rifle and shoot at people. Hoo-ah – oh yeah, they don't say that in the Marines anymore. If Joel reminded me of that one more time I was going to strangle him with his own gun strap.

Roz didn't tell us much more of her story but she listened to us talk about our pasts and asked questions when it seemed like there was a break in the flow. She said it would be a way for all of us to break the ice and get to know each other. Now that we had a couple of kids with us, I guess it made sense.

I know it sounds like I'm planning for the future, but I'm not really. When you get right down to it, our life expectancy is next to nil. When you really think about what we are facing, you'll understand that it's not a good idea to make long term plans.

Especially now.

Especially. Now!

15:45 hours approximate
Location: San Diego CA – Roz's Place

JOEL SNOOZED IN MY CHAIR FOR AN HOUR. I TOOK THE TIME TO EAT and drink as much as my gut could handle.

It was glorious.

Roz was busy pacing the living room. She walked to the front door and then back to the windows that faced the yard. I took the opportunity to check out her ass in a pair of grey sweat pants that seemed molded to her body. I'm glad she didn't catch me. I'm pretty sure she'd have no issue with sticking her shotgun up my ass. Roz peeked out every few minutes. After a while she must have made up her mind to do whatever she needed to do, because she woke Joel up and asked for cover.

Joel popped up like a Marine Jack-in-the-Box, snapped up his assault rifle, and did a quick ammo check. He nodded at Roz and followed her to the door.

"What's she doing?" I asked Joel.

"Her father."

"Oh," I said, and lost whatever little bit of a good mood I'd had a few minutes ago. No kid should have to bury their own parent.

"Should I help?"

"I don't think so. She looks determined to do it herself. Why don't you keep watch out the back."

Roz went into the open garage and dragged out an old carpet. She took the piece to her Dad's body and rolled him onto it. Smart. That way she could drag him easier, and it also created a sort of burial cover.

I went to the back of the house and peeked through a window. This was Roz's room and we'd been forbidden from entering it. I had a feeling she wouldn't mind since we were protecting her.

She wasn't the neatest girl. There were clothes in piles all around the room. Shirts and dresses hung from a homemade wire rack that ran the length of the room. Dresses? That was the last thing I expected to see Roz in. After a few minutes it hit me. What else was she supposed to do with her clothes? There sure as hell wasn't any way to wash them in our new world.

The back room's windows were boarded up but a couple of spy holes offered me a limited view of the world outside the house. Dried up shrubs, a road littered with discarded crap. Broken furniture and empty suitcases. Someone's sports jacket baked in the sun next to a pair of white broken white sunglasses. The only things missing were a few shamblers.

In salute to the dead world I lifted a plastic wrapper, tore it open, and munched on a protein bar. Then I sipped a bottle of water. The only thing that would make this better was an ice-cold beer, but the lone brew we'd saved from our beer-run a few days ago was probably in the coffers of whoever the fuck ransacked our place.

It was early but already hot inside the little brick house. It may be seventy five at the hottest out there, but once the place gets warm it stays that way.

Sound to the west. I was on the east-facing side of the house and couldn't see a damn thing until the helicopter thundered overhead. It hovered for a few seconds over a building and then passed over the house. Did they see Roz? Did she signal to them? Were they going to come back and rescue us?

Over a week in this city and I was sick of being cut off. I was sick of living day to day, meal to meal. I wanted out of San Diego and I wanted to know, more than anything, what in the hell was happening in the good ol' U S of A, because the way we were living could not be the new normal.

I pulled my handgun before I'd even had the chance to think about it. If I could just signal the chopper

I popped the magazine out of habit and checked the load. Full. I lined it up and then fumble fingered the mag. It hit the ground and bounced under Roz's bed. I followed it and dropped to all fours to get it. I got a handful of panties and stockings and stared at them dumbly. I bet Roz would rock this stuff.

I carefully put the naughty clothes back, picked up the heavy magazine, and slammed it home.

The sound of the chopper was long gone. I stared up but they didn't materialize again. Then I looked down.

"Oh. Fuck. Me." I holstered my pistol.

A horde was headed our way. I don't mean ten Z's or fifty of the dead fuckers. It was even worse than the day we almost got stuck in Ty's apartment when Joel's little fuck up seemed to bring the whole city our way. Only speed and luck had saved our ass that time.

There had to be several thousands. Thousands!

"Uhh," I said. Real smart, right?

I was so scared I considered just crapping my pants. Then Joel's voice in my head told me to man up or he'd find an adult diaper and make me wear it. Here we were in a nice safe house where we could silently wait for them to pass us by, and Roz was out on the front yard. There wasn't even a moment of hesitation, no thought of leaving her out there.

I stared and tried to get a count but after a few seconds I dashed out of the room.

I ran at a gimpy pace on my twisted ankle through the hallway. I passed a room where the two kids, Christy and Craig, slept. I made it to the living room and almost crashed into the recliner I'd called home the night before.

"Joel!" I called as loudly as I dared.

He had the door propped open, one foot inside the threshold, the other on the porch. The assault rifle was slung across his chest with his finger poised right over the trigger. Joel wore his New York Fire Department ball cap backwards and the pilfered shades over his eyes.

"Joel!" I yelled louder this time.

"What? I'm keeping watch. Why aren't you doing the same?"

"Dude. We got trouble. Big fucking trouble."

"What?"

"Come look."

"I can't leave Roz out there."

"Roz. Shit."

I didn't have to think about the stupid shit I was about to do.

I tried to brush past Joel but he stopped me with a meaty Marine hand. I towered over him and could have knocked him aside, but for all the shit we give each other, I'd never had a better friend.

"What're you doing?"

"It's bad. There're so many of them I couldn't count the first wave. It's an army and they're all headed in this direction. We need to get Roz back in here now." I looked around the yard. "Where is she?"

"In the garage. Please tell me you're exaggerating a little bit."

"I wish, man. I wish. Did she flag down that chopper?"

"They took off when they saw her."

"Damn."

"You go get her. I'll cover. No, wait. You cover and I'll go. You and your busted leg."

"You're ten times the shot I am. I'll go." And this time I did take his hand, but with more of a handshake grip as I pushed it down. "It's the right thing to do. Stay here and pop anything that gets close."

Joel nodded and clapped me on the shoulder.

I did the stupid thing and took a step outside the house.

16:05 hours approximate
Location: Undead Central, San Diego CA – Roz's Place

THE GARAGE WASN'T ATTACHED TO THE HOUSE. IF IT WAS, THIS might have had a different ending. As it was, the little building was only thirty or forty feet away from the door and only a few feet from the side of the house, but it might as well have been a mile with me naked and armed with a toothbrush.

I swear I could hear them already, even though they had to be at least a hundred yards away.

The morning sun was nice and high in the sky. I shaded my eyes and crunched across the short concrete patio, down the couple of stairs, and onto the sidewalk. Dead grass in all of its yellow and brown glory spread around me. A lone water sprinkler sat next to a dried blood stain which roughly resembled the shape of a man.

The corner of the house erupted in noise. The moans of the dead had reached us much quicker than I thought and that meant one thing.

Shufflers.

A group came into view from the side of the garage. They were a motley assortment of dead, cobbled together by their need for fresh meat. Men and women, boys and girls. The virus had taken everyone in its path.

"Ugly bastards, all of you!" I yelled.

I hoped Roz heard me. I was already headed toward her, so I drew and shot on the move. I missed. My second shot missed as well, so I stopped, took a breath, aimed down the sights and then dropped the Z that was about to enter the garage.

I spun but more of the Z's were rounding the other side of the house. I was trapped.

Hobbling on my bum ankle, I got to the walkway. Joel swung into his super Marine mode by moving onto the porch and dropping the first of the dead. His second shot spun another one around but it completed a halfway decent dance move by turning three hundred and sixty degrees. Joel hit it between the eyes with the second shot.

Another pair right behind the first. I gasped and took a shot. Missed. God I sucked. My hand was shaking like a leaf but I didn't stop firing.

A couple of former soldiers, from the look of their rotted and hanging uniforms. I took out one and hit the other in the chest. He dropped but got a hand out and hauled himself to his knees. I kicked the rotter in the face and dove into the garage.

The bodies from the night before lay in a pile. Roz had executed one at point blank range and most of his head was just gone. Joel's shots had been neater but the bodies were still that —bodies.

"Oh no! Oh shit!" Roz yelled.

"Can you close the door?"

"Shit!" She jumped and grabbed a rope and yanked but the door didn't budge.

The former soldier I'd kicked in the face snarled around a dislocated jaw and came at us. I kicked him in the gut before he could reach the boundary of the garage. He was dead, so he needed to stay on his side of the world. I used the best persuader at my disposal by lifting the hand cannon and firing into his face.

I'd made good use of the gun, but in the heat of the battle I'd lost count of my shots. I went over the action in my head and thought I might have seven or eight rounds left.

Roz grabbed at the door again. I got a hold on the rope with her, this time, and we both yanked. The garage door came loose and slid down with a creak.

The old and heavy slab of wood swung down and dropped into place. It clicked when it was flush with the ground, so I tested the handle, but it wouldn't turn. At least we were safe for now, even if we were trapped in a giant box with no light and four or five bodies. My skin crawled, and that was before I got the first whiff of their bloating corpses.

More gunshots and then they went silent.

"What happened?" Roz asked. She stood close to me, so I reached out to touch her in the dark, just to reassure myself that she was really there. Of all the close calls, this one had been the worst. I was left gasping for air.

"I slipped."

"No, what happened just now?"

"I was in the back of the house keeping an eye out when I saw them coming. About a thousand of those things. I ran out to warn you."

"So you went out on a rescue mission? Are you stupid?"

"You're welcome."

"I didn't ask you to save me. I can take care of myself."

"Yeah, and those things would have devoured you. Where would that leave me and Joel? Inside the house, filled with guilt and your food. That's where."

"Chivalry's dead, man."

"But being a decent human being isn't. Not yet. Not with Joel Kelly and Jackson Fucking Creed on the case."

She let out a light giggle, and that was enough for me.

Roz touched my hand, took it in hers and squeezed. I squeezed back. We stood in the dark and didn't speak for long moments. My breathing was still harsh and came in ragged gasps.

Thumping on the door that grew in intensity. I'd seen this before, the second or third day in the city. The dead had trapped a poor soul in a hotel room and battered at the door and window until both broke. The screams came moments later.

Joel and I had been hidden in a convenience store across the street. The door had probably been busted off the hinges by looters. We crouched and stared at each other with wide, wild eyes. I was scared to death that at any moment one of those things was going to get wind of us.

We managed to keep quiet for a couple of hours while the dead feasted on their prize and then eventually wandered off. Funny how hiding makes you patient. A week ago I would have been going stir crazy from having nothing to do but wait. Back then I had my games and cell phone. I even had a crappy tablet I'd won in a game of spades. I could hang out and read Facebook or surf the web. Being stuck in that store while we contemplated life and death made me shut the fuck up with a quickness.

Roz and I only had one choice and it was in my right hand. Seven or eight shots were enough. I only needed two.

"We're fucked," Roz said.

"No back door?"

"Nope. Dad had this thing delivered and mounted on a concrete slab fifteen years ago. It's not even a real garage. It's just a bunch of wooden siding held together with bubblegum."

"What do you want to do?"

"I don't think making a run for it is an option, yeah?"

"Yeah. I mean no. Think we can kick out a wall?"

"Probably…but the noise."

"Yeah," I said.

Roz folded herself into me and stood there for a minute. She touched my chest and then felt to my shoulder, then down my arm. Shit, was I about to go out with a smile?

Her hand stopped at the handgun.

"How many rounds do you have?"

"Enough."

"Okay, but last resort. If they get in here, do it. Don't tell me it's coming; just do it so I'm not scared out of my pants."

"I bet you look good out of your pants," I said.

"Guess you'll never know in the dark, huh? Maybe we should be quiet. See? I'm coming up with a plan."

"That's the plan?"

"Yeah. If we're quiet, maybe they'll get bored and leave."

I didn't see that happening but I also didn't see anything wrong with holding Roz against me for a little bit longer. It'd been a long time since I held a woman and if I was about to die, I could think of worse ways to go.

Our respite was short lived. The pounding on the door picked up with gusto. I hugged Roz tighter and closed my eyes.

mumble mumble.

"What?" I asked the darkness.

"Someone's yelling."

"Joel. Who else would start making a fuss? Think he's going to go into Marine mode and lead them away?"

"I hope not," Roz said.

"Me too." I nodded in the dark. I liked Joel right where he was – alive and ready to carry on the fight.

More mumbled shouts.

The banging on the door increased and I was sure they were about to break in. The door flexed, so we took up station in front of it and pushed back. It might not stop them for long, but it was better than giving up.

More mumbles but they were overridden by the moans

outside. So many voices and many of them just making guttural sounds. It didn't make any sense. I did, however, make out was the clicks and scrabbling of at least one shuffler.

Something thumped against the garage so hard I nearly jumped out of my skin. I'd like to say we were brave, but I was just about to go find a corner to shit in. If I didn't, my pants were going to be filled, and I didn't want my Mom's worst fear to be realized. She would have to bury my corpse in my dirty skivvies.

Something else thumped. I looked up because the sound had come from there. Jesus, did a shuffler make it that high? I'd seen them leap, but not that damn far. The roof was flat, but it was still a good twelve feet high.

Something smashed into the roof and this time I aimed the gun. More mumbled shouts.

"What in the hell!" Roz yelled. She reached for me and found my hand. I gave hers a squeeze and tried to act brave which was really hard to do in the pitch black.

Light crept under the garage door every time one of the Z's hit it. As the beating grew faster it looked like we were standing under a strobe light.

The door buckled and almost went down. A spring on one side gave way with a twanging pop. The Z's beat at the door even harder. I pushed back, but one hard crash almost sent me to my knees. That would be one of the shufflers.

More noise from the roof.

I tugged Roz to me. I embraced her and put her head against my chest. It wasn't really a romantic way to go out and not something I'd ever plan. If this was some Romeo and Juliet fucked up zombie movie, that's how it would end. I guess I'd just put the gun to her head and pull the trigger, then, if it didn't pass through her head and into my chest, I'd put it under my chin. The dead could feast on my corpse.

Still, I'd love to kill one more shuffler before I went down. I hated those things.

Something crashed into the roof. Something heavy enough to shake the entire building—speaking of shufflers.

Another crash and light poured in from above.

"Get your asses up here!" Joel yelled.

Something sharp smashed into the roof and tore a hole the size of a softball. He was using an entrenching tool to rip the roof an asshole. Son of a bitch, Joel. Son of a bitch.

The dead renewed their efforts to get us. The thumping was bad enough, but now Joel was offering us a way out – if there was time.

"Can you find some way to get us up there?" I asked Roz.

"What about the door?"

"Just make us a ladder. I'll hold the door." I smiled in the dim light because I knew it was probably a death sentence.

She moved away and used the light from above to gather up a few items. Now that I could see, it was clear that the garage was a veritable death trap. Tools lay on benches, and there was a chainsaw that I briefly thought of trying to use if the Z's got through the door.

A couple of mowers lay in disrepair with wheels and machine parts in buckets and bins. There was enough furniture in the room to fill a two-story house, most of it stacked against the wall.

Joel ripped up a chunk of roof and tossed it aside. He looked in and I waved, but with the dust and dark I doubted he could make us out.

"I can see you!" Roz yelled.

She worked at a pile of old wooden chairs, tossing them under the hole Joel was creating. He dug in with the small shovel and then ripped up yet another piece along with a huge pile of pink insulation.

The dead grew furious, judging by the way they pounded at the door. I pushed back, and just when I thought they were going to give it a rest, something hit the door hard enough to knock off another spring.

"Shufflers. We need to hurry!" Joel yelled.

"Then hurry."

"Get your ass up here and dig. I bet they'll let you through."

I flipped him the bird.

The door buckled and almost caved in. I put my back into it but there were fingers wriggling between the frame and the broken door. A hand poked through, so I dragged the gun up, estimated where the head was attached to the body, and put a round through the thick wood. The hand stopped feeling around and went limp.

"Almost got it!" Joel yelled and ripped up another piece of roof.

Roz climbed up onto the contraption she'd built and stood on unsteady legs as the chair wobbled, balanced on two other chairs. Was I supposed to get out on that thing?

She reached up; Joel Kelly caught her hands and pulled. Another pair of hands came down and grabbed her forearms and then she was yanked up. Craig or Christy, those two wonderful kids, had decided to help. I grinned.

My gratitude was short lived.

My skin crawled and my belly clenched when the door gave way. I pulled away and just avoided being crushed under it and about a hundred stinking dead people that wanted to eat me.

Do you know the dread? Can you imagine what their reek is like? It's hell, pure hell and those teeth... Most still have teeth, but others have snapped and cracked chompers that are the nastiest things you have ever seen outside of a pit of bloated corpses rotting in the sun.

I made it two steps, thought I felt breath on the back of my neck, then spun and shot a shuffler in mid-leap. She had both hands up, her mouth a furious grin of madness. I swear she was gibbering. A couple of fingers had been chewed to the knuckle and that was probably what saved me, because her nasty hand wasn't able to keep a grip on my arm.

My first shot missed. I took a few steps back as every fiber of my body screamed that I needed to run. I fired one more time and, this time, did some damage. The bullet ripped through her body laterally but didn't stop the damned woman.

I reached the chairs and crawled up the first level while the garage filled. I had only seconds and one mistake would be the end of me. I'd be pulled into the mass so fast that there wouldn't be time to blow my brains out.

I shot a Z in the chest because I didn't have time to get a good bead. The bullet punched into flesh and knocked it aside.

Up to the second set of chairs and then I could almost reach the roof.

The chair rocked under my feet but I dared not look down. If I did, I was sure one of them would have me.

I leapt up and the chair wobbled to the side.

Fingertips. That's all I managed to hold on with.

Joel grabbed an arm and pulled. Craig grabbed my other arm, and if not for them, I would have gone back down into the mass.

Another shuffler smashed into the chairs and I was left dangling like a side of beef.

"Fucking get me out of here!" I yelled in an unintended falsetto.

"We're trying, you fucking ox," Joel said as he strained.

Joel's face was full of worry, visible even behind his thick shades. He gasped for breath and threw his body into it. I rose into the air a few precious inches and managed to get a grip on the edge of the hole.

I pulled my legs up close to my body as something else grabbed at my boots. A hand got a hold of my pant leg and I was stretched between my rescuers and my would-be consumers.

I'm pretty sure I screamed like a little girl.

Roz leaned over and grabbed a wrist. Together, the three of them pulled me up. I kicked down and dislodged the hand on my pant leg. Another kick caught the shuffler in the head.

It gibbered as it fell away. The bitch's head was covered in wisps of hair and her eyes were sunken in like the orbs of a skeleton. Blood coated her body, but most of it was by her mouth. She struck the mob below and used them as a trampoline.

I was so sickened that I sat down with my feet dangling inside the garage, took aim, and shot her in the head. Her mouth moved and something like words came out, but they didn't mean anything. She stopped making noises when my round split her skull. Take that, you sick fuck.

"Thank you, Joel. Thank you for saving us." I reached out to offer a manly shake-thing that turned into a half-hearted hug until he pushed my hands away.

"You'd do the same for me," Joel said. "You might wish you were still down there."

"Why in the hell would I wish that?" I asked but trailed off when I saw the new horizon.

I rose on shaking legs, my body exhausted as adrenaline faded away. The sun was an unholy blaze that illuminated a fresh nightmare. All around the house there were the dead. Nothing but the dead. On and on the horde stretched, and more were on the way.

We were trapped in the middle of Undeadville with no escape.

"What do we do now?"

Joel shrugged and picked up his AR-15 and popped the magazine. He gave it a quick shake and slid it back home with a click.

"I guess we wait and hope they go away."

Below, the front door to the house gave in with a crash. Great; that was the second fortress we'd lost in two days.

Craig and Roz sat to the side to watch the Z's gather. Roz sat down and touched her fingers to her forehead, then down to her chest, and then side to side while muttering something about el Diablo.

"How'd you even get up here?"

Joel pointed at his entrenching tool and then looked at the house. They'd come out through the roof, jumped the couple of feet that separated the buildings and then gotten us out.

Christy popped out of the hole in the house a few seconds later and slung a couple of backpacks onto the roof. She took a deep breath and pulled herself up. Craig made the three-foot leap onto the home and helped her cross.

They both joined us and collapsed in a heap.

"I got what I could but they broke into the house."

"All that food and water," Roz said and shook her head.

"At least we're still alive." I tried to sound cheerful but it was cut off by the moans of the dead. A shuffler threw itself at the side of the garage and fell into the crowd below.

"Yeah. This is terrific." Joel said.

Joel had managed to make it out of the house with his assault rifle. He sat with it cradled in his arms.

The ocean of the dead stretched around us until they covered the ground in every direction.

REINFORCEMENTS

04:35 hours approximate
Location: San Diego CA

S upplies:

- Food: zip
- Weapons: almost zip

The roof. The roof. The roof is surrounded by the fucking dead. We just need a fire to make the mother....you get the idea.

I'm not much for long speeches. After a while all of the words sort of run into each other and become a drone. Joel Kelly also wasn't a fan of long speeches and beat me to it with this perfect summary: "We are so fucked."

You'd think a Marine would have a little more dignity or some words of wisdom. If John Wayne was playing the part of a Marine at Anzio and the enemy surrounded our little group of survivors, I'm sure he'd have some powerful words for the troops. Big words about glory and how it's a fighter's duty to destroy the bad guys.

Our troops just lowered their heads and hid. It wasn't hard. Since full dark we'd tried to sleep. The effort was there, but I had sand paper in my eyes from listening to the moans all night.

The house was full of dead. The garage was packed with the dead. The area around us as far as the eye could see was surrounded by the dead. So many dead it was like an ocean. They were out there in their rotted masses really stinking up the place. They groaned, moaned, and snarled. Christy lay on her side and tried to muffle them out with her hands. Craig stared back at them defiantly. That's what a kid's bravado is good for, right there. I had no such illusions.

"How did this mess happen?" Roz asked. She was covered in sweat and blood – not her own blood, but that of her dad and the Z's that had chased us into the garage. I'd shot a shuffler in mid-leap and blood had splattered liberally. It was probably the single best shot I'd made in my week in the city and no one even saw it. I should get a fucking medal for that blast. I settled for being alive.

"At least we're alive." I said. I got a whole pat on the hand for that.

"Why don't we sneak back into the house? Close the door. Lock it. Then we kill all the zombies. We'll be safe then," Christy whispered.

Girl didn't realize that we couldn't just take our chances like that. One bite was all it took.

"Will that work?" Craig asked and flipped one of the shufflers the bird.

"Not a chance." I broke the bad news. "We'd probably all die trying."

The shuffler hissed at Craig. He sniffed the air, looked at his slower moving brethren, and then put his hand in his mouth and bit off a finger.

The Z's left him alone while he chewed on his own digit.

Craig lay back down, so I did the same. Maybe if we stayed out of sight long enough the Z's would lose interest and wander away.

"Why do they do that?" Craig asked quietly.

"Why do they do what?"

OUTBREAK

"Act like they're afraid of the crawly dudes."

"The slow ones?" I asked.

"Yeah. They even act like they understand the weird ones."

"We call them shufflers."

"Shuffler? Like they deal cards?"

"No. On account of that shuffle step they use when they walk. It's like a stuttering motion they can't control. We thought they were running around on broken bones or maybe weren't fully turned or some shit."

"Watch your language around the kids," Roz warned.

"Language?" I blinked.

"Doesn't bother me, dude," Craig said.

"How old are you?" I asked.

"Seventeen."

"Probably has worse language than me."

"Dad was in the Navy," Craig said and looked away.

"I'm in the Navy too. It's cool. What did your Dad do?"

"Something with weapons systems."

"Good for him. I bet he had air conditioning." I thought of spending hours and hours in the hundred-degree engine room.

"Shh." Roz shot me a look.

I sighed and patted Craig's hand.

"Sorry, man. I hope your Dad's okay."

"Me too," he said.

I sighed and slipped my logbook out of the backpack that Christy had retrieved from the house, then dug around until I found a beat up pen.

Joel had pulled his NYFD hat over his eyes and snored gently. He was so quiet I couldn't even hear him over the moans of the dead below. How did he sleep in this living hell?

"What's that?" Craig asked me.

"The only thing keeping me sane," I said and set pen to paper to write about how we had escaped the base.

15:10 hours approximate

Location: Remains of San Diego Naval Base

WEAPONS:

- 2 fully automatic assault rifles
- Enough magazines to make them count
- 1 Colt 1911 .45
- 22 Rounds of .45 ammo
- 1 Heckler and Koch MP5-N sub machine gun
- 1 large knife
- 1 vey large wrench

I've heard a lot of situations described as clusterfucks. I've used the term a number of times myself. Generally the word had a lot of meanings, but this was the best example I'd come across yet.

We'd been back on the base for a few hours and all we'd managed to do was run, hide, and shoot a bunch of people that were acting crazed. I know now it was the damn virus that caused the zombie apocalypse but I didn't know it then. If I'd had any clue, I might have done the smart thing and jumped back into the ocean, then would've swam until my legs gave out. With any luck, a killer whale would choke on my sorry white ass.

We'd just run from a barricade that covered multiple streets. There were dead all over the fucking place and it seemed like every one of them had a bead on us. Joel Kelly moved out on point while Reynolds brought up the rear. I stayed in the middle and tried not to trip on anything. Joel used fancy hand signals; after a while, I thought I'd caught on and knew when to stop, when to crouch, when to crawl, and when to haul ass like I was running from a fire.

We came to another cross street that used to lead to a few fast food restaurants. Bodies on the ground. So many bodies. We crouched at the corner of a building and a street missing a signpost. The whole thing had been run over and was tangled in a heap of twisted metal that used to be car. Now that car was a burned out husk filled with bodies. Must have been a family of six. They were all dead, but still smoking. I gagged at the smell.

Joel grabbed the front of my jump suit and dragged me away.

We rounded a corner and ran smack into a band of them. They turned white eyes on us and commenced with snarling and moaning like a bunch of wild animals. Reynolds shot the nearest one in the chest and then his rifle jammed. Joel tapped him on the shoulder, so he fell back while Joel provided covering fire.

Reynolds worked his gun and then came up shooting. He moved backwards as Kelly also fell back, and then we were on the run again.

We dove into what used to be a fast food restaurant. The place was deserted and trash had been hauled out and scattered all over the floor. A bag of sesame seed buns was split open but covered in blood. I was so hungry I considered rooting around until I found one that hadn't been splattered.

"Think they have food here?"

"Fuck if I know. Sweep the kitchen." Joel nodded at Reynolds.

Joel went low but peeked out a window. The others had been broken out so he avoided those. I stayed next to him while Reynolds moved into the other room. He came back a few seconds later and shook his head.

Joel moved toward him but Reynolds shook his head once again.

"Shit," Joel said and followed Reynolds.

"What?" I asked.

"You don't want to know."

"You really don't," Reynolds said and moved ahead.

"I want to go on record as saying I hate this."

"Yeah, yeah. Quit whining and man up so we can get away from this hellhole."

"Think the cities any better?" I asked.

"Can it be worse?"

He had a point.

We moved out of the building and slid past a small store next door. The entire front had been shot to hell. There was a pile of bodies out front and most didn't twitch. Joel scouted and then held out his hand before crossing in front of it.

"Friendlies!" he said in a low voice. He looked back at us once and then dashed across the field of fire of whoever might be manning a gun inside.

No one shot at him, so we stayed low and followed.

We sprinted to the end of the street and then paused next to a burned out bus. It was white, but flames had turned the outside into shades of black. Soot stuck to my back when I slammed against it. Something fell out of a smashed window and grabbed my neck.

I dropped and let out a little scream of horror. Joel looked from me to the hand and smirked. I followed his eyes and got a look at my assailant. It was a hand, all right, but it was covered in blackened flesh.

"Fuck this," I muttered.

Then the hand twitched.

I could have just leapt right out of my skin but managed to hang onto my sanity by a thread. Fingers moved, grasping at nothing, then they went still again.

We pressed on and found ourselves near an administrative building. Shapes moved behind dark windows.

The place looked familiar and I thought it might have been some kind of processing center for those shipping out to new commands.

"Be ready," Reynolds said.

"Who's in there?"

"Not sure," he said. "But they probably aren't friendly."

We crouched behind a car and went over our weapons. Joel popped his magazine and checked it while Reynolds did the same. Joel laid out an extra mag and then came up in a crouch.

"If they rush us, shoot the first few, then we move. They aren't the fastest things, so we should be able to make it across the street."

"You guys move. I'll cover," Reynolds said.

Luckily, we didn't have to turn the street into a bloodbath.

A pair of guys in green moved out of the building. They had guns like Joel and looked like they knew how to use them. Reynolds looked over the side of the car and then grinned. He whistled once and then put a hand in the air.

The guys snapped to and aimed guns at us. From my vantage point, looking through the remains of a blown out window, I feared they were going to start shooting and ask questions later.

Reynolds held his gun in the air and then rose slowly. Joel did the same.

"Good to see someone's alive," one of the guys said.

We moved on the soldiers' position. Other guys in green filed out of the building. Joel Kelly and Reynolds nodded at them and they nodded back. They went into this weird dance where they looked each other's gear up and down, then exchanged this and that. I saw at least two magazines swapped out for other magazines. Rounds were checked and counted out. Someone handed Kelly a pack that looked like food. He tossed it to me then took one for himself.

"You guys with the eight?" one of the other soldiers asked.

"We just got here," Reynolds said.

We'd moved back into the building the guys had just vacated and crouched in the remains of an overturned trashcan. There were quite a few blood splatters but no bodies, for a change. Not even any parts of bodies.

"What?" One of the guys looked them over. He had steel grey eyes and looked like what an action hero should look like.

"We just got here, Gunny. We were on the McClusky before it rammed into the base."

"I saw that. Damn shame."

"What's going on here?" Joel asked.

"It'd take days to tell you. Something's been hitting cities and bases. The first we heard about it was up north around the Portland area. I guess some Black Water types brought back something besides crotch rot from the desert. At least, that's the rumor."

Joel stared at the man like he was looking at a ghost.

"What was it?" Reynolds asked.

"Don't know. Rumors about some new weapon we were experimenting with."

"Bullshit," Joel stated. "I was over there and those guys don't have the tech."

"True, and don't that make you wonder who does have the tech?"

"But what are we even talking about? This shit. All this fucking shit. It's like a horror movie." Joel gestured around.

"Yeah, it's some shit. We're getting off the base. Chain of command is stuck in limbo. Stay, fight, run, fight. We're tired of taking orders from fifteen people so we're getting gone. You guys want in?" Gunny looked us over. "Who's he?"

They meant me. Did I really stick out that much?

"I'm Petty Officer First Class Creed. Jackson Creed."

Reynolds and Kelly followed my lead and gave introductions.

"A squid? Shit."

"Yeah. I know what you mean. I'd trade all my valuable knowledge of making a ship go fast for some combat training right about fucking now," I said, and there was a lot of truth behind those words.

"Well, you're big and you carry a big stick. Sometimes that's all it takes." Gunny nodded at the wrench in my hand. "How many rounds you got?"

"I don't know. A pocketful and one extra clip."

"Lesson number one, squid. It's called a magazine. A clip is what a girl puts in her hair. You a girl?"

Jesus Christ. I'd been recruited into the Marines and this was boot.

"Right. Magazine. Sure, Gunny."

"I'm just giving you shit." He shot me a half grin. "Cooper. Hook this guy up with some ammunition."

Cooper was older and even bigger than me. He wore

enough gear to slow down a camel. Cooper reached into a one of the many pouches that adorned his vest and pulled out a magazine. He looked at my gun and then shrugged and handed it over.

I popped the mag and found the one he'd handed over was a match.

"Here's the drill, gents." Gunny looked between the three of us. "We are getting the fuck out of dodge. Coronado Base is now a death trap, so we're going to leave it behind and take our chances closer to the city. If that doesn't work, then we'll make up the next part, but I will come up with a plan. Got it?"

The guys all Hoo'd and wouldn't you know it? They didn't do a full hoo-ah.

"The plan sounds like shit." Gunny's eyebrows went up at my words. "But it's a hell of a lot better than what we've been doing, which is kind of a circle jerk."

"Right. You're welcome to come up with your own brilliant tactical plan," Gunny said.

The others chuckled. Me and my mouth. If we got off the base, these guys would probably play "string up the squid" and leave me for the dead. That's if they didn't feed me to a horde first.

"I got nothing," I said.

"Great. So, if the General is leaving us in his hands, I suggest we move. Cooper and Walowitz, check the street. Lets get this show on the road."

The two men moved out and advanced up the street. They ran to an overturned car and crouched beside it. One motioned and another team of two went. They ran to an overturned pickup truck and dropped beside it. Two others from Gunny's group took off toward them. When all four were in place, the first two dashed toward a street corner and stuck to the side of the building while the second pair kept watch.

Movement ahead. I snapped the handgun up at the same time as the soldiers by the overturned car. Sounds to the west. Reynolds slipped out and took up position on the corner of the building, then peeked. He slipped his head back, took a couple of deep breaths and peeked again.

Reynolds ran to our position.

"Fuck load of them coming our way."

"Now ain't that a bitch. 'Bout how many?" Gunny squinted into the distance.

"Can't say. Hundred. Maybe more."

Gunny motioned and the others followed. All told, the men plus us made eight. Eight souls that wanted to get the hell out of this area. Seven men better trained than I'd ever been. My on-the-job training had consisted of pointing a gun and shooting. It was easy, the easiest thing in the world. You just had to ignore the fact that there were people on the other end of the barrel.

Cooper split off and went with Reynolds. They rounded the corner of the building and layed down fire. Gunny motioned and we moved toward the fallen car. The two that had been there moved to the end of the street and took up position.

Our routine became one of sending out scouts, shooting whatever dead came our way, and then trying to find an alternate path.

Hundreds had been drawn to the gunfire, but we were also within sight of the base perimeter. The city proper lay out there and it was freakishly quiet.

Eerie.

Dead.

No one trotted over sidewalks. No cars zipped along streets. The navy base was a hub of activity on a slow day. If a ship were returning from a tour, the base would be packed. Now, it was a different story. No one waited at the gate. No one was checking ID's and no one, besides us, seemed to be alive.

"I hate this," I muttered.

"You and me both, brother." Gunny clapped me on the back.

Then they hit us.

It was like everyone I'd just pictured in my mind on a normal day had decided to say hi. They shambled. They crawled. They dragged broken limbs. They pulled themselves along the ground with guts and appendages hanging by scraps of skin. There were so many I couldn't see an end to the mass.

"Not good!" Joel Kelly said.

This guy was a frigging genius.

The Marines opened up on the first row and dropped a number of them. Some got tangled up on their fallen brethren and went down. We angled to the west and then made a run for it. It would actually be more appropriate to say the Marines ran and I tried to keep up. I huffed and puffed and regretted every cigarette I'd ever smoked in my life. I regretted the Thai whiskey I'd inhaled a few days ago.

There was now a mass behind us and another horde to the east. As soon as we hit one more, we'd be truly fucked.

"Movement front!" one of the guys yelled.

We were fucked.

My gut burned and I tasted acid in the back of my throat. If we didn't rest soon, I was gonna puke. If we rested, we were dead.

Gunny yanked his gun and shot a Z between the eyes, then blew another one's head open. I wanted his gun. It had some serious stopping power. They were only ten or fifteen feet away, but he just stood there with his legs spread and dropped two of them. I took a shot as well, but it wasn't as neat. I just wanted to be cool. I wasn't. I was also shaking from being so winded.

The guy I hit flinched to the side, so Gunny shot that asshole, too.

"Move!" he yelled, and his men did just that.

We ran from both herds. A couple of burned out buildings ahead could provide protection but we moved past them.

"What about those?" I huffed.

"Get trapped?" Joel looked over his shoulder to drop the news on me.

That made sense.

We sprinted for a section of fence that still stretched a few hundred feet in both directions. It had a layer of razor wire running along the top and I didn't think any one of us were going to risk getting hung up there, feet dangling while the Z's pulled them back down.

"Get that clear, but just enough to let a man through. We don't want them coming through," Gunny shouted.

Cooper and Walowitz had been on point. They hit the fence and swung packs off their shoulders. Cooper came up with a pair of pliers while Walowitz covered him. A couple of Z's got close so he blasted them. Cooper was one cool fucker. He worked at the fence with quick snips and never lost his concentration.

The pack closed in on us from every direction.

I shot until the gun ran empty, slipped a magazine out and jammed a new one in. Then it was back to blasting. I tried to conserve ammo and take well-aimed shots, but there were just so many and they were so damn close, it was hard not to panic. When panic did set in I did my best to focus on my breathing.

"Good one," Gunny called. He kept the pep talk coming and it helped me focus.

They pushed us toward the fence.

The Marines formed a semi-circle as they fell back.

"We're in business!" Cooper called and slipped through the slit in the chain link fence.

The others crowded around. Panic might have hit one of the guys because he broke rank and dove through.

"Calmly, gentlemen. Christ, Michaels."

I got a push and slithered through the new doorway. Reynolds was next and then Joel Kelly followed him. The others covered us until the Z's were right on them. Gunny shot one in the face, kicked another one in the leg so hard it snapped, then pushed back a pair and shot one in through the throat. Blood exploded and splattered Gunny but he didn't even blink. Two of the men weren't so smooth and got pulled, screaming, into the mess of hands and snarling teeth.

Gunny stood his ground and fought them until his men were through. Then they poked gun barrels through the fence and shot until he could dive under the fence.

He turned, took very careful aim and shot the two men that had been under his command. They both slumped.

"Fuck!" One of the men yelled and shot until his gun ran dry. He dropped the magazine and slapped another one home so fast it made my head spin. He advanced on the fence and fired until Gunny laid a hand on him.

"Move it, people!" he ordered, and we followed toward a road filled with abandoned vehicles.

The outskirts of the base showed signs of battles. There were more bodies but most looked like civilians. We moved among them looking for supplies.

Reynolds moved to point and scouted. Joel stuck by me.

A pair of jets shot overhead. They moved toward the city at high speed and a few seconds later explosions rocked the morning air. We looked up as one and Kelly whistled.

"How bad is it?" Walowitz asked the same question that was on my mind.

"Only one way to find out, and that's to get in the fight."

Men nodded.

"Gunny. My wife's family was staying at a hotel near here. About a mile that way," he said and pointed to the northeast. "I'm going to check on them."

"Stay put, Marine."

"I'm not in your command. Appreciate the assist, gentlemen, but I have to know."

No one said a word as he walked away at a fast clip.

"Gunny?" Cooper asked.

"What am I supposed to do, shoot him in the back?" He looked between the men but they didn't say a word.

Reynolds whistled from ahead and motioned. Gunny moved out and the others followed, but they strung out and kept their eyes everywhere at once.

It was less than five minutes before we ran into a real shit storm.

We slid between buildings and empty cars. Streets covered in debris. Bodies that moved and others that lay still. We moved quickly and used shops or hotels as cover when we had to.

Gunny took us to a four lane cross street that still had a couple of moving cars; they ignored us and navigated between wrecks and abandoned vehicles.

"Let's commandeer us a few cars," Gunny said.

That was the best idea I'd heard all day.

"Shit, Gunny. How are we gonna navigate around all these wrecks?"

"I guess we get out and push when we have to," Walowitz said.

"Are we Marines or Triple A? We'll find a vehicle of sufficient size and drive over anyone that gets in our way," Cooper said.

Gunny chuckled and nodded.

The group spread out. Joel stuck by my side while I checked out a couple of trucks. There was a huge eighteen-wheeler partially on the road and partly on the shoulder. I approached and jumped up on the ladder to see if anyone was inside. A man in a faded green t-shirt threw himself at me. He clawed at the door while I tried to stuff my stomach back down my throat.

We moved away.

Cooper and Reynolds poked inside a pair of cars but shook their heads. Cooper checked three more before finding one to his liking. It was a huge SUV that could probably seat eight comfortably. He pulled a corpse out—an elderly woman with blue hair. She was clothed in a huge dress that was more of a nightgown. When he released the body she hit the ground, but her hand grabbed his arm and she pulled herself up. Teeth clamped onto skin.

Cooper turned, eyes filled with horror. He looked at the wound and then did something I thought I could never do. He dropped his assault rifle, ripped the handgun out of his holster, put it under his chin, and pulled the trigger.

I looked away, and it was a good thing I did. From the base, the mass that had tried to attack us had somehow made it through the fence. They moved toward us, arms extended in claws, mouths snarling, teeth covered in blood.

"Move!" Gunny yelled.

We angled off the road and raced toward the city.

That's when the second mass came upon us.

It was like we were stuck between two groups of angry football fans and we were the opposing team.

We ran.

The second horde was already on us. They got one of the guys whose name I didn't know. He went down with a scream and a few seconds later something exploded.

Bodies flew, but it wasn't enough to stem the tide.

Gunny palmed a grenade and tossed one to Walowitz. They both pulled pins and threw at the same time.

The effect was devastating to the front lines that didn't even know to lift their hands or drop to the ground to protect appendages. Joel and I took shelter behind a car but popped back up. I followed his lead and didn't deviate from doing the exact same shit he was doing. If he dropped his pants and popped a squat right there, I would have been beside him doling out the toilet paper.

Gunny led the charge with Walowitz and the other two Marines behind them. They fired, moved in, fired, and when they were close enough they drew side arms and shot until the entire front line had disintegrated.

Reynolds broke away first and dashed to our side. The others followed, but they fired as they went.

Joel took aim and blasted anyone that fell under his sights. The dead dropped like flies, but still the mass advanced. At least with the first rank down, we had created enough of a mess to hang them up.

That's when I saw the first one.

The guy crept along the ground on all fours. He didn't really speak, he just gibbered like he was talking to himself in a shrieking laugh. It was unnerving. The worst was when he leapt off the ground and hit one of the Marines. They both went down in a heap; the Marine got the best of the engagement, but not before having part of his throat ripped out.

"Retreat!" Gunny yelled and we hauled ass.

We hit a roadblock a hundred and fifty feet later. We came

up along a side street, hung a hard left to avoid a fresh horde, and hit a location that held five or six military vehicles. No one manned them, but they made a hell of a choke point because they stretched between two buildings and blocked the entire street.

Joel leapt on top of a HUMVEE and fired while we stayed behind cover. He took out a few but they were gaining on our tired asses. I was so tired I seriously considered just becoming one of them so I wouldn't have to be scared and exhausted any more.

I scrambled up the side of a transport and swung myself onto the roof. I'd fired my last round and hefted my wrench. The first shuffler that came after me got a face full of steel.

Walowitz and Gunny dove into a transport and shut the door. The vehicle was soon surrounded. Joel and I backed up as Gunny saluted us. A few seconds later the engine roared to life and they backed up. Gunny rolled down the window an inch and shouted at us. "Try for the park in two days at eleven PM."

His truck came to a halt as more and more of them piled on. He shrugged, saluted again, and roared into the crowd. Gunny rolled down his window a few more inches, stuck out his arm, and pounded the side of the cab. "Come on you fuckers!" he yelled.

We didn't wait around to see how far he got.

Reynolds and another Marine joined us as we crawled on top of trucks and then slid down the other sides. The Marine – whose name may have been Jonas – slipped and fell off the side of a truck. He cried out, but before we could get him he was covered in Z's.

They were on all sides now as we stood in the flatbed of a truck that had been used as some kind of transport. Joel tossed his gun and picked up another. I found a handgun but didn't pay attention to the make. I just yanked it out of an unused holster, ignoring the corpse it was attached to, and shot the first dead fuck that fell under my sights.

Reynolds kicked one in the face but she latched onto his leg and her mouth darted in to bite him. I thought the fabric of his camo gear may have protected him, but he kicked her again and backed up in horror.

"We are so screwed!" Joel said.

The rest had reached the truck. A hundred clawing hands on every side.

I don't know if it was the stress of the dying Marines, the loss of Gunny, or just the culmination of the entire day. More than likely, it was the bite. Reynolds got this wild look in his eye and told us to get ready.

I thought he meant that we should get ready to die. Reynolds grabbed a bandolier covered in green balls and slung it around his waist. He took a couple off and handed them to Joel.

Joel Kelly took them and flipped Reynolds a questioning look, then shot a Z in the face.

Reynolds ran to the end of the flat bed and leapt like he was going to crowd-surf. His fingers worked at his belt as he went, and when he came off the truck he left behind a tinkling pile of clips.

"DOWN!" Joel yelled and pushed me to the floor.

It was the most incredible act of heroism I have ever seen. Reynolds threw himself into the maelstrom and saved us.

The blast was immense. What was left wasn't fit to bury. It would need to be scooped up and burned.

We used the explosion as cover and ran through the fresh passageway. When a pair of the dead came around a corner, Joel blasted one in half and then threw the empty assault rifle at the other. I didn't look, but I knew Joel was close to losing it.

Joel and I ran until I was gasping for air and shaking like a leaf. We'd left the mass behind but we were in a new part of the city, somewhere I'd never seen before.

An hour later we found the partially boarded up two-story house and founded Fortress.

05:45 hours approximate

Undead Central, San Diego CA – Roz's Roof

THAT'S ENOUGH FOR TODAY. IT'S EARLY MORNING AND I'D LOVE TO get some more shuteye, but the sun is rising. One of the shufflers keeps throwing himself at the side of the garage. I wish Joel would get up and shoot the fucker between the eyes.

Craig and Christy look miserable. They've already eaten the few snacks they managed to get out of the house. I didn't say anything, but I had nothing stashed in my bag except this log, a few magazines, and my wrench.

Noise to the north. I think it's a chopper. If it comes anywhere near us, I'm giving up the hiding technique and jumping up and down like a maniac.

FREE RIDE

11:25 hours approximate
Location: San Diego CA – Roz's Roof

S upplies:

- Food: zip
- Weapons: almost zip
- Attitude: messy

I tried to sleep. Tried.

It was a losing battle. The moment I closed my eyes all I heard were the dead. They milled, staggered, walked into the garage wall, and every five to ten minutes a shuffler launched itself at the roof.

The truth was that I was too damn scared to sleep. If I were really tired enough I'd have dozed off hours ago. Instead, adrenalin kicked my nerves up a notch. A side effect was that I felt like shit. My muscles ached from being clenched and my mind was filled with all the horrible things I'd seen over the course of two weeks. From a narrow escape aboard the USS McClusky to fighting for our lives in the very garage we were stranded on, and all of the terrible shit in between.

Roz huddled up next to Joel Kelly. I didn't take it as a slight, even though I'd saved her life. Joel had saved my life quite a few times and I'd saved his. I think. Yeah, I probably pulled his ass out of a few bad situations. Kinda hard to survive in this ridiculous world if you aren't helping keep your best buddy from becoming zombie chow.

She didn't exactly invite him she just happened to lay down next to him. Joel was snoring away and rolled onto his side. She was close and they ended up with their arms over each other. How she could sleep through his snoring was beyond me. How any of us could sleep.

I didn't get jealous. Why should I? It's not like she and I were together. We had that little hug and ass grab yesterday in the garage, but we both thought we were about to die. Even if we had made it back inside, I doubted I had the balls to go after her. They were too busy being shrunk up inside my gut in fear.

I rolled over again and tried to fix the lumps that made up my backpack. Then I tried to doze on my arm but it fell asleep. I rolled onto my stomach and got a face full of leaves and dirt. If I wasn't mistaken, there was even a layer of moss up here that I was now inhaling.

"Can you eat moss?" I asked, voice low.

"Gross, dude," Craig said.

"I'm starving, man and pretty soon a bowl of moss stew might look good to you too," I said. "Maybe a bowl of moss stew with pork belly to add some salt."

"Pork belly? Sounds just as gross," he whispered back.

"It's just another name for bacon."

"I'd kill a guy for some bacon."

My stomach rumbled in response.

Hours passed and I may have dozed. My ankle ached like a bitch and the rest of my body wasn't much better. The next time I run into a fucking zombie apocalypse, I plan to bring some serious painkillers to the party. Not to mention a duffle bag filled with Twinkies and MREs. Yeah, I'd eat the hell out of some MREs right now.

We had quite a few of them. The problem? They were in a

house filled with the dead, so that idea was just as fucking dead. Going back into the house wasn't happening unless we figured out a way to go in Ironman-style, complete with metal suit and weaponry. The way these undead assholes acted, they'd probably drag us down, iron suit or not.

I don't remember when, but I finally fell asleep and got an hour or two of REM. Good for fucking me.

06:00 hours approximate
Location: San Diego CA – Roz's Roof

I woke up with a pounding headache. My ankle was swollen from last night's activities. My back hurt from sleeping on the roof. My shoulder barely worked thanks to falling asleep on my own arm.

I rubbed my eyes but it didn't help. They still felt like sand paper.

"You might have gotten uglier," Joel observed.

I didn't have the energy to flip him off.

"I feel like shit."

"Dehydrated. You need water. We all do," he said.

Joel crept to the edge of the roof and looked over the side of the building. He came back up and shook his head. Roz stayed low and stared after him. The kids were a few feet away, conferring in whispered voices.

It was overcast, and from the chill in the air I'd guess it was no later than about 0600 hours.

"Not good. We can't get down. We can't go back in the garage, and we can't get in the house."

"Still full of dead fucks?"

"Yep," he said. "Craig reconnoitered earlier."

"Brave kid."

"And he's light. Don't want a fresh hole in the roof."

Another helicopter thundered against the morning sky. I'd put it at a mile or two out. We could see it, but it couldn't see us, because we were a speck in a big old pile of fuck you. Too bad we couldn't set a home on fire to signal the chopper.

"Anyone got a flare gun?" I asked.

Joel Kelly rolled his eyes.

The chopper cut to the east and then zipped into the distance until we couldn't hear it anymore.

The morning brought some fog and a creepy view of the world below. Where we'd seen the undead on the ground, now they seemed to be creeping out of the mist with heads and arms floating. A shuffler appeared out of the fog with a leap and then was gone, five or six feet away like some kind of fucked up zombie frog.

The nearest house was twenty or thirty feet away and no matter how fast we could run, there was no way in hell we'd make that sprint. The dead were too thick. I'd have a better chance of pogo-sticking off heads than outrunning the tightly packed horde.

"What if one of us put on a lot of clothes? Then the bites wouldn't get through," Christy said.

"You'd be dragged down and torn apart," I said.

Not a good way to go. Sure they might not be able to bite, yet, but enough of those things on top of the kid and they'd have his arms and legs separated from his torso in no time.

"Uh. Yeah. Bad idea," Christy said.

"Can we make a rope out of our clothes and hook it to the house over there?" Craig pointed at the nearest rooftop.

Poor kid. He looked worse than me. His hair was a mess but his eyes were the really sad part. He must have been rubbing at them because one was dark red and he looked as tired as anyone I'd ever seen. Craig lifted one hand to point at the house but it hung limp, almost like a Z's hand. Even his words were slurred.

"One, I don't want to be dangling buck ass naked over those bastards. A shuffler would surely get us. Two, none of us can possibly James Bond the rope over there."

"It was just a suggestion," he said and frowned. Craig lay back down and stared in the direction of the slow rising sun.

"Yeah. It was a good one," I said, but he didn't acknowledge my words.

Joel looked at me but I could only shrug.

The sound of a helicopter again. I sat up and tried to get a glimpse but couldn't tell which direction it was coming from.

"There!" Joel said. He was up on his knees pointing west of San Diego, out toward the water.

The chopper cut across my vision like a fucking messiah. If Jesus himself had risen from the ground and taken to the air, I don't think I'd have been this excited.

The thundering grew louder. The big green military transport did a zig-zag over buildings and roads. As it moved I found myself getting up. First, one foot under a knee. Then I was up in a crouch and trying to ignore the pain in my ankle. I licked my dry lips, but it didn't help, even though I was, for some reason, salivating.

"Is it coming this way?" Roz moved beside me and put her hand on my waist.

I looked her way and tried not to grin like a crazy man.

"Yeah. It's coming our way."

It was. I thought for sure it would go anywhere else but it kept doing a serpentine strut across the sky. Its general direction was still toward us.

I jumped to my feet and waved my hands in the air and started to shout.

"Hey! Hey! We're right fucking here!"

Roz did the same and so did the kids. Craig didn't get to his feet but he waved. His hand was nearly as listless as his body. I hoped the poor kid wasn't sick.

Thank the fuck Christ someone was coming. I was worried about the kid. I'd just met him a day or two ago but he and his sister didn't deserve this crazy new world. I couldn't help but wonder if this part of the country was infected but the rest of the world was fine and dandy. Maybe families were rising even now to have breakfast together. To watch the morning news or sit through children's cartoons. Mom and Dad rushing off to work while the kids try to stay awake in school.

I shook my head and made my brain focus on the task at hand—getting that chopper's attention.

The helicopter must have seen us because they made a beeline straight toward Roz's house.

There was one side effect of our antics and shouts of joy. The horde below had gone into a frenzy. They pressed in on the sides of the garage and howled for our blood. A pair of shufflers flung themselves at the building like we were a side of bacon left out for their morning meal.

The chopper slowed as it neared us. It was green and had large side doors. One was open and had a machine gun pointed out just like they were in a war zone – and that wasn't far from the truth.

The pilot and co-pilot were hard to make out, but I was sure one of them nodded in our direction. A face appeared behind them and studied us intently.

The wash of the blades as the helicopter came to hover in front of us blew Joel Kelly's FDNY cap off his head. He waved but the pilots didn't wave back.

The chopper swung to the side and my gut twisted.

"No!" I screamed. "Don't leave us!"

Roz jumped up and down but I couldn't hear her over the rush of wind.

The side door came into view and with it, the big machine gun. I thought for a crazy moment that they were about to open up on us.

The man that I'd seen a few seconds ago leaned out and waved. He was tall and had dark hair laced with grey. He looked like Gunny, but this man was older. He waved again and we waved back. I felt dumb for it, but it was the best I had in place of a hug and a wet kiss. I'd save that for after we were rescued.

The helicopter hovered just out of reach, then the guy hanging onto the doorway motioned for us to get down. I didn't need a second invitation and dropped to a crouch on my sore ankle. It screamed in pain but I pushed it to the back of my mind.

The man produced a bullhorn and fiddled with the buttons. A woman dressed in combat gear moved beside him and said something. He nodded at her and then lifted a bullhorn.

"Stay down just like that. When we get close make your way onto the craft. When you are onboard sit down and don't move. Got it?"

I gave the thumbs up. He nodded at us and then yelled something at the pilots.

Roz knelt while she talked to the kids. Christy looked at Craig and gave his hand a quick squeeze.

The dead around us went into a frenzy. The shuffler that had haunted us all night tried to leap onto the helicopter but it was a good twelve feet off the ground. The down draft from the blades flattened a couple that were on shaky limbs, or worse, were missing them entirely.

The horde moved in on us again and pressed against the side of the garage. They beat at it and moaned. Even with the immense noise it was truly a fucking chorus of the damned.

Joel prodded Craig and pointed at the edge of the roof. Craig took Christy's hand and together they crept toward the side of the building. He kept his hand in front of his face while she stayed low and let Craig take most of the wash. When they were close enough to step on to the strut, a guy inside reached out, grabbed her arm, and hauled Christy inside.

Craig collapsed when Christy was gone. He didn't move, just sat there with his legs folded under his butt.

The dead went into a fresh frenzy when they saw their prize getting away. The shuffler howled and gibbered. He leapt at the building over and over until he was bloody. The other's pressed from all sides.

Roz was next with Joel helping her toward the end. They tried to prod Craig but he pushed hands away.

The building shook and a corner of the roof swayed, then collapsed as the wall beneath it gave way. Roz made it to the helicopter strut and was helped on board.

The roof tilted but didn't go down. I grabbed Craig and hauled him to his feet.

"Come on. We're almost there!" I yelled.

He nodded once and said something but I couldn't make out the words.

Hands helped him onboard as the roof tilted again. I leaned forward and barely kept my feet. One quick glance over my shoulder told me that this was going to be a very short day if I didn't get my sorry ass on the chopper.

I grabbed my backpack and swung it over my back. The huge wrench got me right in the kidney. I almost doubled over in pain. Then I moved to the edge of the roof and prepared to avoid being zombie chow.

There was a moment where Joel and I met eyes. He prodded me onboard, but I did the same. We stared back at each other like a pair of idiot heroes in a buddy action movie. I didn't feel particularly heroic. All I really wanted to do was get on the helicopter, get to somewhere safe, and take a long shit because my sphincter was not up to the business of me being scared to death all the goddamn time.

Joel pushed and I advanced on the chopper. It was only a few feet away but below was a mass of dead like I'd never seen before. All eyes were on me as I stepped toward the helicopter strut.

The older man's hand came out and I got one foot on the strut while my other was still on the roof. That's when the damn thing gave in. Joel managed to make it to the edge but the second wall crumbed to kindling beneath us.

The shifting caused me to end up stretched between two worlds with hell directly underneath. Someone grabbed the guy in the transport, and with that as an anchor, he hauled me, screaming, into the helicopter.

Joel held on for dear life, and behind him came the dead. The collapsed roof had created a perfect platform to serve him up like dinner. The Z's moved up the newly created ramp while Joel looked on in horror.

"We can't risk it. That building's gonna collapse any minute and probably take us with it!" The woman in the chopper yelled over the "whump whump" of the blades.

The older man looked at us. I had taken a seat on the floor but when I saw Joel's panicked face I came to my feet.

"You can't leave him. He's saved all of us more than once."

"Sorry, son," he said and leaned over to say something to the pilot.

I didn't think. I pushed him to the side and stepped back onto the helicopter strut. I used the machine gun barrel as an anchor and stretched out for Joel.

"Get off! I can't shoot if you're in the way!" the woman said.

"Good!" I bellowed back.

I reached over my shoulder and ripped the huge wrench out and swung it around to lean out as far as I could.

Joel got one hand on the wrench head. Another garage wall went down and took the roof with it. Z's scrambled for purchase but slid down the platform with arms and legs flailing.

Except for one.

The shuffler was nasty. He had long strands of hair but they weren't enough to cover his head. They hung over his face like wisps of white cotton. I shuddered because he made a leap, mouth open, and managed to reach the edge of the garage wall that Joel was balanced on.

I pulled as hard as I could and Joel came along for the ride. The man grabbed my arm and pulled me in. I pulled Joel along until he was on the helicopter strut. The engine screamed above us as all of our weight settled and pulled the transport closer to the collapsing building.

Joel got his hand on the side of the chopper and pulled himself inside. I struggled against the tilting chopper and managed to get one leg in before the shuffler leapt.

We were rising when it caught the strut and managed to hold on. The helicopter tilted once again and suddenly I was looking down at about a hundred hungry mouths.

"Asshole!" I yelled and kicked the shuffler in the face. I did it again and he fell away into the crowd.

They hauled me in and all I could do was collapse as my

heart thundered within my chest in rhythm to the blades above us.

After a few deep breaths I looked up into the face of a grinning Marine named Joel Kelly.

"I am not cut out for this fucking hero bullshit!" I yelled.

"Me either, man. But I love you just the same." He clapped my shoulder one time then took a seat.

The old man looked us over appraisingly but didn't say a word.

"Thanks for saving us," I said after I'd managed to catch my breath. "I'm Jackson Creed and my gay lover there is Marine Sergeant Joel Kelly."

The man nodded at us.

"I'm not his gay...whatever, man. Thanks for picking us up."

"You folks were about to be zombie chow."

"Yeah. Not much choice. We were stuck up there until you came along."

"I'd like to get real friendly but we gotta make sure you're safe. This won't take long so save the introductions. I'd hate to shake hands and then have to blow your brains out." He grinned, but there was no humor behind the gesture.

The guy nodded at the gunner. She slid a silver metal box about the size of a briefcase out from under the metal bench. The guy took it from her and opened it to reveal a computer display. There was a camera attached by a bunch of wires. Shit looked like a science lab experiment.

"We just need a picture of your eye," he said and extended the camera.

"A picture?"

"Yep. We figured out how to spot the virus. Doesn't always set in right away. I've seen guys walk around infected for three days before turning."

"Damn," I said and submitted to a shot.

The flash was bright and left me blinking furiously for a few seconds.

We took turns opening an eye wide while he snapped a shot.

After each picture he typed something on a keyboard and waited.

"Where're we headed?" I asked.

"We have a base but it's not much. Damn zeek's nearly overrun it every day. All the ammo in the world and we can't keep clear of them. Piles and piles of the dead. Never smelled anything so foul in my life."

The sound of the rotor overhead was a constant throb against the cabin as I peered over the lid of the silver box to see if I could get a peek at the display.

"What's going on out there?" I asked.

"Out there? Out in the world you mean? How long you boys been stuck out here?"

Roz cleared her throat.

"Sorry miss." He smiled in her direction.

"No problem." She grinned back but it was just as empty of humor.

"Almost two weeks. Our ship crashed into the base. We've been on the run ever since." Joel filled in the details.

"I'll tell you what's going on out there." He looked at each of us in the eye. "The worst things you can imagine. When you think it can't get worse, it does. When you think that humanity can't get any worse, it does. And when you think the damned Z's can't get any nastier."

The man stared hard at the screen and then swallowed.

"They do."

"Are we good?" Jackson nodded toward the screen.

Craig and Christy looked on with wide eyes. They were huddled together on the hard metal bench.

"Oh, we're good." The guy smiled.

He moved toward the door opposite the machine gun and looked outside.

"Don't be scared, kids." He smiled at Christy and Craig. "Come here, bud. I'll show you something that will make you feel better."

Craig had been slumped against the wall. He stared into space like she hadn't heard the man.

"Here you go." The older man smiled and produced one of those juice boxes with the little plastic straw glued to the side. It was all I could do not to leap across the tiny space and tear it out of his hand.

Craig made a little noise and slipped off the bench.

I slid my backpack off and pushed it into a corner and got a glance at our rescuer's boots. Instead of military issue he was wearing something out of a cowboy movie. Were those snakeskin boots? Talk about an action hero come to life.

Joel had lost his assault rifle in the excitement and looked like his best friend had died. Glad that wasn't true, since I was probably the closest thing to a best friend he'd ever had.

"So who are you?" I asked over the loud thumping of the rotor blades.

The smell of gas and oil filled the cabin but it was whisked away in a blast as air as the man that had rescued us slid the door open.

"Hey man, that's loud."

The guy didn't say a word. He grabbed Craig by the back of the neck, and pulled him all the way off the bench. He looked at the guy in silent shock, but his silence turned into a scream as the man threw Craig out of the doorway.

"The fuck!" Joel Kelly came off the seat just as I tried to stand. He reached for a non-existent side arm. I went for my bag because I was going to haul out eight pounds of metal and bush his fucking head in!

The machine gunner pulled her gun but Joel did some Marine shit. He swiped her arm up and locked his hand over hers. She didn't sit around for that and fought back.

Christy hauled off and threw a poorly aimed punch but the guy slid aside and knocked the girl to the hard floor.

"Knock it off back there!" The pilot turned his head to shout at us.

I ripped my wrench free of the backpack but there was no room to swing it in the tiny cabin.

Roz stared on in shock and then covered her face with her hands and sobbed.

The guy who had just tossed Craig to his death pulled out a huge gun and pointed it at my head. My resolve deflated, as did my grip on the wrench. The fight went out of me. I was done. The days of running and hiding piled on top of the escape, combined with Craig's sudden death nearly made me pass out.

"Stop this!" the guy yelled. "Stop it now or there's gonna be a lot more blood."

"Ouch, bastard!" the gunner said.

"Sails! Enough!" the man with the huge gun pointed at me said.

Joel Kelly managed to get the gun away from the gunner, Sails, and none to gently. He got a look at the big barrel pointed my way and he relaxed his grip on the woman and lowered the gun.

She must not have taken too kindly to Joel's rough handling because she slapped him.

"He's trying to help. You don't know what's going on here, asshole," she said and rubbed her wrist.

"What about what's going on here? He just tossed a teenage boy out the goddamn door. That's what's going on here. I don't know how you people are used to dealing with civilians but you don't just kill them."

"You don't? Is that right, son? How many have you killed since this all began?"

"I killed Z's. The dead. I didn't kill innocent people."

He kept the gun pointed at my head but turned the box to face us and lifted the lid. A laptop screen was set into a hard foam backing. The screen had an image of the inside of an eyeball. I'd seen something like this when I got my eyes checked a few years ago.

"What the fuck are we looking at?" Joel rubbed his face where the gunner had smacked him.

"This is your friend that I just tossed. See the dark spots? Those are dead cells. A lot of dead cells. In a few more days or maybe hours – hell, could be minutes, he would have turned. You want a Z in here? You wanna be stuck with a monster in this tiny little box? No you do not."

"Craig was fine!" Christy went crazy.

She lashed out and caught the guy across the nose with the back of her fist. It wasn't a great shot, but it got the job done. The man fell back and a shot rang out in the cabin. I sucked in a breath expecting a bullet to be lodged in me, but it wasn't. The shot went high and punched through the canopy.

The man pushed Christy against the wall hard, and she collapsed like a sack of potatoes.

Joel wanted to go nuts; I saw it in his eyes and the way his fists clenched on the bench seat. The gunner ripped her gun tight then put it to Joel's head.

"Listen to him. He knows what he's talking about."

Something coughed and the helicopter shuddered. A light flashed in my periphery and then alarms sounded. I didn't need to, but I followed everyone's eyes to the top of the chopper where a hole whistled air. What were the chances?

"Oh shit!" Sails said.

The pilot punched buttons and swore. Our ride swayed one way and then the other. I got slammed against the door and then went flat so it wouldn't happen again. When the chopper tilted to the side I got a look at a huge stadium filled with white tents. Figures moved around the location, but from their wobbling, I assumed none of them were alive. I wasn't sure, but thought it was probably the old Balboa stadium.

Joel held on for dear life as the chopper went into a slow spin.

The pilot did something because we managed to straighten out for all of two seconds before our craft hit the ground. Hard.

I was lifted into the air and smashed into the deck. Breath left my body and I had a hell of a time getting it back.

The gunner had been smashed against the side of the craft and lolled in Joel's lap. The man who'd saved us seemed to be the only one unharmed. He grabbed Christy's form and ripped the door open. The pilot swore, hit some buttons and then ditched.

"This way!" The guy yelled to us as he kept his hold on Christy.

I struggled to my knees while Joel got Sails out of the door. The pilots fell out one after another and then they were on our feet.

I snatched up my backpack and hit the ground right behind them, staggering on my already aching ankle.

No time to rest. No time to worry about the pain shooting up my leg in waves.

"There. It's not far!" The guy picked up Christy and shrugged him over his shoulder. He pointed at a fence

Joel smacked Sails, none too gently. She stirred, looked at him and snarled. Jeez. She looked like one of them for a second. Girl would be cute if she wasn't pointing guns and hitting people.

On the run again? That could mean only one thing.

I looked back and there they were.

There were at least fifty of them. Maybe more. Howling, screaming, and moaning, they walked, crawled, and dragged body parts. They were covered in blood and filth. They were the worst of the worst and they all wanted us.

Not only that, but two shufflers came at us.

I had a vague sense of where we were in relation to the base and San Diego itself, and if I wasn't mistaken, the huge buildings ahead of us were part of the naval medical center. There was a bunch of activity around it as military trucks, transports, and gun-toting HUMVEEs moved around the perimeter of a huge metal fence.

If I were lucky I'd have time to marvel at the construction later. For now I had to actually make it.

We ran our asses off.

If we were in good shape, fresh off the rack, it might have been a cake walk to sprint to the finish line. Not today. I was running on empty. Joel was in bad shape and he had Sails to carry. Roz looked like someone had just punched her in the stomach. The only one that seemed capable of moving was the asshole and he was carrying Christy over his shoulder. I had the urge to sprint and bash in the fuckers head and leave him for the Z's but my ankle barely left me room to stagger at a half sprint.

We might not make it anyway. None of us.

The first of the dead were on us.

Joel slung Sails to the side and fired her gun. He hit a Z right in the chest, dropping him for now. The guy carrying Christy turned and fired a couple of shots dropping a zombie that snarled in our wake.

Roz paused but I motioned her on. There was no point in here trying to be a hero with no weapon.

A shuffler jumped.

I ripped the wrench up in an arc that terminated with the bastards head. He went down, but it was a temporary respite. There were dozens of dead on our heels.

More gun shots and I used what little energy I had left to sprint forward until I reached Roz. I touched her shoulder.

"Just like last night, eh?"

"Fuck this!" she said in reply.

It wouldn't be long now and I didn't even have a gun to finish me and Roz off before they got us. The horde was going to rip us apart.

Gunshots from ahead and several Z's fell. More shots and more bodies dropped.

Holy shit! The cavalry had arrived.

A full contingent of military advanced on our position. Beautiful men and women in full combat gear and packing enough heat to start a war in some third world country.

I did the smart thing and dropped to my knees, dragging Roz down with me.

It was over in seconds. They must have fired five or six hundred rounds but they stopped the horde in its tracks. Even a shuffler, so frightening to us before, was taken down with at least half a dozen bullets.

The trek to the base wasn't as hectic now that help had arrived.

The guy that had rescued us and killed Craig talked to someone that looked like they were in charge. He pointed at us and at the helicopter. A group broke away and headed toward the transport no doubt to see if it was worth trying to fix before being overrun with dead.

The grass here was trampled flat. There was a road running near the base but it was packed with military transports either coming or going. Engines rumbled around us and it felt good to not only be alive but to be back near something resembling civilization with living people moving around.

The guy met us as we stumbled to the bases entrance and he didn't look happy. He'd handed over Christy to one of the men at the gate. He spoke to the man for a few seconds then shrugged the listless body off his shoulder. Another soldier joined them and helped carry Christy into the base.

The man spun on us.

"Listen to me and listen well. This ain't fucking lala land. You know that if you been in the city for any amount of time. There is a shit storm of hate just waiting to suck us all in and we can't take any chances. Got that? No chances. On any other day I'd leave all of you to the dead. That stunt almost cost us all our lives. You do some shit like that again and I'll put a bullet in your head myself."

"You didn't have to do it!" I yelled back. This guy could have been a fucking admiral for all I cared. All I wanted to do was kick his ass.

"This base is secure. No one with a hint of the virus gets in but they get out. In pieces."

"Fucking asshole," I said.

Joel touched my shoulder to pull me back but I wasn't having it. This guy was tall and he looked commanding but I was still a hell of a lot bigger than him. I hefted the wrench but Joel pushed my hand down. I looked at him and he shook his head.

"I am that, but I'm also one alive fucking asshole. Now do yourself a favor and stay alive too. We need every able body we can find. Don't forget. I'm the one who rescued you."

"Oh I won't forget everything you've done. What's your name, anyway?" I gritted my teeth.

He turned to leave, snake skin boots kicking up dirt as he strolled away. He looked over his shoulder and fixed me with his eyes.

"Names Lee and that's all you need to know for now. Good luck, soldier," he said and strolled into a gate that opened for him.

"I'm gonna kill that son-of-a-bitch," I muttered.

"Get in line," Joel said.

Together with Roz, the injured gunner named Sails, and Joel, we limped into the base before the sliding chain link fence rattled closed.

NEW FRIENDS

10:30 hours approximate
Location: Undead Central, San Diego CA – San Diego US Naval Hospital

S upplies:

- Food: warm and enough to fill our guts
- Weapons: plenty to go around
- Attitude: I want to punch stuff

ALL THROUGH OUR LOUSY TIME ON ROZ'S GARAGE ROOF, I thought we were going to die. I thought we were going to slowly starve to death or the Z's would figure out a way to get at us. Instead we were rescued. The dead were doing their best to batter down the house and even succeeded, once the chopper arrived. I don't know if it was all the noise or us being visible. They went into a frenzy and smashed down the damn walls as we flew away.

The entry to the base was so heavily fortified that we had to be escorted in. Every couple of feet there was a pole covered in razor wire and a lot of that wire was covered in flesh, blood splatters, and strips of clothing. It was the perfect trap. If some of the shamblers made it as far as the base, a lot of them would get hung up, then shot by the heavily armed guards patrolling the massive chain-link gate.

The entrance had fortifications and machine guns. Big fuckers with barrels large enough to take down any target on foot. Men and women stood at guard or knelt and stared down barrels. A few shot us dirty looks. Not my fault! I wanted to protest but it seemed prudent to get my smelly ass into the base and blend in, then figure out how to introduce Lee to my eight pounds of wrench.

As we approached the entrance a squad met us. They had an apparatus similar to the one Lee had used. They didn't point guns at us but they looked ready to draw and shoot at the slightest hint of trouble.

After getting the eye treatment we were escorted to a table where a woman took our name and a drop of blood.

"Does the blood tell you if we got it?"

"Maybe," she replied. She looked tired under a mess of black hair.

"That's reassuring," I said.

"I wish we knew more but we don't. We just look for certain anti-bodies. It's easier to see with the magnifying glass. The disease sets up shop and causes clots. Clots show up as red spots. The clots die and the eyes turn white."

"Thanks for the lesson, Doc." Joel said.

"Oh, I'm no doctor." She attempted to smile and then went back to writing notes on a pad of paper.

They tagged us with some numbers and sent us on our way in the general direction of food and water. I limped behind Joel on my screaming ankle.

By the gates were a huge pile of fence sections and a couple of pieces of heavy equipment, including a huge bulldozer and a crane.

Our rescue had been messy, but that's been life since we arrived in Undeadville, USA. At the time I was actually hopeful that when we set foot on the chopper, our would-be rescuer, Lee, would take us to safety. All of us, not just some of us. Then that fucker threw Craig out of the chopper like he was a bag of trash.

The question ate away at me, though. Was Craig one of them? If we'd been stuck on that roof for a few more days would he have changed? It's possible, but he said he was fine, even if he was tired and just plain out of it. Since we'd found the kids they'd been sorta upbeat all things considered.

I didn't see any bite marks on Craig so how the hell had it happened? Was the disease being spread by some new mechanism? For the last ten days we'd seen men and women bitten, look horrified, and within moments become one of the Z's. Now there was a new way for victims to carry the virus?

After the chopper crash, they let us in the front gate. From the looks, as we hauled ass toward safety, I had a feeling they wanted to send us a bill and make us haul the remains of the chopper inside the base.

I was happy that the pilot and co-pilot weren't near us. I was afraid they'd point the finger at us and say it was our fault. The entire battle inside the chopper had taken half a minute. Then we'd struck the ground. I asked Joel Kelly later if he'd ever been in anything like that before.

"A chopper crash? Shit. Been in a few. That one wasn't bad. I'd call it a shaker, but not quite a bone rattler."

I grinned back at his grin and wondered if he was bullshitting me. Only a boneshaker? When we hit it felt like someone had picked me up and thrown me against a brick wall.

Roz moved alongside us while Christy fell into step but she kept glancing over her shoulder as we made our way toward the base.

"Don't think about it," Roz said.

"What if he's okay? We weren't that high; maybe Craig hit something soft." Christy whined from behind us.

"He didn't survive." Roz fell back a step and put a hand around his shoulder. "I'm sorry."

Christy shrugged it off and moved a few feet away.

"Nothing we can do about it now except get that son of a bitch that killed Craig." I tried to sound reassuring.

"He's out there. I know it," she said. "Everyone else in my life is dead. Craig was all I had left."

She had a point, but I couldn't think of anything to say so I let her talk.

"We didn't ask for this. None of this. I shouldn't even be here. I should be home doing school work or playing video games with my friends. I'm so sick of this. So sick of all of this. I hate this world."

"Yeah. Me too. But you gotta go on and honor Craig's memory. If you're gone who's going to remember him?" I asked.

When we were all gone, who would remember us?

"You guys lost?"

I turned to find an unexpected face. With her helmet off she wasn't bad looking, in an "I'll rip your balls off if you cross me" way that I kinda liked. What I didn't like was the fact that she'd helped Lee kill a kid. I also didn't like that she'd hit me hard enough to make me see stars. I guess I could forgive the second one with enough time.

"Well look who it is," I said and came to my full height.

She looked up at me but wasn't intimidated. She didn't look mad or sad. In fact, she had no expression at all.

"Yeah. Look who it is. You guys looking for a shower and chow? Because you need it."

Roz crossed her arms and stared at Sails. Sails met her gaze and didn't flinch.

I leaned over and whispered in Joel's ear, "Girl fight, bro."

He pushed me off.

"You seen Lee?" I asked Sails.

"No. If you want to thank him I'll pass along your message. Do yourself a favor and let it go. It sucks, but it was for the best," she said and moved away.

Joel got in her face.

"It was for the best? He was just a kid. What if it was your kid, huh?"

"It was my kids, but now they're gone. If you'll excuse me," she said and moved away.

Shit.

Joel looked like he wanted to say something but he didn't. Anna glanced between us and didn't say a word before moving off into the crowd.

The base of operations was made up of a hospital and a bunch of smaller buildings. People scurried around, most of them armed. I hadn't seen so many people in one place in a long time and it was comforting.

Hand painted signs hung on hastily constructed signposts indicating in which way lay food and supplies. I spotted one in particular and almost broke into tears.

'Showers.'

I smacked Joel and pointed. He nodded but couldn't seem to take his eyes off the departing figure of Anna Sails.

"You like that?"

"I'm not happy, bro."

"Join the fucking club."

I pointed at a sign that read "food" and we moved toward it.

"Chow first. Then I'm going to shower so long I turn into a giant prune."

"Squids and water," Joel said and then led the way.

They fed us in an overcrowded mess hall filled with a mix of military, military wannabes, and civvies. There were lines drawn, like a prison mess hall. A group of survivalist types complete with "been in the mountains for months" beards sat near a couple of families but the groups didn't look at each other. The military men and women strutted around with weapons on open display.

"Pass the salt?" a man asked me.

He sat with four kids and a wife who hovered over the little ones while they ate dry cereal and stared around the room with wide eyes.

The kitchen had canned supplies and boxes containing even more boxes of crackers. There were five-gallon jugs of bug juice and sliders that tasted like slimy vegetarian fake meat. I don't know where they got the stuff but my stomach thanked me. My guts weren't so happy an hour later but I rode it out and then came back and begged for more. I'm not a little guy and it takes a lot to feed this zombie killing machine.

The rest of the partially formed base was obviously in transition when we arrived. A steady stream of cars and trucks roared into and out of the base. There was a constant unholy racket of helicopters thumping at the sky as they roared in and then back out. Most delivered supplies but a lot of them carried away people. Folks that were dressed in civvies and carried bags or stuffed suit cases. Where was everyone headed? If it was somewhere safe I wanted to go there now.

Like the empty field we'd flown over yesterday this place had tents everywhere. They told us to go to some section that me nor Joel Kelly could make heads or tails of. Might as well have been some Sudoku puzzle for all the sense it made.

I wasn't complaining. I can't say how relieved I am that I'm somewhere surrounded by guns and people who know how to use them. The food might not be the best but it was food. I've been so hungry over the last ten days I'm sure I've lost about fifteen pounds.

We ate and tried to talk but we didn't get a lot of answers. I turned to the guy that had asked for the salt and asked him what was happening in the world. How far had the virus spread? Were all of the other states affected?

"When the televisions and radio stations died we lost touch with the outside world and just waited. We ran out of food a few days ago and started moving around. A convoy found us and rescued me and the family. Thank god for the military."

"So you don't know what's going on in the rest of the world?" I had so many questions but everyone I talked to had a similar answer. Even the military guys didn't know what was going on.

One thing I learned was that there'd been mass desertion, as the enlisted grew worried about families and just left their posts and stations.

"All I know is I got food and water and a warm place for my family. That's good enough for me." He turned away.

I resisted the urge to grab him by the shirt collar and demand answers. Instead I snapped my plastic fork in half. I probably just needed to go find a place to curl up and sleep for the rest of the day. First we needed to spend some time trying to clean off two weeks of blood and filth.

The tent was huge and sectioned off for men and women.

It wasn't warm and the soap were cakes of white with other people's hair in them. I didn't care, and judging by the sounds of others near me (including Roz, who hummed a song in a bad falsetto) no one else did either.

Not much of a shower, but I was left grinning and shivering. Piles of clothing, most of it military, were in a corner. I pawed through it until I found something big enough to fit me. Must have been someone's shitty idea of a joke because the only pants my size were a pair of old dungarees that were loose in the waist and too short by a few inches, but they were better than my beat to hell overalls. The shirt was digital camo and had enough arm pockets to hold a few odds and ends. I filled one with .45 ammo and another with 9mm.

I strapped my trusty .45 around my waist, then grabbed a huge pea coat and fell into it. Warmth eventually set in while we stood around talking about the wonders of running water. Christy looked dour and when Roz suggested looking for a bed we followed.

"Sleep. I need a week of it," I said.

"Me too, man. I'm as tired as I've been in my whole damn life. Even boot wasn't this much work."

Together we went to find a couple of cots.

10:30 hours approximate
Location: San Diego US Naval Hospital

Roz and Christy found a cot and a sleeping bag right next to each other; no one else had claimed them, so they settled in. Joel and I nodded at Roz and moved on to find a corner of our own.

I settled back on the cot and stared at the ceiling. Someone had left a pile of magazines in a corner but who cared about that shit anymore? Damn world was gone and I was supposed to read celebrity gossip? Hell, most of those chumps were dead anyway if Los Angeles went down like San Diego.

The enclosure was huge and filled with sorry sorts. We walked up and down aisles before deciding that if someone came for this pair of cots they'd have to be bigger and meaner to make us move.

People moved in and out of the area. Kids cried. Babies howled. Mothers shushed, and fathers looked dour.

"When do we tell them we're enlisted?" I asked Joel quietly.

Joel leaned over close and whispered. "I don't know if we should. Something weird about this base."

I had to agree with Joel's assessment. Since we'd arrived no one had answered our questions. They told us there'd be time for that later. We should settle in, relax and eat. No one would come clean about what was going on.

I'd tried to ask a few people, but they were all tightlipped. Then I found a guy named Edward Bowls. He was in his mid-fifties and coughed all the time. One time I thought I saw his hand come away with blood but he covered it up.

"It's bad out there," he'd said when no one else was around. "They try to make it seem like this is isolated but it's not. The states are falling fast and there doesn't seem to be anyway to stop the spread of the virus. It doesn't get everyone but it gets most. Some have managed to setup battle lines and quarantine zones. I heard that Montana is pretty clear but there ain't shit in that state to begin with, just a bunch of open space. Plus everyone's got guns."

"So not everywhere is as bad as San Diego."

"Yeah but some places are worse. I heard Lee was up north and is heading back up there. Lee's in charge I guess, cept he ain't military." Edward leaned over and coughed until he was out of breath.

"He's not? He sure seems like it." I tried to play it cool.

"Some group of mercenaries. That's what I heard. I guess he was over in Afghanistan spreading freedom with a machine gun before his boys got called back home."

"Mercenaries." Joel swore.

"That bad?" I asked but neither one answered.

"I heard stuff and it wasn't pretty," Joel said and put his arm over his eyes.

I lay back on the hard cot and tried not to think. That lasted for about fifteen seconds.

"So mercenaries, like Black Water. US has been using them for years, right?"

"I guess, man. I never ran into them when I was over there."

What if Lee had been right? What if Christy was one of them? What if monkeys flew out of my ass? One thing I'd learned in this new world was to stop dwelling on the what-if's. All those got you was a big cup of regret and not much else.

But questions swirled around my head. Craig was fine all day and the night before. What was different about the disease when it attacked him? Why was it delayed?

Then it hit me. He'd gone back to Roz's house and secured some of our gear. What if one of the things had gotten at him and he kept that part of her trip quiet?

Shit.

"Are you sure you didn't you see any sign of the virus in Craig?" I asked Joel.

"You've asked me that a hundred times. I don't know, man, I was there too and I don't know."

"Right? I know he was fine. I know it. Lee had no right to do what he did."

"Lee's probably gone now, so what are you gonna do?" Joel asked me.

"Go after him? Wait for him to get back. I don't care. I just want a chance at his ass."

"He seems to be in charge or something. Weird that he doesn't wear any insignia but everyone knows who he is."

"He's an asshole," I said.

"Truer words, brother."

Joel rolled over and covered his head with his pillow.

Asshole.

We woke to screams.

I sat up in semi-darkness and felt around for my side arm. It was under my pillow, that's right. Tucked next to a backup mag. Joel was on his feet and checking over his own weapon. We weren't the only ones. There were so many armed folks you'd think we were at an NRA sleep over.

A guy dressed in fatigues ripped the tent entrance open and shouted over the rows of cots.

"Up. Everyone up. Move quickly to the landing pad. Choppers are arriving. When you get the sign, you keep low and get on board. Got it? You don't listen and you get left behind."

I shook my head and rubbed my eyes. My head felt like it was full of cotton and my eyes were gummed shut. Joel was already strapping on his gear and appeared to have been up for hours. I wished I had a double dose of energy drink, then a bottle of whiskey to wash that shit back with. Thai whiskey. I'd crush a few heads for some.

The civilians around us rose and packed quickly. Kids were quieted and shuffled out. It didn't turn into a panic until the guns started to boom outside.

I pushed through the throng with Joel Kelly close behind. Roz was on her feet with a backpack over her shoulder. She tugged out a handgun and held it at her side.

Christy stuck to her side but she was clenching her fists open and shut over and over again. I dropped my pack to the ground and opened it. Moving things around, I found what I was looking for.

"Don't shoot anyone. You know how these work, right?"

It was the little Sig Sauer 229 I'd found on Monster Ken an eternity ago.

Christy took the gun and looked it over. She racked the slide back to inspect the chamber and then let it slam shut.

"I've played a lot of video games."

"Good," I said. "Now don't shoot anyone unless they're a threat."

"Yep."

She lifted her head and nodded at me. Confidence, though a spark at best, showed.

"What now?" Roz yelled over the noise.

I tried to smile at Roz but it came out as a sneer. She thumped me in the chest, then kissed her fingers and smacked me across the cheek, not too hard, kind of a love tap. Then she did the same to Joel Kelly.

"Let's go kick some ass," Kelly said.

"Or haul ass," I said.

Together we navigated the throng and moved to the entrance.

Our quarters weren't even two hundred feet from the entrance to the base so we got a quick appraisal of the action and it wasn't good. Not good at all.

Joel must not have believed his eyes because he moved toward the gate. The wrong way. Stupid jarhead.

Civilians streamed past us in a panic, clutching children close. A man lugged a huge suitcase a few feet then looked over his shoulder and gasped. He tossed the bag to the side of the pathway and started to push through the crowd.

Men and women, some in white gowns and others in wheel chairs spewed out of the hospital doors. Other's watched from windows with huge eyes.

I watched too. I watched and I got scared.

As far as the eye could see they came. The mass was the largest I'd seen yet, even surpassing the horde that we'd spotted moving through the city. They stumbled toward the fence in their greed for human flesh.

It wasn't an easy task to navigate the traps and bodies left to rot from the previous incursion, but they came at us anyway. They poured over the remains of the crashed chopper we'd arrived in. They came even though gunfire smashed into them from a running squad making their way for the gate.

An enemy with any sense would have ducked and moved as they sought to find firing positions. These had no care in the world for tactics. These monsters just wanted to eat.

The dead numbered in the thousands, or maybe even the tens of thousands.

Guns opened up in force this time. They fired without respite, .50 cals along the outside walls and men positioned over the newly constructed mesh gate. If we thought we were safe, it was an illusion. As soon as they hit the chain link, our safety, that illusion was gone.

Joel dashed to the line and tapped a gunner on the shoulder. The other man didn't look at him, just kept on shooting. Joel pulled his pistol, took careful aim, and fired.

Joel was like that. If there was a fight he was there. I wasn't like that. I would fight if I had too but this was too much. The men and women defending us were looking at a painful death.

If I left now I could probably slip into the mass of people and use my size to my advantage to fight my way to the front of the line. If there was a truck or chopper headed away from this mess, I wanted to be on it.

Who was Joel Kelly anyway? Just a guy I'd been stuck with since our boat was overrun. We'd put up with each other for days. We'd argued, fought together, and even come to be friends. I'd saved his life and he'd saved mine.

"Take the kid and go," I said to Roz. "Just go. I'll be there soon."

"Fuck you, sailor boy. I'm getting in this war."

Christy grinned up at her. Who the hell was I to tell them to run away?

Jesus Christ, was I the only sane one? Now was my chance. I hadn't asked to be shackled with this bunch. I might be better off on my own.

Who was I kidding?

"Oh, fuck a duck!" I said and went to join Joel.

I wasn't the only one. A number of civilians did the dumb

thing, like me, and moved toward the action. They carried what weapons they could gather, mostly melee, but some had guns. Military guys roared up in jeeps and spun to expose beds laden with huge cases. These were dragged into the center of the action and broken open. Automatic weapons gleamed back at us. Cases of ammo and magazines, some full, were also left out for us.

I grabbed a machine gun of some sort, probably some gun Joel could wax poetically about for days telling me the exact length of the trigger action and round capacity. In another box I found full magazines. I picked up a box of shells and went to find a nice corner to plan my death.

The horde came on and was answered with lead. As the horde closed, and even picked up speed, it became apparent that we had minutes at most. You'd think that twenty or thirty people shooting could handle anything but we were outnumbered. For every body that fell there were five to take its place.

And there were shufflers. A lot of shufflers. They were in the pack but many of them held back as the slow ones went to do their dirty work. I swear those goddamn things still have half a brain.

The fortifications outside of the gate did a lot to help slow the dead. They got hung up on barbed wire and stuck to posts. Some were fired upon while others left to lift their hands and reach for us in vain. Losers.

I ducked and moved toward Joel Kelly. He was outside the gate, on one knee, aiming and firing with grim determination. His position was right next to an overturned truck. I touched his shoulder and he looked back and shot me a wink.

"Glad you could make it, bud." He aimed and dropped a woman dressed in the remains of a nightgown. She fell without a sound and was quickly trampled beneath the mass behind her.

Next to him was someone I didn't expect. Anna Sails fired in rapid succession with a gun as long as her legs, and she wielded it like a pro. She fired, shifted, aimed, fired again, and every time her gun boomed one of them dropped.

"Civilians are being moved out in trucks. Buy them time. Fall back when the horde gets close. We got a surprise for them." A man with a bullhorn shouted at us. I thought it might be Lee and had a hastily constructed plan where he accidentally takes a bullet, but when I looked back it wasn't him.

It didn't take long for us to create a wall of bodies but it didn't do much to deter them. A couple of shufflers leapt off the top and came down near some of our guys. They were quickly shot down, but it was close.

The first line must have gotten some signal. They dropped down low while the line behind them stopped firing. They scurried back and the second line opened up again. We were about fifteen feet from the gate and when they called for us to do the same.

Five or six guys ran out as we retreated. They carried bandoliers covered in metal globes. They stopped, pulled pins, and tossed a wave of grenades at the approaching horde. I was already on the run when the explosions shook the ground and I didn't look back.

We were cutting it close. The dead were only a few feet away when Anna Sails stowed her weapon on her shoulder and ran after us. I kept an eye on her and even shot a shuffler as it leapt out of the mass. I hit him with three or four bullets but they only ripped into his body. He was blown to the side, but he was a quick one and rolled to his feet. With an Olympian leap he managed to take down one of our guys. The soldier howled in fury but got off a shot and hit the bastard in the head. Brains exploded and one of his buddies stopped to pull him out from under the corpse.

"Everyone in, now!" The guy with the bullhorn roared, so we hauled ass.

As we cleared the gate the heavy machinery we'd seen earlier in the day roared to life. A pair of fences sections had been tied to the bulldozer. It rammed into the horde with a sound that will haunt my nightmares for years to come. It came to a halt after crushing a great many of them, and then backed up with a flash of yellow lights and piercing alarm.

Joel helped Anna in but she shrugged off his hand and went to stand with a group she seemed to know. They set up a new firing line behind the fence while the rest of our guys filed inside. It was all high fives and way to go's but not everyone was happy. Edward, the man I'd met in the mess hall, looked haunted. He also looked like he needed to find a bucket.

Behind us, civilians moved onto trucks that lurched away. Some didn't wait and tried to crowd on to full trucks or jump on board before they had stopped moving. When the Z's hit the fence it was pandemonium.

"We should go, Joel," I said and grabbed his arm.

He pointed toward the crane we'd seen when we first arrived.

Its arm moved into the air, lifting a huge claw and then it swept own and cleared a path. Not even a hundred Z's could stand up to the crane's power as it swept back and forth.

The mass was here, though, and it was a matter of time before this entire base was overrun.

A shuffler hit the fence and tried to climb it, but Anna Sails shot him through the head.

"Yeah, it's time," Joel said.

I looked around and spotted Roz and Christy. She'd abandoned the little handgun in favor of a machine gun. It has huge in her hands as she moved away.

Our pace was brisk and soon we ran into others that were fleeing. We had to slow, but at least we were moving toward safety.

Then I heard a sound to my left. The horde had swung around or broken off and had reached the fenced in there. Reinforced by long metal bars the chain-link still wasn't strong enough to withstand the impact. A pair of shufflers launched themselves at the top of the wall and one managed to reach the razor wire. He got hung up. I took a lot of joy in pausing for a minute to shoot it three or four times. No headshot but he slumped after the last bullet ripped through his upper body.

"The fence isn't going to hold. Move!" A soldier said and then broke into a run.

The crane swung its arm back and forth but the driver must have seen the futility of his action and decided it was time to make his getaway. The crane backed up and all those tons of metal began a slow crawl through the dead. None rose from where it passed.

"Come on, you big idiot." Roz grabbed my arm and pulled.

I joined our motley group of five even though I was sure we were about to be over run. Thousands of them behind, and thousands to on our flank. We weren't going to last much longer unless we found a transport.

A pair of HUMVEEs pulled into the street to my right and then opened up with machine guns. The guys on the guns swept back and forth as they shredded the front ranks.

A rending crash behind. I didn't have to look around to know that the fence was gone.

We ran with me in the lead because I was the biggest. We hit the mass of other survivors looking for a way out and I wasn't shy about pushing through them.

The line of trucks and cars took on as many as they could. It was a full blown panic as people fought to get on anything that moved. Women and children were pushed aside. Anger boiled but this was no time to crack some heads and teach manners.

Some ran. They just bolted in every direction, barreling into anyone blocking their way.

Explosions behind. I looked over my shoulder and found a group of soldiers tossing more grenades at the mass of Z's. Bodies and parts of bodies flew.

We were brought to a halt by a couple of guys trying to sort the evacuees.

"Civilians that way." One of them pointed at a scrambling mass.

A second line fed to huge military transports that was at least somewhat organized. Men and women in uniform jumped onto transports, some as they roared off.

"We're enlisted, man."

"Right. Move your ass or we'll drop you right where you stand."

A couple of people picked that minute to try and break through the line and run toward the military trucks. They were met with the butt of rifles. Another civilian got wind of the action and screamed.

"They aren't letting us out!"

Joel and I exchanged glances just before the first shot rang.

A civilian in ragged jeans and a white t-shirt covered in holes pulled a pistol and pointed it at one of the guys in green. He pointed back and shouting broke out. The guard looked at us and lowered his gun as well.

"It's cool, man. We'll just find another ride," Joel said.

Didn't these guys have a secret military code or something? Joel was dressed in the remains of his combat gear and if there was a man with more military bearing, he wasn't here.

I backed up a step, taking Roz with me. Then a figure pushed between us.

"Lower that gun, soldier," she said.

Anna Sails to the rescue.

"They can't join us, ma'am," he replied.

"These guys are with me and they're enlisted. Just make a hole," she said and pushed forward.

The two looked at us in confusion. Then it evaporated as shots broke out near us.

"Oh, fuck this shit," Joel said and grabbed Roz's hand.

The two sides got tired of shouting at each other and someone fired. I couldn't tell which let the first bullet fly but it was a massacre after that.

I backed up and then grabbed Christy's hand and tugged her after Joel.

Anna Sails followed and together we ran back toward the horde.

Chaos behind. Chaos to the sides.

It was either risk a bullet or run.

We ran.

The fence on the east side of the little base went down. I fired a few rounds as we ran but it was like trying to stop a wave with a BB gun.

Shots continued to ring out as we hauled ass. The pair of HUMVEEs we'd seen earlier backed up as they fired. I smacked Joel's arm to get his attention. He veered toward the transports.

Joel waved his hands to stop the trucks. They slowed as they fired.

I turned and shot a Z in the neck as it came at us. There was another behind him and when I fired a burst, the bolt slapped open with a clang as I ran dry. I reached for a mag, but realized too late that I was totally out.

Fuck that. I swung the gun around, burned the shit out of my hands on the barrel, ignored it to turn the gun into a bat, and hit the Z so hard it did a mid-air summersault and landed in a splatter of crushed head and leaking brain matter.

Five or six more were right behind.

"Nice shot," Anna said beside me. She turned to her side, raised a huge hand gun and fired. Seriously, it was like something Dirty Harry would carry.

A shuffler leapt out of the mass and was on Sails before I could fire. They tumbled to the ground and the bastard went at her. Sails was good, fast; she got her gun in the way and smacked the Shuffler across the mouth. He howled and dove in for her neck.

I grabbed him by the back of his ratty-ass clothes, and lifted him straight off the ground making my ankle want to screech in pain. He was covered in open sores and bled some kind of mucus from multiple wounds but I didn't give a shit.

Sails might be a pain in the ass but none of us were going down under a shuffler. I'd put a bullet in her skull first.

She pulled herself across the ground, looked up, and blew the head off one of the dead that was headed straight for me.

The shuffler fought like a man with twice his strength. He got me good across the gut and most of the air left my lungs. Then his elbow connected with my head and I saw stars.

I lifted him above my head with both arms and then flung him down on the back of the HUMVEE so hard his head split like a fucking melon. Sails had to pull me away from kicking his twice-dead ass.

"I'm Marine Sergeant Joel Kelly. Got room for us?" Joel stood near the front of the transport.

"Pretty fucking full, Sarge. We got…" I couldn't hear the rest because the machine gunner blasted a line of lead across the approaching dead.

There were so many of them that we didn't stand a chance. The walls were down and we were being overrun.

Joel grabbed Roz and Christy and stuffed them into the back of the Humvee. I scooped up Sails and dragged her to the other side of the truck and banged on the door. It opened and the face of a young soldier poked out.

Anna was having difficulty breathing and gasped when I picked her up.

"I'm staying with you guys," Sails said.

I ignored her.

"Put her on your lap. You're welcome," I said and pushed her toward the door.

"Idiot! I don't need saving! Just let me stand and fight with you guys."

"Get in or I'll put you in," I said as I towered over her.

The machine gunner opened up again and dropped at least a half dozen.

"I'm staying!" She pushed against my damaged chest.

"Anna, please. Get in. We're all getting out of here," I said.

She looked me up and down and then nodded and crawled in.

"Better than being tossed to the dead," I said. Thoughts of Anna backing up Lee made me second-guess my actions. Maybe I should have tossed her to the horde.

The back was stuffed and there was no way for me and Joel to squeeze in. Joel winked at me through the opening and then slammed the door shut. He came around the side of the transport firing.

I closed the door and joined him.

"Hold on, gents!" The machine gunner roared and pointed at the back of the HUMVEE.

A whole world of hurt ran at us. The dead were here and we were screwed.

Joel was the first to make the leap. He got on the back of the transport and shimmied up the angled back until the gunner helped him. Then he hung onto the plates on the side of the gun.

The HUMVEE lurched into motion with me standing in the middle of the zombie fucking apocalypse holding my dick.

"Wait for me!" I yelled and leapt.

I missed.

The first Z came at me so I clothes-lined the asshole. A shot and something buzzed past my neck. I looked over my shoulder and there was Joel Kelly, holding onto the back of a giant machine gun while he somehow pulled his side arm and shot a dead fuck through the head.

This guy should be in a video game.

I hauled ass, jumped for the back and started to slide back off. Joel dropped his gun, grabbed the machine gun mount with both hands and stuck his boot right next to my face. I grabbed hold and tried to haul myself up but a Z got my leg.

I kicked back a few times and got him in the face. Bone crunched as his nose was crushed but I didn't have time to gloat because the truck lurched into motion and I had to hold onto Joel Kelly's leg for dear life.

I crawled up the back of the HUMVEE until I was able to reach the gunner. Him and Joel reached out and pulled me the rest of the way then I was clutching the back of the gun mount.

"Haul ass!" The gunner pounded the top of the truck.

We broke across a parking lot, ran over a tent, hit the side of the building and that almost knocked me clear but I had a death grip.

Then we were past the little base and behind the line of trucks.

"Next stop, L A." The gunner grinned.

"Great. I need some new underwear," I said over the roaring wind.

The gunner smiled again and patted my shoulder. He ducked back into the vehicle for a minute.

"Joel, man. I owe you."

"Yeah you do. Dumb squid."

"Words hurt," I said. "Especially from a dumb jarhead."

"Don't get all mushy on me. Christ. I've had enough of this day and if you start bawling I'm going to have the gunner shoot me in the fucking head."

"Okay man, I won't, but I want to tell you something."

"I ain't marrying you."

"Thank the fuck Christ." We hit a bump and I came down on my sore chest again. After an epic swearing session I got my breath back.

"Gonna make it?"

"As long as you got my back I think I'll be okay. You're like a brother, Joel. Nah. You are my brother." I said it and meant it. We'd seen a lot of shit over the last few weeks but one thing hadn't changed. One thing had been there to help me survive and cope with this new world and that was Marine Sergeant Joel "Cruze" Kelly.

"Know something?" Joel asked.

We bounced up the road, slowed at a cross street, and then maneuvered around a wreck.

"Huh?" I asked, expecting some kind of brotherhood of war speech.

"I'm glad we're moving. I just farted and it's a reeker. Sorry about that." He looked at me with a smirk. "Brother."

I couldn't help it. I laughed until tears streamed down my face.

"Can you guys drive faster? Something died back here!" I roared at the driver.

"Sure, man." The driver called back.

"I can't hang on that long."

"Hitchhikers take what they can get." He laughed from inside.

"I hope he's kidding." I said to the gunner.

He didn't answer, just looked up.

Overhead, a helicopter roared away from the base and headed north. If Lee was on it I wished him well, because when I found him again he'd answer questions with my size fourteen boot up his ass.

This is machinist mate Jackson Creed and I am still alive

EPILOGUE

The series continues in:
Z-RISEN: OUTCASTS

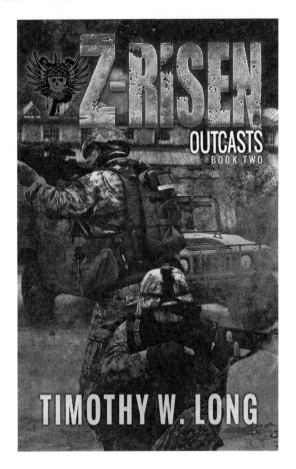

AFTERWORD

I've written a lot of zombie books over the years and had a lot of fun doing it. Z-Risen was born out of a conversation, over beers, with my friend Craig DiLouie in mid 2013. I had an idea to do a military themed series based partially on my own time in the United States Navy and pair up a Navy Engineer with a Marine. The two forces have always had a friendly rivalry and I thought it would make for a good story.

The book was initially written as a free web serial and it was set in the same world as my Permuted Press book Beyond the Barriers--the books can be read independently.

I'm an indie author and I work very hard on my books. I hold down a full time job, have a family, and still manage to get in a few hours a day to write. I love hearing input from readers and the best way to provide that is via a review.

When you leave a review on Amazon, Barnes and Noble, Smashwords, or where ever you purchased a book, it helps other readers. This also helps the author out more than you can imagine. It's hard to be a successful independent author but when a book sells well it is likely to get sequels and that's what I have planned for the Z-Risen series.

So please, friends, if you can spare a few minutes of your time, go and review Z-Risen: Outbreak on amazon.

Afterword

Click to review

Be honest and know that I read every review and use feedback to better my writing as well as have a positive impact on future books.

11:15 hours approximate

Seattle, WA – currently free of dead

This is author Timothy W. Long and I am still alive ... and writing.

OUTCASTS

Z-RISEN BOOK 2

PREFACE

In the event this log is found with my corpse, I'm Machinist Mate First Class Jackson Creed and it's been a week or more since we arrived in San Diego following the event. With me is Marine Sergeant Joel "Cruze" Kelly.

We were both stationed on the USS McClusky, an Oliver Hazard Perry-class frigate out of San Diego. Our ship was overrun by the dead and we barely escaped with our lives.

Now we live in the middle of Undead Central.

GO TIME

08:35 AM Approximate
Location: Somewhere outside of San Diego, CA

We came upon the worst wreck yet about an hour after sunrise. Before that it was stop and go – mainly stop – as we hit accident after accident. No one bothered to stick around and guard his or her car.

Since hauling ass out of San Diego and taking a full day to make twenty miles, we'd pretty much had it with the road, the cramped military vehicle, and each other.

The driver hit the roadside curb so hard we bounced and came down cursing. The guy spun the wheel to the left and then kept on going until the road cleared up enough for the HUMVEE to crawl back onto.

Joel and I rode up top with a guy named Greg Bailey. He sat behind the big .50 caliber machine gun and chewed on a huge hunk of tobacco. Every couple of minutes he'd spit over the side and Joel or I would move so we didn't get hit. After a half-day of this, I was ready to rip the load of chew out of his mouth and stuff it up his ass.

The main thing that saved him was the fact that he'd pulled our asses out of the shit on the way out of the naval hospital earlier in the day. Plus he was a hell of a friendly guy from

Dallas, Texas, and had a good-natured way of looking at the world.

"World's gone to hell. I get it. Thing is, we're still alive and know where there's a big ol' base full of big ol' men and women with big ol' guns. We make it there and we're in the green, boys. We call that 'go time'."

I tried to grin back but every inch of my body was a mess of bruises and sore muscles. All I wanted to do was find a hole in the ground and sleep for a week. Dodging tobacco-bullets wasn't helping.

Shitty aiming aside, Bailey was a nice enough guy. Too bad he didn't make it.

We stopped to stretch our legs and Roz told me she'd sit up top for while so I could get some rest inside. I'd argue but didn't have the energy. She wanted to hang with Joel, I got it. We'd had our little bit of touchy feely when we thought we were about to join the dead; she seemed to have forgotten all about that.

I hunched over and crammed myself into the back, but fought a smile when Sails settled in next to me. Christy wanted to look outside while we picked our way over the terrain.

"You okay, dude?" I asked her.

"I'm fine. I miss Craig, is all. I wish we could go back and look for him. That's stupid, right?"

"Sorry, dude. I know how you feel. I hate what happened, but we can't go back."

"Stop calling me dude," she said and almost cracked a smile.

"You got it." I waited two seconds. "Dude."

The other guys in the transport were Donny and Markus.

Markus had black hair shaved close to his head and wore a bunch of scars on his face. One creased his forehead and then zipped across his nose. He'd been driving when we made our escape and didn't talk much.

Donny was ill-tempered. Even though he smiled a lot, I didn't trust him one bit. He was far too content to shoot Z's. I hated it. I hated popping these things in the head or bashing in brains. He did it with that easy smile.

"You guys Guard?"

"Not really," Markus said.

"What? Army?"

Sails was particularly quiet when the subject of enlisted men and women came up. She shifted in her seat and then stared out the window without saying a word.

"Nope. Isn't it enough that we have a nice thick roof, protection, and food?" Donny responded, still smiling.

That was all I got out of them.

There wasn't a lot of talk in the HUMVEE. After a while, you get so damn tired you don't want to be bothered with shit like chatting about the weather or how you killed the last Z. You want to just sit back and try to think about better times.

I'd been doing that for the last fifteen minutes. Then I realized how quiet it was inside the vehicle. Although I was pressed against the not-unpleasant shape of Anna Sails, doing anything about it was the last thing on my mind. I was fond of my balls and had no doubt she'd shoot them off if I even attempted to drape an arm over her shoulder.

My half-musings didn't last. All I had to do was glance outside to be reminded that we may have escaped with our lives, but how long could we last? How long until we became permanent fixtures in Undead Central?

Bodies everywhere, some of them moving. Cast out luggage, clothes, shit that used to mean the world to some little kid. Now it was all fodder for the zombie fucking apocalypse.

We passed a pile of the dead that smoldered. A few of them were still twitching as the smoke lazed into the morning air. We stopped for a bio break near an overturned school bus. I stretched my legs and then limped off to relieve my aching bladder.

Joel and I stayed together, one keeping watch while the other took care of business. I stared at the front of the shattered bus and nearly pissed all over my hand when the driver sat up and reached for me. Other figures moved around in the murky interior, so I shook it, zipped, and dragged Joel to a nice Volkswagen Bug that had somehow survived the seventies and the apocalypse. The doors were open and nothing moved inside. While Joel took a leak, I went through the glove box and kept an eye on the road.

Nothing approached us and I came up with a couple of packs of Reese's cups that were a melted mess. Joel and I squeezed out candy that looked like turds and licked the wrappers clean.

Back in the HUMVEE, it was business as usual. We drove off the road, got back on it, cut across creeks, got out and pushed cars out of the way, and generally did whatever we could to get as far from San Diego as possible.

We drove a few miles from the freeway and found a gas station. It had been looted. A small city spread out behind it on the flat landscape; I didn't see anything moving.

Joel and Donny got out and then got real creative with the hatch over the diesel gas tank. They used a military-issue big ass crowbar to bust it open. Roz returned from the side of the building with a hose.

"I got this." Bailey hopped down from his station.

"You should stay on the gun," Joel said.

"We ran out of rounds back at the hospital. Blew through the last fifty when you boys got on board."

"You've been manning an empty gun?"

"Habit," Bailey said and turned his head to spit.

He dug around in the back of the transport and came up with a hand pump.

"That thing gonna work?" I asked.

"Damn straight. I used to work at a Chevron back in the halcyon days of my youth. I've done worse to get gas out of a hole in the ground."

I didn't ask what "worse" meant.

We set up a perimeter, then watched the road and each other's backs. Bailey and Roz managed to monkey a couple of hoses together and pump diesel into the HUMVEE. It was slow going; as the minutes ticked by I got more and more nervous. I felt like we had a giant fucking bull's-eye painted on our location.

"We got this," Bailey said after I came over to check on him for the third time.

I nodded and walked toward the perimeter.

That's when they came out of the woodwork.

I don't know if it was us; we were speaking in low voices. The sound of the pump or the clang when we popped the cover and dragged it off? Hell, it might have just been bad luck.

"Zulu's at three o'clock!" Donny yelled and went down to one knee.

The first shot was shocking in the quiet morning. I drew but didn't have a clean look until I moved around the backside of the HUMVEE.

"Everyone back in, now!"

"Almost got her; buy me a minute," Bailey said and pumped like a madman.

Joel fell back shooting as Markus closed in on their position to set up a screen. A hail of bullets met the Z's but there were many hands and hungry mouths.

The snarling mass didn't have a shuffler behind them, but what was back there was almost as bad. Fresh dead. They poured in on our position. I tried to get a count but gave up at eighteen or nineteen.

If we had a wall or roof or a fucking piece of artillery, we might have been able to drop most of them but there were just too many and more were coming.

I fired three rounds at a staggering guy dressed in a pretty nice set of PJ's. Not your dollar-store variety – these looked fresh and pressed. Too bad the asshole wearing them was missing most of his throat and shoulder. One round went and one caught him in the chest. He was blown back but that made my third shot miss. I don't know how action heroes make killing shots in movies. When you got a bunch of fuckers bearing down on your position, you might as well be trying to shoot a bulls-eye off a jumper at a goat rodeo.

"Up, Bailey! Let's get motivated!" I yelled as I ran back and grabbed him by the shoulder.

He looked up, pumped a few more times, and then yanked the hose, still drooling diesel, out of the HUMVEE.

Sails was up on the side of the transport. She had one hand on the door and her gun in the other. The .357 banged slowly; she was careful to clear her field of fire, aim, and then blow a Z into the mass.

The trickle had expanded and now thirty or forty swarmed. They were on us before we were loaded. Joel scrambled up the side of the vehicle. I joined him, shimmying up the back until I found my grip on the edge of the gun turret. The HUMVEE roared to life as doors slammed shut. Sails kept her cool and kept blasting.

Joel sat up and covered Bailey while the man tossed the pump aside and jumped to his feet. The Texan rocked forward and grabbed onto the back of the HUMVEE. He almost got his foot onto the metal bumper but slipped and slammed his knee into the hard exterior.

"Son of a mother fucker!" he screamed.

"Wait! Bailey's out there!" I yelled, but the vehicle had already lurched into motion.

"Not good!" Joel shouted.

I rolled to the side and prepared to jump off the truck, even though I knew it would probably be a death warrant. Joel Kelly grabbed my shoulder and yanked hard to get my attention.

"Lemme go, Joel!" I tried to bat his hand aside.

"Look, it's too late, man. I know, it's Bailey – but it's too late. You go down there and you aren't coming back."

Sails shot a female crawler in the shoulder, adjusted, then blew her rotting head back. A pair of festering males were right behind the woman. Sails shot one; the other fell onto Bailey.

Bailey got his forearm up to stop the zombie's descending mouth and managed to hold it back, but another of the crawlers attacked.

Bailey screamed as the Z sank its teeth into his arm and ripped.

Sails's gun rang out again.

Bailey slumped forward a moment after a hole appeared just above his nose.

I pounded the top of the HUMVEE in frustration.

21:45 approximate
Location: Somewhere south of Los Angeles

Supplies:

- Food: A lot, but the mystery men in our new outfit are keeping it under guard
- Weapons: Plenty to go around
- Attitude: Not a happy squid tonight

WE STOPPED FOR THE NIGHT A FEW MILES OFF THE MAIN ROAD. WE rolled over hard, desert-like terrain. The driver found a little gulley off the beaten path and backed up so the ass of the HUMVEE sat over the little depression in the ground. We piled out and set up camp. I volunteered to take first watch, but Joel Kelly took one look at me and told me to sleep.

I ate a cold meal from an MRE while Sails and I sat in silence. She picked some chicken crap and I took some beef brisket that tasted like leather dipped in barbeque sauce. We exchanged our desserts. She had spice cake and I had oatmeal cookies. After we were done, I told her it was a great first date, then rolled up in a green blanket that smelled like fuel and promptly passed the fuck out.

04:15 approximate
Location: a big hole in the ground

DONNY WOKE ME FOR WATCH. I ROLLED OVER AND TOLD HIM IF HE touched me again I'd rip his head off and shit down his neck.

Sails punched me in the side and told me to get up and stop bitching.

I'm really starting to like this girl.

I patrolled the perimeter but it was about as lively as a desert could be. Little creatures ran around in the dark and did a good job of scaring the crap out of me. Donny handed me a pair of NVG's and showed me where the power switch was located. I adjusted them for my head and took in a world of green hues. The restricted view they afforded was only a little bit better than walking around with a flashlight. At least this way I wasn't calling out to every Z within a five-mile radius.

I stared at a rock for a while and contemplated whether these godless undead fucks could even see light. Their eyes were milky white, like the irises had been covered in full size cataracts. How in the world did they sense us, unless it was just noise?

I almost fell on my face and realized I'd completely zoned out.

I shook my head and went back to pacing.

05:15 approximate
Location: a big hole in the ground

AN HOUR LATER THE OTHERS ROSE.

The sun , like me, was in a piss-poor mood, and hung out behind a couple of clouds. I thought for sure we were bound for rain but it hadn't quite cracked the sky yet. We pulled out and went back to picking our way across what little road we could find.

Joel told me to squeeze in the back. Roz took to the gun turret and he stayed on top of the vehicle to keep watch. I didn't ask if he was keeping an eye on the enemy or on her.

Christy clung to my side; Sails sat in silence next to Christy. I tried to talk, but she told me to shut the hell up so she didn't have to think.

An hour later we came across a small town that wasn't crawling with the dead.

The town of Clairemont was about thirty miles from San Diego and probably a hell of a nice place before the world died.

Worried about supplies, we hit a couple of diners but found them picked over. The second shop, Heart Stop Café, had been cleaned out with the exception of a few boxes of powdered cocoa. A couple of people missing the back of their heads were decomposing on the floor. Shells lay all over the floor along with chunks of glass and broken mugs and dishes. The two had obviously put up a fight.

Whoever had shot up the shop was long gone, but I kept looking over my shoulder. My neck crawled like it was covered in spiders. I felt like someone had a gun trained on me and they were going to open fire at any moment.

Back on the road, we ate cold MRE's again and talked about our dwindling supplies. Frankly, I was surprised the two others hadn't kicked our asses out of the transport and made for the base alone.

Maybe they were thankful to have extra eyes and guns. Maybe they had their eyes and dicks set on Roz and Sails. I didn't envy them if they tried anything. Sails was likely to gut one while putting her .357 in the other's mouth and blowing the back of his head off.

We chatted briefly about how long it would take to reach the base in LA. I was worried that, by the time we arrived, it would be game over – the base would be a smoking ruin like the one we'd left behind.

"It's a tough spot they got set up. The Marines, Navy, and Bright Star brought in a lot of hardware to build the walls. Got moats and everything. It'll be there." Markus sounded sure.

"Speaking of bases, we should set up a base for a day and then do some scouting and build up our supplies. We can move out again in the morning," Joel said.

"Damn fine idea," Markus said from the front seat.

"Agreed, boss." Donny smiled over his shoulder.

If he got touchy feely with anyone, I was going to put my foot in his mouth.

WE PULLED ACROSS SOMEONE'S LAWN AFTER BOUNCING OVER A couple of roads clogged with cars. The town sported a shitload of cookie-cutter houses and strip malls. We passed a Mexican restaurant that had been burned to the ground. Across the street, a Krispy Kreme was also a smoking ruin. The bank next to it had all of its windows smashed in.

Night had arrived and talk of sleeping outside was quickly shot down. None of us wanted to be exposed, so we picked this place out of a half dozen we passed.

FORTRESS, MARK II WAS A DILAPIDATED HOTEL OFF INTERSTATE 5. IT had been a piece of shit before the world went to hell. The (former) Hotel Palomino had two floors and a metal gate we'd managed to wedge shut. On the top floor we'd found adjoining rooms and made our nest for the last few days but it was temporary.

"Why are we locking ourselves on the second floor? We should set up camp on the first floor so we don't get bottled up," Donny opined.

"Back the HUMVEE right under the railing." Joel pointed at the second floor. "That's our escape route. See those metal gates at the end of the hallway? That'll buy us a lot of time if a horde locates us. Slow, but we can get in the transport through the gunner's portal."

"It's a solid plan," Markus said.

He spun the transport around while we pushed an electric hybrid out of the way.

The five of us – Joel, Roz, Christy, Anna Sails, and me – stuck together in the larger room while Markus and Donny took the room with two twin beds.

There were other empty rooms, but not a single one had less than one body. We got lucky with our set. There was a Z with an arrow through its head blocking the door, but we hauled his corpse across the landing and tossed it near a dumpster overflowing with trash.

I guess Joel was feeling cocky. He pressed Markus and Donny for info about their outfit, but they were tightlipped. When Joel pressed harder we got an earful.

"You guys want to sit out the end of the world right here or do you want to stick with us and our armored vehicle?" Markus said. His scars gave him a sneer but I had a feeling he would wear the look, regardless.

Half an hour later we took stock of our gear and I did a proper ammo and weapon count. My .45 was down to one backup mag and a couple of spare rounds. One thing I'd kept handy was my pipe wrench. Damn thing had been worth its weight in gold.

Joel laid out a couple of magazines. He slipped over the side of the balcony and came back a few minutes later with nondescript boxes of fresh ammo. Joel tossed me one and gave one to Sails.

Roz dug out a handful of rounds from my box and filled her 1911 .45. She checked the action and then asked Joel for a quick lesson on how to strip and clean it. Jesus Christ. The way she said strip and clean made Joel's eyes go wide.

Later we joined the mystery men in their room and took stock of our other food supplies. Donny carried up a satchel full of Meals Ready to Eat and we used water from the toilet to fire up the little chemical pouches. I waited a full two minutes, saliva filling my mouth, before ripping open the brown packet. I devoured it by squeezing the contents from the pocket into my mouth while it was steaming hot.

Joel ate his cold with a plastic spork.

Show off.

Donny and Markus studied a map while they ate from the various pouches.

"We're here and Bravo is here." Markus pointed out two big red splotches.

"Bravo?" I asked.

"Home base, for now. That's where we're headed." Markus said.

"Safer than the place we just left?"

"Better be. That was a cluster fuck, man. We knew that horde was on the move, but they got there a lot faster than we'd anticipated."

"Might have been the noise. I heard a chopper crashed the night before," Donny said.

I coughed and didn't say a word. Anna Sails kept her poker face while Joel Kelly's eyes tightened.

Donny had this reedy voice that was like nails on a fucking chalkboard. He also had pinched in features and a long nose. He wore digital cammo that bore no insignia and he carried a huge bowie knife strapped to his side. He'd set his Mossberg pump action shotgun across the map while we chatted. I studied it with interest.

"Can I check out your piece?"

"Yeah. Just don't blow your head off," Donny handed me the gun.

"Beautiful." I said.

"That's a special order right there," Donny went on. "It's a Mossberg 500 with a tactical upgrade. Holds five plus one in the chamber. It's got a sweet grip, feel it. Gun wasn't mine. It belonged to that Bailey guy."

"You say Bailey like you didn't know him."

"I didn't. He was guard and that was his personal weapon. He was a prepper I guess."

I lifted the gun and put it to my shoulder. The front rail was fitted with a sloped grip. Bailey had outfitted the shotgun with a rail near the chamber and it contained six rounds. The rear rail held five more.

For a split second I had the desire to turn the gun on him and blow his fucking head off. Then I'd have to kill Markus because he'd probably be pissed about me shooting his buddy.

The thought left pretty quickly. These two might have questionable agendas, but they'd saved our asses.

The shotgun felt good in my hand and probably packed enough load to disintegrate a Z at close range.

"I gotta get me one of these."

"Look at that. Creed's got a crush," Kelly said.

"Love at first sight, I'd say," Anna added.

"Oh, haha. Sight. I get it. You two should write a comedy routine and go on the road."

I stared back until they both looked away, but Sails wore a little smirk.

"We'll crash here for the night and then scout in the morning. We may get lucky and find enough supplies to get us through a few days. Then we move out around noon." Markus said.

"We might stay here for a while longer," Joel said.

That was news to me. I liked the sound of us going somewhere safe. I liked the thought of having a bed and water. Food was great but I was so thirsty I was ready to start making some kind of piss filter.

"Suit yourself," Donny said and looked at Markus. The big guy shrugged his shoulders and went back to chewing on a straw that poked out of his camel pack water system. It was dry as a bone, but I didn't blame him for the wishful thinking.

"We haven't discussed staying anywhere. I'm with you guys," I said, but wondered if I meant it.

Joel, Roz, and Anna looked at me.

"Or I guess we'll talk about it."

"Do what you gotta do. All I know is we're headed toward safety. The base has a real command and control structure, and they're taking orders from Washington. Someone over there is still calling the shots." He trailed off.

That was the first we'd heard about any kind of authority existing. Didn't really matter. Everything was so fucked it wasn't like they were looking for me, Joel, or countless other enlisted.

"Is the President still alive?" I asked.

"Don't know. I just know that we got orders. They come into the vehicle from time to time but the system is on some kind of repeat, so we're hearing what a lot of others are hearing. They keep rattling off safe havens in different parts of the country."

"So…military."

"Yeah, let's go with that," Donny said.

"Just tell us what the fuck is going on. Come on, man, be straight with us," Joel said.

Markus sighed and went to sit on the side of a bed.

"Your call," Donny said.

"Fine, man. We're with a group of peacekeepers called Bright Star. We were in Iraq and then we went into Afghanistan. We take care of security when the U.S. pulls out."

"So, you're like Blackwater." I thought out loud.

"Not quite. We're smaller and better organized. Right, Sails?"

"I only did one tour, man. Lee asked me to join his last mission because I was having issues," Sails said.

She took a seat at the table and toyed with the rest of the pouches in her MRE. Sails tossed me her pepperoni sticks so I gave her my crackers and fake cheese spread.

"Lee? What do you know about Lee?" I couldn't help it. My face flushed at the mention of his name.

"Lee's in charge for now. He went ahead to LA to help secure the base. I heard that he's got family there. Heard he had them flown all the way across the country," Donny said.

"Lee's an asshole. He tossed my friend Craig, just a kid, out of our helicopter."

"He was infected, Creed, you big dummy. Get it through your head. I saw the test results myself and I know what they meant. That kid could have turned at any moment. Any second. Then we could have had a Z right there in the helicopter. One bite and we were all going to be fighting for our lives," Sails said.

I couldn't believe she was defending Lee.

"So what, you all got a nice little brotherhood thing going on here? Got your secret name and decoder rings? Tell me how this makes the world better," Joel Kelly demanded. He gripped the edge of the table so hard I thought it was going to snap.

"Secure that shit, Marine," Sails said.

Markus and Donny nodded. Was that it? Did Sails outrank these two yahoos?

"Look, man," Markus said. "The military is fragmented and it's got no command structure. No way to gather forces in one place and enact some kind of plan to deal with this threat. Two hundred years and we've never had an occupying force on American soil. That changed a few weeks ago when someone attacked us."

"Wait. This was an attack?" I couldn't believe it.

"Something hit multiple locations. Some virus, and I swear that's all we know."

"Fuck me." Joel Kelly said before I could.

"We were already here and preparing, ready to deploy, when the main bases were hit. The military took devastating losses. Did you guys see what happened at Coronado?"

"We were there." I said.

Markus expelled a breath.

"Then you know first hand what happened. Bright Star is new, small. We were under the radar so now we're doing our best to cope. That's why you should stick with us if you want to survive and fight back. Fucking do what we tell you for a few more days."

"That's terrific." I choked back a snarl. "Sounds like you guys have all the answers. Don't need us, right?"

"We need everyone." Sails put her hand on my arm.

She didn't wear that usual frown and looked like she meant it. I resisted the urge to yank my arm away.

"And only my unique skills at bashing in Z heads can help save the world, right?"

"You'd be surprised what one man can accomplish with the right motivation," Sails said.

Shit. This was not the way I wanted the conversation to go. I wanted to stay mad at these people for killing Craig, but there was that little part of my brain that kept telling me that there was truth to what they'd told us—that Craig had been one of them. Infected.

I got sick of thinking about it and changed the subject.

"We need water," I said.

"Should be an ice maker on the floor. If it's still got water, we can use these." Donny produced some filtration tabs in little brown packs.

Joel smiled and snapped up a couple.

"Come on, Creed. Lets scout."

"Fuckin A. I hate it when you say those words."

"The fuck do you want, squid? A love poem?"

"Yeah. Serenade me."

"You guys are both idiots," Sails said.

"You'd be surprised what two idiots can do with the right motivation," I replied.

Sails actually smiled. Well, score one for the good guys.

"Great. Now we're all friends again. Hey Sails, if you get bored you can always bunk in with us," Markus said. "Right guys? There's enough of the women to go around."

Sails moved like a whip. Her hand shot to her side and in the blink of an eye she came up with her Smith and Wesson M&P R8. Ten and a half inches of dark steel met Markus stare.

"Say 'the women' one more time." She spoke through gritted teeth, and then she did that cool thing they do in the movies where she cocked the trigger. Silence fell in the room while we waited to see if Markus would lose his head.

"Just fucking around, Sails." He gulped. "You used to have a better sense of humor."

"You used to not be an asshole," she replied.

Sails arm still hadn't trembled. She holstered the gun, shot everyone in the room a flat look, then went to the adjoining room and shut the door.

"Woman is out of her mind," Donny said. "She used to be more fun."

"Sails had a fun side? What the hell happened?" I asked.

"She was on her way back when she heard about the outbreak. Her husband ran off a year ago but her kids were at her mother's house. It was right in the middle of the first horde that razed San Diego. She was on her way to the house when it was overrun. She got there just in time to see the worst of it."

"Shit," I said.

Joel echoed me.

"What did she do in Bright Star? She seems like she's used to being in command," I said.

"She was, in a fashion." Markus took the gun from me and put it back on the table but didn't bother to elaborate.

"She's a badass," I said.

"She's got a sweet ass," Donny said.

I thought about hitting him hard enough to make him talk stupid for the next week.

"Let's go, Creed. I'm thirsty." Joel interrupted my little fantasy.

10:15 AM Approximate
Location: Clairemont, CA

Joel and I did a perimeter sweep and verified that any Z's hiding out in the other hotel rooms were dealt with.

We kept it quiet by using close-in weapons. We cracked open a door three rooms down from ours. She was facing a wall and didn't even move until we stepped inside. That was enough to creep me out. She spun, looked at us with those milk white eyes, and then stumbled toward me. Joel stuck his big Marine knife into the woman's head and she went down without a sound. The woman's suitcases had been emptied all over the room. The refrigerator was a bust. We didn't stay to investigate further because the smell wasn't worth it.

The next room held a man dressed in rags. From what we could tell, he'd been stuck in there from the very beginning. He had a couple of bullet wounds to his chest, and in the room we found a single snub-nosed .38 and a pair of shells. I pocketed the gun and we moved on after a quick inspection turned up

nothing but more gore. The poor son of a bitch had tried, as best
we could tell, to kill himself. He had one bite mark on his neck.
He'd chewed his fingers to the second knuckle and then started
on his arm.

I put him out of his misery by driving the pipe wrench
under his jaw. His mouth shattered, and when he fell back I
moved in and crushed his skull like it was a thick egg.

When Joel and I entered room 223B, we found what had
probably been a husband and wife wrapped in a fatal embrace.
She had eight inches of steel buried in the back of her skull.

I stared at them and then turned to inspect the room.

That was a mistake.

The guy wasn't dead. He lurched to his feet and nearly
tackled me. Joel wove in for a slice, but I grabbed the Z just as
his nasty mouth was inches from my shoulder and tried to toss
him away.

He got ahold of my shirt and wouldn't let go.

His face darted in again and I fought my gag reflex. Of all
the rotted stinking things I'd smelled over the past few weeks,
this was the worst. His breath was a horror. His teeth were a
horror, and his nose was a crushed horror that had dried blood
crusted all over his mouth and jaw.

I hit him in the temple, but the blow was short and it barely
rocked him. He fell backward, almost taking me with him.

"Out of the way, Creed!" Joel cried.

"Think I'm not trying?"

The biter dove in again, and this time I hit him across the
face. His jaw snapped shut, but he managed to fall back against
the bed and pull me with him.

I rolled to the side but he stuck with me. Something closed
on the back of my shirt and I think I screamed like a little girl.

I whipped my elbow back and cracked him across the shoulder. He fell away and I was free. Rolling to the other side of the
bed, I let Joel do his thing.

Kelly moved in and stuck the guy in the throat with his
knife. He ripped the blade back so forcefully that the Z's head

nearly came off. The guy's second life ran out as he fell off the bed and onto his wife's half eaten corpse.

I sat up and gasped for breath. Nothing like fighting for your life when you're already exhausted, hungry, thirsty, and pissed off.

"Goddamn," was all I could get out.

Joel wiped his blade on the bedspread and then sheathed it.

"That's why I never got married." Joel stared at the dead couple.

At least the pair were in something resembling a loving embrace.

PANTING AND SHAKING, I SAT FOR A MINUTE AND CAUGHT MY breath. Joel looked me over and pronounced me still alive. I wobbled to my feet and checked all my extremities. No bite. Christ. That was not how I wanted this scouting mission to begin.

I moved to the refrigerator and opened it to find green and rotted store-bought sandwiches still wrapped in plastic. The prize turned out to be a half empty bottle of schnapps. I'd never in my life thought about tasting the stuff, but after almost making a one-way trip to Undead Central, it looked pretty inviting.

Joel poked through their luggage and came up with an open bag of chips. He took one out, sniffed it, then ate it. He grinned and handed me the bag after digging out a small handful.

"Yeah? Look what I found."

I took the top off the schnapps, took a tentative sniff, and then decided it probably wouldn't kill me. I'd had hooch on the ship that could strip the side off a destroyer; this shit was like lemonade by comparison.

"Early for drinking?"

"I'm a sailor," I said and tossed back another shot.

The chips were spicy and that suited me fine. Thoughts of

bringing some back for the rest of the crew evaporated as we handed the bag back and forth.

The room had a pair of prints on one wall depicting the coast. Clothes had been left in the closet but nothing my size. I found a bright red dress that would probably look great on Sails. Instead, I held it up for Joel.

"You could rock this."

Joel snorted.

Joel pawed through the luggage and found a brown bag. He opened it up, looked inside, and then dropped it.

I took a long pull while Joel wiped his hands on his tactical armor.

"What's in the bag?" I asked.

"It's for you."

I took another shot and then handed the bottle to Joel. He eyed it, smelled it, and then took an equally long pull. He lowered the bottle with a sputter.

I pushed the bag around with my foot until something slid out.

"Oh my fucking God." I laughed.

It was a huge black dildo.

"I thought you Navy pukes were into that kind of thing."

"Nah, man. I like a Marine penis. Small, but stands at attention with a stiff breeze."

"That is the gayest thing you've ever said, Creed."

Joel handed the bottle back, and I took another shot because it was going fast. It felt good. One more, and then Joel finished the bottle.

I picked up the brown bag and moved to the couple on the floor. The dead guy's mouth was stuck open, so I slid the rubber penis in between his teeth.

"Hey Joel, I think I know why these two weren't getting along."

"Dude. That is just fucking morbid." Joel sat down on the side of the bed and laughed until he nearly fell off.

THE NEXT ROOM HAD A SIMILAR DÉCOR AND WAS COVERED IN enough blood to make Hannibal Lector himself swing by to congratulate the former occupants.

Joel had jimmied the door with his knife and let it swing open. The room was dark and smelled rancid. The sound was what got to me. I wanted to turn and puke, then gouge out my eyeballs. A pair of Z's had been munching on the inhabitants for God knew how long. They tottered toward us on shaking legs, but we did them the courtesy of putting them down.

The room was a bust and so were the two after.

After making our way to the icemakers, we found that one was full of water. The other had blood on the side; we didn't bother opening it.

The next few rooms turned up a few items. A couple of bags of peanuts slightly larger than the samples they pass out on airplanes. A handful of tootsie rolls in some guy's fanny pack. He also had a wad of bills, though, so Joel and I split them up. Probably useless, but five hundred dollars was still five hundred dollars.

The last room was empty of inhabitants. A set of suitcases had been stacked in the closet. I worked on one while Joel pried the lock of a smaller bag.

It was just clothes and toiletries. I took out an electric shaver and tested the battery. It ran at full speed so I spent a minute buzzing the fuzz off my face in a darkened mirror.

Joel found an unopened tube of strawberry lip balm. I didn't even ask when he slipped it into his pocket. There was a two-liter bottle of soda that had been opened and then resealed. I unscrewed the top and was met with the sound of released CO_2. I sniffed and then decided that if the Z virus was living in cola, we were all doomed.

In a desk drawer I found a bag of corn chips and added it to our haul.

Joel returned from the bathroom with a pair of cups still wrapped in plastic. We toasted each other and then drained our portion in a couple of gulps. It was flat, warm, and fucking delicious.

AFTER FORTY-FIVE MINUTES OF BREAKING INTO ROOMS WE HAD pitifully little to show for it:

- A couple of protein bars
- A liter of generic soda
- 3 small bags of roasted peanuts
- An unopened bag of corn chips
- 15 tootsie rolls (I stashed a few in my pocket)

We returned with four pitchers of what I was sure was rancid water, but after the purifying tabs did their work I was the first to down half a container. After we'd drunk our fill, we went out to fetch more. I didn't even complain about the chemical taste.

Markus asked if we'd found anything else that might be useful.

"Nah," Joel said.

"We found an unhappily married couple but they weren't very chatty," I said.

"Probably due to the dick in the guy's mouth," Joel said.

After that it was my turn to burst into laughter.

"Glad you guys had fun. Now we got a serious issue. One of the boxes of MRE's turned out to be filled with ammo. That's great in the long run, but it means we're down to four full meals and there are a lot of mouths. We can probably make it last the day. So what's the plan?"

"I'll take Joel and the big squid here on a scouting run tomorrow. Did you get coms working?" Sails asked.

"I think so," Markus said and held up a large black band.

"That's good. Real good," Joel said.

"We'll be able to stay in contact. I'll take up station on the roof and provide over watch with an M14. It's a solid weapon with a range of five hundred yards. One bummer? I got limited ammo so don't expect me to pick off twenty fucking ZULU's, got it?"

"How many rounds?" Joel asked.

"About thirty five. You guys get into the shit too deep and you haul ass back here, got it? Roz, Christie, and Donny here will be backup."

"Sounds like a plan." Joel nodded.

21:15 hours Approximate
Location: Clairemont, CA

IT'S LATE AND I CAN BARELY KEEP MY EYES OPEN. TOMORROW WE are going to expand our area of operations and hopefully come back with a bonanza of food for the next few days. That's if we don't join the crawlers first.

And so the fuckening continues.

GAME FACE

12:45 hours approximate
Location: Just outside of Los Angeles

Supplies:

- 3 MRE's
- 1 box of chips and candy
- 1 half-gallon of water requiring purifying tablets

The following day would have an early reveille and I was already exhausted. I pretty much dragged my ass to the next hotel room, Joel in tow, and took in our new vacation spot.

Our room had a pair of queen-sized beds that looked – and worse, smelled – like something had died on them. Joel turned over one of the mattresses and rolled out a sleeping bag he'd grabbed from the HUMVEE. With Bailey gone, we had some extra gear. Joel lay down and broke out a manual about some type of communication unit.

Christy moped and took up station in the remnants of what had once been a very luxurious spa tub. At least it was clean. She dug a couple of blankets and pillows out of the closet and set up a cozy little nest. She hadn't been talkative since we left

San Diego, and I couldn't blame her. Two weeks ago, she'd been home with her parents and brother. Now they were all gone and she was with a bunch of strangers. I remembered my childhood. Dad used to drink a lot. Sometimes he and Mom would disappear for a day or two and then show up like nothing was different. Like I was supposed to ignore the fact that they'd abandoned me.

I hated the feeling of abandonment. I knew it had to be much worse for Christy, so I took every opportunity to speak with her and make her feel at ease. Roz was like a foster mother to her and did her best to keep Christy happy.

I tried to joke with Christy, but she rarely even smiled. She just looked scared and lost, and no amount of dumb things I could say would ever make her feel better. Craig had been a big loss for her. A loss for all of us. I'd never had kids and, quite frankly, didn't know the first thing about being a dad. Still, I felt like I owed her something, even if it was just a kind word or a lame joke.

"You holding up alright? You look like a princess in that tub."

"My kingdom used to be bigger."

I smiled and dug around in my pockets. I sat on the side of the tub and held my hand behind me, then looked over my shoulder and winked at her.

"Oh my gosh," she said, and scooped up the handful of warm tootsie rolls. "Thank you."

"Don't let Joel see. A Marine hopped up on sugar is scary as hell."

"I've seen enough scary sights for a lifetime," she said, and settled back to unwrap a treat.

"I'm sorry, Christy. Really sorry. I know they're just words, but I hope you understand that we're here to help and look out for you, okay? I can't imagine how hard it's been, but I promise you – nothing is going to happen to you. Me and Roz will be Papa and Mama Bear—with automatic weapons."

She looked at me from beneath a mass of dark curls; tears streamed down her face.

"I miss them so much and I'm so scared. Every place we go is worse than the last. I just want to go home, you know? I just want to go back to my old life."

"I'm with you." I dug a napkin out of one of my pockets. I inspected it and found the inner fold clean, so I used it to dab at her cheeks.

"Papa bear, huh? That's good, Creed." Roz joined us.

I rubbed Christy's head because I didn't trust myself to hug her. If I did, I'd be in tears, too, so I left and headed for bed.

My head swirled from too much schnapps and not enough food. I sat on the side of the bed and just stared at the slit in the curtains. Daylight snuck in, but it didn't make me feel any better.

The events of the last few days crashed down on me. Sleeping on a roof, a half-day of rest in a ratty half-assed cot under an equally half-assed tent, surrounded by civilians with no hope in their eyes. Stuck on top of a HUMVEE while it leapt away from an army of the dead. Clinging to the gunner's portal for an hour, leaving my arms and shoulders feeling like they were lead bars. Watching Bailey fall.

Anna Sails had stayed to talk with the other mercenaries, but joined us a few minutes later. I wanted to ask what they'd talked about, but I didn't think I'd like the answers. Besides, I was exhausted and didn't feel like fighting. She closed the door behind her and looked at our pitiful space.

I offered to sleep on the floor, but I used my best puppy-dog eyes on Anna. She glared, but then looked at the mattress.

Anna rolled out a sleeping bag while her eyes burned holes in me.

"Creed – I don't have to say it, do I?"

"Say it? What's 'it'?"

"You stay on your side. Got it?"

"Sails, you're nice and all, but it's the zombie fucking apocalypse. Know what the last thing on my mind is?"

"You're a man. I know the only thing that's on your mind."

"You kill me, Sails. Now, if we were out in the world, the real world that existed a few weeks ago, I might take a shot. I might show up with flowers, most of them in one piece, and I might even say nice things. You know … assuming you're my type, and all."

"You have a type?"

"Yeah. Cute and armed."

Sails expelled a breath and fought down a smile.

"You and Roz could bunk together," I suggested. "I'm used to the smell of Marines by now."

Roz was sprawled out on the bed next to Joel, watching as he stripped her .45. He showed her a couple of things, stuff he'd taught me a week ago.

"They look cozy over there," she said.

They certainly did. How quickly Roz forgot about our little moment in the garage. Come to think of it, that was probably a moment only in my mind. I was probably the only one who gave that time any importance.

"Fine. That shit's sorted. Now keep the snoring down," I said, then pulled up a blanket and promptly passed the fuck out.

06:30 approximate
Location: Clairemont, CA - Undead Central

MY ALARM CLOCK WASN'T THE OLD-STYLE RINGER. IT DIDN'T HAVE bells. It had two hands, and they were attached to one very grumpy Marine. Joel "Cruze" Kelly shook me again. I pulled one arm out of the sleeping bag to punch his fucking lights out and then realized that wasn't a great idea, because he'd probably hit me over the head with his assault rifle, then stab me in the gut with his knife.

My pissy mood was justified; I'd had little sleep. About an hour ago, I'd half-woken to sounds in the distance that my brain couldn't clarify. Might have been screaming, or it might have been a nightmare. After that, I tossed and turned while

Anna Sails lay next to me in her own sleeping bag. Our little quad sure as hell wasn't the Hilton, but we were alive.

"Let's go find some supplies," Joel said as he moved away.

"What's wrong with him?" I asked Sails.

"Don't know. Maybe he got his period," Anna said.

"I need coffee."

"You're in luck, Sailor," Anna replied.

She held up a couple of packets of Folgers instant coffee, and that got my attention. I swear I was almost drooling.

"Well, I'll be goddamned. Where'd you find those?"

"In the bathroom, of course. Don't you ever stay in hotels?"

"Nah. I live on a big floating hotel." I looked down for a minute. "Lived, I mean."

"How long were you in and what ship were you on?"

So I told Sails a little about what had happened on the ship. I told her about how it was overrun and how Joel, Reynolds, and I had all jumped into the ocean just before the USS McClusky hit land and exploded.

I dumped the packets of coffee into a glass that looked more or less clean, and then poured in enough purified water to make a triple espresso. I swirled the mess around for a minute before tossing it back. The flakes of coffee had barely dissolved and ended up stuck in my throat, but I thought it was better than any Starbucks coffee I'd tasted in my life.

"That was delicious." I burped.

"I've tasted asphalt with more flavor," Anna said as she finished her own dose.

"Really? I bet there's an amazing story behind that, and I bet it starts with 'So, I was drinking'."

"Yeah, something like that. Now put on your game face. It's time to go."

Joel was geared up and stood near Roz. He looked like he wanted to say something, but she shook her head, so he kept his trap shut. Ugh – fucking high school drama. Not how I wanted this mission to start.

We piled into the mercs' room to gather gear and go over the plan one more time. If we ran into a mess, Roz, Donny, and Christy would come out to provide backup.

Joel tested his communication gear, and Markus gave him the thumbs-up when the Marine's voice came in loud and clear over the walkie talkie.

Before we left, Donny offered me his friend.

"Do not lose this."

He handed me his Mossberg and a box of shells. She was already loaded, and the rails were filled with shells. I hefted the piece and grinned.

"Thanks, man. I hope I don't have to use it."

I'm pretty sure he knew I was lying.

07:15 approximate
Location: Clairemont, CA

THE MORNING SKY WAS OVERCAST; THE COLOR OF THE CLOUDS matched the sidewalk. It had rained the night before leaving everything damp. If we were going to be staying we needed to rig up some contraption to capture the rainwater.

Joel took the lead while Anna studied the keys we'd found on various corpses. She finally settled on one car after finding a match.

The Chevy Nova looked like something I would have been in love with when I was sixteen. Out of the seven vehicles – some of them high end – the Nova was one of two that opened with a key. A beat up Jeep with plastic side windows went to Roz. If we got in the shit, this was our way back to Fortress— assuming she and Donny could get us out.

Our car had been dark blue at one time, but the paint was faded and splotchy. The fender was dented, and we found out that the driver-side rear window only rolled down five or six inches, but the engine roared to life after Anna pumped the gas and cranked the ignition a few times. Once it had run for a bit, she shut it off and then fired it up again.

"Just making sure we don't get there and the damn thing dies," she told me.

I spun as a loud noise drew my attention. Markus had figured out how to get up to the roof and was now taking up station to watch over us. His rifle looked old, but he'd sworn that it would do the job.

Joel triggered the communication device around his neck and checked in with Markus. They spoke "go shoot stuff" jargon for a few seconds, and then Joel nodded, indicating that we should head out.

"There's movement east, but they're still a klick out. About thirty of them, and they won't even converge on this position if they keep following their current course. If they swing around a few degrees, they'll be on us," Joel relayed.

"How long do we have?"

"About twenty minutes, so we need to make them count. We hit the first few places that look promising and then we haul ass back here. If things look clear in a few hours, we can go back out. Anna's volunteered to drive. Creed…if anything comes near the car, you stick that BAMF out the window and eliminate them. I'll take care of the upfront action."

"Wait. B, A…" I started to spell out the letters.

"Bad Ass…"

"Mother Fucker. Got it." I racked a shell into the gun's chamber. Talk about a satisfying sound.

Anna poked the Chevy out of the hotel parking lot, saw that the road was clear of Z's, and took a left at the first cross street.

Half a block later, we came across two of them. They were as young as Christy, but they were old in terms of time spent dead. Both were desiccated corpses that barely managed to stay on their feet. The pair of creepers wandered toward the sound of the car, but they couldn't keep up.

The next street over was a big mess. Houses smashed in. Furniture and appliances tossed onto yards. Clothes torn and discarded onto browned grass.

"Why do they drag all their crap out of the house?" I wondered out loud.

"Probably treasure hunters looking for money hidden in the walls, or maybe just looking for cool shit," Joel said.

"This is like little Mexico. Ain't no one stashing money in walls," I said.

"You know this how?" Anna asked.

I didn't have an answer to that one.

We hit a couple of houses and came up empty. A little rambler looked promising, as its blue front door was still bolted shut. When we approached, however, a very angry voice yelled out in Spanish that, best I could tell, we should move the fuck on.

We did.

After a fifteen-minute circuit, it was beginning to look like we weren't going to find a damn thing – but then Joel had an idea.

"Bet that T J Max had a vending machine."

"Goddamn genius," I replied.

Anna pulled into the parking lot and around to a side alley that led us to the back of the building. When we'd first hit San Diego, we'd gone into a Walmart, not knowing that it was full of Z's. The entire nightmare in that giant dark building had stuck with me ever since. For a while, I even wore a ridiculous orange wristband, pilfered from the sporting-goods section, as a reminder to take nothing for granted. The band eventually got crusty with sweat and blood, so I left it in our original Fortress. Now we were thinking about going into another darkened warehouse-style building.

Wish I'd kept that sweatband. Maybe I wouldn't have gone for a repeat.

———

07:20 hours approximate
Location: Clairemont CA, Undead Central

JOEL WEDGED HIS BIG MARINE KNIFE INTO THE DOORFRAME AND worked at it for a few minutes. I kept an eye out by scouting our

OUTCASTS

perimeter while Anna watched Joel's back. I came across another door, but it was locked and had a security pad and card-reader. I'd have been screwed, anyway, because the power was out. I tested the door but it didn't budge.

The exterior of the building was surrounded by some well-tended shrubbery and a few trees. I felt somewhat secure, but if more than one or two Z's got wind of us, we'd be hauling ass for the car.

It was strange being out in the open and in a location I'd never visited before. Here we were, survivors of a world gone completely insane, and we were trying to break into a department store.

The big Mossberg felt awesome in my hand. It was like something I'd been missing my entire life. When I was a kid I got to fire a shotgun a few times, but it was nothing like this. It was probably a smaller 20 gauge, but it still bruised the hell out of my shoulder. This baby was different. If I played it smart and let them get close, I'd be a ZULU killing machine. I also wore my trusty M45A1 as a backup, and had one extra mag stuffed in a back pocket.

With all the firepower, I'd done something I hoped I wouldn't regret. I'd left the pipe wrench back at Fortress. I guess that, if it came down to fighting hand to hand, I'd just use Joel Kelly as my new wrench.

Something rustled near a dumpster about fifty feet to the west, but I didn't go to investigate. That would lead to shooting, and shooting would lead to Z's. I thought a dirty face peeked out, but it was gone before I could get a clear view.

I hustled back to Joel's location; we'd already been in the open for too long.

Joel had his arms crossed while Anna worked at the door.

"Give up?"

"Damn thing's stuck as hell, man. I can't even get the blade in there deep enough to pry the door open."

"Need the assistance of a Navy engineer?" I asked.

"Do you have a tool kit hidden somewhere in your clothing?" Joel smirked.

"Just one," I said.

I planted my leg on my aching left ankle, then lifted my right foot and bashed the door. It swung in hard, but Anna dashed in and managed to stop it from whipping around and crashing into the other side of the frame.

"Real fucking subtle," Anna Sails said. She tugged her gun out of her holster and backed up a few steps, then did a quick sweep.

Joel slapped me on the back, and in we went.

The place was dark. Really dark. There wasn't even an exit sign to help us poke our way around. It was dead quiet, which was actually good news for us. If nothing was moving around in the place, we were probably safe from being rushed by Z's.

"First stop is the flashlight department," I whispered.

"Shhh!" Anna and Joel shot back.

I shrugged and stayed close.

We moved fast, but I kept my head on constant gawk as I swiveled around to check out the fading slit of sunlight streaming through the cracked-open doorframe. I wanted to shut the door, but apparently I'd damaged it too much to even prop it closed. At least we had a little bit of light.

The back of the building was constructed as a long hallway with metal shelves for inventory. Most shelves were covered in boxes. I opened a few of them and found they contained clothing. Lots and lots of children's clothing. I thought about grabbing something for Christy, but none of the stuff was her size.

We moved down the hallway with Joel's tactical light poking into the dark.

We tried a few office doors, but they were locked. We crept further down, away from our point of entry.

"Jackpot," Joel whispered as he opened a door.

The room held a few round tables with chairs arrayed around. To my relief, it was free of Z's.

Joel played the light around the room and revealed a bulletin board and counters boasting a coffee maker, microwave oven, and sink. There was a small window set high in the rear wall. A little bit of light filtered through, so I went through the drawers. After opening the third one, I came up with a prize: a couple of handheld LED flashlights. One was weaker than the other, but they'd help. I gave the brighter one to Anna. Gentlemen that I was, and all.

We split up and grabbed what we could. There was a soda vending machine, but it was locked up tight. I'd kill for a fucking Coca-Cola right about now. The snack vending machine was filled with potato chips, candy bars, and crackers. I stared through the quarter-inch-thick glass and just about drooled.

Joel moved to the door and shut it. He motioned with both hands like he was stabbing someone.

"What the fuck?" I whispered.

"Break the glass, dummy," he shot back.

"Then gimme your knife, if you can part with it long enough."

"You can't break it with a blade."

"No shit. Just gimme the damn thing."

Joel walked over and handed it to me while Anna Sails walked the perimeter and kept watch.

I took the big knife, reversed it, and hammered the hard metal cap into the glass.

My hand bounced back and I nearly stabbed myself in the shoulder.

"Another idea, genius?"

"Do you want to eat this shit or not?" I glared back.

Joel smiled.

Anna left the room and returned a moment later with a couple of garments. She tossed them at Joel.

"What should I do with these?"

"Wrap them around the muzzle of your piece and shoot the glass, dummy."

I chuckled and Joel glared.

"Shit. Yeah, that's a good idea."

Joel had acquired a Springfield XDM 9mm sometime during the escape from the base. It was a small handgun, designed for conceal and carry, but he'd taken to it just the same. He chambered a round, checked the safety, and then wrapped a couple of shirts around his hand and the weapon.

I looked away when the muzzle flashed. Even with the fake silencer, the shot was still ridiculously loud in the tiny room, but it got the job done. Well, close enough.

The bullet struck the glass and left a small hole with spider-webbed cracks radiating outward.

This time, when I hit it, I was not denied.

Glass shattered and fell in an unholy clatter. We looked at each other, holding breath for a moment, and then moved with a purpose. Joel tossed open cabinet doors and found a box of garbage bags, then he quickly backed up and stared hard at one of the open storage spaces.

Christ, was there something in there?

"Bingo as fuck." He said and tossed me the bags.

"What is it?"

"A bunch of plates and utensils." He grinned. "Oh, and these."

I wanted to hug him as he took out a case of bottled water. He placed it on the counter and then followed it with a case of iced tea. Joel stacked another case of water on top of that and then looked at me.

"Right!"

I had to put the Mossberg on the counter so I could hustle precious fluids to the doorway. I peeked outside, into the sunlight. That wasn't my smartest move; I was practically blinded. I took a moment to let my eyes adjust, using the opportunity to crack open a bottle of warm diet Snapple and down it in three massive gulps. I didn't even care about the aftertaste of artificial sugar.

I'd stumbled halfway back down the hallway when I remembered I had the small flashlight in my pocket. I took out the palm-sized unit and felt around until I found a button. I clicked it and was met with a beam of light that first flickered, then flared.

"Shit!" I tried to yell, but began to choke and cough as I went down.

The Z was almost on me. She was a snarling mess of blood and gore. Someone had stabbed her in the chest, and the knife was still stuck there, jutting from one of her breasts. Her silky print shirt was ripped to shreds and hung wide open, but – even in a lacy black bra – she was about as sexy as a sweaty linebacker.

I fell back on my sore ankle and went down hard, sprawling on my ass. I lifted my right hand and then remembered I'd left my pipe wrench at home. I went for my side arm, but the Z wasn't waiting. She fell onto me.

Even this waif of a girl, who couldn't have weighed more than a hundred and ten pounds soaking wet, still had the snarling rage. She wasn't as crazy as a shuffler, but she was fresh dead – and if she was fresh dead, she wasn't the only Z in the building. Unless she stabbed herself in the boob.

I pushed her to the side and rolled the other way. She lay dazed for a few seconds and then moved up on all fours. The girl stared at me with those white eyes. I swore, but pulled my gun, aimed, and squeezed the trigger.

The fucking Z dodged to the side like she knew I was aiming for her! It didn't matter, though, because I'd forgotten to turn the damn safety off, too.

The Z leapt into the air and smashed into me. She snarled as she pummeled my chest. I was on my back again, the air driven from my body.

She bit down on my arm and I shrieked. She tore upward, but came away with a mouth full of cloth. I got my knee into her chest, and then she rammed her elbow into the side of my head.

I rolled and took her with me, but she skittered away.

In the dark it was hard to see her form. I snapped the safety off and aimed.

She came in low, from the direction of the door, and I was again blinded by the sliver of bright sun. She hit me just as I fired. The shot went wide and smashed into the door.

This chick was really getting on my nerves. If I was going to make a one-way trip to Undeadville, it wasn't going to be at the teeth of a hundred-pound girl who wore fashionable clothing.

Then she hit me so hard that I saw stars.

I grabbed her around the neck and tried to hold her away. Her teeth came within inches of snapping my nose off, but I turned my head enough to avoid that. Her breath reeked of rot. I gagged and held my stomach in check.

She flailed, hitting me in the sides with both of her hands while I tried to keep her from biting me.

I yanked the knife out of her chest and drove it into her side. I tugged it back out and made a stab for her head, but panic overrode a controlled aim and the blade split her cheek open. I turned my head to avoid getting a mouthful of gore.

Something grabbed the girl and she was suddenly lifted off of me. She flew to the floor but was on all fours in a split-second.

A gun boomed and the girl was driven into the ground. It boomed again and the girl's head popped.

I gasped for breath, and then rolled to my side and managed to get to my feet.

STANDING OVER THE Z, WITH HER GUN STILL EXTENDED, WAS MY hero: Anna fucking Sails. Her eyes were tight as she looked me over.

"Creed. If you're about to join the crawlers I'm going to be very fucking disappointed."

"Sails. Jesus Christ. You saved my ass." I got to my feet and limped toward her.

"Now we're even. You saved me at the hospital. Call it good?"

I stood with one foot cocked, because it screamed in pain every time I put weight on it. A few days out and I was already a damn cripple. I'd strained it while helping Roz dispatch a few Z's at her house and had been on the mend ever since.

Sails grabbed my arm and dragged me to the door, propping

it open with her hip. She examined the torn shirt and probed at my skin.

"I guess I don't have to kill you." She let my arm drop.

"Ow." I tried not to fall over.

I put my hand on Sails's shoulder and then draped my arm over her in an embrace. I liked how she was strong and tough but also had all the right curves. Her back tensed, but then she let the tension go.

"Thanks, Sails."

"We're not married. Get your hand off me," she said, but didn't push me away.

"Sorry. Hurt my ankle. Help me back to the break room so I can finish the load-out?"

"You're about an idiot, know that, Creed? How are you going to help with a busted leg?"

"Yeah. Good point. I'll just wait here while you guys bring up the..." I didn't get to finish my sentence because something screeched in the department store.

Joel appeared a second later, took one look at us, and the corpse, shrugged and deposited a box of goodies next to mine.

"Movement in there. Lots of it. We need to haul ass," Joel said and turned to go back in.

"Wait, man, where you going?"

"One more box. I got it. Just get this shit in the car." He turned back. "Can't you two wait for a touchy feely moment until we're at least back in the hotel?"

"He hurt his vagina and needed my help," Sails protested.

"Ankle. It gave out when she attacked. Just go. Stand around discussing all this bullshit and nothing will get done." I didn't let go of Sails.

Joel went back. I swallowed when my friend left, but if anyone could take care of himself, it was Joel "Super Marine" Kelly.

I let go of Sails, limped to the pile of goods, then picked up a box and hobbled to the front door. Sails moved ahead and opened it. She looked both ways and then hustled to the car and popped the trunk.

"Got to be fucking kidding me!"

"What? Z? Dead hooker?" I wanted to know what was causing the look on Anna's face.

She left the trunk open and as she left to retrieve another box.

I staggered to the trunk with the box in one hand, and then gasped and gawked. Now where in the hell were we going to put our goods?

The space was filled with boxes of canned goods. Someone had already crammed the trunk with corned beef hash, canned tuna, mixed vegetables, and – of course – spinach. There also were bags of noodles and boxes of instant mashed potatoes.

The irony of our situation really sank in when I heard the first Z round the corner. It staggered into sight, followed quickly by another one. They stared with milk-white eyes. Sunken cheeks. Matted hair. Blood-splattered clothing.

"We need to go now!"

Gunfire erupted inside; I knew the sound all too well. Joel was using his AR. Anna's booming .357 sounded next, but then stopped, presumably so she could reload.

I lifted the .45, took very careful aim, and shot the first Z. The bullet spun the guy to the right, but I'd missed a direct headshot and only taken off an ear. I fired again, the count in my head ticking to four. Joel had taught me well. Four more and I'd have to reload. I shot the second Z, and this time scored a headshot, but the bullet punched through its cheek and tore a path of destruction. The Z's jaw half-destroyed jaw unhinged as he continued to advance.

I dispatched that one, and then, with shaking fingers, reloaded.

From around the back of the building came at least a dozen more, and just to show how really unfucking lucky we were today, there were a pair of shufflers in the bunch.

"Joel. We need to go. Now!" I called into the building, no longer worrying about loud noised drawing a horde. They were already here.

DO OVER

08:00 hours approximate
Location: Clairemont, CA

The nearest Z went down as I emptied my magazine. I reached for a fresh mag, slapped it home, and went on firing. I got lucky with the first shuffler. Real fucking lucky. If the real world were still around, I'd go out and buy a goddamn lottery ticket.

As the shuffler left the ground, I squeezed off a pair of shots. The first one missed by a mile, but the second one caved in the fucker's head. I didn't have time to let out a whoop, though, because the other shuffler was rounding the corner.

The shuffler flopped to the ground like a rag doll. Blood hit the pavement, splattering across my boots. I staggered back from his twice dead corpse, and almost went down on my bad ankle.

Gun shots rattled inside the department store. I didn't bother moving toward the blasts. If there was one guy equipped to take care of a few Z's, it was Joel "Cruze" Kelly.

I reached for a fresh mag when I remembered I was out. I had a few shots left, but not enough to take down the half-dozen Z's headed my way.

I pushed boxes around in the trunk until I could get my

hand under the floor mat; I felt around for a tire iron. Found it in seconds, but the thing was one of those cross-shape deals, which are really convenient when you need to change a tire, but not so much when you need to bash heads.

I wanted to go back to the start of the morning and have a do-over, Groundhog Day style. Then I'd have brought my damn wrench. Like a genius, I'd left the brand new pump action shotgun in the break room.

I had five rounds left in the magazine and a few in my pockets, but that wouldn't help me. I'd have to reload while attempting to not get bitten.

I shot a Z in the chest and blew it off its feet. The bastard, dressed in nothing but a long t-shirt, rolled over and crawled toward me.

More shots echoed from inside, and I decided that it was probably a good idea to get in there where I had some backup. I moved to the door and slid it open.

"It's me, Joel! Don't blow my head off!"

The Z's, somehow sensing that I was going to slip away, quickly converged on me. I turned with a fire lit under my ass.

I ran right into Sails as she slammed another case on the ground.

Joel came around the corner, firing.

"So glad to see you guys!" I must have been a sad sight, but I was damn sure relieved.

Sails didn't reply; she just pressed something against me. I looked down at the Mossberg that Donny had entrusted to me.

"Go kill some stuff, Creed." She said as she let go of the shotgun.

I made a mental note to never leave my primary weapon out of reach. If I had to strap it to my forehead, I was going to always be prepared in the future. Then I made another note to hug Sails—if we managed to survive this latest clusterfuck.

I pushed the door open as I holstered my sidearm. Sails moved at my back. She pushed the door all the way open and dropped to a crouch. I lifted the Mossberg 500, aimed in the direction of a Z covered in gore, and blew a hole the size of Texas through its chest.

I worked the grip as I hammered shell after shell into the breach. After I unleashed five rounds, I fell back. Sails covered me while I reloaded from the front rails.

Joel made it to our location with a box of goodies over his shoulder. His AR was strapped across his back, and he was firing with his handgun as he moved. BAMF indeed.

"No room. Trunk's full," I told him.

"Full?"

"Yeah, didn't you guys check it before we left? It's got enough food to last us a week."

"The fuck?"

"Donny looked over the car after I found it, but he's a lazy ass. He probably never even looked in the trunk." Sails rolled her eyes.

Joel shrugged and ran to the vehicle. He kicked the rear door all the way open and tossed two cases of water and tea into the back. I moved around him as I reloaded.

Sails grabbed a box of bagged potato chips and candy bars and tossed it in among the mess.

"Sails, I'll take the shuffler. Concentrate on the others and don't let any of them near me."

"Done."

"And don't shoot me in the ass."

"If I do, I'll kiss it and make it better."

"Wait. Really?"

Sails shot me the finger, then buried a pair of rounds into a woman whose bad day must have started 72 hours ago.

The shuffler was a greedy bastard, but he was smart. He leapt around behind the horde while I tracked him with the pump action. I dropped a Z by taking out his knees, and then ducked so I could see where the jumping asshole was hiding.

"Let's just go, Creed!" Joel yelled.

"Right," I said and backed up a few paces toward the car. "Right after I eliminate this shuffler."

The horde had been down to five or six, but then a fresh

bunch arrived to refill the ranks. There were at least twenty other Z's when I finally got a clear look at the shuffler.

In life, he probably wasn't more than five-foot-six. He was built, though, like a tiny linebacker. His arms were crisscrossed with wounds and his head was partially bashed in on one side. His one good eye swiveled to find me, so I lifted, aimed, and fired.

The big gun bucked against my shoulder.

My shot was off by a foot. It struck another Z around waist level and crumpled the guy.

Joel let off a burst of rounds as he closed in on my position.

"Let's go, man."

"That fucking shuffler. I swear he's playing with me."

"Ain't no damn zombie smart enough for mind games. Get in the car, Jackson."

"I can take him."

"Dude. We need to evac." Joel was ready to go.

Sails hopped in the car. It roared to life as I fell back. Joel grabbed a few more items and stuffed them in the trunk before slamming the lid closed.

I hit the side of the car with my butt, then felt around until I found the door handle. I popped it open and slid inside. As I maneuvered, I never lost sight of the shuffler's location. He'd been hobbling along behind the mass of Z's while I worked the shotgun.

I was barely in the seat when Sails gunned the engine.

That's when the shuffler showed me just how wrong Joel had been.

It had managed to move among the horde, up on two feet. I saw him just before he dropped to all fours. Then he was in the air and sailing toward us like a freaky jack in the box.

I didn't have the chance to shoot it, because Sails slammed into reverse, then spun the car around in a neat half donut. The smell of burning rubber filled the air.

I was thrown against the door as she came to a halt. She worked the gearbox, and then I was pressed into the seat.

"Hang on to your nut sacks!" Sails yelled and the car lurched forward.

She only drove for a few seconds before she slammed to a halt.

Ahead of us, a fresh horde had arrived. There were more than thirty, and even if we had a freaking tommy gun, there was no way we could shoot our way free.

"Eagle One, we're bottled up." Joel spoke into his throat mic.

At least that damn thing was working, now that we were out of the building.

"He doesn't have a shot. We need to get to the west side of the building so Markus can assist," Joel said.

"How?"

The two hordes closed in, and there was that damn shuffler. I leaned over, stuck the barrel out, and fired at him.

"The hell, Creed!" Anna yelled.

Joel rubbed his ears.

It sounded like someone had tossed a hand grenade in the vehicle. My ears rang and everything came in like I was stuck underwater—muffled and far away.

The shuffler fell back. I hadn't even managed to hit him.

"Sorry! This son of a bitch is fast and smart. I don't suppose you have a grenade stuffed in one of your pockets?"

"Even if I did, you'd probably set the damn thing off in here."

"Gimme a little credit." I had to shout to hear myself over the ringing in my ears.

"Can you go over?" Joel turned to Sails and pointed at the median separating the parking lot from the street.

"I think so. I'll have to go slow or we'll be tossed out the window when I hit the little hill."

The "little" hill was made of eight inches of curb that rose into a hump which was covered in shrubs. Even if we got over the initial bump, I was concerned that we'd be stuck.

"Wait, we might…"

Sails hit the gas and eased up onto the curb. When she was over the hump, she punched it, and we bounced up and over the curb. I held on to the seat while also holding my breath. There were so many Z's behind us that this was about to become a very bad day.

I leaned out of the car, my body perched up on the door frame, then aimed the shotgun and blew a Z backward.

The shuffler faded into the crowd.

Joel Kelly popped out of the passenger side window so he could shoot a few Z's.

We were in trouble.

The car managed to scream up the curb and make it onto the easement. That's where we got stuck. Sails hit the gas, but the rear wheels just spun.

"Joel! In the back, quick!"

"What?"

"In the back! If we can get some weight back here, the car might move."

He slid back inside and then slithered over the back of the seat to join me.

Two Z's got wind of me and rushed. I shot one in the chest, pumped, and then clicked on an empty chamber.

Joel tossed me his sidearm and I shot until it was dry.

They still came at us.

"We need to haul ass!" Sails said, opening the door.

"I'm not leaving our stash," I replied.

And I wasn't. There was no damn way I was about to just run, knowing that we'd busted ass to get this stuff. Besides, my ankle was shot, and I wasn't going to get very far unless my Marine buddy carried me.

"Let's sit on the back of the car. It'll move."

"That is the stupidest damn idea ever," I said, but I was already opening the door.

We dashed out of the car and hopped onto the trunk. Memories of barely holding onto the HUMVEE as we exited the naval station a few days ago flashed through my head. Joel fired while I reloaded the Mossberg.

Six or seven of the shambling corpses were right on us. A guy missing part of one arm flopped his good hand onto the trunk and managed to get a grip on my pant sleeve. Joel lashed out with his boot and kicked the guy to the ground.

Anna leaned out and shot a Z through the head, then gave the car some gas.

Show off.

Joel and I held on for dear life while the rear tires finally found purchase. I grabbed hold of the space between the trunk and the rear window; I managed to hold on even though it felt like my fingers were about to be ripped off.

Joel wasn't so lucky.

He was bucked off the back as the car shot forward.

We hit the other side of the easement and I was nearly thrown off.

Sails slammed to a stop and jumped out of the car.

I rolled over and dropped to the ground. The pain was immense as my leg crumpled under me.

I managed to roll over, grab the shotgun, and fire at a Z that was less than three feet away.

I also managed to miss the fucker by a mile.

"Up, sailor!" Sails to the rescue.

I got to my feet, slammed a fresh shell into the Mossberg, and shot the Z that was closing in on Joel. The explosion lifted the fat man off his feet and drove him backward into another Z.

I dropped to Joel Kelly's side and rolled him over. He coughed, and then reached for his side, but his sidearm was still in the car.

"Where's our backup?"

"Nothing on coms."

Nothing on coms? Markus was supposed to have our back. Roz was also supposed to be waiting to drive out and help us. What was happening back at Fortress Mark II?

Joel looked like hell. I helped him to his feet just in time for him to lunge forward and bury his blade in the head of a female Z. She fell away, dragging his knife with her.

Z's to the side and now a few to the front. I reached for another shell and realized I'd exhausted all of the rounds on my pump action, so I turned it around and used it as a club.

The first Z to reach me took a face full of tactical stock. He staggered away but wasn't dead. I kicked the legs out from under another while Sails got Joel Kelly into the car.

I dove back through the rear door as Sails slammed hers shut. She hit the gas, and we ripped over the easement and hit the asphalt hard enough to bounce me into the roof.

"Gun!" Joel said and reached over his shoulder.

I looked around and found his piece on the floor. I handed it over. Kelly did a quick inspection, and then leaned out of the window and fired two rounds.

That's when the shuffler hit the car.

He must have been in the mass of Z's, because I didn't even see him until he was on the trunk. He held on as Sails slowed to maneuver around the fresh hell that had arrived from the road. This mass wasn't as big as the one we'd left behind, but there was no way we could just plow through them.

The shuffler howled at me, so I howled back. He was an ugly fucker with lank hair that hung just above his eyes. There was that look of something...intelligence? Anger? It seemed to nestle there in his gaze, and I saw, for the second time, the hint of green, like he had some kind of dye in his eyes.

"Gun!" I yelled.

Sails handed back her big .357. I took the handgun, lifted it, and then fired. The explosion in the little vehicle was like the soundtrack to the end of the world.

The shuffler fell away, but he'd moved as I'd lifted the piece and aimed. I slammed the gun into the rear window, near the bullet hole; most of the safety glass fell into the car.

I sank back into the seat as Sails found an open spot of road. The only problem? We were headed away from Fortress Mark II.

08:20 hours approximate
Location: Clairemont, CA

THE WIND TORE INTO THE CAR AS SAILS PUSHED THE VEHICLE UP TO speed.

"We'll hit the freeway and then double back around the outskirts of the city. Go the way we came in, yeah?" Joel spoke to me and Sails, his eyes darting around.

"Sounds like a plan." My voice sounded weird, like I was talking through a gag.

My ears rang like a bitch from all the gunplay; shooting at the shuffler had nearly made me deaf.

Just when I thought we were home free, the car came to a screeching halt. Joel and I were both thrown into the seats in front of us with a few healthy howls and curses. I got my arm up, but still managed to kiss leather.

"Christ on a crutch, Sails!" Joel was wide-eyed.

"Wow, gee. I must really suck at this driving shit. Now shut up and look!" Sails sounded like she wanted to rip our heads off. I peered forward and saw why.

I exhaled a long, slow, weary breath, then swore. Joel looked through the cracked front window and joined me. Great. We'd gone from one fuckening to another in the space of two minutes – and this one left us completely exposed.

Ahead lay a sea of dead.

THEY'D TAKEN TO THE ROADS LIKE A PARADE OF THE DAMNED. Moaning, lurching, covered in filth and blood. Missing arms, ears, lips, and cheeks. Damaged bodies, torn skin, mangled limbs. They had the telltale white eyes; most swiveled to take us in.

"How the hell do we get back to Fortress, now?" I wondered out loud.

"We may have to go through them," Sails said.

"That's not much of a plan," Joel responded. Can't say I disagreed.

So our choices came down to either going back, or going around them.

"Fuck it." Anna punched the car into reverse and backed down the ramp, then flipped around and drove until she found a bit of shoulder that wasn't covered in bodies, busted cars, or the remnants of looted supplies. She slammed the car to a halt, and this time I was ready. I got my hand up to stop my forward momentum, but before I could, she gunned the engine and shot down a side alley.

Joel tried his throat mic again. This time he got through.

After speaking in a low voice for a minute, he shot Sails a look of fear.

"What's wrong?" Sails looked puzzled.

"Fortress. We need to get back now."

"Dammit! How many Z's?"

"A few, but there's another problem. Some locals came by and wanted to look around. Sounded like they had eyes on the HUMVEE."

"How many?" I asked.

"A couple, but there may be more on the way. That vehicle is prime property."

"There's plenty of cars to go around," I said.

"Yeah but how many are armed and armored? With enough ammo, you could go just about anywhere."

"Haul ass, Sails." I gripped the back of her seat.

"If you say that one more time, Jackson Creed, I'm going to pull this car over and shove my gun down your throat."

"I love it when you talk dirty." I grinned.

She responded by slamming on her brakes hard enough for me to nearly end up in the front seat.

A pair of Z's were right ahead of us, blocking the street like they were out for an afternoon stroll. Sails moved around them. They reached for the car, but Joel kicked the door open and knocked one of them to the ground. We maneuvered beyond them and were on the move again.

The city was new to us, but the center of town was still at our backs. From there, it was easy enough to triangulate the hotel's location. Sails drove over a couple of cross streets and ended up finding the freeway we'd come in on. Then it was just a matter of pulling off and retracing our tracks.

As if Markus sensed us talking about him, the sound of a really big gun spoke in the distance. It rumbled over the car, followed a moment later by a second shot.

"That's probably Markus." Joel did not look happy.

Sails sat behind the wheel and gripped it tight.

"This is not good. We don't want a blood bath, but can we even assist?"

"We're low on ammo and we have a car full of supplies," Joel replied.

"We can't just abandon them," I said.

"We ain't abandoning anybody. I just mean, we can't let our supplies fall into the other guys' hands. We worked too hard for them."

"Yeah, well, most of the food was already here. I hope Donny survives, so I can punch his lights out. We could be sitting in a hotel room right now, eating canned green beans and catching up on sleep," I said.

"Probably wouldn't stop the locals," Joel replied.

"Coulda, shoulda, woulda. Let's get motivated, people. We gotta make a decision," Sails said.

"Pull up a block away. I'll scout." Joel went over his gear, checked his rifle, and adjusted his combat armor.

I sat in the back and felt like punching stuff. With the Z's there was always that sense of dread, like we were in constant danger. But Z's were slow and you could take them out if you were careful. Fighting other survivors was a different matter. They planned and strategized just like us. When the bullets started flying, it would be a clusterfuck – a big old cluster, and one of us would probably end up shot.

But there was no way they were getting Roz and Christy, not to mention our armored transport.

Anna Sails pulled away from the curb. The car made a weird thumping noise as she pushed it up to about fifteen miles an hour.

"Stop." I had a sinking feeling.

"Flat?" Joel looked over his shoulder.

"Might be something worse." I said.

"We're in the middle of the zombie fucking apocalypse, as you like to say. We don't have time to swing by a repair shop," Joel said. "Abandon ship and find a new ride."

"No time. Let's just go. All this bullshit and our friends have their asses hanging in the air. Fuck the car if it gets us there," Sails said.

She pushed the Chevy up to a little over twenty-five, but the ominous thumping got worse and worse. Sails had to take a left at the next intersection and then maneuver around a pair of stalled pick up trucks. I used the time to feel around under the front seats until I located the box of shells Donny had handed me on the way out of Fortress Mark II. I reloaded the Mossberg and then filled the rails with rounds. Then I stuffed as many as I could into my front pockets.

I handed Sails her M&P R8.

The next street was totally clogged with stranded cars. Sails let out a grunt of frustration and moved to an alley that was remarkably empty—except for a dumpster that had been left in the middle.

"Fuck that." She moved on.

Could have been a trap. Who knows? She was driving, and I trusted her judgment. Not that I'd tell her that.

The next cross-street was also clogged, but Sails eased up onto the sidewalk and then back down to the road. Each time we went up or down, I worried that the car would just stop, the transaxle cracked.

We were a block from the hotel before we saw familiar landmarks. Joel motioned for Anna to stop.

"Keep your head down, and if you run into trouble, drive away, but keep an eye out. Joel and I will check out the situation at the hotel."

"The fuck you leaving me in the car for? Cause I'm a woman?"

"Nah, I got Creed for that role." Joel said and winked at her.

"If you want Joel to sit up here and help with the get away then be my guest. I know you're capable, Anna," I said.

"Well, all you had to do was ask nicely." She wore a little sarcastic grimace.

"I'll give the all-clear when things are safe. If someone starts shooting, you gun it and roll up on them while firing into the air. That should spook them, maybe give us an advantage," Joel said.

"How about if I shoot at them?" I asked.

"As long as you don't hit me" Joel replied.

I lumbered out of the car and wondered why in the hell he wanted me along.

Sails grabbed my wrist as I moved away from the car. She pulled, so I leaned in.

"Creed. Stay sharp out there, and don't do anything fucking stupid."

"Fucking Stupid is my middle name."

Sails smirked.

"Make it back and maybe I'll let you hold my hand and take me to a movie."

"I'd like to take you to…"

"Creed, let's move. You're in the Marines now, bitch," Joel said and moved out.

"Yeah. You too, Anna…be safe." Then I patted her hand like she was a two-year old or something. Fucking brilliant.

08:25 hours approximate
Location: Clairemont, CA

"WHY DIDN'T YOU TAKE ANNA?"

"Because you and I've been a team for the last two weeks. I don't have time to train a new guy. Or girl. Besides, I don't trust the mercs," Joel said as we huffed it toward the hotel.

Joel picked his way around a series of low shrubs, then faded from tree to tree as the gate came into view. Since the pair of gunshots, it'd been mercifully quiet. Joel triggered his throat mic a few times but he didn't hear a response. What the hell was Markus doing up there?

"Sails is cool. I think she might like me. Don't say anything."

"What are you, in high school?" Joel laughed.

"No, I mean she's cool to me. I'd like to get to know her."

We dashed behind a bus stop and Joel poked his head around the corner.

"Clear." He moved inside the little shelter.

I wished a bus was on the way to carry us to anywhere that didn't host a shitload of Z's.

"Just don't think with your dick, Creed. There's enough going down without having to get attached. Next thing you know, you're going to worry about a girl every five minutes."

"Oh yeah, so if Roz decided to go her own way, what would you have to say to that?" I asked.

"That's low, Creed." Joel barely hid a half smile.

"What the fuck ever. Let's go get your girl."

"Roz isn't my girl."

"Right."

Joel moved out with me close behind. He double-timed it toward the remains of a fast food restaurant. My ankle screamed in protest, but I kept up. I leaned against the building to catch my breath. All of the windows had been broken out and someone had sprayed a name on the brick wall. "Looking for Ellen Bates. Fred and Mary are at the La Jolla refugee center."

"So what's our play?" I asked.

"We're blind, and that's not good. Markus could be down, and that's even worse. You cover my back. If anyone gets close, give them a warning. If they show a weapon, shoot them."

"Wait. I've never shot anyone before."

"The hell you talking about, squid? You've killed dozens of Z's."

"Those weren't people. They were problems."

"These guys are about to be a problem. Do you really want to let them get to Roz and Christy?"

"No."

"There's your pep talk. Now let's take care of business." He abruptly moved ahead.

I limped after Joel.

08:35 hours approximate
Location: Clairemont, CA - Undead Central

WE KEPT THE SUN TO OUR BACKS AS WE PICKED OUR WAY OVER THE flat terrain. Old strip malls and more than one apartment complex provided enough cover for us. I kept the Mossberg pointed away from Joel as I covered his six. My eyes went where the gun barrel went. My hands were tense on the gun as I kept it steady against my shoulder. I would have been in a crouch as I moved, but shuffling on my busted ankle wasn't making that part easy.

Joel was silent as he faded from doorway to doorway, from car to car. He moved and motioned after he'd swept the area with his eyes. By the time I reached his location, he was already on the move again.

The hotel was in sight.

We found an overturned suburban to take cover behind. Joel peeked around the back of the big vehicle, and then ducked back around and crouched next to me.

"There's a couple of cars in front of the gate. I can see three people."

"So what do we do?"

"Fuck."

"You're not my type," I said.

Joel snorted, then looked thoughtful.

"If this was Afghanistan we'd go in hot. Shoot, scoot, and cover. Problem is, we don't know these guys' intentions."

"We're both dressed for battle. How about this?" I laid out the plan.

Joel thought about it for a minute.

"It's not bad. There is one problem."

"Yeah. I might get my ass shot off."

"That's it."

I grinned as wide as possible and wondered where in the hell my sudden bravado had come from. Then I strolled out from behind cover and walked toward what might be a firing squad.

CLUSTERFUCK

08:45 hours approximate
Location: Clairemont, CA

I t was time to put up or shut up. Joel wanted to go in
shooting. I wanted to try something else. We glared at
each other until, after a few seconds of trading comments
about why both ways out were a shitty idea, Joel relented.

I took a deep breath, put the shotgun barrel over my shoulder, and casually strolled out from behind cover. I moved as if I
didn't have a care in the world, even though I might have a
hundred gun barrels pointed at me.

I ambled around a stalled car that still had moving occupants inside. From the appearance of the two Z's, I guessed
they'd started chewing on each other out of zombie boredom.

The walk was only fifty feet, but it seemed to take forever.

I neared a pair of cars. Both were newer, and one of them
still had a sales sticker on the window. Whoever these guys
were, they were smart. Hitting up a car dealership and taking
whatever we wanted should have been our next move.

"Stop! Hold it right there!"

The kid couldn't have been more than twenty. He wore a
wind breaker and a cowboy hat. At his side was a holstered six-

shooter hanging from a wide, crooked belt. He looked like he was trying out for a modern-day Western.

"Whoa, man. What's the deal? Me and the boys are hungry and need to get back to our base of operations." I spoke with a calm confidence.

The kid was quickly joined by a pair of guys not much younger than him. They carried assault rifles.

"Boys?"

"Yeah. Who are you guys?" I asked.

"Uh. We're from the University of San Diego. We were trying to find a safe place to rest. We saw the military vehicle."

"You guys should move on. I'm with a bunch of Marines and they're twitchy fuckers. They see all those guns and they're likely to start shooting. In fact, see that truck over there?" I turned and pointed.

The guys followed my gesture and the cowboy gasped.

"Yeah, that's my friend Joel. Marine sniper. I've seen him shoot the arm off a Z from three hundred yards. That's what he did in the war. He shot people."

"Oh shit, man. We aren't looking for trouble; we were just looking for help."

"Are you sure there aren't any lurkers around? Backup? You guys wouldn't be trying to steal our shit, would ya?" I leveled my best stone-cold-killer gaze at the kid.

"No, man. No. It's just us."

I turned and waved the all-clear for Joel. If these guys had laid in some kind of trap, they were the best actors in the world.

"Joel's calling it in. If you guys are legit, no one gets hurt. Cool?"

"I swear, it's just us. We're just lost and hungry," the youngest of the bunch said.

He had pale skin, freckles, and red hair. He was so skinny I wondered if a stiff wind would knock him over.

"We got a warning over coms that our little home here might be in danger," I said.

Joel kept his assault rifle at the ready as he advanced toward us.

"That wasn't us."

"Yeah? You wouldn't lie to me, right? What are your names, anyway? I'm Jackson Creed and that mean motherfucker is Joel Kelly."

The three exchanged glances. They looked like they wanted to get the hell out of here, and I didn't blame them. I was bluffing, sure, but if I thought a bunch of hard ass Marines were bearing down on my location, I'd leave a rooster tail of dust.

"We should just go," the skinny guy said.

"Free country," I said.

"It *was* a free country a few weeks ago," the kid said.

"You mentioned some others?"

"Yeah, man. A bunch of guys on motorcycles and in trucks. They exchanged words with whoever is up there and then moved out. They didn't look happy."

I looked into the hotel parking lot and found out why. Donny was in the gunner's seat, and he had the machine gun pointed in our direction. They couldn't know that he was out of ammo.

I lifted my hand and waved. Donny waved back.

"Do you know who those guys were?"

"Just a bunch of mean looking guys. Bad asses. They wore leather and looked like they had a gang before this shit went down. They had swagger, man. Tons of swagger. Their leader's named McQuinn."

Joel joined us and he didn't look happy.

"How many?"

"Just a few, but last night we were camped a mile or two from here and we heard this loud noise. We saw lights on the road, so we kept out of sight. There were probably fifteen or twenty vehicles."

Joel moved toward the gate. He waved once and got the all-clear from Donny.

"Creed, let's go."

"Sails?"

The Chevy crept up on our location from the west. She came

in real quiet, and I noticed right away that the thumping was gone.

Donny ran out and opened up the gate, and Sails drove in. Joel motioned for me.

"You guys have any supplies?" I asked.

"Not much. We got a case of refried beans and some salsa from a shop that wasn't picked over. Also found some beer, but Edgar's been hitting that stuff pretty hard at night."

The third guy wasn't as tall as me, but he was wide. Even with his gut, he looked like he was in decent shape.

"Gotta feed the machine," he said and belched. "I play football. I used to."

"Bring your stuff. We're moving out soon, but we have some food. Got any ammo?"

"Not much. A few boxes."

Joel stormed toward me.

"What the hell, Creed? These guys need to move on."

"Oh."

I hadn't even thought about taking a vote.

Rumbling sounded in the distance and Joel got a worried look.

"It's cool. We don't want any trouble," the skinny guy said.

The other two followed suit and hopped into the cars. I wanted to say something, but Joel was right. We didn't need more mouths, but that wasn't the only reason. They didn't look like they were capable of taking care of themselves. They were just a notch lower than me on the zombie fucking apocalypse totem pole.

I moved toward the gate and shut it while Anna pulled up next to the HUMVEE.

"You fixed the car?"

"Yep. It just needed a woman's touch."

"Really?"

"Nah. We picked up an arm along the way, and it was thumping under the car."

I actually laughed at that one and gently punched Sails.

"I hereby grant you the rank of First Class Engineer in the United States of Undead America."

"I better get a damn pay raise," she said.

"Oh, you will. I'll put in a call to the President immediately."

"Wow, Creed. You're all heart."

"True story. Now about that date?"

"Yeah. About that," she said and turned.

I followed her gaze; a moment later, a rumbling sound reached me.

Engines. A lot of engines. And they were heading in our direction.

09:25 hours approximate
Location: Clairemont, CA

OUR MINUTE OF CHITCHAT ENDED ON A SOUR NOTE, THANKS TO A bunch of assholes determined to crash our party. Over the last few weeks, we'd run into good people. Mostly good people. There were a few exceptions, of course, like Ken and his bat-shit insane buddy, who were holed up in a little house when they weren't grabbing female Z's off the street. Fucking a Z? In the case of Monster Ken and his jackass-in-training, they must have been crazy before the whole end of the world thing occurred.

From time to time, we'd even come across some looters, but – as Joel pointed out – it wasn't our job to play sheriff. We weren't cops. It was a dog-eat-dog world, and the meanest dog would want to find the biggest bone.

As far as I could tell, we were the only bone in town. A few stragglers were making a living by scrounging, but for the most part, this little town had become full-on Undeadville.

It'd finally happened. It was bound to. The mercs had mentioned moving fast, but Joel and I had talked them into staying for a day while we did a food run.

Fuck me.

09:35 hours approximate
Location: Clairemont

"SORRY ABOUT THE COMMUNICATIONS, MAN. THE BATTERIES started to die about the time you boys left," Markus said.

He held up the dead unit and then tossed it into the back of the HUMVEE.

"Do we have more batteries?"

"Don't know, man. There's still a lot of shit in the back of the transport. We can check later, but right now we have a bigger problem."

I nodded and moved around to the back of the Chevy to help load food into the HUMVEE. I grabbed a box of juice bottles, stuck one of the bottles into my pocket, and maneuvered the rest of the box into the truck. Christy grabbed it and shifted the contents into the back.

Roz came down the stairs in a rush. She had the last of the supplies from the hotel room in one hand and her handgun in the other.

"You guys get fucking lost out there?" she asked as she breezed by.

"We got in some trouble," I said.

"Imagine that. You and trouble."

"Come on, Roz. We found a great stash of food, but the place was crawling."

"I'm sure. This whole town is crawling. Now let's go before those assholes get here and I have to start shooting fools."

Too late. They were already here.

09:45 hours approximate
Location: Clairemont, CA

THE KIDS IN THE TWO NEW CARS ROARED BACK TOWARD US. I didn't really think about options for them. If they were caught, they'd probably be killed, or at least get their asses kicked. The guy in the red sports car did a little wave as he drove past. I waved back.

Then they were gone.

The carnival arrived a minute later.

Donny had been busy moving shit around in the back of the HUMVEE. He whooped once and then slammed a heavy box on top of the transport. Markus conferred with Joel Kelly. Markus nodded and then disappeared up the stairs.

I waited around with my dick in my hand, wondering what in the hell I should do. Donny called my name.

"What'd you find?" I asked.

"Got some frags. Best fucking thing? I found a few rounds for the fifty cal. We can spook 'em. Now who's going to go out and bullshit our way out of here?"

"I guess you're staring at me because I have the duty?"

"That would be real Christian of you, partner," he said.

"What if they start shooting?"

He tossed down a box of shells. I caught it and read the tops. He'd given me about thirty fresh rounds for the Mossberg.

"Shoot back," he said and loaded the big machine gun.

Donny handed down another box to Joel.

Joel opened the green metal box, extracted a few round items, and then handed a couple to me.

"These are M67 frag grenades. You've seen this on TV a million times, right? Pull the pin and throw. After it hits, you've got anywhere from three to seven seconds before the blast. When you throw, make sure to yell 'frag out,' especially if we're around you."

"What's the range of the explosion? I don't want an ass full of shrapnel."

"Fifteen meters immediate blast zone, but shrapnel can travel as far as a few football fields, so you make sure you're behind something. This will scare the fuck out of anyone on the other side of the fence."

"Scare them worse than a bunch of zombies?"

Joel winked.

We moved toward the perimeter.

He checked the fence and figured out a way to lock it with a metal bar. It wouldn't hold up to a halfway-determined assault from even a small vehicle, but they didn't know that.

Brick walls rose on either side of the fence. Joel found a spot out of sight, then loaded rounds into magazines and secured grenades to his tactical armor. I refilled the rails and breach of my shotgun. Standing, I couldn't see over the wall. I limped to the front office, dragged a chair out, and placed it next to the wall. I climbed atop it to get a look at the approaching force.

The wall was old and pitted and made of red bricks. I found a couple of places where the grout had eroded, so I was able to view the road through the small holes.

What I saw was a scene straight out of a Mad Max movie. Trucks, cars, and motorcycles closed on us. Someone had mounted a head on the hood of one of the trucks. From a distance, I couldn't tell if it was male or female.

Maybe they would just hang a right and keep going. I scanned the parking lot and saw that everyone was hidden, either behind cars or in the Chevy, which had moved to the side of the building and was out of sight.

The lead pickup truck came to a halt, and a guy hopped out and took cover behind his door. Another man slid out of the passenger side and took cover behind his door. He wore some kind of camouflage gear. As far as prospective allies went, this was not looking promising.

Then at least fifteen motorcycles roared up behind them.

They were a motley bunch, but they were well supplied with guns. I saw more than a few women among them. They all had hard faces.

"We know you're in there. Just give us the military vehicle and we'll be on our way. We don't want anything else."

"That's not cool. What if we need it?" I called out from behind the wall.

Joel shot me a questioning look.

"What?" I whispered.

He shrugged and pointed toward the guys on the other side of the fence then showed me a fist.

"I don't know what the fuck you're trying to say." I whispered back.

"Be a hardass," he shot back.

Jesus. Why wasn't *he* talking?

"How many are there? Maybe you guys can join us. We could use a few more men," the guy said.

He wore a pair of reflective sun glasses even though it was overcast. His hair was steel grey and about an eighth of an inch long. He wore a giant gold cross around his neck on an equally huge gold chain. He also had about five guns strapped to various parts of his body. Topping that off was an assault rifle bigger than anything I'd seen since this whole shit-fest started a few weeks ago.

"Yeah. We can use ya." His buddy spoke up from behind the other door, then chuckled.

"State your intentions." I deepened my voice.

Joel shrugged. Thanks a lot for the vote of confidence, pal.

"Name's McQuinn, Frank McQuinn, and we intend to take that HUMVEE and go."

"Do you see that big gun on the HUMVEE?"

"Yep, sure do, and no one's behind it. Run out of ammo?"

"You don't want to find out."

"Look, man. There's, what, two or three of you? And one's a chick. We scouted you earlier at the shopping center. Good moves back there."

"Yeah, thanks. I got all my Christmas shopping done in one day."

McQuinn chuckled.

"Just give it up. We don't want to have to do things the hard way. Right Roscoe?"

"Goddamn right," his companion said.

"Just go away and no one gets hurt," I said.

"You said that already." McQuinn sighed. "Have it your way."

He motioned and a couple of guys moved up behind his pickup.

A shot rang out and the side mirror, right next to the man, exploded. He fell away from the door, hand up to shield his face. He was back on his feet in a split-second and behind the pickup just as fast.

"Hey, man! I thought we were having a friendly conversation here." McQuinn yelled as he rubbed his cheek.

More men moved in toward our position. I counted nine and relayed the information to Joel. He nodded and made some hand gestures of his own in the direction of the hotel. That made me feel better. At least they had a plan of some kind.

"The next round is through your fucking head. Now turn around and go."

Donny stopped hiding and popped up in the gun turret. He yanked back on the release and then fired five rounds at the pickup truck. The sound of the huge machine gun thundering in the mid-morning sent shivers up and down my spine.

So much for my shitty attempt at diplomacy.

This was bound to happen. The zombie fucking apocalypse was going to bring out the worst in people; it was inevitable. The same thing would happen during any catastrophe. You'd get your share of people helping out, of course. We saw that when the bombs exploded in Boston. We saw it when tornado after tornado leveled parts of Moore, Oklahoma. A lot of people helped out.

Then there were the other guys. Those who only gave a shit about themselves or how they could fuck others over. That's who we were facing now.

I lifted the shotgun, held it over the top of the fence, and blasted. I wasn't aiming for anything in particular, since I couldn't see a damn thing. I just wanted them to know that we were all armed and ready.

I peeked back through my little hole and saw guys scrambling. They dropped to the ground in shock. Some thought to drag out weapons, but they'd just have a wall to shoot at. Or

Donny, and no one seemed interested in taking on the HUMVEE.

Donny let loose with another short burst. The booming gun scared the shit out of me, and I couldn't imagine how bad it would be out there, in the path of those huge rounds.

The lead asshole's truck took all of the damage. Bullets punched into the hood and steam erupted through the grill.

Joel Kelly slipped to the gate, took a breath, then popped out and laid down a few rounds. He aimed low and hit a tire. Just like that, he was back behind the wall.

Donny stopped firing and all was quiet—except for the sounds of glass falling to the ground and guys calling back and forth in fear and confusion.

McQuinn ran to the choppers. He didn't even look back.

"Get the fuck out of here or we'll kill every one of you!" I yelled.

He jumped on the back of a motorcycle. The driver spun the bike around and roared off. A second truck backed up and attempted a half-donut that ended with the driver planting the ass of his pickup into a telephone pole. It fell over with a crash and crushed part of the truck.

Just like their arrival, their departure was fast and ugly. Within a minute or two, they were all headed back the way they'd come from. I wanted to cheer, but settled for shooting Joel Kelly a thumbs up.

Too bad our victory would be short-lived.

10:05 hours approximate
Location: Clairemont, CA

I SAT DOWN AND WIPED SWEAT OFF MY FOREHEAD. SO THAT WAS A battle? It was more like a one-sided ass whipping.

Joel stood over me as the last of the motorcycles roared away.

"Think they'll be back?" I asked.

"Probably. We should clear out."

"Are we safe?"

"Brother, we haven't been safe since you carried your big ass down the stairs and interrupted my game of spades back on the McClusky."

"But you have to admit, I have my moments."

"Was that one of them? What were you trying to hit with the shotgun, a building? I think you even missed that."

"Fuck you, Marine. I laid down cover fire."

"When you lay down cover fire, you need to actually hit stuff."

"Noise was on my side."

Joel looked at me and then his eyes clenched tight for a split-second.

"What is it?" I asked.

He farted.

10:15 hours approximate
Location: Clairemont, CA

WE WERE CRAWLING INTO OUR LOADED VEHICLES WHEN THE rumble returned. We'd only taken ten or fifteen minutes, but it was long enough for the assholes to return with new trucks and their egos pumped up. I ran back to the wall and found my peep hole. What I saw scared me.

Markus was already hopping into the driver's seat. He got back out, took a look, and swore.

"Shit. Just got the gun packed up." He rummaged around in the HUMVEE again.

"I can only provide a little more fire. Maybe three or four bursts. We need a way out, and we need to stop as many of them as we can. Let's make them pay for ground," Donny said and slid in the back.

"We need a back door outta this place," Joel said.

"Fence in the back. Can we blow it?" I asked.

When we made our new home, Fortress Mark II was the perfect location to keep Z's out. The fence extended all the way around the building and the small parking lot. It wasn't all that high, old cast iron, painted black, but it stopped the casual creeper from hitting us on our six.

We ran to the back of the building and made for the fence.

"Why the fuck won't those guys leave us alone?"

"It's gotta be the transport," Joel said as I tried to keep up with him. "And maybe they think we have a lot of supplies. I think the main problem is that we hit them. We fucked with their pride and now they're motivated."

"Damn. Still doesn't make sense."

"That HUMVEE is worth its weight in gold right now. You've seen the world, Creed. You've seen what it's become. The population's been cut down to almost nothing and only the strong will survive and right now those guys want our strength."

"So we should run."

"They might not be trained and we are. Problem is, we're a few and they're a lot. Same shit happened on patrol. You'd have a bunch of well-trained Marines and all of the sudden you're facing a larger and very determined Al Qaeda."

The grass was all but dead where Joel knelt down and checked the fence. He pushed against it, rattled it, and then stood and rammed his shoulder into it. At ten foot intervals, metal posts had been driven into the ground. That made for enough reinforcement against even Joel Kelly, super Marine.

"Can we blow it up? Couple of grenades?"

"It's worth a shot. We could put one at a post here." He pointed.

"Another one here," I said and stood ten feet away.

There was another parking lot next to ours, but it was for a small Mexican restaurant that had been gutted by fire. The open road lay beyond that, a clogged freeway even farther away.

"I'll get Sails and the Chevy. You go and provide covering fire."

I hobbled along behind Creed, my leg screaming with pain

every time I took a staggering step. I'd turned my nose up at some Aleve earlier in the day, but right about now I'd pop half the bottle.

Joel explained the plan while Markus loaded his rifle. I stuck around for a few minutes but moved toward the fence when I heard rumbling.

They had a moving truck and it was coming up to speed. They'd put a piece of corrugated steel over the windshield with a small view-hole cut for the driver. Behind them, cars were flanked on either side, along with a couple of motorcycles.

"Christ, what did we do to these guys?" Roz asked.

"Like I said. We hurt their fucking pride," Joel replied.

SHOTS ERUPTED AND BULLETS WINGED OUR WAY. THEY HIT SOME OF the parked cars but none of them struck the HUMVEE. A window shattered in the hotel. Falling glass tinkled around us.

Donny aimed the big gun and shot at the truck. He splashed hits across the hood, and a few punched through the corrugated shield. Against a .50 cal, it might as well have been paper, but we couldn't see the driver. For all we knew, the guy was lying down and just keeping the wheel straight. If we had unlimited ammo, Donny could have turned the entire front into Swiss cheese. That would have bought us time.

Joel grabbed Christy and Roz. They dove into the Chevy with Sails once again behind the wheel. She gunned it and they zipped around the side of the building.

"Fall back. Move from cover to cover, but lay down lots of fire, Creed," Markus said.

He lifted the sniper rifle and took aim.

Bullets splashed around him and that's when I noticed a couple of guys were firing from inside cars. One of them was leaning all the way out so his entire torso was exposed. He wore some kind of armor like Joel.

It didn't help.

Markus fired, and the big round punched into the guy's

chest. He didn't throw his hands up in pain; he just slumped to the side and then fell out of the moving car.

Markus aimed again and fired at the truck.

Donny shot a few more rounds but the truck wasn't stopping. In fact, it was gaining speed, and it was aimed right at the fence.

"Go time!" Donny yelled out and Markus moved.

He was almost at the HUMVEE when he spun around.

I moved behind a little hybrid we'd pushed out of the way yesterday and fired a few rounds, but it was like shooting at a brick wall. I hit, sure, but the truck wasn't stopping.

Markus staggered to the HUMVEE, his hand on his shoulder. He managed to crawl inside and back the transport up. Donny shot until the .50 cal ran dry. He lifted an assault rifle, but slumped back as a round slammed through his head.

Blood blew out in a mist, something I'd become all too familiar with since this whole fucking nightmare started.

The HUMVEE kept backing up, even as the truck hit the fence. The rending crash shook the ground. The metal buckled and the gate flew apart.

I ran as fast as I could, damning my ankle, expecting to take a round in the back at any moment. I ducked around the corner of the hotel and got a face full of brick for my effort, thanks to a bullet exploding next to my head. I dove to the ground, rolled to the side, and got my back against the wall. The Mossberg flew, so I leaned over and snapped it up by the stock.

I blew out a quick breath and risked a look. The HUMVEE kept backing up as the truck came through. The collision stopped the HUMVEE and pushed it forward until it hit the side of the hotel. Markus opened the door and staggered out. He had his sidearm in hand and started firing before he was even on his feet. His shoulder bled, and he looked like he was in shock. It didn't last long; a couple of rounds found him.

Fuck! If Joel didn't get the fence down with a pair of grenades we were so screwed. These assholes wouldn't bother to talk. They'd probably shoot Joel and me down and then go after the girls.

Wait. Grenades. Frags. I had a couple jammed in my pockets.

I practically whooped as I pulled one out and turned the nearly one pound ball of explosive. I gripped the handle against the side and yanked the pin. I slipped from behind the wall and threw like the big truck was home base.

The grenade sailed through the air but I was already taking the next one out. I pulled the pin and repeated my throw even as shots rang out and rounds exploded around me. I'd forgotten to yell "frag out!"

Then I was on the move.

My ankle screaming in pain, I put everything I had into getting out of the area and into the car. As far as I knew, Joel and crew were already blowing the fence and leaving me behind.

I bolted around the corner and almost took a round in the face, thanks to Sails. She had her handgun raised, and it was just as steady as it had ever been. How that small woman managed to hold a .357 with an eight inch barrel and not even show the strain was something else.

Behind me, the first explosion sounded. Two seconds later, the other grenade went off, followed by an even larger explosion that rattled my spine.

Joel and Roz were running like they were on fire. They dove behind the car, and Sails gave me a quick motion that seemed to say "get the fuck down!" I dropped to the ground.

The pair of grenades on the fence went off at about the same time. One tore the post away, but the blast must have nudged the other grenade, because it rolled away before exploding. I covered my head and hoped a piece of metal didn't find it. Then I was back on my feet and staggering toward the car.

The chunk of fence was still in place, but was sheered away on one side. If the car missed, and hit one of posts on the left, the car wouldn't go anywhere after that.

Joel looked at me, but it was Sails who broke and ran to my side.

I got to my feet and hooked my arm over her shoulder for support.

"Creed, ya big dummy. What did you do?"

"What had to be done," was all I could think to say. Real heroic, right?

I might have been mistaken but I swear she turned her help into a halfhearted hug.

I crawled into the back right next to Christy and tried to shoot her and Roz a grin, but I was rattled. In the last fifteen minutes we'd gone from having a cozy home to driving off marauders, to facing almost certain death.

Sails hopped in the Chevy, and instead of ramming the fence she ripped the car to the right and did a one eighty.

"Down, you ox," she said.

I dropped lower and Sails, eyes intent, punched it.

We raced backwards until the Chevy hit the curb. The car bounced up and I almost went with it. Roz got her hand up, and Christy reached for me and managed to grab my arm. She hugged me tight. Before I could think to catch my breath, we hit the remains of the fence and it slammed to the side. The rear of the car crunched, but we were free. Hitting the other parking lot was just as hectic, and this time I was bounced into the top of the car.

Sails yanked the car around and then shot between a pair of abandoned cars. She found her way out of the parking lot, and, instead of dealing with side streets, she made a beeline for the freeway, which lay over an expanse of dying grass and weeds.

"You okay, dude?" I asked Christy.

"I've never been so scared in my entire life." She held onto me like I was going to fall out of the car.

"Me too," I said.

"What happened?" Joel turned to ask.

I gave them a quick account of the scariest two minutes of my life. Joel looked at me for a few seconds after I'd finished the story before cracking a smile.

"Goddamn Jackson Fucking Creed. I knew I'd make a Marine out of you. A couple of big ass transports hit, and that means a lot of gas. A lot of gas means a bigger explosion. Way to use your head, squid."

"Oh yeah. Totally planned that."

"What about…" Roz trailed off.

"Donny bought it while he was still behind the fifty cal. Markus came out shooting, but they got him. He didn't even look surprised."

Sails struck the dash a couple of times.

"I tried, Sails, really," I said.

"It's not that. Those guys were assholes, but they deserved better. Everything's gone. The HUMVEE, our ammo, guns, food, water." She trailed off, frowning.

"We have stuff in the trunk. Enough to get us by for a few days. I say we keep trying to make it to Los Angeles," Joel said.

I nodded, then looked through the rear window.

We weren't clear yet; the cars and motorcycles were finding a way around the hotel and heading toward us.

OVERDRIVE

13:50 hours approximate
Location: Clairemont, CA

We ran for our lives.

The Chevy was a busted up mess. The hood was creased and we were leaking some kind of fluid. The bumper held on for dear life. At least one tire was losing air, and we were overloaded, so the car took forever to get up to speed. Then, just as we got some momentum, Sails would have to slam on the brakes and maneuver around an abandoned bunch of cars.

Joel Kelly cursed. I cursed. Sails cursed. Roz was the only one who kept her cool, looking over her shoulder at the mob of pissed off civilians behind the car.

The Chevy was running in the red. We'd hit empty. If the car was like most, that meant we had maybe a gallon of gas. Two if the car's manufacturer planned for idiotic moments.

The other vehicles closed in on us.

I motioned for Christy to move closer to Roz and lowered the armrest. I had to lean all the way over but managed to work my arm into the trunk. I shifted stuff around until I got my hands on some bottles. Coca-Cola, a diet Sprite, and a Snapple. I handed them around, reached back in, and snagged water. Joel took the tea and practically drained the whole bottle in a couple of huge swallows. We might be minutes from death, but at least we'd die hydrated.

"We don't have much time," Joel said.

"We can make it to an exit, maybe find a way to ditch them. Find an open garage and hide. If we move fast, we can get the door shut," Sails said.

I ripped through one bottle of water, then drained another.

Anna slowed once again and had to hit the shoulder to get around a pair of cars. The sports car must have been in a hurry, because it had hit a Fiesta so hard that the front looked like an accordion. It had flipped over onto its side. A car like that probably ran in the six-figure range. Like being stuck in the apocalypse wasn't bad enough, this guy had wrecked his pride and joy.

No one moved in either wrecked vehicle.

"I don't like it. Means we have to take a chance on finding the right neighborhood. We might make it a half mile off the road and run into a road block we can't get around. Or we do make it around and then run out of gas. Those guys are going to be able to spot five people on the run. Bet on it," Joel said.

I couldn't argue.

"What if we jump out and let the car keep rolling? We can get to the other side of the freeway and find a new ride. Look at all those cars. Hell, there's a Suburban that's just ripe for the taking. Big and black."

I grinned at Joel and waited for him to shoot me a one-liner, but I guess the stress had gotten to his sense of humor and shut that shit down.

"That's good," Roz said. "Beats the hell out of getting caught in the open."

Sails got up to almost twenty miles an hour by driving over all the white reflective turtles and swerving between a bunch of wrecks, then she slammed on the brakes so she could cut to the left and find a way onto the shoulder. She had to get around a dozen-car pileup that would have been big news a few weeks ago. Now it was just a bunch of scrap metal that no one cared about.

The road behind us was a river of cars under a dull grey sky. Rain was coming. If we got stuck somewhere, we'd be cold and wet AND on the damn run.

The car sputtered and then caught, but our valiant steed managed to puff up another few hits of gasoline and carry us onward.

I didn't know the first thing about horses, valiant or otherwise, but I bet they didn't run out of gas unless you didn't feed them.

"Shoulda got horses," I said under my breath.

"Do you know how to ride?" Roz asked.

"Not a clue."

"They wouldn't be much use. Can't exactly outrun a motorcycle."

"I was just thinking out loud. Hell – horse, helicopter, gunship, big-ass tank, something other than this piece of shit car that's running on fumes."

"This car's been a champ," Sails said, glancing in the rearview mirror to catch my eye.

"I have a stupid idea," I said after another few seconds of silence.

"Yeah?" Joel glanced at me.

I told them what I had in mind. Sails looked at me like I was bat-shit insane, but, after meeting my eyes once again, she nodded.

14:00 hours approximate
Location: Clairemont, CA

THE EIGHTEEN-WHEELER TOOK UP MOST OF THE ROAD. THE DRIVER must have really slammed on the brakes; the trailer had come to a stop at a thirty-degree angle. Sails hit the shoulder, then spun her wheel to the right and slammed the car to a halt the second we were obscured from view. Joel was already moving, grabbing his rifle and backpack. Roz jumped out with Christy in tow.

"Later dude," I said and waved at Christy.

She tried to say something but her words were lost as the door shut.

"Don't do anything fucking stupid out there," Joel said as he kicked his door open.

"Fucking stupid is his middle name," Sails said, cutting me off.

Joel reached over the seat and gripped my hand in his.

"Just stick to the plan."

"You too, motherfucker. Don't make me come find you and piss on your corpse."

Joel was out the door and we were zipping away. Any longer and the gang on our ass would have caught on. This was a terrible idea. A horrible idea. I was hurt, could barely walk, but if Joel didn't go with Roz, how would they get Christy away from the approaching shitstorm? I'd do just about anything to protect her.

I watched them fade against the side of the trailer, then take cover behind the wheels. Joel poked his head out and motioned. Roz and Christy kept low and rolled into the little gully that separated the two sides of the freeway.

I wondered if I'd ever see Joel Kelly again.

When I'd presented the plan, my great plan, the others had looked at me like I was crazy. Then Joel had nodded and pronounced it sound. Sails said she'd drive because she already felt like a chauffeur.

"I'll go it alone," I'd said.

"Don't even think about it. You can barely walk."

"It's okay. I'm fast. I'll just pull off the road and then disappear into an apartment complex or mall."

"That's your big play? Just disappear? I never figured you for the hero type," Sails said.

"I have my moments."

"He does. Like taking out those trucks at the hotel. Fucking brilliant." Joel backed me up with a wink.

"I'm going with you, so let's just jump to the part of the conversation where you stop saying no."

"Oh, Sails. I'd never say no to you."

She'd shot me an unreadable look in the rear view mirror.

Sails pushed the pedal to the floor; we burned out before the rear tires caught. Thirty seconds later, she had to slow down. Christ. We were back to the slowest cat and mouse freeway chase of all time.

We drew a quarter-mile away, then a half-mile. I waited, breath held, for the first of the jackwads to find Joel and company. If the Marine and the girls stuck to the plan, they would be pressed against the side of the gully, waiting until the road was clear.

My first order of business, as Joel had taught me, was to count rounds and weapons. We didn't have a lot, thanks to losing the HUMVEE, but we had a couple of handguns and I still sported the Mossberg shotgun.

I counted out shells and found enough to reload the Mossberg and fill the rails.

I'd used all of the frag grenades.

I still had my Colt M45, but I was low on ammo.

"How you set for weapons, Sails?"

"Not great. I've got about twenty rounds for my three-fifty-seven. Joel left another gun. I think it's a nine. Some kind of Sig. Cute little piece."

"Sexy."

"What?"

"Nothing, just an inside joke between me and Joel. We picked up the gun last week. It's a long story."

"Tell me later," she said, but I couldn't read her tone.

"Any rounds for the nine?" I asked.

"A spare mag, and I think we have a couple of boxes in the trunk. Keep digging."

I did, but Sails had to yank the car to the left and right a couple of times and I nearly ended up on the floor. I reached into the trunk again and felt around until I found my backpack, then dragged it through the tiny opening. I pulled out my giant wrench and placed it on the seat next to me. There wasn't much else in here. I'd had a small stash of food but that was gone. I still had the logbook, and I had a bag of weed I'd completely forgotten about, the brown bag that Joel and I had found during one of our missions, back when we'd been safe and sound inside of Fortress Mark I.

I glanced outside.

The jackwads were closing in at an impressive rate. One of the pickups was pushing through smaller wrecks to make a path. A couple of high-end motorcycles zipped around, but they seemed hesitant to close on us.

I went back to scrounging and finally located some shells. 9MM. The next box turned out to be a heavy one, packed with 5.56 shells. I put those in my backpack under the assumption that I'd be seeing Joel in the near future.

I wanted to keep feeling around but we were running out of road. Ahead of us lay a huge pile up of cars and trucks – so big that there was no way we'd be able to get around them.

I focused on the eighteen-wheeler we'd left far behind and was gratified to find that the jackwads, my new name for the assholes in pursuit, hadn't stopped. That meant that Joel and the girls had managed to evade detection.

Part one of the mission accomplished.

Part two was going to be a bitch.

14:10 hours approximate
Location: Clairemont, CA

"WE'RE OUT OF TIME, CREED," SAILS SAID.

"What about there?" I pointed just ahead.

The off-ramp was jammed with cars. Rotting bodies lumbered between the abandoned vehicles. I marked the exit on my internal map, then reached for my log book and quickly jotted it on the back.

"No way we can get through that mess," I muttered.

I looked back again, but the eighteen-wheeler was too far in the distance to make out.

The jackwads weren't. They were closing, but they also had to pick their way around cars and wrecks the same way we'd had to. They had numbers on their side, though, and could take alternate paths where available. We had maybe a quarter-mile of breathing room, and I didn't see how we could possibly stop the car and be effective on foot. My big play had been with the knowledge that my ankle and foot were a throbbing mess and that I'd be unable to run. I was hoping something would just pop up, some stroke of genius.

Turned out, that was Sails' department.

"No. Look at where the railing is broken. Someone pushed over the curb." She motioned to a part of the freeway a bit closer.

She was right, but the opening led to a big drop. Even if we did manage to survive, we'd surely have broken bones, maybe a snapped neck or two to contend with. I could see it now: lying in a pool of blood while those asshole stood over us and laughed at our soon-to-be corpses. Maybe they'd be nice and give us a quick exits, bullets to our brains. More than likely, we'd have to face that McQuinn guy, his bald head gleaming in the morning sun while he pummeled us, laughing maniacally.

"Are you crazy, Anna? That drop'll kill us."

"We're not going to be in the car, Jackson."

"So now that we're on a first name basis and all, mind telling me how you plan to get the fuck out of a moving car?"

"We're going to dive out just before it hits the overpass and we're going to be going fast. It has to look real, like we made a mistake."

"Are you crazy? That shit wouldn't even work for Bruce Willis," I groaned.

"Just hear me out," she said and then laid out the entire plan.

"Alright, Sails. I got nothing better."

"Jackson, what's wrong with using my first name? Too confusing?"

"Yeah. I got a one track mind. Guys in the military use last names, but friends use first names - sometimes. There aren't any rules."

"Call me whatever you want, Creed. Just don't call me late for a three course meal at Sizzler."

"You didn't use my first name that time. What, we aren't friends?"

"You have two last names. What's your middle name? Oh… right." She shot me a shit-eating grin in the rearview mirror.

14:15 hours approximate
Location: Clairemont, CA - Undead Central

I DUG OUT SOME SODA AND STUFFED A CAN IN MY FRONT POCKET. Anna popped the top of one and drained it while we maneuvered around a car that had bodies lying across its hood. As we roared away, one of the bodies twitched. A head covered in gore – one eye smashed in the socket, the other dangling by its nerve bundle – turned after us.

A motorcycle closed to within fifteen feet, so I lifted Anna's hand gun, aimed through what was left of the rear window, and fired three rounds at his bike. The last one hit the front tire, and then he was flying through the air.

My ears rang like a bitch, but it was worth it. That would teach them to stay back.

We neared the section of the road Sails had pointed out. It was just before the off-ramp and, with the exception of two vehicles, was clear of major debris. Now that we were away from the city, lines of trees were starting to form up on either side of the freeway. We would be smart to get lost in them if we survived the next few minutes.

I moved to the right side of the car while she worked the

case of soda around with her feet until she got it where she wanted it – right next to the gas. Stupid crap car didn't even have cruise control, so we settled for something a little more permanent: a weight on the pedal.

I put my backpack on, held onto the wrench with one hand and clutched the shotgun to my chest with the other. Sails holstered her gun and leaned across the long seat to pop open the passenger door.

"After we hit, we move fast. Duck and cover. Got it?"

I cracked open the door and eyed the ground as we sped over it.

At ten or fifteen miles an hour, I knew it would probably hurt. That was logical. I didn't, however, count on it feeling like I was being tossed against a brick wall by a professional wrestler.

The asphalt met me with gruesome glee. I struck it with my elbow, rolled as I tried to bleed off some momentum, and ended up smacking the back of my head into the ground. I got a glimpse of a pair of clouds, but they disappeared as I tumbled on. It was like they were mocking me.

Anna Sails did a lot better than me. Where I was all battering arms and legs, she was an elegant dancer. She made the art of jumping out a moving car look like a modern ballet. She hit the ground on her side, tucked her arms, and spun over three or four times.

I came away with enough bruises to look like I'd been pounded by a boiler tech.

Our car found its way between the two others in its path, hit the overpass, and sailed into the air. It crashed below with a crump. There was no special-effects explosion, no rending of metal. It just fell with as much grace as can be expected from a thirty-year-old Chevy that was rode hard and put away wet.

I staggered to my hands and knees and shimmied behind the nearest vehicle. I was still seeing stars but at least I was mobile. Anna looked me over, then nodded.

We'd ended up next to an SUV that housed a couple of the dead. Two bodies hung out of a broken passenger window. A line of cars stretched all the way to our position at the very beginning of the off-ramp.. I spotted the first of the creepers a second and a half later. He was covered in gore and being followed by a kid a few years younger than Christy. They were about a hundred yards away and didn't see us. I let out a sigh of relief as we continued to pick our way from hiding spot to hiding spot, but with each step my foot screamed in pain. My knees hurt and my elbow was numb.

I'd done a good job of holding onto the Mossberg. The stock was banged up pretty bad and the sides were scraped, but I didn't find any sign of the barrel being blocked.

We kept the bikers on our six and hustled. Up in a crouch, we moved from the cover of one car to another. The jackwads would be here soon, and I had a feeling our little stunt wouldn't fool them for long.

A fresh group of Z's broke from the tree line. This time it wasn't just a pair. There were six, and they were playing follow the leader just like the previous two.

"Not good," Anna Sails said.

We had them at twelve o'clock. McQuinn's guys were closing in.

"Any way we can go over the side, maybe hide?" I tried to peer over, but even if there was a small ledge we could hide on, anyone checking out the wreck would just have to glance sideways to see us. Then it would be a shooting gallery, and we would be the targets.

"Don't think so. Shit, Jackson, this is not what I had in mind."

"Really? Because I thought this whole jumping out of the car thing would end well for us."

The traffic jam was so bad that, even if we managed to find a car with the keys in it – and we managed to get inside and the gas hadn't gone stale and we cleared the bodies out and the car started – we'd still be stuck, because the cars ahead or behind were either separated by a few inches or had actually been stopped due to impact.

The next mob of Z's was four times the size of the last one.

They came out of the trees and staggered after the first two groups.

"Last stand?" Sails pulled a handful of shells out of her pocket.

"Wait. I have an idea. It's a shitty one, but I can't think of anything else."

"Yeah? I'm all ears," she said.

I didn't have time to explain, so I called out to the army of the dead.

"Psst!" I hissed loud enough to catch one or two Z's attention. A little noise went a long way in this undead world.

A man craned his neck around to get a look at me and then broke from the pack. A woman, bloated with rot, followed.

"What the fuck!" Anna hissed.

"Follow me," I said and moved around her.

I hobbled to a pile of corpses next to a blood-splattered Suburban and tugged out the freshest looking corpse. He'd been dead for a few days, at least, and was already smelling pretty wretched. The guy was big and round. I dragged him off the pile. Another body lay next to the big truck, so I grabbed his pant leg and pulled until I could see beneath the vehicle.

"Under. I'm right behind you," I said.

Anna Sails looked at the bodies, looked at the tiny space, and then turned pale.

"No fucking way am I getting under there."

"Want to stay here and explain to the guys we just shot and blew up that you aren't looking for any trouble and just want to be on your way?"

She stared at me for a full five seconds. Motorcycles closed in on our location with a loud rumble, and that really got the army of undead's attention.

They came toward us in a slow stagger, milky eyes focused on our flesh.

Sails made a disgusted noise and crawled under the truck. I watched her slim form until it was completely out of sight.

I yanked out my knife and placed the point on the dead guys belly, pushed it in, and cut up until I hit his rib cage.

Putrid intestines erupted from the wound, carrying shit and black blood. I used his shirt sleeve to dig in and grab his stomach. I dragged that out and let it flop across his lap.

A form lurched inside of the car and slammed hands against the driver side window. Eyes, green and wild with hatred followed me as I dropped to the side of the big vehicle. Before I slid under, I smeared blood on the door handle and door. I slid in next to Sails and then pulled the body next to me. There was barely any visible light thanks to the pile of bodies on either side of the SUV.

I turned until I was facing Sails but didn't say a word. I swear that I could still feel her eyes burning into me.

We waited. I did my best to keep the contents of my own stomach in place.

14:25 hours approximate
Location: Clairemont, CA

"So they went over the side. Great. Let's call it a day. I told McQuinn this was a shitty idea. 'Just let 'em be,' I said. 'They got a big ass gun in there and those are some hard looking men.' But noooo. He just had to stop by and say howdy, then start tossing threats around."

"He's just doing what's best for us. We can't keep this moving around stuff up forever. That HUMVEE was priceless, man. With enough ammo we'd have been able to hold off hundreds of the dead."

The two men had stopped their bikes a few feet from our hiding spot, hopped off, and pushed their kickstands down. They walked up and down the line of vehicles, peering into cars, and pushing at the bodies on the ground.

I watched them from under the vehicle, my eyes finding a space between a corpse's broken arm and a dead woman's arched neck. Sails was moving next to me, her hands busy. I didn't need to see her to know that she was removing her gun from its holster. We were in a terrible spot with the other side of the SUV butted up against the side of the off-ramp's concrete wall. We had one way out, and that was the way we'd come.

"Look at this. Guy's been ripped open."

"Maybe their car hit it?"

"No, look at him. Blood everywhere and his guts ripped out."

"Zombies, man. Here they come, too."

"Something's not right."

The sound of lurching feet. Chattering of teeth. Groans and moans. The Z's I'd called to were closing in on our position. This could go a couple of ways. The men would run or the Z's would keep coming and overwhelm them. Something told me that the guys would take off. It'd been weeks since the zombie fucking apocalypse arrived and survivors didn't last for long if they sat around waiting to be eaten.

"Let's go, man. Fuck this. Tell McQuinn that they went over the side and that's that."

"Yeah. Maybe you're right," the guy said and poked his gun inside the SUV as he opened the door.

Wrong move, asshole.

He screamed and fell back as a corpse shot out of the truck.

The woman was small and fast. Wiry. I got a look at her arms as she flailed, and they were all ripped skin and exposed sinew. Muscles and tendons flexed as she moved.

The second guy let out a little scream and then fired. His shot went wide.

"Easy," I whispered to Sails.

She had moved right next to me and put her arm over me with her big .357 in hand. She rested it on my chest while she pushed her body against mine and craned her head over my neck to see the action. As well formed as Anna was, the last thing I could think about was how good she felt pressed into me.

The first guy went down while his buddy maneuvered around them, trying to get another shot. The shuffler thrashed its arms and legs, bit, snarled and spat. Its mouth dove in for a taste and got one in the form of the man's nose – just the tip, but it was enough.

The shuffler was lifted off and tossed to the side by the man's companion. They opened up with their guns, but the shuffler did something I never would have expected. Instead of going for an enraged attack, it hopped behind the cover of a car. The two men advanced, firing, and disappeared from my limited view.

"Jesus Christ, Jackson. We need to get the hell out of here," Sails whispered next to my ear.

I grabbed her forearm and held on tight. I meant it to be reassuring and not restraining.

"Just hold on. They'll move on soon, or die trying," I whispered.

"What if that shuffler figures out that we're hiding out under here?"

"Then we shoot it in the fucking face," I replied under my breath.

The men drifted back into view as they looked for the shuffler. Noise behind Sails made me turn my head. I couldn't see anything, though, because the other side was completely dark.

More shots rang out. The pair came back into view. The guy who was attacked spat blood.

"Hank. Damn, man. Did that thing get you?"

More shots, but the shuffler danced away.

The two men stood side by side, hands up as they pointed their guns. They backed up together, but the bitten one staggered. He fell to his knees. I could see him staring right at us as a bubble of blood touched his lips and then drooled down his chin. He tried to say something, but the words were choked off by another burst of blood.

The guy raised his gun and tried to aim at us, but his arm faltered and the barrel dropped. He reached for his neck, like he couldn't breathe. His eyes clenched in pain and he bent over, coughing until it turned into a choking sound.

"I'm sorry, Hank. Real sorry, man, but you know the rules."

A single gunshot rang out. The guy collapsed to the side as the bullet tore through his head.

There was a scream and the shuffler was on top of the shooter. They went down in a heap, the man fighting for his life. His gun went flying but he managed to jam his forearm into the shuffler's neck. He pushed.

The monster was lifted briefly, but then it drove down with freakish force. The man's arm collapsed and the shuffler's head dove in, seeking flesh.

The man let out a scream of horror and tried to wrap his legs around the shuffler. His hands held the Z's neck and squeezed, but the shuffler thrashed from side to side and slipped loose.

The shuffler ripped into flesh, tearing chunks out while McQuinn's man continued to howl in pain. The first Z arrived and fell forward to gorge. A few moments of struggling ensued and the guy tried to scream, but it came out a gurgle from the hole in his throat.

The shuffler turned its head as it chewed a chunk of flesh and looked me right in the eye.

I swear the nasty fuck smiled at me through blood and drool.

I didn't dare breathe, didn't blink, and didn't move. Every muscle in my body was tense. Anna moved her gun as she tried to bring the shuffler into sight.

Before she could start shooting, the rumble of cars and motorcycles reached us. The rest of McQuinn's men had arrived.

SECLUSION

14:40 hours approximate
Location: Clairemont, CA

When McQuinn's men arrived, it was in force, and they weren't shy with their weapons. If the shuffler got away, I didn't see it. After what seemed like forever, the bullets stopped flying.

Then it was just a waiting game.

I closed my eyes and dozed as the men we'd been evading moved around the area. Sure, you're thinking that I'd be nuts to try and get a few winks, but let me tell you about life in the US Navy. I'd been on more than one fast cruise and I'd gone for days without real sleep while the ship was put through her paces. Constant drills, people always up in our shit, and never-ending cleaning. No one got rest, because it wasn't exactly a nine to five job. I remember the longest I'd stayed awake was a consecutive thirty-six hours. After that I'd crawled on top of the oil storage containers, safely hidden from roving eyes, and taken a nap.

Of course I got caught, but that was to be expected. I did my job in the Navy but I was also kind of a fuck up. That little nap cost me a couple of days in Thailand.

I didn't sleep; I just drifted while Anna Sails lay beside me.

I'd have preferred a bed or sleeping bag, but as long as we were alive I'd settle for her arms around me and the hard cold asphalt.

"Don't get any ideas," Sails reminded me more than once.

"I have an idea. After this, let's get pizza," I whispered.

"Gonna kick your ass when we get out of here," she whispered back.

"If we get out of this, I'll let you try."

"You'll let me?" She poked me in the side.

"Yeah. You're all of five-foot-four, right? If I take your gun, how will you get it back when I'm holding it seven feet off the ground?"

"How about I just stab you in the groin?"

"How about you don't. I like my groin."

And on it went as we whispered back and forth to keep from going insane.

McQuinn's men swept the area a couple of times while they put down the Z's I'd lured to the scene. There wasn't a lot of talk. A couple of guys went over the wall, checked on the car, dragged our hard-earned supplies up, and tossed them into trucks.

The action had drawn a lot of attention. They came from around homes, beside cars, and from the road below. The dead got wind of the jackwads and wanted to eat. The moans rose around us as they closed in.

Finally, a beat-up truck puttered to a halt, and out jumped someone familiar.

Sails and I lay in silence as the men above spoke.

"Did you find them?" It was McQuinn.

"Nope. Not in the car. I don't know how they survived that," one of the guys said.

"Probably crawled out and got dragged away and eaten," another chimed in.

"Hmm," McQuinn muttered.

"You guys sweep the buildings down there? Could be they got out before the car went over the side."

"Yeah. We looked, but gave up when the fucking rotters showed. We should go."

Sails kept her arm steady on my chest, hand in a death grip on her gun. The weight of the long barrel wasn't really reassuring. If she started firing, I'd probably lose some skin.

McQuinn didn't move. From our vantage, I couldn't tell what he was doing.

"I hope they survived," he said.

"Why?"

"I want to personally execute each one of them while the rest watch."

"That's cold, man."

"Fuck them. They cost us a lot," he said.

After a minute of silence he finally got back in his truck and roared away. Other engines joined them. We waited in breathless anticipation for something to go wrong. I was tense because I was convinced this was some kind of trick. As soon as we came out they'd be waiting with guns and shit-eating grins. I shifted the shotgun out of the crook of my arm because the pressure had cut off the blood flow and made my hand numb.

I reached up, found Anna's hand, and gave it a quick squeeze. She squeezed back.

15:40 hours approximate
Location: Not-sure-where, CA

"THAT GUY'S AN ASSHOLE. HE REMINDS ME OF SOMEONE WE RAN into last week. Joel and I came across these two guys who were dragging female Z's off the street and using them...you know. Fucking animals."

"What the hell? What did you guys do?"

"Me and Joel took care of them, and I don't mean we left them breathing. But is that what the world's come to? Monsters like that?"

"So, what, you took matters into your own hands?" she asked.

"Yeah. We did."

"How is that different from what McQuinn and those clowns are doing?"

I'd planned to have some catchy one-liner for when she called me a hero. Something cool, like "mess with the best, die like the rest." Instead, I choked on silence. Warmth rose into my cheeks.

"Were we supposed to just let them keep that shit up?"

"I don't know. Probably not, but who made you the sheriff?"

"No one. They started shooting first."

"So why not fuck off and leave them alone?"

I didn't have an answer, so we lay in silence for a few minutes.

"It was wrong. Just wrong. I don't care if those things are mindless animals. They deserved something better than being tied to a couch and screwed by those rapist assholes."

"Jesus."

A creeper lumbered past our hiding place. His left foot was cocked at an angle and he dragged it with each staggering step. My tiny window allowed me to track him for a few more seconds before he faded from sight.

"I'm not going to apologize. Besides, we left them alive. Kind of."

"Kind of?"

"The leader took a shot to the gut. I hit the other one so hard he couldn't talk right. So we dragged them to the pile of rotting Z's they'd created in the kitchen and left them."

"Always going to be good guys and bad guys. Which are we?" she asked.

"Me? I'm a bad guy trying to be good." I tried for my best Clint Eastwood impression and came up lacking.

"That's real deep, Jackson. Have you thought about writing a book?"

"I am. Kinda." I told her about the log book I'd been writing in every day.

"What did you say about me?"

"That you're a gun-wielding, take-no-shit ball buster."

"I am not!" She elbowed me, but I thought she might be smiling.

"I wrote that you were pretty cool even though you did hit Joel in the face and threaten to shoot him when we were back in the helicopter."

"I overreacted. Lee's the kind of leader that doesn't like to be called out."

"Yeah. About that."

"Don't start that again. I told you, I saw the results myself. If the kid turned inside that helicopter, what would happen? What if he was laying there, all quiet, and you leaned over to ask him how he was feeling? Kid sits up and takes a bite of your face, then we have to shoot you and him."

"His name was Craig and he was just a sad kid. He'd just lost his family," I said.

"He's not the only one that's lost people."

I wanted to find anger, but it was hard to when I knew she was right. I settled for staring at the underbelly of the SUV a half-inch from my nose.

18:10 hours approximate
Location: Not-sure-where, CA

AFTER WHAT SEEMED LIKE A WHOLE DAY I DECIDED WE'D WAITED long enough.

I pushed the body away from the side of the car, then shimmied out and shoved away a couple of body parts.

I had my head sticking out in the air like fresh bait. If a couple of Z's had been near us, I'm sure they would have been on me in a heartbeat.

I heaved myself out of the coffin-like space and took a deep breath. It still smelled terrible, but at least the light breeze made the odor a little thinner. I leaned out and offered my hand to

Sails. She looked at it for a second and then accepted, so I pulled her out.

We stood and stretched, looking around for movement.

I considered our options. If we walked back, it would take hours. If we found a new ride, we'd probably be able to get back in thirty minutes. I pointed at a gas station near the off-ramp. Behind it were a few trees and a large complex of some sort.

"Try for it?" I asked.

"Might as well. I don't want to be out in the open for any longer than we have to."

We moved out.

18:30 hours approximate
Location: Not-sure-where, CA

WE COVERED EACH OTHER AS WE MADE OUR WAY TO THE BOTTOM OF the ramp. Anna moved with the same precision and self-awareness I'd seen Joel exhibit on many occasions. She was cautious, but she strode forward when she saw openings. We neatly avoided a group of Z's intent on devouring the remains of a family of four. They'd gone down fighting, but they'd gone down.

We used abandoned cars for cover and avoided looking inside. Seeing a Z'd-up kid scratching at the glass was a sure way to get creeped out, even after weeks of being around the crawling corpses.

I followed Sails' lead as she gestured for me to move ahead or guard her back. We avoided another small pack intent on chasing down a dog. The dog was smarter and a hell of a lot faster than any white-eyed snarling Z.

I wished I had fast legs like that. The dog cut to the right and stopped. He sat back on his haunches, tongue hanging out as he panted, and he...what? Waited?

The Z's closed in, one falling only to be stomped by his uncaring companions.

The dog barked and then took off again.

He was fucking with the dead.

The dog led them off and I made a mental note to find something for the guy to eat if he came back our way.

We dashed down a tree-lined side street, past houses spray painted with graffiti, doors hanging open, windows broken, and innards tossed onto yards and porches.

At the center of the avenue we found a building that boasted a gated entryway. The front door was open, but the building itself, while looking like every other piece of shit apartment complex I'd ever seen in California, hadn't been entirely beat to hell.

A pile of bodies lay at the bottom of the stairs; maybe that was the warning to any who ventured there. With Anna covering me, I tiptoed inside and then waited in darkness for many long minutes. Silence. Nothing stirred.

With pounding hearts, we made for the stairs.

18:40 hours approximate
Location: Not-sure-where, CA

WE CREPT TO THE STAIRS AND MADE OUR WAY TO THE SECOND floor. The first had been ransacked. Doors stood open, and I didn't want to try sneaking into one to find a pack of Z's or worse, a few shufflers.

The second and third floor had been hit as well, but at least the apartments hadn't been completely picked over. I finally chose a room at random and poked my head inside. Anna took position beside me and then dropped low. I went in with the Mossberg ready, the stock planted against my shoulder.

The kitchen was on the right and a hallway ran to the right. I held up my hand and Anna stopped next to me. She closed the door with a soft click and we waited in the dark for a few minutes. When I felt like I had my night vision up to par, I leaned into the kitchen and tapped the barrel of the shotgun against the counter just once and then we waited.

Sounds filtered in from the outside. The moans and howls of the dead sent chills up my back. If they'd seen us and were headed our way, we were now officially stuck. We might be able to go out a back window, but how would we get down? Probably not enough time to tie sheets together.

Nothing moved inside the apartment, so we made a sweep.

The first bedroom had been tossed. Sheets torn off the bed, blankets in a pile, drawers open, an empty and discarded suitcase, clothes everywhere. Someone had left in a hurry.

The next bedroom looked about the same, except for the addition of a rotting body on the floor. Sails pushed it with a foot, and when it didn't get up and try to devour us, she covered it with a blanket. We closed that door behind us, cutting off some of the cloying scent of rot.

The last bedroom was in one piece. I checked under the bed, because don't fucking judge me.

The living room had a two piece sectional in some kind of off-white leather. A little bit of daylight filtered in through the rear sliding glass door. There was a balcony with a small grill and a satellite dish. What I wouldn't give to crash on the couch with a dumb action movie playing. On second thought, I was living an action movie.

We moved a chair into the hallway and wedged it under the doorknob. If someone wanted to get in, they'd make a hell of a lot of noise.

I took a breath and sat on the couch. My ankle ached, so I put it up and then just zoned out for a minute – or maybe an hour.

Sails moved around the apartment checking kitchen cabinets and drawers. She gave a little whoop, then brought back a few items and tossed them onto the couch. She went back and brought more.

My stomach rumbled to life when I found little bags of chips, granola, some fruit roll ups, and a couple of flat packets containing tuna fish. One of those went into my mouth first, right after I'd ripped the top open with shaking hands.

We didn't talk for the first few minutes as we ate. On a scale of one to ten, I'd give this one about a five for healthy eating. It got a fucking eleven for deliciousness.

"How is it that this place still has food?" I wondered out loud.

"You saw the bodies below. I think the building was well guarded until recently," Anna said.

"Maybe. Or could be someone else is away from his post but will be returning soon."

"Maybe. The way I see it, we have about twelve hours. Wanna watch a movie?" I gestured at the big screen mounted on the wall.

"As long as it's not a fucking zombie movie," Anna replied.

I choked on a cracker, then took a swig of one of the warm Cokes she'd found in the fridge.

Anna moved to the hallway and poked through a few closets. She returned a minute later with a couple of LA Kings blankets and tossed me one. I wrapped it around my shoulders and reveled in the feeling of warmth returning to my body.

"I'd sit by you, but you smell like a car mechanic," Anna said.

"That's not so bad."

"And death. You literally smell like death."

"Oh."

"I wonder if the toilet would stand up to a flush. I'll test it first," she said and left the room.

I sat in silence and thought about what we'd lost in the past twenty four hours. The HUMVEE. Markus and Donny. We'd lost our new fortress and now we'd lost our way. We knew that there was a force in LA, and we could probably find refuge there. But as far as I knew, Anna Sails had no idea where they were located. So we had no next play. No safe haven waiting for us. Like the first week or so, we were on our own.

"Holy shit!" Anna shouted.

I heaved myself to my feet and snagged my wrench, then hobbled down the hallway.

She was standing in the bathroom, staring at the sink. The water was running and she had her hand under the stream. Sails, with her hair hanging over her face as she stared in shock, looked beautiful.

"What's wrong?" I asked, and then realized just how stupid I was.

I rushed to the other side of the vanity and tested the other sink. Water, cold and flowing freely, hit my hand. I ducked my mouth next to it and took a tentative sip. Then I gulped.

"How's this even possible?" she asked.

"Probably residual water pressure. Maybe it'll take a little longer to go out. Could be days. Could be hours, for all we know." I honestly didn't have an explanation. Did this place have some kind of backup generator hooked to a pump?

Anna drifted to the shower and stared at it for a few seconds before sliding the glass door aside and turning on the water. She let it run for a few seconds and then shut it off.

"You first, and don't be shy with that soap."

I laughed when I looked at the wire rack hanging from the shower nozzle and found some decidedly feminine products like conditioner, pre-conditioner, and liquid soap with a bunch of flowers on the label.

"Gonna be cold, but I don't even care," I said, unbuttoning the nasty shirt I'd worn for the last few days.

"We should wash those," Anna said, looking up at me.

I slid the shirt off and held it out with two fingers. This damn thing would be better in the trash than in the wash. Maybe I'd turn up some clothing that fit once we went through the rest of the apartment. I missed my overalls. They had been thick and kept all the gore off.

Anna watched me from the doorway but didn't say another word. I reached for the button on my pants, and that's when she turned and closed the door.

I shrugged and leaned over to drop what was left of my pants. I nearly fell as I tried to balance but keep the pressure off my sore ankle, and managed to stumble into the sink, banging my leg into the sharp edge. That got a few choice words.

"You alright in there?"

"Yeah. Just having trouble with my damn leg. Ankle gave out." I gritted my teeth.

"I'll see if I can find something to wrap it."

I turned on the shower and spun it all the way to hot, then had a brief fantasy of steaming water belting out.

I put my hand under the cold stream and sucked in a breath. This wasn't going to be much fun. I manned up and stepped under the water. It was like I'd been tossed in the ocean off the coast of San Diego all over again. I gasped and hooted then went for the soap.

I was halfway through scrubbing my face when I heard a noise. Blinking away suds and water, I found a shape in the room.

"Don't even say a damn word, Jackson. Not a word," she said as she slipped, naked, into the shower with me.

She pushed me aside and let the water run over her hair and face.

Anna stood there, her pale form all hips and legs, waist and butt, for me to gaze at. She grabbed the soap and then scrubbed as quickly as she could.

I turned her around and pushed her against the wall. She looked up at me and used both hands to brush water off her face. We both shivered. I didn't say a word, just like she'd asked. Instead, I leaned in and kissed her.

21:00 hours approximate
Location: Not-sure-where, CA

WE LAY TOGETHER ON THE COUCH, BURIED UNDER A PILE OF blankets. I was exhausted but grinning like a guy caught in a cookie jar filled with gold. After our shower, I didn't feel like braving someone else's bedroom, so I took her hand in mine and tugged her to the main room. Then Anna had showed me that she had a very soft side, and for a while we didn't have to talk.

"Can I speak now?"

"I don't know if I should let you start. Will you shut up at some point?"

"You hurt me, Sails." I chuckled.

"Not yet, but I might."

She pushed against me and got me all worked up again. She sat on top and looked down at me.

"Okay," I said. "Hurt me."

21:50 hours approximate

Location: Not-sure-where, CA

"Are you ever going to tell me about Bright Star? Do you guys have a secret decoder ring or something?" I asked before I drifted off.

"Not much to tell. I came in a few weeks ago. Fresh recruit. They don't talk a lot. We just go where we're told."

"But this thing. This nightmare that's killing the world. Where did it start?"

Anna didn't move for a half-minute, then she spoke. "I heard it was Afghanistan. Some kind of test, but not by us. Someone brought it there. We followed some leads and found a village that was occupied by something like the Z's we've seen. The villagers had them tied down, but the things were just... Fuck. They were barely human."

"Like we've seen."

"Not quite," she said and blew out a breath. "They were still alive. They had big open sores, but their eyes had gone milky white. They had a pulse, but it was so slow it was barely there. We took blood samples while those that were unaffected screamed at us to leave their family members alone. The things barely moved except to reach for us."

"That is messed up."

"I thought they were begging, but now I know. They wanted flesh. It's like they see what they used to be and want to have that back."

"I don't get it. How did they become infected?" I asked.

"Not sure. Rumors. Some kind of chemical attack and an experimental drug to help the wounded. We didn't do it. The Afghani's brought it in from somewhere. Lee thinks it was used in a coordinated attack against the US."

"Lee, huh."

"He's a good leader and knows when to make tough choices."

It was all I could do to clench my jaw shut and not say a word.

"We responded when things started to break down. We gathered as much of Bright Star as we could and established a pair of bases here," Anna continued.

"The first base is gone."

"Yeah. But I hope the second is still there."

"Where?"

"Near LA. I know the general area, but it's a big city. We might drive right past it," she said.

"So you knew the location that Donny and Markus had in mind?"

"I think so. Like I said, I know the general area. It'll be better than this."

"Better than being in bed with me?" I gave her my best wounded look.

Anna thumped my chest.

"Shut up, you," she said gently. "It's better than running and hiding. What if that gang comes back and finds us? What if we run into five hundred Z's? It's dangerous, and our best bet is to be with others. They have a chain of command and, hopefully, a plan."

"No one plans for this," I said.

"You'd be surprised what they plan for."

"I didn't plan on this," I said. "You and me."

"Yeah, well...shit happens. Just go to sleep, Creed, before you say something fucking stupid."

"Fucking stupid is my middle name," I quipped and got another thump.

It was worth it.

I can barely keep my eyes open. Anna sleeps next to me, but I can't stop thinking about this amazing turn of events. Damn Anna Sails. A few days ago, I wanted to hate her. Now I am sleeping with her.

Tomorrow's going to be a long walk back.

Time to call it a night.

NEW ATTITUDE

07:20 hours approximate
Location: Not-sure-where, CA

I woke up feeling like I'd taken a beating. My back was a mass of knots. My legs were so sore I could barely swing them off the side of the couch. My neck ached and my head was pounding.

Anna was already up and moving around the apartment, dressed in nothing but panties and bra. I decided that I could watch her all day. She shifted the living room's blinds to the side. I groaned when the sun hit me.

Birds chirped and called. Somewhere, a crow was bitching about something. He was probably trying to peck the eyes out of some corpse and the corpse tried to eat him.

Last night this room had been a refuge. In daylight it was barely above shit hole material. The couch was worn and the recliner, which had looked so inviting, was half-covered in blood. The rest of it was a flattened mess of what had once been cushions.

"Just kill me now," I mumbled.

"Get up, lazy squid."

"Why don't you come over here and make me," I said.

Anna's eyes darkened and she moved to the couch. Most of

me was still buried under a pile of blankets and had no interest whatsoever in leaving them.

She leaned over and stared into my eyes for a few seconds. I stared back.

"How about if I stick a knife in your balls?"

"That's what I like about you, Anna. You're hot when you're angry."

Her lips parted in a smile that she tried to quickly hide.

"Just because of last night. Just because of that. Don't think that you have any power over me. It was mutual."

"Then let's mutually agree that you need to get back under these covers."

Anna knelt next to me and put one of her hands on my cheek. She ran it over my head and scruffy beard, then she leaned over and planted a quick peck on my chest.

"I don't want to get too close to you. Do you understand that?"

"Why not?"

She looked away for a moment. Her eyes tightened and her lips parted. She sucked in a breath.

"Because it's dangerous. It sucks out there, Creed. I've seen what happens to loved ones. Seen it firsthand. Seen them dragged into a pile of dead and devoured and not been able to do a fucking thing about it." She trailed off.

"So you're going to live the rest of your life in a bubble? Fuck it, Anna. We might both buy it today. Enjoy life while you can."

"It's not that easy. I had a family. Kids. I saw them die. Devoured. And there was nothing I could do. They died screaming. Do you know what that does to a person? It breaks them, Creed. It kills them."

I swung my legs over the side of the couch and took her in a gentle embrace. She held me for all of fifteen seconds, then stood and went into the kitchen. Her eyes were tight and they didn't meet mine.

07:30 hours approximate
Location: Not-sure-where, CA

ANNA HAD GONE THROUGH THE APARTMENT EARLIER AND DUG OUT some clothing. She left me with some fresh boxers that were a little too small but still welcome. She'd found some white socks and even a few T-shirts. Those were also too small, but I slid a shirt over my chest and stretched it out.

I was dressed and testing my swollen ankle when Sails came back. She had a ball of something in one hand.

"Give me your foot," she said and pulled a footstool next to the couch.

She poked and prodded at my swollen ankle.

"Ow," I said, even though it didn't hurt that much. I was so used to hobbling around and ignoring the pain that this was nothing.

"Not good. I'm going to wrap it. I found a bottle of ibuprofen. That should help with the pain and swelling a little bit."

"Didn't know you were a nurse."

"I'm not, so pray I don't have to dig a bullet out of you."

"You can dig a bullet out of me anytime." I grinned.

"Were you dropped on your head at some point?"

"Probably."

She wrapped the bandage around my foot and leg until she had my ankle secured.

"Put your leg up for a while. I'll bring you some food."

"That's real domestic of you, Anna," I said.

"Be nice or I'll add rat poison," she said and headed back to the kitchen.

07:55 hours approximate
Location: Not-sure-where CA

OUR BREAKFAST COULD HAVE BEEN WORSE. WE ATE PROTEIN BARS and washed them back with some silver packs of juice. I bit the corner of the first one and drained it in one go. Despite claiming to be some kind of fruit juice, it tasted like sugar-water, and that was just fine by me. The second one went down just as smooth. This shit would be perfect with some vodka.

"I don't suppose you found any booze in this place?"

"Some cooking sherry."

"Some cooking what?"

"It's some kind of sweet wine."

I made a face.

There was a canister of smoke-flavored almonds. They were stale but I ate them by the handful. Fruit wraps were next, then we moved on to a couple of cans of peaches.

We'd been passing the food back and forth with a little "try this." "This one is good." I think it was because we didn't really have anything to talk about. I tried to ask Anna about her life before the event, but she just brushed off my questions or changed the subject.

"It's going to be a long walk back," I said.

"I don't think it's going to be too bad," Anna said.

"Because you have me to keep you company?"

"Because I found something very useful in a closet."

"If it's some kind of funky jetpack, I'm all ears."

"Come with me," she said.

"Yes ma'am!" I saluted.

We didn't head to the bed. Instead, she stopped in front of a doorway and pointed.

"The rocket pack is in here?"

She opened the door. My mouth fell open and my lips curled into a grin.

"Perfect, right?"

"Anna, I could kiss you," I said.

Then I did, and she didn't punch me.

I unhooked the first bike from a hanger and brought it into the hallway. It was an expensive looking bicycle with sculpted lines and fancy brakes and gears changers. The second bike was smaller. It was white and had pink stripes along the body.

"You'll look so cute on that thing," I deadpanned.

"I happen to like pink."

I blinked.

Then I spotted something else on the shelf and took it down.

"That'll work," Anna said.

08:15 hours approximate
Location: Not-sure-where, CA

WE SAT SIDE BY SIDE ON THE COUCH, WEAPONS LAID OUT BEFORE US. Joel had taught me enough about caring for my guns so that I didn't feel like an idiot. Anna stripped hers like a pro and used a cloth to wipe down the components.

The half-empty bottle of synthetic motor oil I'd turned up in the closet would have to do. We scrubbed down all surfaces. I worked a couple of layers of lubrication into every sliding part, and then reassembled. The Mossberg also got a layer of oil. I used an old metal skewer I'd found in the kitchen to lightly scrape away any carbon buildup.

"How do you like the shotgun?"

"We were made for each other," I said.

"It suits you."

"How so?"

"Because you like to bash stuff. How many heads has that wrench crushed?"

"I lost count on the third day. By then it didn't seem to matter any more," I replied.

"Do you ever think about the people on the other end? The ones we end up putting down?"

"Not anymore. To me, they aren't people anymore. They're a threat and they need to be dealt with. If they have any humanity left, I haven't seen it."

Anna reassembled her M&P R8 and reloaded while we chatted.

"So if one of them got me, you'd handle it, right?"

I frowned.

"You're really fucking morbid."

"It's a valid question," she said. "I'd do the same for you. Unless you want to live out there like one of those things."

"Maybe I'll get lucky and turn into a shuffler. Then I can still chase you around."

"You think you're chasing me?"

"I'd say I caught you," I grinned.

Anna rolled her eyes and snapped the revolver's cylinder shut.

"Just remember. If I turn, I want it done quick."

"Yeah. Sure, Anna," I said.

We scrounged up a couple of backpacks and stuffed them with food, anything that was dry or light. I added a couple of cans of fruit for Christy and almost regretted my choice, since my backpack weighed about twenty pounds. It might not seem like a lot, but after a few miles on a twisted ankle, I'd be hurting.

We slid the dresser away from the front door but a noise stopped us on the spot. I slipped to the door and listened but didn't hear another peep. I peered through the fish-hole and saw only an overcast day. I moved around, trying to see what else was out there, but nothing appeared in my line of sight. I turned, looked at Anna, and shrugged.

I put my finger to my lips and she moved her head in understanding. We waited a minute and then a minute more. I didn't hear any other noises, so I nodded at her.

Anna un-holstered her pistol and aimed it at the door. I lowered my wrench and slowly turned the lock. The door slid open a crack.

I expected to see a Z or two on the landing, maybe a shuffler creeping around – in which case, I was going to put him down before he had a chance to get a fucking attitude. I had it mapped out in my head. He turns, gets that gleam in his eye, and then BAM! My wrench takes him to the ground and leaves a pile of goo.

Instead, we were greeted by the dog from the day before, the mutt that had been teasing the Z's, leading them off by barking and then dashing away when the foul creatures got close. She whined and shifted from foot to foot.

"Well goddamn," Anna said before I could.

I set the wrench against the wall and lowered my hand. The dog leaned forward, sniffed, and then her tail thumped against the floor.

"Okay, get in here," I said and motioned.

The dog looked like it was mostly Labrador Retriever, but definitely had something else mixed in. She was a yellowish-tan with white around her eyes and nose, a good looking dog, but far too skinny. I understood that. Hard enough for humans to be out scavenging for food. I didn't want to think about what she'd been eating to survive.

I glanced both ways to make sure there were no Z's on the landing, then I closed the door with a soft click.

Anna dropped to her knees and gave the dog a rough scratch around the ears.

"You smell," she said.

"Lets get her some food."

"Then what? Leave her here?" Anna rubbed the dog's neck.

The dog's tongue lolled out.

I took her to the kitchen and dug around in the pantry. No dog food. Since we weren't able to carry all the heavy stuff, I made her a meal of baked beans and beets. The pup went at it while keeping her eyes on us. I found another bowl and filled it with water.

"What else are we going to do?"

"We can't leave her here. We'll have to let her go before we move out."

"Okay, but what is she going to do?" I asked.

"I don't know. Dog stuff, I guess," she said.

"We could leave more food out and leave the door open. She'd be good for a day or two. Maybe she can sleep on the couch," I said and patted her side. "I bet you've always wanted to sleep on a comfy couch."

"You two make a cute couple," Anna said.

"I thought you and I made a cute couple," I said, expecting her to flip me the bird.

Anna looked away in discomfort but I caught a glimpse of color on her cheeks. I did the smart thing and shut the fuck up.

08:45 hours approximate
Location: Not-sure-where, CA

WE PUSHED THE BIKES OUT OF THE APARTMENT AND ONTO THE landing. I'd dumped out a few more cans of food into bowls and left them for the dog, but she'd eaten her fill and now seemed more interested in following us.

"Stick around here and don't let any stupid boy dogs get up in your business," I said in a baby voice while she licked my face.

"Up in your business?" Anna stared at me.

"Yeah, unless she's looking for some action. I mean...I guess it is the end of the world," I said and shifted attention back to the dog. "Just make sure he wears protection."

"Are you preparing a speech for your future kids?"

"Kids? I'm not really the dad type."

We moved to the stairs. I hoisted the bike up to my shoulder while Anna followed. She stopped at the top of the steps and covered me while I went down. The dog stuck with Anna.

"She'll probably stay after we start peddling," Anna said.

"I don't think that's gonna happen."

"I hate to say it, but we may need to do something about her. Can't have her barking when we're near a bunch of Z's."

"Whoa," I said. "What do you mean 'do something'?"

"It's for the best."

"It is not for the best. That dog's a rock star. You might as well put a bullet in my skull."

"Like I haven't thought of that a few times."

"Pardon?" I asked.

"Just…when we met, you were kind of a dick. All puffed up because of the kid."

"That kid was my friend."

Anna parked her bike and lowered the kickstand, then came to me. I half expected her to start a fight.

"Jackson. I'm sorry, okay?" She reached up to touch my cheek.

I stared back at her, wondering what she was about to do. She surprised me.

Anna got on her tiptoes, put her hand around my neck, and pulled me into a kiss.

"Uh."

"Don't be such a dork after last night. I was upset when I met you. I didn't like what happened to the kid, but it was the right thing to do. He was one of them. I'm sorry, but that's the way it is now. I don't want a dog barking at the wrong moment and getting us killed."

"Don't use the dog as a fucking bargaining chip."

"I'm not," she said. "And you know it."

Christ, she was right. But right or wrong, I wasn't going to kill a dog that just needed some attention. Man's best friend and all.

"Let's see what happens. Maybe she's not a spaz."

"A spaz? Who says that?"

I shrugged.

"No barking," I told the dog.

She wagged her tail and sniffed the air.

Anna and I hopped on the bikes and started our trek back.

09:00 hours approximate
Location: Not-sure-where, CA

THE DOG FOLLOWED US AS WE MADE IT UP THE OVERPASS AND PAST the SUV we'd hidden under the day before. There was no sign of McQuinn and his crew, but we kept a cautious eye out.

The weather was turning and it looked like it might become a sunny day after all. The morning air still had a chill, but there was a mugginess lurking under the light breeze that hit me. If it weren't for the zombie fucking apocalypse, you might think that me and Anna Sails were just a couple of lovers out for a morning ride. I wondered what it would be like to have a normal life with a girl like her. Would we bike to coffee shops? Go on picnics? Go for long drives? Hang out and watch bad movies on the SyFy channel?

I knew one thing for goddamn sure. Our nights wouldn't get boring.

The dog kept to our side and sniffed the air as we headed for the other side of the freeway. A pile of bodies blocked our way at one point, so we moved to the shoulder and tried not to look. The dog whimpered as we moved past it but then dashed ahead a few meters.

We made it to the highway and stuck near the shoulder, veering off the road when we had too. It would have been easy to weave between cars, but I was concerned that we'd end up getting snagged by a Z that was hanging out in one of the vehicles. One minute we're cruising, the next a hand is in our spokes and one of us is flying. We got up to a decent speed and the miles flew by, but then we happened upon a huge wreck.

The dog dashed ahead and then stopped and looked back at us. Her hair rose on her neck and she snarled but kept still. We stopped beside her, but she just stared.

The pair of Z's slid around the side of a blue Monte Carlo and stumbled toward us. The dog backed up and didn't make a sound except for a low, rumbling growl.

Anna and I jumped off the bikes and went to work.

I took the bigger one out with the wrench. It was a beauty of a shot, too. I stepped aside just as the slow creeper came at me. He wasn't long dead and still had a lot of kick in his lurch.

I hit him in the head and he fell away. He didn't even have a surprised look on his face – he just looked...blank. He managed to land on one knee and get a hand down. I stepped behind him and brought the wrench down with a loud crack.

Anna pulled her knife. She thrust, arm extended, to take the other Z right in the throat. She moved in, knocked his hand to the side, and ripped the knife to the away, taking most of his throat with it. The Z dropped but kept twitching.

The dog still stayed behind us and growled.

"It's cool, dog. We got 'em. Thanks for the assist," I said.

The dog showed her teeth.

From now on I'm paying attention to the mutt.

The second wave clambered out of a bus and made for us. They snarled, white eyes locked on our flesh. There were only two at first, but then the rest of the bus unloaded.

"Let's go, Anna," I said.

We rolled our bikes around the wrecks, hopped on, and made a beeline for the rendezvous point. The dog moved alongside us but glanced over her shoulder a few times. Once she let out a low growl. I followed her gaze and saw a Z following us in the distance.

"Dog's a keeper," Anna said.

We rode a few feet apart.

"She needs a name," I said.

"How about Frosty?"

"What the hell kind of name is that?" I asked.

"She didn't even blink. Just stopped, stared, and growled. She's cool under pressure."

I grinned at Anna. "That's a damn good name."

09:30 hours approximate
Location: Near Clairemont, CA

WE HIT TRAFFIC FIFTEEN MINUTES LATER.

The pack of Z's was the biggest I'd seen in a long time. They moved in our direction, but we saw them long before they saw us, so we ducked off the road and dashed to the thin tree line. The growth here was sparse and we didn't really stand a chance of hiding if they took a real interest in us, but I'd found that even partial coverage was better than nothing. It could help to confuse them, with their milky white eyes and lack of ability to smell us.

Frosty stuck to our side and sat on her haunches while the parade of the damned marched by.

The Z's were a mix of old and young, men and women. They moved at a slow pace. Thankfully, I didn't see any fucking shufflers. At least fifty of the dead meandered past our location. Their destination, if Z's could have a destination, seemed to wait in the same direction as ours. One thing was for sure – we'd have to deal with them on our way to LA unless we found another way, and I didn't know shit about this area. Without Google maps or even a GPS, we were just hoping to stay near the highway and to make it to the big city and whatever salvation it represented.

A boy meandered through the crowd, but he was just as dead as the rest. In one hand he carried some kind of a stuffed toy that was covered in blood, and he still wore little kid pajamas. It was just about the saddest damn thing I'd seen in days.

Anna looked away but I caught a tightening of her eyes. I reached over and put a hand around her shoulder. She didn't flinch, and after a minute the tension went out of her and she leaned into me. She didn't look at me, but she sobbed in silent heaves against my arm. I held on until she was done. When the group passed, we moved on. I didn't say a word.

09:50 hours approximate
Location: Near Clairemont, CA

"This is the truck," I said.

"No it's not. We haven't gone far enough. There was a big yellow truck next to the semi. I remember that."

"There's a big green truck. Are you sure it was yellow?"

"I'm sure," she said but sized up the truck just the same.

I moved around the semi while Sails covered me. When we

got around to the other side I stopped because Frosty growled.

A Ford truck that was at least thirty years old had smashed into the semi and the driver had been tossed against the side of the bigger truck. Most of the top of his head was gone. At least he wasn't a damn Z.

A hand reached out for me and grabbed my ankle.

In my life, I have never let out a sound like that. It was filled with revulsion and fear and I sounded like a six-year-old when I jumped back and fell on my sore ankle.

Frosty wasted no time. She darted in and grabbed the Z's hand and shook. I got myself loose and unlimbered the wrench. When the Z, a girl in her forties and covered in blood and goo, came out from beneath the vehicle, I bashed in her head.

Frosty took a seat next to me and panted.

I did the same thing I'd done to Anna. I leaned over and put my arm around her neck. She smelled like a dog that had been outside for a few days and I didn't give a damn.

"You two really are cute together. Well, hell, Creed. I thought we were a thing. Looks like I've been dumped for that bitch."

I stared at her for two seconds before I burst into quiet laughter.

10:00 hours approximate
Location: Near Clairemont, CA

AFTER LOITERING IN THE SHADE OF THE TRUCK FOR A BIT, WE TOOK to the bikes and headed down the freeway again, weaving off the road and onto the shoulder until we'd gone at least another 2 klicks. As much as I willed the truck to appear, it did not.

"We have to be close," Anna said.

I nodded and scouted ahead.

We'd come up on a slight rise that obscured the rest of the freeway. I struggled to try and remember anything that looked slightly familiar but it was like one big paint-by-numbers, minus the damn paint.

The rise gave way to another graveyard of abandoned vehicles. In the distance, about a klick way, lay another semi. Frosty stayed next to me and whimpered a couple of times. I leaned over and patted her head. She looked up at me and then her head snapped front as her hackles rose. With a soft growl, she dropped her head.

Among the cars, something prowled.

I found a car to duck behind and put my hand on Frosty's shoulder to keep her calm. My leg ached from foot to knee but the ibuprofen had taken the edge off. With my other hand I motioned for Anna to join me. She pushed her bike the twenty yards that separated us and squatted beside me.

"See that?" I pointed.

"Shuffler?"

"Yeah. I think it's the one that attacked the car yesterday."

"No goddamn way," she said but squinted into the distance. "How do we play it?"

"I've got an idea, but I'm not sure how to get her to understand." Anna patted the dog's head.

"We could point and make dog noises."

"You try that, Creed," she said.

"I'll go and I'll take Frosty. Maybe she'll get the message and draw the asshole away so I can move in for a quiet kill."

If I went in swinging in the open, I was looking at a tough fight. As much as I'd like to say I was a badass zombie fighter, the fact of the matter was that shufflers, even one, could be a handful for a pair of people. This guy was one of the worst I'd seen.

"I should go. I'm not hurt," Anna said.

"I got this. Just stay here and stay safe. If I get into trouble, you come in with gun blazing."

"Two things, Jackson." Her eyes were tight but she spoke with passion. "One – just because we did what we did last night doesn't mean I'm some little teapot that you have to protect. I can take care of myself. Two – if I shoot, it will bring that group our way. Then we're really fucked, unless we can manage to take out the shuffler and fifty or sixty Z's."

She made all kinds of sense. If she was Joel, I'd have no issue, but I knew Joel and I knew how capable he was. Anna Sails was different. She was good with her gun, but I'd never seen her take on a shuffler by hand. I got nothing against a girl kicking ass. In fact, I fucking love it. But if this was the same shuffler, then he was too smart for just one of us. He didn't just jump into battle. Yesterday I'd seen him use a bunch of Z's as cover while he crept around and tried to flank us. Then he'd leapt on top of our car and tried to smash in the back window. Only Anna's quick moves behind the wheel had shaken him loose.

"I know you can take care of yourself. But things are different now. I get to worry about you."

"Worry about yourself first, you big dummy," she said.

"Words hurt."

"So does my foot, so if you want to keep it out of your ass, just play it cool."

"Fine, Anna. See that blue compact? I'll hide behind it. You draw him out and then we can both take him down."

"Not enough cover and it's at least thirty yards. How are you going to ninja your ass over there?"

"I got skills. I had a good teacher," I said.

"You can barely walk. I'll go but I'll use the red Mustang. See it? The convertible?" She pointed.

"Yeah."

"You hide there. I'll draw him out. I'm going to go out in the open and when he closes in I'll fade back. You whack him when he comes after me."

"Worst plan ever."

"Got a better one?" she asked.

"Nope. Let's get this ambush ready."

10:10 hours approximate
Location: Near Clairemont, CA

I HOBBLED INTO POSITION WITH FROSTY. I STAYED NICE AND LOW AS I did my best not to stumble into cars. I kept my eyes wide for the smallest hint of a Z hiding out in a car. Last thing I needed was to have one of them snag my shirt and drag me down.

Frosty wagged her tail while I crouched next to the car. She kept looking in the direction of the shuffler but she didn't bark or freak out. In fact, she was cooler than me. If this dog was smart enough to keep a level head in the face of a freaking shuffler, I should be cool enough to wait for Anna to draw him out.

Anna moved toward the shuffler's position. She kept low and faded from car to car, always keeping the shuffler in sight.

I crawled to the front of the car but popped up to keep my eye on the bastard. He was dressed in rags and covered in filth. His long hair hung in stringy clumps that covered his face. He kept close to the ground and did the fast crab walk I'd come to expect from a shuffler. But what was he doing? Sniffing something out?

Anna bumped into a vehicle's side mirror and dropped out of sight. The shuffler moved as quick as a whip toward her position. I had the urge to jump up and call him to me. I had my wrench, and chances were I could get in a good blow when he came at me.

All in all, our half-assed plan had gone to hell in about six seconds.

The shuffler wasn't waiting around for Anna to get into position to drag him my way. She was at a twenty degree angle to me and there were only a few cars separating us.

The shuffler must have been a goddamn mind reader. He latched onto her hiding spot like he had internal radar and leapt toward it. Anna went for her weapon as the shuffler hit the roof of the car she'd been hiding behind.

I moved.

Anna ripped her knife free of its sheath and dropped into a fighting stance. She kept the blade in a reverse grip, pommel next to her pinky, and got her other arm up as a guard.

I put too much weight on my ankle as I tried to break into a run and nearly went down as pain ripped up my leg.

The shuffler leapt off the car, but instead of directly engaging him, Anna slipped to the side and ripped the knife along his ribs. It turned with a snarl and came at her again.

I lifted my wrench high and strode toward the action.

If the shuffler was hurt, he didn't show it. He dropped to all fours and then leapt again.

Anna dove forward and came up behind him. The shuffler turned and got a face full of blade. Anna was probably aiming for his throat, but the slash was still a beauty. I didn't know if I was supposed to cheer or feel worried.

I was still twenty-five feet away, but moving fast.

The shuffler had learned his lesson and didn't go on the offensive right away. He dropped to his hands and knees. His face, sunken in and small, was a horror of wounds and ripped flesh. He looked bizarre, like some strung-out fanatic.

Anna dropped to her fighting stance again, but this time she didn't wait around. She advanced on the bastard.

He faded back, but not far, and then rushed in on all fours. Anna seemed to be caught off guard. Instead of moving to the side, she slashed down.

The shuffler bowled into her and took her to the ground. She fell hard and her breath was expelled in a big "whoof."

I extended my legs, ignored the intense pain in my ankle, and almost reached the shuffler.

His head darted in, but Anna got her knife up and his mouth closed on the blade. She ripped it to the side, splitting his face open. Her other hand went to his throat to hold him back.

He flailed at her, punching her in the side with both fists, his legs locked tight. Goddammit!

A shape flashed past me and barreled into the fray. Frosty. Snarling, lips drawn back over teeth, she got her mouth around the shuffler's arm and yanked.

Anna seemed dazed. She lifted her hands and tried to roll to the side.

The shuffler went after Frosty and gave her a glancing blow. She yelped in pain, let go, and backed up. Her lips drew back again as she bared teeth and growled, low, in her throat.

Furious, howling, and spitting blood, the shuffler leapt into the air, Anna his target.

I won't say that it was pure luck. It was also a lot of adrenaline and anger mixed with fear. When I swung the wrench, it was with intent.

I hit the shuffler so hard that his head separated from his body. What was left of him collapsed on top of Anna. She rolled to the side and pushed him off. To my horror, his body still twitched. I grabbed the shuffler's leg and dragged him a few feet away. Anna helped by pushing him away with her feet.

"Fuck me." She tried to sit up and moaned.

"For the record," I panted, "that was a terrible plan."

I dropped beside Anna and helped her up. I looked her over, then met her eyes, which were filled with something like fear. I put my arm around her and held her close.

"If you and Frosty had taken a few seconds longer, I would be one of them now."

"I tried to get here as fast as I could," I protested.

"Creed, you were right on time. Thanks."

Our moment didn't last long. The moans of the dead reached us. Staggering to our feet, I was horrified to see a dozen of them coming at us. Frosty rumbled deep in her chest while her dark eyes stared, unblinking, at the threat. I put my hand on her neck and rubbed, but she didn't take her eyes off the Z's.

Anna and I struggled to our feet. We had about thirty seconds to make it to the bikes and then hightail it out of here. She held her hand at her side and grunted when she took a step.

The Z's stepped up the pace when they got wind of us. Mouths wide, they moaned and groaned for our flesh. Arms up, feet staggering under rag-covered legs, eyes white and devoid of intelligence, they came on.

I dragged Anna after me, intent on reaching the bikes.

Then someone let out a quick short whistle.

I spun to the side as fear filled my gut.

It took a couple of seconds for me to connect the dots. Joel Fucking Kelly.

"Let's go." He gestured for us to join him.

ROTTED FLESH

10:30 hours approximate
Location: Near Clairemont, CA

"Joel! You scared the ever-loving shit out of me. Asshole."

"What did you want me to do? Jump up and down to get your attention?"

"How long have you been watching us get our asses kicked?" I asked.

"Not long. I was near the rendezvous point, just hanging out, doing my hair, checking my nails, and wondering if you two were still alive. Then I saw you on the bikes with a dog in tow. I was about a hundred yards away and saw Anna take on that shuffler."

Hanging out, my ass. Joel had probably constructed some kind of sniper hole and covered himself in weeds and dirt, and was sitting there, unmoving, while his Marine eyes never blinked.

"Fucker." Anna looked back and grunted, leaning on me as we followed Joel at a quick pace. "But we got you, didn't we?"

She gave the mangled corpse the finger.

"You did alright," I said.

"We need to pull a disappearing act, then we can sort all this shit out. Just follow me and we'll be out of this in no time. Nice dog," he said after noticing that Frosty was still following us.

I didn't argue with Joel. If he had a plan, I was all ears, because nothing we'd done today had been anything worth bragging about.

"Dog's great. Her name's Frosty. She's smart."

"Smart enough to keep quiet?"

"Yeah. I named her Frosty for a reason."

Joel considered the dog.

Frosty sat, panting, while she stared back at Joel. She licked her chops and then thumped her tail a couple of times.

"Dog seems risky. Any barking..."

"Like I said, she's smart." I recounted how we'd first watched her tease a bunch of Z's.

"Just keep her close and quiet," Joel said.

He led us to the side of the road and then down the embankment. The ground was covered in refuse and luggage. Most of the bags had been ripped open, leaving the clothing and personal items of a dead world scattered on the grass and dirt. Joel pointed at a bunch of bushes.

"Push them aside, then cover up when you get in. I'll lead that pack away." He never took his eyes off the approaching group of Z's.

They staggered in our direction, moaning and snarling. Flesh pulled tight against bone. Limbs rotting or altogether missing. If this bunch got too close, we'd have to haul ass. The wind shifted and carried their scent our way. Even after weeks of this shit, it still made me want to gag.

Anna moved to the little copse and tugged shrubs aside. Behind them lay a huge drainage tunnel that ran under the freeway. There had been a metal grate at some point, but most of the bars had been battered aside. Anna and I moved into the dark space. I couldn't speak for Anna, but I was holding my breath. If the Z's found us in here, they couldn't come at us en masse, but I was beat and Anna couldn't have much left after her fight with the shuffler.

Joel moved away from our position and waited for the Z's.

They stalked toward him in an unorganized group of hungry mouths and milky white eyes.

"Yo, dead fucks. Come here often?"

They started snarling and groaning when they got sight of fresh meat. Joel was a rock.

Once they began to focus on him, Joel backed up a few steps. The grisly parade marched after him.

He waited until the first straggler was upon him, then whipped the butt of his gun around and smashed the Z in the head. It dropped, but a second one was just a step behind. Joel backed up again and then struck that one. The blow was glancing, spinning the Z to the side. Joel moved in and hit it one more time.

Joel moved back another step and clobbered the next one so hard it dropped like a rock.

The fresher Z's bunched up on each other, and some went down in a tangle of limbs. He had their full attention now.

I moved in the tunnel but Anna put her hand on my arm and squeezed. I looked at her in the dark and could only see her shaking her head. I knew that Joel was capable of taking care of himself, but damn.

Frosty sat next to me and growled gently. I put my hand on her snout and then patted her head. She didn't relax, but she was smart enough not to bark.

Joel turned and moved away from the bunch. Of the dozen that had been after him, only half were on their feet. He whistled at them and they came on, staggering over their fallen comrades. They moaned for Joel's flesh.

He again turned and moved away, and they followed.

"Stay here," I said.

Anna shook her head. "Don't. He said he'd take care of it, Jackson."

"It looks like he's trying to take out the entire bunch by himself."

"He's thinning the herd. Making it easier to run if he has to."

"Looks more like he's trying to kill them all."

"Can't kill the dead," she whispered.

Joel tugged his big knife out of the sheath. When the first Z was within reach, Joel slid to the man's side, slammed his blade into the rotting neck, and yanked it out just as quickly. Gurgling, the Z went down.

Joel moved toward the second one. He knocked her hands down and then thrust his blade into the woman's head.

Two down.

The remaining Z's were still coming at him, so Joel turned and moved off another twenty feet until he was in a small cluster of trees. He was out of sight, but – even from our hiding place – I heard the dead falling.

The dog's entire body was tense. I put my hand on her neck and rubbed her. She growled again.

"Stay," I told Frosty.

I tugged free of Anna and pushed aside bushes to leave our hiding spot. Anna hissed after me but I ignored her.

With aching and battered body somewhat under my command, I advanced on the slowest Z and took him out with one swing. The next one fell against a third staggering dead dickhead, and they both tumbled away. I briefly rested my hands on my knees to catch my breath, then hefted the wrench and brought it down on the third Z, which was struggling to disentangle from his blood-covered comrade.

I moved behind Z's like the world's noisiest ninja. The wrench went up, and another Z got the thick side. I whirled again and caught one across the shoulder, then corrected on the follow-through and turned his head into mush with a back-swing. Each 'thunk' brought blood and brains.

I followed the noise of Joel taking out Z's and managed to drop two more. Anna was then standing beside me. She didn't say a word, just shot me a nasty look. I ignored it and advanced on another poor bastard.

Anna took one out with her blade while I bashed another to the ground. The trail of bodies led us right to Joel.

I'd been fearful he would be surrounded, maybe over-whelmed, but he was very calm as he pushed one over to tangle up with a big guy dressed in rags. The Z's scalp was torn and bloody. It had so many wounds, I wondered how he was still on his feet. One of his calves had been ripped almost to the bone but he staggered on, arms up, hands clawing toward me.

I bashed in his head and he went down in a heap. Joel moved in on another and stabbed deep into its eye-socket.

Then it became a mop-up operation as we finished them off. The work was gruesome. It was one thing to take them out from a distance; it was another being this close to their rotted flesh and stinking, pus-filled wounds. They were some of the nastiest Z's I'd seen since San Diego and that was saying something, considering we'd spent part of yesterday next to a pile of putrid corpses.

The last one was a kid that couldn't have been older than seven or eight. I moved behind him and pushed him to the ground. He tried to get up, so I leaned over and pressed my hand against his back. The wrench went high as I concentrated on my target. I couldn't swing. I wanted to, but the world was suddenly swimming before my eyes. The Z tried to turn over, but he couldn't have weighed more than fifty pounds. What there was of the kid had been eaten away by the virus, the elements, and other Z's before he turned.

Joel shouldered me aside and plunged his blade through the back of the kid's skull.

"Why are you hesitating?"

When had Joel come up alongside me?

"Dizzy," was all I got out before I went to one knee.

"Jesus. You're a mess. Let's get you safe."

"Sounds good to me," I muttered.

"Thought I told you idiots to stay out of sight."

"There were so many. I got worried about you. Sue me."

"Idiot. I was going to loop back after I lost them in the trees."

"Well, I didn't know that."

"There wasn't time to draw you a map of my battle plan. Plus I'm all out of crayons and construction paper," Joel said.

"Very funny, smart ass."

"I learned from the best." Joel patted my shoulder.

On my feet again, I was grateful for Anna's help. I draped an arm over her shoulders and we staggered after Joel. I felt as much a zombie as any one of the group we'd just put down.

10:50 hours approximate
Location: Near Clairemont, CA

THE TREES WERE SPARSE WHEN WE FIRST LEFT THE HIGHWAY, BUT AS we moved farther away, they grew closer together. Undergrowth snagged our feet as we crunched over twigs, soggy leaves and soft ground. There was no beaten path to follow.

Joel paused to check on us. I nodded at him, so he pressed on. Frosty had taken a liking to Joel right away and moved beside him. She broke away to sniff at trees and to push up piles of leaves. She found a spot she liked and took a crap. We averted our eyes until she was done. She walked around in a circle then dashed back to Joel's side. She looked proud of her shit spot.

"Must be the beans," Anna said.

"Did you just make a joke?"

"No. She probably hasn't had anything decent to eat for days and we gave her baked beans."

"I don't give a shit what we fed her," I said.

"Stop."

"Just saying. It's a shitty location."

"Ugh."

"I wasn't trying to give you crap," I pressed on.

"Are you five?"

"Poop jokes never get old. It's a scientific fact."

"I think you're the one who's full of shit, Jackson," she said and poked me in the side.

We broke out of the tree line and came upon a long section of chain-link fence. On the other side lay a deep pool of water. A mallard was chasing around a smaller duck, no doubt trying to get laid.

There were recreational vehicles scattered around the area. I counted at least ten, and they were of all shapes and sizes, from giant brown land-cruisers to tow-behind campers with pop-up tents. An old silver Airstream sat next to a white Winnebago that had seen better days a decade ago.

The camp, as far as I could see, was surrounded by chain link fencing. Our welcoming committee sat just outside.

As we walked toward the camp, the people came to their feet. The men and women were holding hammers, axes, and blades. All of the folks were old and older, wearing anxious looks. They studied us with interest. A couple nodded at Joel.

"They were supposed to help. I just needed to lead the last of the bunch here."

"None left?" One of the men spoke to Joel with a slight accent that I couldn't place.

He was dressed in shorts and a red and black-checkered shirt. He wore hiking boots and looked to be in better physical shape than I'd ever been. He also had to be in his seventies.

"This is Claude. He's French, but he's cool," Joel said.

"Mon Dieu. I'm a gentleman. A French gentleman," the guy said.

A woman stood next to him. She was younger, but not by much, and when he spoke, she wrapped her arm around his waist.

"That's Belle. Annabelle, but she likes Belle."

"Good. We already have an Anna," I said.

Anna Sails shot me a look. "Already got one?"

"I didn't mean it like that," I said. "Although I got you last night."

"Jackson!"

I shrugged and moved in to shake hands with our new friends.

Friends. There's a word in short supply these days. Our last companions were killed when McQuinn and his jackwads decided that they wanted our shit. We turned the tables on them, and I ended it with a fiery explosion that nearly cost me my life.

Now we had at least ten new friends. Make that ten well-armed new friends.

"You two need some rest and first-aid," Claude said.

"How about the extra camper? It's not much but it's got room for two," Belle said.

"Anna, you can stay with Roz and Christy. We have a good-sized RV. I'll bunk with Creed."

"No need to kick you out. We survived out there. I don't think one more night together will kill us," Anna said.

I practically sighed with relief. Nothing against my buddy Joel Kelly, but Anna was a much sexier roommate.

Joel shrugged then winked at me as he turned his head in the direction of the camper.

"Over there. It's the white one on top of the big ass truck."

"As long as I don't have to sleep under the truck, I'm good," I said.

"Why the hell would you sleep under the truck? Musta had the sense knocked out of you by that shuffler. You gonna be alright?"

"Yeah. I'll tell you about it tomorrow, after I've slept for about eighteen hours."

Joel nodded. "Just take it easy. We'll rest up for the day and then move out late tomorrow night if the Z's don't gather." He turned away and checked his assault rifle, pulling back on the receiver and inspecting the gun's load. "Keep the noise down and stay inside. They've managed to survive by keeping indoors for a whole week. Damn good strategy."

"Better than running around shooting stuff?"

"Much better plan."

"How are you set for food?"

"They're mostly travelers and they've done well with supplies. We lost one the other night because he got drunk and went to find his dead wife. His RV turned out to have a shit load of food in it. Ain't gonna last forever, though."

"Did he find her?"

"What?" Joel asked.

"Did he find his wife?"

"Let's just say she found him."

"Sorry to hear that."

Claude turned up his nose. "He was a bit of an asshole, but he was still one of us."

I shrugged out of my backpack and put it on the ground.

"I can add to our supplies. Got a few dried goods, couple of cans of fruit for…"

"Jackson!"

I turned, and there was Christy. She and Roz stepped down from a big brown RV that looked like it cost more than I'd ever made in all my years in the United States Navy.

She broke from Roz's side, ran toward me, and crashed into my chest. Her arms wrapped around my waist.

"Good to see you, dude," I said and hugged her back.

Christy looked good. She had cleaned up and found a change of clothes. The haunted look had vanished from her eyes. What a difference a day makes when you aren't running for your life.

"Don't call me dude, dude." She smiled.

"I brought you something," I said and unsnapped my backpack.

I dug around and came up with a can of mandarin oranges.

Christy ignored me, her eyes on Frosty. The dog wagged her tail. She sniffed Christy's hands. The two stared at each other like they were long lost best friends.

I held the oranges up lamely, then put them back in the bag for later.

"What's her name?"

"I call her Frosty because she's cool under pressure. She doesn't bark at Z's and she's great in a fight. Saved Anna's life."

"She's so cute!" Christy said and hugged the dog. Frosty looked back at me, tongue lolling out, then licked Christy's face.

"Ah, dude. She's got shuffler all over her face," I groaned.

Frosty took to Christy quickly and followed her to their camper. I told her to remember to walk her and feed her only the best. Turkey and bacon were preferred, but she'd probably settle for anything canned.

11:45 hours approximate
Location: Trailer Park

OUR "CAMPER" WAS A METAL AND FIBERGLASS ENCLOSURE
mounted on top of a F250 truck. It had a bunk that rested over
the canopy. The interior was sparse, but it did boast an L-
shaped couch that doubled as a dining room table for three.
Two, if I stretched out. There was a tiny sink and even a toilet.
The little space had a feminine feel, but I could care less.

Belle made us take off our outer garments and inspected our
wounds. Anna had a nasty bruise running up her side that
would be purple and yellow by tomorrow. I had a few scrapes
here and there, but nothing that wouldn't heal in time. Belle
dressed our wounds. She was thorough, and I knew she was
looking for any hint of a bite.

"I'll bring some food by. There's a package of diaper wipes
you can clean up with, but you two get some rest. Are you okay
sleeping up there?" she asked us.

"No worries," Anna said.

Belle left us alone with a few words of warning.

"Stay inside as much as possible. If you see a group of
infected, keep out of sight. Make as little noise as possible. Do
that, and they leave us alone. If things get tight, you'll hear
bells in the distance. That's Joel running out to distract a
horde."

"Say what the fuck?" I asked.

Anna elbowed me in the side.

"What, I'm a foul-mouthed sailor."

"I've heard much worse living with that French firecracker,"
Belle said.

"Coulda gone my entire life without hearing that," Anna
said under her breath.

This time I elbowed her in the side.

"Claude used to do it, but Joel is younger and can handle
himself. There's a set of bells a few hundred feet away. Sound

them and the infected go in that direction. We run a tight ship here."

"Of course Joel does it. He's a super Marine. He eats Z's for breakfast and then spits them out."

"Right," Belle nodded. "He's very spry."

"That's our Joel. You should remind him that he's spry," I said. I tried to imagine the look on Joel's face and nearly cracked a smile.

"I will if I see him. He patrolled last night. We haven't seen him much since he arrived."

"I bet you sleep better," I said.

"Are you like Joel? Can you help protect us?"

"He's not like Joel. He's more like a fish out of water," Anna said.

I started to protest.

"But Jackson Creed has his moments," she said and met my eyes.

I looked away first.

"Get some sleep. If you hear bells, it's all hands. Remember that."

"So we hide if we hear bells or we go out there?" I asked, genuinely confused.

"Do what the situation calls for," Belle said and left, closing the door quietly behind her.

Anna and I made use of the baby wipes and managed to get most of the blood and grime off. I helped her and she helped me. She ran her hands over some of my wounds and I touched hers. We didn't talk much, just sat and got comfortable. I could get used to this domestic shit.

"They don't have a plan. They don't have a clue. No wonder Joel has been wired since he got here."

"This place is defensible, but if they get cornered it will get messy," Anna said.

"Messy isn't the word for it. This camp is a bunch of retired travelers. All they know about surviving the zombie fucking apocalypse is to stay inside and stay quiet."

"Wouldn't hurt you to be quiet," Anna said.

"What, and have you miss my stunning insights and wisdom?"

"Write them down. I need my beauty sleep."

"You're already beau-"

"Just save it, Creed. I'm who I am and you don't have to sweet talk me."

"I wasn't trying to sweet talk you. You're a damn fine looking woman, Anna," I said. Christ, what was I doing, checking out a car?

"I wish I could say the same for you."

"What's wrong with me?" I protested.

"You're kinda scruffy and when you take off your shirt you look like you're half werewolf."

"Where wolf? There wolf!" I said and pointed at the window.

"Shut up and eat."

"Yes ma'am." I grinned.

I chowed down on a couple of strips of jerky while she went at the granola. I ate most of a tin can filled with tuna, then Anna helped me finish it off. Crackers, a couple of fruit strips, and I was beginning to feel like we might actually be safe for a while.

After we ate, we crawled up into the bunk. There was an old red blanket and some kind of comforter. I tugged them over us and settled back.

I put my arm around Anna, half-expecting her to push me away, but she snuggled into me.

That's all I knew for a long time, because I fell asleep as she muttered about how we should rest, there'd be time for other stuff later.

I dreamed that I was on the run. The road stretched on forever. The sun hung low in the sky and it was the color of blood. I was alone and the road didn't end, so I ran and ran and ran, but always behind me were the sounds of moans and groans as the dead pursued.

22:30 hours approximate
Location: Trailer Park

I woke to voices, sat up, and bashed my head into the overhead canopy.

"Mother…"

"Dude. You should take it easy," Joel said.

Anna was dressed and sitting at the table with Joel and Belle. They had a map stretched out. Belle was marking spots while Joel studied it intently. A pair of candles held down two corners and provided flickering illumination. The windows had curtains, but they'd been taped down so no light could get out.

I glanced at my beat up watch and did some quick math in my pounding noggin. I'd slept for almost twelve hours and my body felt like I could sleep for twelve more.

I swung my legs over the side of the bed and shrugged into my pants and shirt. My head pounded from a nasty headache that a full bottle of Advil might make a dent in if I washed it back with a fifth of whiskey.

"Damn head hurts."

"I think you broke the camper, Creed. What part of keep it quiet didn't you understand during orientation?"

"The fuck, Joel. You guys come into our…shit." I looked sheepish. This wasn't my place. I was a guest at best.

"Just messing with ya. Now get your ass down here and help us strategize."

"Big word for a Marine."

"So's machine gun, ya navy puke."

"That's five words, Joel," Anna said helpfully.

"Ah, Christ. I thought you two were just being polite last night when you offered to take the camper together."

I kept my poker face but Anna blushed a furious shade of red. Joel looked between us and sat back on the couch.

"Just shut the fuck up," I said, staring at Joel, but there was no anger.

"Yeah. Okay. That your pick up line?"

Anna and Belle burst into laughter.

"I'm serious. What did he say, Anna? That he had a crush on you, might be the end of the world, all that shit?"

"Jackson Creed was a perfect gentlemen," she said.

Now who was keeping a poker face?

"Just tell me what we're doing so I can get back to sleep," I mumbled.

"Sleep, huh. Remember the rules, keep the noise down."

I rolled my eyes and joined them.

With the couch and table in use, there was little extra room, and I had to hunch over to peer at the map. I gave up on that uncomfortable position and got on my knees.

"We're here," Joel said and pointed at a red dot. The area around it was mostly rural but the highway was easy enough to follow, and it led straight to LA.

"Where's the nearest Starbucks?" I asked.

"This is where Bright Star may be located," Joel pointed at a blue dot that was just outside of the big city.

I found the legend and studied the scale. We were a long way from that dot. On any normal day we'd be able to drive up the coast in an hour. Now, with the freeways jammed, it could take days.

"So why not stay here? This is nice enough, and they have a plan. Just stay quiet." I said.

Every time I thought about the old folks here using that to avoid detection, I wanted to groan. There were just too many of the things out there, and if they became fixated on the survivors, these people would be dead in no time.

"Roz and Christy want to stay, but I'm going."

"Going where? To Los Angeles? How do you plan to get there? Fly?"

"I ain't going to LA. I'm going here." Joel pointed out another spot on the map.

"Camp Pendleton?"

"They train Marines, but they might let you in."

"The fuck would I want to go there for? You can have all the saluting and shooting stuff with your hard-on assault rifle. I'm sick of it," I said.

What I didn't say was that I thought the idea of staying here was pretty damn good, especially if I could talk Sails into staying. She might be a pain in the ass, but right now she was my pain in the ass. Or so I surmised after our one night together. I was under no delusions that I could keep her here if she didn't want to stay.

"I'm sick of it too, but I need to know what's going on out there. I need to know if my brothers are still there. I've been thinking about it, Creed. This shit, this running around shit, I'm done with it. I want to get back, get in a unit, and get in the damn war."

"So you're going to abandon us and drive, what, forty miles away to a Marine base? How do you plan to get there?"

"Side roads, off road, whatever I have to do. I'm taking this camper."

I looked at Belle but she just shrugged and went back to studying the map.

"It's a good plan," Anna chimed in.

"It is?" I asked.

"What do you want to do, Jackson, stay here and start a family? It's the end of the world. If I can live a few more weeks, fight for a few more days, it's worth it. I've got nothing else left," Anna said.

That stung, but I coughed to cover the lump that had formed in my throat.

Anna met my eyes and then she must have realized what she said because she looked surprised.

"Anna," I started.

"Come on, Belle. These two got stuff to sort out." Joel rose to his feet, hunched over to avoid the roof, and made for the back door.

"Joel. Can't you think of any other options? We're a team, man."

"We are, but you have to do what's right for you."

"That's your big speech?"

Joel shrugged, peeked out the back window and then

cracked the door open and hopped down. Belle followed, and then the door clicked softly shut.

22:45 hours approximate
Location: Trailer Park

"DON'T START WITH ME. I'M GOING," ANNA SAID.

"Fine. You don't have anything here, right?"

"Oh Jesus, Jackson. I didn't mean it like that. What're we doing, anyway? Last night was just a way to blow off stress, right?"

I dug out a bag of crackers and munched on a couple. Anna handed me a bottle of water which I drained in one go.

"Sure, Sails. Just blowing off steam. Couple of people just out for a zombie joyride jumped in the sack together."

"You better not fucking fall in love with me, Jackson. I'll kick your ass."

"Who's talking about love? I just like being around you, okay? And you can try to kick my ass anytime you want."

Anna covered her look with a drink of water.

"Idiot," she muttered.

"Maybe, but I'm the idiot that's here right now. Why don't you think about staying? Give it a day or two. After yesterday and today we deserve a break."

"I don't want to stay here. I'm going with Joel because it gets me closer to LA, and that gets me closer to Bright Star. Roz and Christy are staying, so you'll have someone to keep you company."

"I need to watch over Christy. I owe her after what happened to her brother." I tried to cover the disgust in my voice but it was there and it was bitter.

"I've told you a million times."

"You can tell me a million more times and it won't change the fact that he's dead and that fucker Lee is responsible."

"Enough about the kid. We're talking about us, right? If you're so bitter then I'll no longer be around to be a reminder."

"Fuck!"

"The hero would stay," she said. "You saved us all back at the hotel."

"Enough with the hero bullshit. I just did what was right and it sucked. How many of those guys did I kill? Joel probably shoots a guy and doesn't think twice. That's not me."

"It was us or them. I'm glad it wasn't us," she said.

I met Anna's eyes and pondered what kind of a future she and I might have. The way the world was now, it wouldn't be a good one, but at least we'd be able to watch over one another. Sails wasn't what I'd expected. Back when she was running with Lee, she'd been a hardass that punched my Marine buddy and then pulled a gun on him. Even I wasn't that fucking stupid.

She didn't take shit and I liked that. She was tough and I liked that as well. I'd never planned far enough into the future to think about settling down with someone. Never thought twice about what I'd do beyond the next port of call or the next bar hop.

But here I was.

"Just tell me what you think we're doing and I'll tell you if you're right," she said.

"Don't put that shit on me. It takes two to make a couple. Math. I may be a dumb squid but I can count."

"See, Jackson, that's where we differ. I don't see us as anything like a couple. We're just here to watch out for each other," she said.

"And that's it?"

"You don't know me, Jackson." She looked down. "You don't know what I saw or what I did. In the end it didn't matter, because they were taken from me. Everyone. First my husband when he ran off last year. Then my kids when they were killed by those things."

I reached across the table and took her hand in mine. Anna looked down and her hair covered her face. I knew she was fighting tears and I didn't know the first thing to say. She gripped my hand for a few seconds, shook her head, and looked up at me.

"It's okay. We can talk in the morning. Okay?"

"Yeah, sure, but I'm sleeping by the door in case you try to pull a disappearing act."

"Clingy doesn't suit you."

"Running away doesn't suit you."

"Just shut the hell up, Jackson. I've done enough talking today."

So I shut up.

We ate in silence for a few minutes. I grabbed a magazine off a pile and saw the date was from a few years ago. After flipping through a few pages I realized it was all about golf, something I was not at all interested in, but it was better than sitting around glaring at each other.

"I'm sorry," Anna said.

"Me too."

"What do you have to be sorry for? I'm the one who's being stupid."

"Forget it, you don't have to apologize."

"Yeah, Jackson. I do need to apologize for treating you like shit. For treating you like you don't matter," she said. "You do matter, Jackson."

After a second I shut my mouth. "You better not fucking fall in love with me, Sails."

Anna didn't say anything for a few seconds, then she laughed, and just like that, the tension was gone.

"Come on, let's just get some rest," she said.

Anna stood up and stretched. She checked the door and turned the lock.

"Z's can't open doors."

"Yeah, but others can," she said.

Anna took my hand and led me to our bunk.

LAND OF THE FREE

11:30 hours approximate
Location: Trailer Park

We didn't stay for just one day. We stayed for a few.

I dug out one of the shirts Anna had found at the apartment and went to town with some duct tape, covering my arms. I applied it liberally but left space for my elbow so I could bend my arm without difficulty.

"Very fashionable," Anna observed.

She sat on the side of the bed dressed only in panties and bra, looking hot as hell. Sadly, she slid into more clothing. I watched her dress and she watched me back. We didn't speak but I was getting used to that. She had her demons and there wasn't a lot I could do about it except to be there for her. Sounds useless, but it was all she wanted. She told me a little bit about PTSD while we lay together the night before and it sounded horrible. Then it dawned on me that we were probably all suffering from the same thing. She asked me to be patient with her and I promised that I would.

"Look, Anna," I said. I took her hand in mine and just held it for a minute. "I'm not under any delusions here. I know we're a mess, but we're here for each other, right?"

"Yeah. We're here for each other. Fucking hell, Creed. If you go out there and try to collect flowers for me I'm going to be really disappointed," she said.

"You don't have to be a hardass all the time."

"I'm not a hardass. I'm just me."

"Fine. I'll go find some nice weeds for you."

Anna kicked at me with one slim foot but I sidestepped it and tugged her off the bed and into an embrace. I could get used to this. Anna might be a time bomb. She might be a hardass. But there was a lot to like about her.

I wondered how hard the new world was planning to work against us.

12:05 hours approximate
Location: Trailer Park

THE FOLKS THAT MADE UP THE LITTLE CAMP CAME FROM VARIED backgrounds. Most were senior citizens. We'd met a dozen the first night. By the next day a third of them had drifted away. Safety in numbers was Claude's credo, but some argued that they were better on the move. Campers left at night, and besides the puttering of motors, we didn't hear another sound out of them as they faded up the road.

Claude was a natural-born leader and wasn't shy about getting the people to work together. He'd organize groups of three or four and have them outside for a few minutes, gathering supplies from abandoned RV's, or collecting water.

Joel and I ignored the politics and worked during the day to go out on patrol, shore up the fence, and put a better lock on the gate. They'd used a piece of twelve gauge wire to loop a couple of links together, but I found a chain that might have been used to hold the gate closed in the past. Someone had cut it cleanly. I dug out a couple of pairs of pliers and worked at the links until I had a half-ass lock. It performed by someone sticking a screwdriver into a pair of links and using the smaller wire to keep the length of metal in place. It wouldn't keep out a determined intruder, but it would keep a Z out.

The gate was made of chain link and was eight feet tall. Z's occasionally gathered, so we taunted and bribed them with our bodies until they followed us near the gate. Then Joel, Anna, Roz, and I went out and killed them.

Roz was in good spirits and stuck to Christy like they were sisters.

"How's the leg, Jackson?" Roz asked.

"Ankle. Still hurts but I've had some good care." I lifted my pant leg and showed off a bandage that wrapped around my calf and down into my boot.

"Good care, huh? You and Anna seem to be pretty friendly."

"Yeah," I agreed. "Friendly."

"You two make a good couple. You're kind of a mess and she's kind of a badass."

"That's what I like about her." I smiled.

I didn't ask about her and Joel. This wasn't high school and, frankly, it was none of my damn business.

Christy spent a few minutes running Frosty ragged before ducking back into the RV with the wet dog in tow. Frosty followed, tail wagging. True to the camp's rules, they stayed out of sight as much as possible.

The weather sucked. Rain fell in a light mist that got heavier as the day wore on. Joel and I rigged up some tarps over a pair of RV's to capture the water. Claude pointed me toward some old PVC tubing. I ran it into Joel's temporary home.

Christy was interested in what I was doing, so I showed her how to make a basic water filter.

"Rain water's clean, but if you ever need to drink water and you don't know if it's safe, just make a filter. The best way is if you have charcoal," I told her.

We requisitioned an empty two-liter bottle. I cut the bottom off and then cut some fabric into strips. Christy and I went out near the pond and dug down until we found a little bit of sand. She gathered a few handfuls while I loaded up on pebbles.

"We're going to make clean water with dirt?" she asked.

Christy wore a long red dress with black tights. She had a light windbreaker on. Her hair was drenched in minutes.

"Yep. You can go back if you're cold," I said.

"I'm fine. I want to learn this."

She and I dug out enough sand and little rocks to complete my project. The rain picked up, so we hightailed it back to the camper with our treasures.

Back in the big RV, we laid our collection in neat little piles on the counter. Belle 'tsked' at the mess, but I promised her that Christy would clean up after we were done. Christy shot me daggers, but I stuck my tongue out and she smiled back.

Belle, Anna, Roz, and Joel had all escaped the rain and were sitting inside the RV. They laughed as they played high-stakes poker for millions of dollars. Christy glanced at the game, but was more interested in what we were doing.

We filled the filter with five layers: pebbles, sand, crushed charcoal from a fire, sand, and more pebbles. The little strips of old bedding we'd converted into strips separated each layer.

"Why all the sand?" Christy asked.

"The little rocks and sand filter out dirt and particles. The charcoal gets any chemicals out. By the time it passes through, the water is safe to drink."

I used more strips of cloth to attach one end of the filter to the tarps, then I dragged the other end of the PVC tube into the RV. I untied the knotted end and watched as the first few drops fell out of the tube and into the sink.

"Get a cup."

Christy grabbed a coffee mug off the counter and held it out.

I tasted the next few drops, smacked my lips together, and then motioned for Christy to try. She filled her mug halfway to the top and then took a sip.

"Tastes weird, like it's got wood in it or something."

"Probably the charcoal. If you want to filter rainwater, all you really have to use is a coffee filter. Duh," I said.

"Jackson, you jerk." Christy laughed.

"And it falls from the sky. Just stand outside with your mouth open. If you stand there long enough, you'll get a full belly of water. Plus, you'd look like a crazy girl. The Z's might just leave you alone."

Christy giggled as I tossed my head back and opened my mouth wide and stuck out my tongue.

"Is that what he did to impress you?" Roz asked Anna.

"Something like that. The tongue part is good," she said, then her face went scarlet.

Roz sat back hard in her chair and laughed.

I ignored them.

"Mad person disease, that's what Z's call it when they don't want to eat someone," I said.

"What makes the person mad?" Christy asked.

"When they can't build a good filter, I guess."

"I won't get the disease, then."

"Just remember this filter in an emergency."

"I will. I'll write it down. I write down all the survival stuff I learn."

"Learn how to shoot straight yet?"

"Joel showed me but I haven't actually fired a gun since the hospital," she said.

"Anna's an ace shot. You should ask her to teach you."

Christy glanced up at Anna and then looked away quickly.

"Joel's fine," she said under her breath.

After the last few days I'd come around on Anna, but my change of heart hadn't spread.

"Just something to think about," I said lamely.

"Do you like my dress? Belle said it was her daughter's. It's a little big but the color's pretty, isn't it?"

"Of course it looks good on you, dude. I'll have to start calling you princess."

We joked around for a few minutes and then talked about video games while the poker match went on. After Joel was in the hole for a half a billion dollars he called it a game and asked if I'd make a quick perimeter run with him.

Roz stood as he made for the door and said something close to his ear. Joel shot her a quick smile and whispered something back. I looked at Joel but his face didn't betray anything. Whatever those two were up to wasn't my business.

It was time to get to work.

13:30 hours approximate
Location: Not-sure-where, CA

WE SET OUT ON PATROL, LEAVING THE CONFINES OF THE LITTLE trailer park. We ranged a mile out and then circled around, avoiding the highway and its dangers. We found a small town, much like Clairemont, but without map or GPS we couldn't determine the name.

A pack of Z's wandered the streets. We perched behind a bunch of shrubs and waited them out. Neither of us moved until the group was well away from us, then we rose and hustled to a shattered storefront. The shelves were bare of anything useful, so we exited through the back door.

We passed a pair of bodies. Both had been placed on the ground with the back of their heads caved in. A crow bar lay next to them, the curved end covered in blood and matted hair. It was possible that the pair had been Z's, but I suspected they'd instead been shop owners and had put up a fight when looters arrived.

Joel considered the bodies but didn't say a word.

"What's up with your tactical gear?" I asked.

"I added plates after our last encounter. Getting shot at wasn't my idea of a good time."

"Plates?"

"Ceramic. They're light, but break up if a round hits them."

"Where in the hell did you find plates?"

"Did some digging around in the supplies in the camp. They have a communal drop off for goods. Turns out some-one's kid was in the military and saw action. These were packed away in a box. They aren't a perfect fit but I made them work."

"What about me, Joel? Shouldn't I wear something like that?" I asked.

"Sure, man. If you can find them."

"Well, shit. What's the alternative?" Joel had worn his IMTV tactical gear since we'd been on the USS McClusky. I'd worn one messy bunch of clothes after another.

"Don't get shot." Joel winked at me.

We moved to another storefront and found it empty save for bodies. In this case it was easy to make out the features of the dead. They'd been Z's, but now they were just moldering corpses.

Another horde wandered in our direction so we took care to stay hidden. A shot rang out from somewhere and one of the Z's dropped. Joel and I ducked behind a countertop and watched.

The men came into the streets from the north. They were dressed in leather and carried bottles of alcohol. They bore automatic weapons and seemed to take great pleasure in gunning down the horde.

One of the men stepped out of a building and I knew him right away. It was McQuinn.

"Son of a bitch," I whispered to Joel.

He nodded but didn't do anything stupid. If I had his gun I probably would have picked McQuinn off—or at least tried to. I was under no delusions that I could even hit the building, let alone a single figure.

"I hope he doesn't find the camp. Dammit. We should warn our new friends," Joel said.

"They aren't exactly hidden. If McQuinn's men do any further exploring, they're likely to find the camp."

Joel chewed on that for a minute and then moved. He kept low, peeked out of the back, and gestured. I followed him across a street and we slipped into the woods.

14:45 hours approximate

Location: Trailer Park

ARGUING WITH CLAUDE WAS USELESS. WE TRIED TO IMPRESS ON him the fact that McQuinn was a threat.

"But what can we do except to hide? If we leave they may hear the noise of the campers," he said. I'd noticed that when Claude spoke in a rush, his speech took on a thicker accent.

"You got no choice, man," I said.

"We do have a choice. Besides, we are reasonable people. Maybe they will be reasonable with us."

"That shit didn't work out too well for us," Joel said.

Claude shrugged and left us. He moved back to his RV and shut the door quietly behind him.

"We should pack it in."

"Yeah. I'm down with that. Been thinking about that abandoned RV back there. No one investigated because they thought there was a Z inside." Joel pointed toward the back of the camp. The vehicle would have looked old a decade ago.

"What about it?"

"Could be it's full of food. If we don't check it out before we go, we might regret it later."

"Ah hell, Joel. I hate it when you make sense."

"So you're going to go with me?"

"Just because I don't want to get shot at anymore doesn't mean I want to be a fucking Marine with you and your pals at Pendleton," I said.

"Yeah, but think how great it would be, man. Going from squid to badass."

"Because that's what I want out of life," I said sarcastically.

"Yer goddamn right," Joel said. He clapped me on the shoulder and moved out.

I stood in the drizzling rain for all of a half-minute before sighing loudly and following. Quick check, get any goods, and then haul ass out of here. I was game.

14:55 hours approximate
Location: Trailer Park

WE SLIPPED OUT OF THE RV AND DID A QUICK PERIMETER SWEEP. A pair of Z's were wandering by. When they got wind of us, they lurched toward the chain link fence.

"Come on. They'll leave in a few minutes if we pull a disappearing act. Damn things aren't too bright," Joel said.

We ducked behind the truck/camper that Anna and I were calling home and waited them out.

"So you and Roz, huh?"

"None of your damn business."

We crouched in silence for a minute.

"So you and Anna, huh?" Joel asked. I wondered when he'd get around to giving me shit.

"None of your damn business."

"Hey man, I'm glad you made it back, but we've complicated things. Women," Joel said.

"It's not that complicated to me. I like Anna and she seems to like me."

"Yeah, but it makes us weak as a unit. We're likely to do stupid shit if they get in trouble."

"Joel. If you're out with a bunch of Marines, doing Marine shit, do you ignore your buddy if he gets in trouble? What if he's hit? Do you abandon him?"

Joel snuck a look at the Z's.

"That's not the same," he said.

"Not the same because your buddy doesn't have tits?"

"That's different. We work as a unit."

"And we don't?"

Joel chewed on his gum.

"They ain't leaving," Joel said and nodded toward the pair of Z's.

I gave up on trying to talk sense into him.

"We could flank them and take them from behind," I said.

"You'd like taking a couple of Z's from behind. That way you don't have to smell their rot breath."

"That's not what your mom said last week,"

"Low blow, brother. I ain't talked to my mom in a long while," Joel said.

"Ah shit, man. I'm sorry. I was just fucking around."

"I know. It's cool. We're tight, right?"

"Tight as a nut on a six-fifty-five valve."

"You'd like that, wouldn't you? Being tight on my nut."

I snorted out a half laugh.

"We could go out and take them, but I'd rather not risk it. For all we know, the woods could be filled with Z's. Last night I went out there and heard a lot of movement. Besides, McQuinn is nearby. Best we be gettin' on."

We moved, low, toward a pair of abandoned RV's on the outskirts of the camp. They were in the corner of the fenced-in camp.

"You haven't checked these out yet?"

"Nah. Claude usually leads a group around but these were ignored because there're too far back. Plus, Claude thought he heard something in the older one and worried it was occupied."

"Occupied by something with a pulse?"

Joel shrugged and sprinted toward one of them. The gravel covered road was hard under my feet, and even though my leg was feeling like I could put pressure on it for a change, the running hurt. I sucked it up and followed.

"Where'd that come from?" I pointed at an ambulance.

"They found it abandoned a half-mile from here and drove it back to the camp."

"Claude did?"

"Not sure."

"Anything else in the truck? Damn, man. That should be filled with medical stuff."

"It was already cleaned out when they found it."

"Not even a bottle of Percocet?"

Joel snorted.

To our right sat our goal. The pair of vehicles were older and hauled by trucks. I checked the first vehicle by peering into the windows; there didn't seem to be anyone inside. I tried the door but it was locked. I could break the window with the wrench, but it seemed a shame to go around bashing in a perfectly good truck. If we found the keys inside we might be able to make use of it.

The RV itself looked like it had been built in the seventies. It was brown with one large white stripe running down the center of the body. Dirt clung to the sides, doing its best to cover up all the dings and dents.

Joel moved next to the RV's door and rapped lightly.

I moved to the other side of the door and waited for his lead.

He tried the door handle and found that it was locked. I pressed the side of my head to the RV and listened. After a half-minute I hadn't heard anything moving, so I shook my head at Joel.

"Guess we do it the hard way," Joel said.

He put his AR-15 next to the door and then pulled his knife. The blade was dented in a few places, but I'd seen him use the knife on a number of doors and it always managed to hold up to the task.

"Breaking and entering. Just like old times," I said.

Joel jammed the blade into the doorframe and tapped it a few times then ripped it to the side. The door lock popped and it was go time. I moved back to cover Joel while he grabbed his rifle and poked it into the darkness.

"Yo," he called through the doorway.

We waited for the count of fifteen.

Joel switched on his tactical light and moved up the first step. I followed his lead.

The smell was bad. The tiny space reeked of refuse and rot, but there was something worse hiding in the stench. I knew that smell all too well. A body didn't take well to being half-devoured and then left lying around. The problem with Z's was that they were still ambulatory, even as the damn things continued to rot and degenerate.

The interior looked like a tornado had hit. Cups, silverware, and plates were scattered over the floor along with several bags of trash. A suitcase had been ripped open so hard the top hung on by threads. Blood was splattered on the walls and floor.

Joel poked around and found a body lying next to the bed. He toed it and the hand twitched. The Z was a mess. Most of her face was gone and one of her arms was bent under her body. From the weird angle I guessed it had been practically ripped out of the socket. Her neck had been partially severed, and that left a lot of blood, most of which had soaked into blankets scattered next to her. A large kitchen knife lay next to her body.

"Jesus," Joel whispered.

"How'd that happen?"

"She tried to kill herself. Look at the wound."

"I've seen enough. Let's just do her," I said.

Something thumped.

My blood ran cold as I tried to take in the entire interior. Where had the noise come from?

Joel flashed his tactical light around the space. I lifted the wrench, ready to bash anything that leaped out at us.

Joel motioned toward the bathroom door. It was closed but it bucked as it was hit again.

"Fuck. Shoot first, man," I whispered.

Joel put his finger to his lip.

He moved to one side and motioned toward my wrench. I moved to the other side of the door and lifted it as high as my head. Any higher and it would hit the ceiling. Joel shone his light at the floor. I grimaced because a puddle of blood had seeped out from under the closed door.

Joel reached for the door and triggered the lock.

The door swung open on silent hinges. Joel moved back, gun aimed at the interior.

I didn't even get a chance to swing.

The Z was small, smaller even than Christy. It jumped off of a partially devoured body and hit the kitchen counter. I swung wildly because the monstrosity had scared the f'ing shit out of me.

I caught its leg as it tried to scurry toward the front of the RV, but it ripped free with astonishing strength.

Joel followed it, his light playing over the small body.

"Shoot that thing," I said.

"Too noisy. And look how small it is." He slung he gun around his shoulder and tugged out his big blade again.

"Shuffler," I said.

"Can't be."

Joel was wrong.

Had to be a kid, but that wasn't what horrified me. The little form was a shuffler and it was fast. Too fast.

With a howl it leap-frogged from behind the passenger seat, landing on me in two hops. I swung up but he hit me low. The little bastard was covered in gore and his hair was matted against his head with blood.

I tried to step back and my weakened ankle picked that moment to give. I fell, rapping my elbow against the linoleum floor, sending a wave of pain up my arm. Joel moved in and slashed at the little shuffler, but it was too fast. The kid hit a wall like he was some kind of ninja and then was on the floor behind my Marine buddy.

I rolled to the side and tried to heave myself up. Something touched my arm and I recoiled in horror. The corpse in the bathroom was still moving. A goddamn Z. The kid had been eating a Z! I wanted to scream in horror but I didn't get the chance.

I'd had the bad fortune to land on my right arm, so I shifted the wrench to my left. I was strapped with the Colt .45, but in the tiny space I was afraid I'd miss and maybe hit Joel.

The shuffler lived up to its name by shooting forward on all fours. Joel abandoned swinging with the knife and kicked the kid. He didn't get his whole boot into it, but the shuffler was smashed against the wall. He rolled over and stared at us from a few feet away, and his head turned quizzically from side to side.

His mouth was a horror of broken teeth and torn lips. His nose had been smashed at some point and was a purple knob.

But that wasn't the worst of it. As the little fucker prepared to leap again, his mouth opened up and a hiss came out.

"Diiieeee."

My wrench caught him across the shoulder as he jumped. The little form hit the wall again and collapsed against the floor. Joel didn't wait. He moved on the shuffler and crouched down to lock his knee over the kid's throat.

The shuffler thrashed under him but Joel had at least a hundred and twenty pounds on the kid.

"Did that fucking thing talk?" I asked in shock.

"I don't know," Joel said and put his knife next to the boy's temple.

The shuffler settled down and glared at us.

His eyes weren't the milky white we'd come to expect. They were probably brown at one time, but now they were so bloodshot they looked like they were covered with little red spider webs. But there was something else back there, some hint of color that was unnatural.

"Joel. Look at his eyes."

"What?" Joel looked up at me.

"His eyes. Am I seeing things?"

Joel stared hard then he jolted upright.

"The fuck?"

"Green? I swear I've seen the same glow in other shufflers, but I let it go as a trick of my imagination."

"What are you?" Joel asked.

The shuffler gritted his teeth together and bubbled blood. His chest rose and fell.

"He's breathing."

"This shit isn't real. Every one of the damn Z's we've seen are animated corpses. This thing is something else. We should bag him."

"With what?" I asked.

The bed had the pillow and blanket but both were splattered with blood that had dried into obscene patterns.

"Maybe we can wrap him in something," Joel said.

"Yeah, we'll put a leash around his neck and stick him in a

box. On weekends you get to walk him." I was done with this thing. He'd already knocked me on my ass once. I was ready to put him down.

The kid had been still for a few seconds, but launched a surprise attack. His hands whipped up and struck at Joel, but they hit the tactical armor and I doubted Joel even felt it. Then the little shuffler grabbed Joel's leg and used his body as a lever to twist Joel to the side.

The kid fought like a demon and managed to get loose. I reached for him and caught his pant leg but he kicked free and was out the door before I could draw my gun.

Joel and I rushed to the entrance. He skipped the stairs, but I had to hobble down them like an old man. The shuffler leapt across the ground like a frog until he reached the little pond. He splashed into the center, like he was giving us a big "Fuck You," and then leaned his head back and howled.

The sound rolled across the camp. Joel raised his rifle and rushed toward the shuffler. I couldn't run so I dragged my handgun out, ready to shoot the little bastard.

"Don't shoot! That's the water supply!" Joel yelled back at me.

The Shuffler went quiet for a few seconds and then howled again.

Faces appeared in windows and doors opened. The shuffler splashed around up to his waist and then howled a third time.

Anna and Roz ran toward our location. Anna stopped long enough to pull her gun, then she was on the move again.

"No, Anna!" I called out.

Anna shook her head and pointed toward the back of the camp.

I looked toward the rear fence surrounding the park and gasped in horror.

The dead had arrived and they weren't alone.

15:15 hours approximate

Location: Trailer Park

AMONG THE HORDE THAT POURED OUT OF THE FOREST WERE shufflers. A lot of shufflers. I'd never seen so many in one place. Back in San Diego, Joel and I had run into a small group of Z's with a pair of the faster creatures almost herding the group along. Of course they weren't actually directing; that would have been ridiculous. These were mindless creatures.

Ten, twenty, thirty – they kept appearing, and the only thing keeping them from us was a flimsy chain link fence.

Claude poked his head out of his RV. He looked from us to the shuffler and made a cutting motion with his hand next to his throat. He stepped out, a pistol in his hand, but then stopped and stared in horror at the Z's.

"What have you done?" He was ashen.

Joel ran toward Claude. It was only a hundred feet but I wasn't as fast. A few days of rest had done me good, but I was still in a lot of pain.

Anna stalked toward the water.

The shuffler lifted his head to howl again, but Anna didn't wait around for him to unleash another one. She lifted her .357, aimed, and blew a hole through the kid's chest.

The shuffler was blown off his feet and thrown a couple of meters across the pond. He splashed down into the water and floated on its surface before sinking. A few seconds later he floundered out of the water and hopped to the shore. He flopped over in a pool of blood. His hands clutched at the ground as he tried to drag himself toward his brethren at the fence.

Anna moved in on him.

He tried to get out another howl but Anna finished him with a shot that drove his forehead into the ground and left a mess of blood and brains. I'd been moving on the kid's location and maybe I was seeing things. Maybe it was just grass, but I swear I saw green among the muck left by Anna's bullet.

"That's our drinking water!" Claude yelled.

I spun from the sight of the kid and clambered toward him

and Joel. Anna seemed to be more circumspect and simply stared at the mass of gathering Z's.

"Anna, come on!" I called to her but she didn't seem to hear me.

Joel and Claude were well into a heated argument. Jesus, we didn't have time for this shit.

"This place is blown. Get your people together and get ready to move out!" Joel ordered.

"What have you done?" He stared in shock at us.

"It wasn't us, it was that damn kid. He went insane when we opened the last RV."

"Our home, our water – it's all gone now."

Anna finally moved to join us, checking her handgun as she walked. She spun the cylinder open, removed a couple of spent shells, and reloaded. She did it like a pro, hands moving but her eyes on us. She slapped the cylinder into place and reholstered.

"This is a fucking mess," she said.

"Hey, man," I continued to argue with Claude, "It was that kid. He's some kind of weird and smart fucking Z. He called them here."

Anna stared at me like I was insane.

"It's true. Damn thing went crazy, busted loose, and then ran into the water and started howling," Joel said.

"That's why I took out the threat," Anna said, but her tone left no doubt that we were idiots for letting the shuffler get away. "Smart or not, he was just going to bring more of them with all that noise."

"He called them here. The shuffler called them," I said, not really believing it. What Anna said had to be true. It was just the noise. Z's that could call other Z's to them? It was horrifying.

"Never heard one of those things make a noise other than moans or groans," Joel observed.

"There might have been an army of Z's out there but they were shamblers. They weren't banding together like that until the little shit called them," I told Joel.

"That is unfuckingthinkable." Joel shook his head.

"Fools. I told you to leave things alone," Claude said and stalked away.

Joel unslung his AR and dropped to one knee. He completed a quick inspection, lifted the rifle to his shoulder, and switched on his holographic site. The gun bucked against his shoulder.

The first shuffler took a shot to the head and flopped back, lifeless, into the horde. Joel fired again but a second shuffler moved too quickly and the bullet ended up catching a Z in the groin. The milky-white-eyed fuck didn't even feel it; he just staggered back and then went at the fence again.

"Creed, get them organized and get them out of here. Everyone in his or her RV and ready to move as quickly as possible."

Joel fired again and took a Z in the head. The guy had been thrashing at the fence, trying to get his hands through. The moans grew louder.

Claude had gathered the other travelers together and began issuing instructions punctuated with hand gestures.

"Everyone get ready to move. There's too many for us," I said.

"I have a solution," Claude said.

He gave me a look that was pure hatred and then stomped away with Belle in tow. She glanced back at me but I couldn't read her look. Was it pity? Sadness? Understanding?

How the hell was I going to get through to this guy? Someone would have opened the RV at some point and let the shuffler out. Too damn late to go back in time and just shoot the kid while he was stuck in the bathroom.

"We should fight," one of the men said. He was dressed in shorts, a tropical shirt, and white tennis shoes. He looked like he was going to pick up a racket and find a court to play on.

Even if we set up a line of fire and everyone had automatic weapons, there was no way we could take them all out, and the noise would continue to draw others.

Joel's gun rang out a few more times and that did not help matters. If anything, it only helped to reinforce the idea for these folks that they might have a chance here.

"Joel, that might draw more here," I said.

"I'm going after the shufflers."

"Edgar, let's pack up," an older woman said. "We're too old for this."

"I know a thing or two about fighting," he said.

"You did when you were nineteen. Now come away," she said and tugged at his hand. Her eyes pleaded with him.

He nodded at her and the two left the group. The others watched them walk away and that seemed to stir them to action, because they moved toward their RV's.

Claude came back from his RV and he had an actual machine gun in hand. It was straight out of an old war movie. I'd seen a "Tommy Gun" before, but never up close. Over his shoulder hung a large green bag. He reached inside and took out a long magazine that resembled a stick instead of the curved mag's I'd grown used to seeing.

Claude moved past Joel, toward the water.

"Claude, you can't get them all," Joel called.

Claude ignored Joel. He stopped when he was twenty-five feet from the fence and put the stock against his shoulder.

The gun was ripped up to the right as Claude unleashed a full magazine on the Z's. Some were hit, but he mostly ended up shooting a whole lot of air. He slipped the magazine out, put it in a back pocket, and slapped another one home.

The Z's were undaunted and more of them arrived. They were now a real threat to the fence. It buckled and nearly caved in as they pressed forward.

We didn't have long.

"Anna, you with me? I'm taking the camper and leading this parade out of here."

"Yeah, let's go," she said.

Joel gave up on shooting them and went to join Roz and Christy. They conferred for a few seconds.

"Joel?" I pointed at the truck we'd been occupying.

He gave me a thumbs up.

Others came out to join Claude. The shooting rang out all around us, and for a split-second I wondered if they had the right idea. If we put enough fire on the group of Z's they all be cut down in minutes.

I realized the futility when others poured out of the woods all around us. They came in their disgusting masses, filthy, shambling, clothing hanging in shreds. Missing some body parts and dragging some others. There were fifty, then seventy-five. I gave up on counting and instead grabbed Anna's hand.

"Leg good?" She looked up at me.

"Hurts like a bitch but I'm managing."

"I told you to take it easy."

"Ain't nothing easy about surviving the zombie fucking apocalypse," I replied.

Anna snorted but she kept her eyes on the men that were trying to stop a tidal wave with nets. Gunfire rang out over and over again, but the Z's kept on coming.

"I got the fence!" Joel yelled and ran toward the gate.

"Meet you there," I said as we reached the truck.

Then a sound reached me and my blood went cold.

"Oh no," Anna said.

A huge truck rumbled up to the gate and stopped. Around it came a flood of cars and motorcycles. Claude's gun continued to fire but he didn't once look back. I could only guess it was due to the noisy gun and not because he no longer gave a damn.

HOME OF THE BRAVE

16:05 hours approximate
Location: Trailer Park

We'd tried to warn Claude. Hell, we were at fault ourselves. Instead of just leaving, we'd stuck around and pissed away any head start we might have had on McQuinn and his men. For all we knew, they'd been stalking the camp for a while. Had they seen Joel and me earlier in the day?

"Joel!" I yelled. "Regroup, now!"

Joel didn't need a second warning. He was already running back toward us.

One of the guys took his helmet off and stared. I got a glimpse of a bald head, a thick mustache, and a dark goatee. Ah hell. It was McQuinn, and I had no doubt that he'd recognize us if he got a clear look.

If these guys were smart they'd see the threat of the Z's and just piss off.

I ducked around the truck with Anna, but McQuinn spotted us and pointed.

Another pair of vehicles roared up on our location and stopped near the gate. We were completely blocked in.

Claude stopped shooting and turned to watch the new

arrivals. He smiled and waved and started to walk toward the men.

"Mon Dieu!" he called out. "Just in time."

He moved to the gate.

McQuinn's men hopped out of their rides and formed a line near their leader.

McQuinn gestured as he directed his men. They weren't interested in the Z's at all and pointed at the RV's. Why else would these guys be here if not for our supplies? We'd seen just how much they cared.

"No need to come any closer, old man. Just clear out of here. We'll take all of those lovely vehicles and be on our way. Before you ask, this isn't up for discussion."

"You cannot take our homes! Are you animals?" Claude called back.

"McQuinn, we ain't got time for this shit," one of his men said loudly enough for us to hear.

Frank must have agreed, because he drew his gun and shot Claude through the chest.

The old man fell back, a look of shock on his face. Belle rushed to his side with a scream.

Joel reached us and ducked as the men that had been shooting at Z's turned to take in this new opponent.

"Just leave and you live," McQuinn yelled. "Walk away and don't look back. Like I said, this ain't up for discussion."

I'd be exposed, but I didn't care. I laid the Mossberg on the truck's hood, snatched out my Colt, stood, aimed, and fired at McQuinn. Fuck this guy.

My first shot went wide, but my second blast got his attention as it whizzed right next to his head. McQuinn dropped, and that's when the shit really hit the fan.

16:10 hours approximate
Location: Trailer Park

Say one thing for McQuinn. His timing always sucked.

If we'd been left alone we could have escaped this new hell. We'd have piled into RV's, campers, trucks, or anything else with wheels and left the camp. Now we were blocked in. To the east lay the highway that we'd been stuck on for a day. To the west lay the unknown, so it made sense to head in that direction. The problem was the treeline and how to get through it. Our camper, even at full speed, would become a pile of warped metal if we challenged the growths.

So that left one direction out, and that was through McQuinn.

I'd like to say that there weren't many of them and we could just shoot our way out, but as the seconds ticked by we were forced to observe the arrival of more and more trucks. Men and women with guns jumped out and formed up with something approaching military precision. They were the same motley assortment we'd seen before we had to blow the hotel location, and they were all well-armed.

Joel and I dove behind the truck. Anna dug out a handful of shells and did a quick count. Joel did the same. He was dressed in his IMTV tactical armor and wore an assortment of magazines, but even if he had a completely covered position, there was no way he could take out a quarter of this army.

I didn't have to do much of a count. I knew how many rounds I had in the big Mossberg. I had even fewer for my Colt M45A1, but at least the mag was full and I had one in the breach.

Roz was caught out in the open with Christy. They ran, Roz dragging Belle by the arm, and hid behind the RV that Claude had occupied. Belle screamed and tried to dash back to her to her husband but Roz wasn't having that and hauled her back.

"Can we bullshit our way out of this one?" I asked Joel.

"After you just tried to kill the man? I don't fucking think so."

"Good point," I said and rolled to my right.

I didn't have a good angle but I fired anyway and blew a

windshield out. Maybe we could spook McQuinn's half-ass force into leaving us be, but it would take a lot of firepower.

"I wish Donny and Markus were still here. Those guys might have been dicks but they had a lot of experience," Joel said.

"And weapons," Anna finished.

"What's the plan?" I asked after the two quieted down.

I popped my head up and got a quick look before ducking again.

"Six coming in. They're at the gate. They've stopped to open it."

Behind us, the dead howled for our blood and pushed on the fence. Several shufflers moved through the horde and tested the fence by jumping at it, but even they couldn't clear the top.

"They will move fast. They aren't dumb and know the Z's are a threat, so we won't have much time. We can spook them, make ourselves seem bigger than we are," Joel said

"It's like you can read my mind," I muttered.

"There's only one way out I can see and it's currently blocked," Anna chimed in.

She had her big .357 in one hand and took a peek around the side of the camper.

"I've never thought I'd wish for the Z's to break through a barricade," I said.

"Huh?" Joel said.

"If the Z's broke through, it would keep the guys busy. We could probably make a run for a section of fence next to the gate."

Joel chewed on his cheek while he mulled something over.

"That's a solid plan," Joel said and looked back the Z's.

There had to be seventy of them now, and at least a dozen of them were shufflers.

"I didn't come up with any plan, Joel. What the actual fuck are you talking about?"

"The Z's. That's the answer. We just need to get them on this side of the fence."

Anna grinned at me for some reason.

"No, man. I told you. Enough of this hero bullshit. I'm not cut out for it. Besides, as soon as they see me, they'll know who we are and nothing will stop McQuinn. Guy's got it in for us. Let's take our chance on hopping in an RV and making a new gate."

"He's got it in for you because you nuked half his trucks. That was a really brave move back there, Jackson," Anna said.

If she started batting her eyes at me I was going to run into direct line of sight while screaming.

"That's our Jackson Creed, man of the people and hero to all. He's got women throwing panties at him." Joel clapped me on the shoulder.

"Inappropriate," Anna said. "I let him take them off."

"Fucking kill me now," I groaned.

I had about thirty more seconds of red-faced embarrassment before McQuinn's voice interrupted us.

"Run. All ya'll rabbits need to run. Run!"

"This is the play," Joel said.

He leaned in and pulled us close.

McQuinn fired a few rounds into the air for effect. It had the effect of making me keep my head down.

When Joel was done laying out his plan I just stared at him.

"On three?"

"Ready," Anna said.

"Wait one goddamn minute," I protested.

"If you got something better, speak up. Otherwise, it's go time," Joel said.

I had nothing.

16:20 hours approximate
Location: Trailer Park

JOEL MADE A BUNCH OF HAND SIGNALS AT ROZ. SHE LIFTED HER hands in the air in the universal "what the fuck are you talking about" gesture. I mimed shooting at McQuinn's men and she gave me the A-Okay signal.

"See how much easier that is?"

"If she'd have paid attention when I taught the signals, she would have gotten it," Joel said.

"Was she paying attention to something else?" Anna asked pointedly.

I snorted.

"On three," Joel said.

I counted down then popped up.

"Hey McQuinn, suck on this," I said and opened up with the Mossberg.

The gun boomed in my hands as I laid down heavy fire on him and his men. They dove for cover, which meant kissing the grass. Roz poked around the corner and opened fire. She was shooting left handed and hit a whole lot of air, but to the guys on the receiving end it was probably terrifying.

Joel and Anna broke from cover and ran toward the camper we'd investigated earlier, even though that wasn't their goal.

One of the car doors opened and someone returned fire. I did the smart thing and ducked behind the truck, then made myself small behind a wheel.

Then a couple of other jackwads opened up with assault weapons.

Roz dashed around to the other side of the RV when bullets ripped into metal and fiberglass near her position. She popped out and emptied her gun.

Rounds flew. Metal screamed. Guns boomed. It was the single most terrifying experience of my life and I'd seen some shit. I'd been chased by shufflers, stuck in a house with Z's, and faced down Monster Ken and his idiot protégé. Nothing had prepared me for having ten guns leveled in my direction and fired at me. Not even the hotel had been this crazy.

The sound of an engine trying to fire up told me that Joel and Anna had reached their destination. It turned over one more time but all the starter did was grind. Well that was just fucking great.

Another try and the engine started with a backfire, then roared to life as they gunned it. Grass and gravel flew as the ambulance shot forward. Anna was probably behind the wheel.

Poor Joel.

The ambulance pulled around a large black RV, and then the sound of wheels biting into grass ensued. The tires spun until they caught on the soaked ground. I rammed a couple of shells into the Mossberg and did something stupid. I moved to the front of the truck and used the hood for cover as I popped up and unloaded. I was aiming at anyone dumb enough to move, but all I hit was metal. Still, it did the job of making them drop behind cover.

McQuinn had taken cover near the fence. I could see the side of his head, so I shifted the barrel and shot a blast in that direction. He flopped toward the ground but was back up in a heartbeat.

As I dropped behind the truck something stung the side of my head. I slid to the ground and reached for my ear. My fingers came back covered in blood. Then the pain came as I realized I'd been shot.

A line of fire cut across the side of my head as my nerves woke up to tell me what the blood was showing me. I probed desperately and then realized I'd been grazed.

Fuck this. The next shot might finish the job. But what was I supposed to do? Run? They'd cut me down in seconds.

As if they sensed my predicament, the jackwads subjected the truck to a number of hits. I crawled behind a wheel and tried again to make my big frame small.

Some of the residents didn't take too kindly to strangers shooting at the camp. Gun barrels appeared from windows, and within a few seconds, gunfire was returned.

I wanted to dig a fucking hole and hide in it.

TAKING A COUPLE OF DEEP BREATHS, I POPPED UP AGAIN AND FIRED at one of the cars. Buckshot peppered the side and left little holes. A man who had been hanging out of an open window ducked back inside.

Blood dribbled down the side of my head and onto my shirt. I brushed at the wound with my arm but that made it hurt more. Fine, I'd just go ahead and bleed all over the damn place.

The ambulance roared as it backed up. Twenty-five feet, then fifteen.

One of McQuinn's cars moved to the west side of the fence to flank us. I took a breath and wondered how long I'd last if I hid under the truck.

I loaded the last five rounds into the Mossberg and leaned it against the side of the truck. I tugged out the .45 and checked the breach. One ready. I lifted the gun and carefully aimed at the new threat. The first blast blew off part of their side view mirror. The next punched through the driver side window and exited through the windshield.

The driver hit the side window and shattered the safety glass. I aimed at him and fired. Missed.

The ambulance roared back until it hit the fence. The sound of rending metal reached me. I didn't look. Instead, I steadied my aim. One thing I'd learned from Joel was that in the face of these kind of odds it was a good idea to make yourself as much of a thorn as possible, so I laid down more fire.

One of the RV inhabitants caught on to what I was doing and fired on the flanking vehicle as well. The barrel was long and dark and probably belonged to a hunter. The sound of the gun's explosion was deafening even as others fired here and there. A pause, and then it fired again. The round punched into the side of the vehicle. The passenger rolled out while the driver ducked down.

A barrel appeared over the hood, and it was aimed in my direction.

I shot until I was dry, then slid another mag in with shaking hands. Any second now and one of those rounds was bound to find me. And this time, it wouldn't just graze me.

The ambulance's siren howled over the noise of gunfire, buying me a short respite.

I aimed again, shot at the door, then shifted to the left and fired in the direction of the car's passenger. The hunting rifle boomed again, and that must have spooked them, because they didn't return fire right away.

Even if I were able to run without pain, I'd never make it around the side of the RV that would offer shelter. I could try for the door but there was no telling if they'd even let me in.

Gunfire peppered the side of the truck again so I ducked back down.

The ambulance had done a job on the fence and on the Z's around that section. The chain link was down, but the vehicle was half-stuck, unable to move forward.

Shufflers howled and raged toward the ambulance. It backed up a few feet to crush more of the fence into a group of Z's, and that must have provided enough traction because it suddenly shot forward.

They'd accomplished the first part of the mission. But now our solution was likely to bite us in the ass. Z's poured in, and they were led by a small army of shufflers.

16:30 hours approximate
Location: Trailer Park

"STAY DOWN!" A MAN CALLED TO ME FROM AN RV.

I looked up to nod but he was already gone.

The flanking car's occupants opened up on my position and I had no choice but to drop low and hide under the truck. Now I was exposed if anyone caught wind of my big frame. Not to mention the fact that if they managed to hit the gas tank, there was a real chance of a fire and I was not looking forward to running from flames only to get shot in the ass.

I slammed another magazine into the .45 – my last – and said a quick prayer. I wasn't one to ask God for help, but what the hell. I was probably going to die in the next few minutes, so it couldn't hurt. My dad used to say that, if the rapture happened, he was going to be a begging-for-forgiveness fool. Before that, everything was fair game. Thanks for the advice, Pops.

The RV came alive with the sounds of a large diesel engine turning over and the stutter of pistons firing under the hood. Wheels bit at the wet ground, and then it was moving. It picked up speed as it approached the fence, then swerved to the left as the driver aimed for a section between posts. I guess they'd decided that this location was fucked and it was time to retreat.

The jackwads fired on the RV, so I used the opportunity to lean out from cover and take very careful aim.

My target wasn't much older than me. He wore a beat up camouflage jacket and sunglasses.

I exhaled and pulled the trigger.

The gun bucked in my hands and the guy, surprised, spun to the side and dropped his rifle. He tried to stand up, hands going to his upper body. He stared down at his chest. A second later he slumped to the ground.

The RV hit the fence and swerved again to swipe the car. As the RV struck, the car's hood was smashed and the body of the vehicle was ripped to the side. The RV came up to speed again and roared toward the road. A few men took shots but they hit the back and sides of the big vehicle.

The RV spun to the right, nearly lost control, then corrected its course and headed for open road.

The ambulance had moved slowly to draw the Z's after them. The back door popped open and gunfire echoed from the rear. A shuffler took a pair of blasts but was back on its feet in no time.

The rest charged the ambulance in a rush.

With siren wailing, it revved up and hit the gate. Lights exploded and the front of the ambulance crumpled as it plowed through the chain link and into a car that was blocking the way.

The ambulance spun the car to the side but came to a screeching halt.

Shufflers and Z's poured into the camp.

The RV that had just made a rear exit was followed by an

older truck towing a camper. It hit a small rise and I thought the camper would fly off, but it settled. The driver spun the wheel to the right and was on the road.

With chaos all around, I decided it was now or never.

I rose to my feet and peeked over the front of the truck.

The ambulance backed up a few feet and then wheels spun as it got stuck again. Do something! I wanted to shout at Joel and Anna. They were only a few yards from the men with guns, and it wouldn't take the jackwads long to fill the cabin with lead. I shot at a man closing in on the truck, and then the first shuffler arrived.

He leapt into the air and landed on a man dressed in a thick leather jacket, driving him to the ground.

McQuinn himself stalked toward the fight, ripped the shuffler off the man, and then shot the enraged Z in the face.

The sound of Joel's AR was unmistakable in the riot. He fired at some men and they kissed the ground.

The ambulance shifted into reverse and then backed up with spinning tires. It hit a shuffler and crushed him, but the vehicle couldn't move forward.

Bullets peppered the cab and I caught a glimpse of Anna dropping to her side. The driver's side window exploded in a puff of safety glass.

I tossed the empty Mossberg to the side and drew my .45 again. The handgun was running on empty, but I had some rounds in my pocket. Dropping to the ground, I reloaded the magazine with shaking hands.

I dug my wrench out from under the truck.

The Z's bypassed the RV's and were more interested in the fresh meat behind the line of cars. The fence provided a stopping point for many of them, but the shufflers were smarter and took to the downed gate, spreading out in their hunt for victims.

"Fall back, regroup at the rally point!" McQuinn called as he ran for a car.

The son of a bitch was still out in the open and trying to give orders when the ambulance started to wail. Now he wasn't so damned cocky, not with a hundred Z's closing in on his ass.

I moved to the rear of the truck and aimed at McQuinn. I tried to lead with the barrel, but when I fired my last few rounds, I knew I'd missed.

A pair of Z's closed on me.

"I don't have time for this," I growled.

I took the first one with a swing of my wrench, connecting with the side of his head. I knocked the other to the ground and stomped his putrid head with my good foot.

Roz poked her head out and shot a Z, hitting it in the chest. She grabbed Christy and hauled her in my direction.

Christy looked terrified, but at least she had a gun – the little Sig that Anna had taken care of for a while.

The girls reached me, huffing and puffing, and Christy threw herself at me. I hugged her close, then let go and flattened a Z that had taken an interest in us. The man fell and didn't get back up. Christy stepped back as a Z closed on her. She looked terrified but she stopped in her tracks, took a wide stance, lifted the gun, and shot the woman in the head from ten feet away. She fired again for good measure but the Z was already falling.

"What do we do?" Roz asked.

"Get in the camper and go. I'm going back for Anna and Joel," I said and pointed at the crushed ambulance.

"You can't do that! There's a hundred Z's headed this way. You won't even get close."

"I have to try."

Christy looked up at me and she shook her head. Her eyes were filling with tears. "Don't leave us, Jackson."

The kid was right. I didn't stand a chance, yet every bone in my body wanted to do something dumb. Something brave. I wanted to wade into the mess of Z's, swinging left and right until I'd cleared a path.

Frosty growled low and the hair on her back stood up like a Mohawk. She bared her teeth and took a step away from us.

I spun around just in time to catch the shuffler as it leapt off the camper. A second one followed behind.

I fell back, swinging as I went and missing by a mile. The first shuffler hit the ground and was back in the air before I could think about getting into some kind of a fighting stance.

I got lucky and pushed it away as it tried to sail into me. His momentum carried him in the side of the truck I'd been hiding behind.

Christy shrieked and tried to aim the pistol, but she wouldn't shoot. I knew what the problem was. Roz and I were in the line of fire.

The shuffler darted one way, then went in the other direction as Christy tried to compensate with the gun. It was almost on her when I reached the little fucker and grabbed his leg, jerking backward. He flopped flat to the ground so I picked him up by what was left of his waistband and lifted him into the air.

The second shuffler hit me from behind and drove us to the ground.

I rolled to the side and wasn't gentle with my knees and feet as I fought them off. I connected with something soft, then drove my elbow back into the other shuffler's face. Frosty darted in, grabbed a shuffler's foot, and shook. The shuffler kicked back and Frosty let go with a whimper.

Roz waded into the fray and pulled a shuffler off me. She tried to shoot it in the head but missed when it darted forward and took her legs out from under her. Roz fell forward and landed on top of the shuffler. The gun sounded between them, and for a second I thought she'd shot herself.

Roz rolled to the side and I realized she'd hit the shuffler with another round. Instead of giving up the fight, it was more enraged.

My shuffler came at me again. She was slight, but not much smaller than Anna. I hauled off to punch her, but she was around my guard in a heartbeat and going for my face.

Her breath was rancid, reeking of rotted meat. As she closed in I saw, for the third time, something Joel and I had tried to deny. It was there in her eyes, some hint of intelligence hidden behind a light green glow. There was no mistaking it this time. Her eyes were not natural, not by a long shot.

I got my hand around her throat and held her up, but she drove her knees into my gut, almost bouncing up and down. My blood and skin were inches away and she wanted a taste.

Frosty dove in again, bit the shuffler in the leg, and jerked her whole body back. I used my sudden advantage.

The wrench came around in an arc as I gave up my guard. I hit her across the shoulder. I lowered the wrench and then shifted her head to the left. What little strength I had left went into the swing.

I hit her across the head so hard that part of it caved in. The shuffler shuddered, and then whatever had been driving her on gave up the ghost as she flopped, lifeless, across my body.

I had nothing left. I was exhausted, beat down, bleeding, and now I was covered by a damn shuffler.

Christy screamed again and fired but I couldn't tell where she was firing from. I rolled to my side and tried to find my breath but it wasn't there. The ground swam before my eyes as exhaustion hit me like a brick wall.

"No time for this shit," I muttered and heaved myself to my feet.

Roz kicked the second shuffler in the head and Christy darted in. She pointed the little sig and fired. The bullet hit the shuffler in the side of the neck and ripped away skin and sinew. The shuffler wasn't down, though, and looked like it was ready to leap again.

I lifted the wrench in both hands and then fell on her, the massive metal bar cracking across her back. I put everything I had into it and the shuffler let out something like a squeal as its spine was shattered.

She hit the ground and squirmed around us, so Christy shot her again. This time her aim was true and the shuffler was still.

"We need to go!"

Roz grabbed my hand and pulled. I staggered after her and looked back toward the ambulance. Something had gone wrong because it was no longer trying to move. I stopped in my tracks. A rush of Z's moved in on the cars.

I decided that I'd use the hole the first RV had left in the fence and circle back around for Anna and Joel. No way I was leaving them behind.

Gunfire erupted around the ambulance. Anna popped up and fired at someone. They fired back from the safety of their car. Anna slumped to the side again.

I remember yelling her name, screaming as she fell. I remember breaking Roz's grip on my hand and trying to reach Anna. Christy yelled at me but I didn't hear her. All I heard was Anna's voice in my head. I heard the things we'd talked about this morning. I heard her telling me I was an idiot for getting mixed up with her.

Roz slapped me so hard it rocked my head to the side.

"We. Need. To. Go."

"Not without Anna. I have to save her."

"No, Jackson, you have to help save Christy."

She was right. I had to save Christy. I had to get them out of here.

We managed to pile into the truck. I barely remember Roz starting it. Christy tried to press the Sig Sauer into my hand but I just stared at it dumbly. The path ahead was filled with Z's. Roz wove around packs and ran over those who were in the way. The truck bounced up and down as she gunned it.

I rolled down the window to get a look at the ambulance, convinced that we'd spin around and go back for them.

Then it exploded.

I lowered my head.

That's when the shakes kicked in.

THE ROAD AHEAD

17:00 hours approximate
Location: Not-sure-where

Roz and Christy were safely seated in the back of the camper with Frosty. I looked toward the passenger side seat and thought of Anna Sails. I should be sitting over there while she drove and peppered me with dark looks every time I asked stupid questions. There was no way around it. We might not have been perfect for each other, but I felt her loss with a hollowness I'd never experienced before.

Anna had been ready for any fight but I'd also found something else in her, a fierceness that was hard to define. I'd learned a lot during our short time together, and it was with a heavy heart that I shifted into drive and found a section of road I could roll onto.

And Joel.

Joel "Cruze" Kelly, the best friend I'd ever had. When we first ended up in this fucking zombie wasteland we hadn't been the best partners, but we'd made do and even become friends. He'd taught me how to field strip an assault rifle, given lessons on flanking maneuvers and laying down suppressive fire, and always had a comeback ready for my dumb jokes. I was a much better man for having him in my life.

Sappy, sure, but I'm not the same guy I was a few weeks ago. Back then, I'd been an alcohol swilling, foul-mouthed engineer who cared only about where we were headed and when we were getting underway.

I looked in the rearview mirror again, but the ambulance was a smoking ruin. The gunfire had torn the vehicle apart before it had caught fire. Then the Z's had arrived, led by a full pack of shufflers, and made short work of McQuinn's crew. Some went down, but many simply piled back into cars and roared away. I didn't know if McQuinn was alive, and I didn't care at this point. If he was out there and I ran into him again, I'd be more than happy to go slow while I took him apart. I hoped he was a fucking Z.

I pulled out to a crossroad where a couple of bodies lay next to a car. I took a right. The plan was to run parallel to the freeway for as long as possible and hopefully come across Camp Pendleton. Along the way I'd stop and pick up a map.

I looked down because my vision was suddenly cloudy.

17:30 hours approximate
Location: Not-sure-where, CA

WE WERE A FEW MILES OUT WHEN I CAME ACROSS THE CAR. IT HAD most of a Z hanging off the back and it had been shot to hell. I was going to pass it when curiosity got the better of me. If one of McQuinn's men was in the car, I wouldn't mind dealing out a little justice with my wrench.

If I got lucky, it was Frank himself, although I was sure he'd gone down under a shuffler.

I stopped a few hundred feet from the car and stared for a minute. Nothing moved.

Roz slipped out of the camper and ran to my side of the truck.

"What's up?"

"I think that's one of McQuinn's cars."

"So let's drive past it. Come on, Jackson. I want to be as far away from this place as possible as quickly as possible."

"Me too," I mumbled.

But I didn't. Sudden white-hot anger filled me and the world swam in front of my eyes. I might have been crying again or I might have been overcome with rage.

I jumped out of the still-running truck and drew the little Sig. I ducked down and angled toward the car, ignoring the throbbing of my ankle.

I kept the gun up. The second anyone showed their face, I was going to blow it off.

Roz hissed at me to come back but I ignored her. She groaned and followed, flanking the car from the other side.

I moved up on the abandoned vehicle and found it empty. There was blood on the seat and some splashed on the door, but there was no one in sight.

The shops along the sides of the street were a mess. Most had smashed in windows and battered doors. A gas station bore graffiti that read, "Aim for the Head." If the occupants of the car had found a store to hide in, there was no way I was going to find them unless I went door to door.

Something moved near the hood.

The car had come to stop next to a solid concrete barricade that might have been used to block access a few weeks ago. I'd heard from other survivors that the government had tried to quarantine entire cities but the virus had spread far too rapidly.

A gun barrel suddenly angled over the barricade so I dropped to the side of the car. I rolled my eyes when I realized how stupid I'd been. We could have driven by this car without a second thought.

"You better be an ace fucking shot because there are six of us," I bluffed.

"What, you teach that dog how to shoot?"

I gasped and stood up. The gun barrel lowered and I rushed to the barricade.

I'll never be able to explain the rush of emotions I felt when I found Joel Kelly with his back against the barricade, clutching his chest. But that wasn't the half of it. Next to him, holding her arm as blood ran down her side, was Anna Sails.

"Oh fuck!" Because I'm good with words like that.

"Good to see you too, buddy," Joel said.

"Anna, my Anna," I said and reached out to brush the hair off her face.

"Jesus, Jackson, it's been thirty minutes and you're already a weepy little bitch," Anna said through clenched teeth.

"I thought you two were dead," I said.

"If I don't get this bound, I may be in a few hours."

"Are you hit anywhere else?"

Anna moved her hand aside to show where a couple of wounds were puckered along her upper left arm. I crouched next to her and put my hands on her neck and felt down to her shoulders. I went over her chest and then hips as I probed for wounds, but she didn't gasp, she just stared at me.

"If you don't stop feeling me up, you're the one that's going to get hit."

Roz dropped next to Joel. She smiled at him, then put her arms around his neck and pressed her forehead against the side of his face.

"Are you okay?"

"Armor saved me but I feel like I was kicked by a fucking mule. I might have a broken rib."

"How in the hell did you escape? I saw the ambulance explode."

"We weren't in it. We got the hell out of that piece of shit and then used it for cover. One of McQuinn's men was trying to crawl into his own car, so I borrowed it," Joel said.

I imagined Joel Kelly politely asking the guy to give up his car. I had the feeling it didn't go over like that.

"I got you, baby," Roz said and kissed him on the cheek.

"Jackson," Anna said, "It's not that bad. Get Joel to the camper and then come back for me."

I ignored her and put my arms under her legs and around her back, then gently lifted her off the ground.

"Shut up, Anna. I'll get you fixed up. You'll be back on your feet in no time, you'll see."

"Yes sir," Anna said and put her head against my chest.

I carried her to the camper and ripped up a piece of bedding for her to press against the wound. It would have to do until we could find something better. Christy greeted her with a small smile and Frosty's tail thumped against the floor so hard I worried that every Z within a half-mile radius would hear.

In the distance the shrill call of a shuffler broke the silence.

"I'll be right back, Anna," I said next to her ear. I didn't want to take my eyes off her.

"Go get your pal before those Z's show up and make this day into an even bigger mess."

"Anna, I—"

"Shut up, Creed. Just shut up and come back to me. We'll talk later," she said.

"I was just going to say that I'm so glad you're here. That's all."

She grimaced through the pain and managed to hit me with a smile that was something I don't think I'd seen yet – because it was genuine.

07:30 hours approximate
Location: Not-sure-where, CA

It's dark outside and this candle is just about burned to the table. We found a copse of trees off the road and pulled under them. The gas tank is still half-full so we have plenty for the next day or more. With any luck it will be enough to carry us all the way to Camp Pendleton. I never thought fifty miles would seem like such a long distance, but there's a whole world out there just waiting for us to screw up. Just waiting to devour us.

Anna thinks she knows where Bright Star is camped but she's worried about how long they were planning to be there. It could be that we arrive and the entire group is already gone.

Joel's cool with that because he's convinced that the Marines would never give up Camp Pendleton. I didn't bother reminding him what happened to the naval base in San Diego.

Joel and Roz insisted that we take the bed because Anna needs to sit up during the night to keep pressure off her wounds. Christy fit in alongside Anna, so I'm taking what's left of the bed, and that's more than good enough for me.

I can feel Anna's eyes on me as I finish this entry. I've looked up to catch her staring at me a number of times even though she tried to feign sleep. With her injuries, she is in a lot of pain but she doesn't complain.

Tomorrow will be a fresh start. We'll drive all day if we have to so we can reach the base.

For tonight, I've got this book. I've got food and water thanks to the camper. I've also got great friends and even a dog that thinks her place is with her head in my lap or in Anna's. I've got Joel.

Best of all, I've got Anna, which is reason enough to keep getting up and kicking ass. We're hurt, but we're alive, and that's enough for now.

This is Machinist Mate First Class Jackson Creed and I am still alive.

POISONED EARTH

Z-RISEN BOOK 3

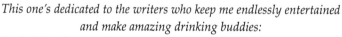

This one's dedicated to the writers who keep me endlessly entertained and make amazing drinking buddies: Craig DiLouie, Jonathan Moon, Cheryl Dyson, Peter Clines, Eloise J. Knapp, and of course, Katie Cord.

PREFACE

In the event this log is found with my corpse, I'm Machinist Mate First Class Jackson Creed, and it's been a few weeks since we arrived in San Diego following the event. With me is Marine Sergeant Joel "Cruze" Kelly.

We were both stationed on the USS McClusky, an Oliver Hazard Perry-class frigate out of San Diego. Our ship was overrun by the dead and we barely escaped with our lives.

Now we live in the middle of Undead Central.

SSDD

05:35 hours approximate
Location: Just outside of L.A.

The sun rose over a desolate road, and that's the nicest thing I could say about the morning.

Abandoned cars and trucks lay across the road like an obstacle course in hell. Suitcases had been emptied and tossed to the side. Glove boxes hung loose and had long since been vacated of all but papers and melted tubes of lipstick. I no longer bothered to check under seats.

After a vehicle had sat in the sun for a few weeks, anything that had been edible became something mushy and frequently sported mold or, as a real bonus, maggots and rot. I once found a bag with a freaking severed hand inside. The hand didn't move, but I damn sure did. What kind of a wacko cuts off someone's hand and leaves it in a goddamn bag?

There was enough debris littering the road to remind me of a war documentary. I used to watch the History Channel. They always showed men and women on the move, dragging kids and belongings. That wasn't the case now. We were in the midst of a full-scale war that none of us were truly equipped to deal with. We did our best, but it was hard to handle the shitstorm we'd endured for the past month.

The level of Zs had decreased as we moved away from the city on our journey to Los Angeles. That didn't mean we could be any less vigilant. One wrong move--one careless step like forgetting to check under the camper before everyone was out-- and it could be the end for one or all of us.

I'd seen a Z try to grab Christy when she dropped to the ground. Either we'd run over the bastard or he'd crawled under there during the night. He'd sent Christy stumbling back and screaming. I wasn't too quick with the wrench, because bashing something that's got its head under a vehicle is like the most fucked up game of Whack-A-Mole ever devised.

Just another day in paradise.

The night before, we'd spent our time huddled in the camper, backed up between two houses so we had an easy exit. The pair of ramblers was so close together that the truck slid between them, leaving very little room on either side of our mobile home. If the Zs came, we'd have a fighting chance.

Following our escape from a shitload of shufflers and an asshole with an army, we'd spent a week plus change on the road. We didn't move all that fast. Didn't try to. It was a time to lick our wounds and press on. Los Angeles had become some kind of quest. It was our fiery mountain in Mordor. It was where we'd find warm beds, food, and acceptance. We had talked about it so much and for so long we no longer considered what would happen if the town was like everywhere else we'd visited: fucked.

Frosty--our newly adopted dog--was the only one that played it cool. She nosed around the little camper, and I took her out when she sniffed at the door. She always kept on guard, and still didn't bark when Zs were near. I was tempted on more than one occasion to let her tease some Zs like she'd done the day I found her. Seemed like she loved nothing more than taunting the undead and leading them on a chase. But she was also smart enough not to let one of the rotters get a hold of her.

When I went out, Christy went with me, and hung around asking questions every minute. Never knew a kid could have so many random thoughts in her head. When will we find a place to sleep? Where are we going to get some fresh fruit? Could we grow a garden somewhere? Would I ever tell Anna how I felt about her? That last one got me, but I ignored it, because Anna was aloof about what had happened between us. Two could play that game, so I kept my mouth shut for a change.

When we found our safe place for the night, Christy took Frosty out to play. With the dog outside, I knew that if she got a whiff of more than one or two Zs she'd sound the alarm and we'd hightail it to a new hiding spot.

07:20 hours approximate
Location: Vista

JOEL HAD SPENT A COUPLE OF DAYS SITTING AROUND LOOKING miserable while we all did our best not to get on each other's nerves. Bunch of hardasses in a tiny space meant tempers could quickly flare. One time I was so sick of being cooped up with them, I took a walk just to clear my head. Cleared my guts, too, because I had hellacious gas. If it was just me and Joel, we'd fart and play it off, give each other an earful and then look for a window to open. But Anna and Roz had this way of looking at us like we were a couple of thirteen-year-olds.

It was so early the crickets were still making a hell of a lot of noise. I'd been outside stretching my legs when I'd realized that the new world had a weird smell. Fresh and clean. Kinda ironic considering all the dead stuff we'd seen over the last few months. After I found a place to piss, I headed back to the camper so we could gather around the small table and plan our next move.

Anna rested on the edge of the bed. Her arm was a mess from the gunshot wound. Roz sat in the tiny alcove, curved in a display of terrible posture, one knee cocked back and her other leg under the table. Christy was trying to teach Frosty to hold a treat on her nose until she was given the command to eat it. The treat was just some dried-out food from the night before. Frosty thought it was the shit, but didn't seem to think much of the game.

Joel stood over the table like a limp-dick general. His ebony skin was sallow. After taking a couple of rounds to his IMTV armor he'd been left bruised and battered. We'd had a hell of a fight on our hands.

Now, a week of rest had done little but irritate him. We studied a beat-up map of the area, looking to stick to any roads that were off the main drag.

This plan didn't always work out so well. Looking at a map was one thing. Actually finding our way was another. We'd pick a side road, head toward a larger road, and then learn the hard way that "progress" had screwed up anything resembling what we found on our fifteen-year-old paper map. One thing the zombie fucking apocalypse did not allow for was GPS.

The day before, Roz and I had raided a little convenience store. Miraculously, the place had only been mostly picked over. We found some dried goods, but not so much in the canned food department. Roz did turn up one of the most disgusting things I've ever seen in my life: a whole cooked chicken in a can. When that abortion slid out of the tin, I thought I was going to puke up all the stomach acid my empty gut had to offer.

It'd tasted worse than it looked. It was so bad I dreamed of some mid-rats back on the McClusky; that stuff tasted like boiled shoe leather, but beggars can't be choosers. You either get used to eating shitty food or you starve. You get used to being on the run, constantly looking over your shoulder. You get used to the moans and groans of Zs. You get used to hiding and keeping quiet. If you don't, it's a quick trip to zombieville.

And that's why I'd choked the stuff down and been thankful for the protein.

Frosty had nosed around, so I ripped off a few ounces and fed her. She licked my fingers and whined for more.

"I know, dude. Good shit." I rubbed her head.

A half hour later we'd headed back to the camper where we shared the meager contents from our backpacks. Roz had inspected Anna's wound and "tsked" a few times. She then took a turn feeling up Joel's chest to check for cracked or broken ribs. She told him the bruising and swelling were going down.

"Hear that, jarhead? You're going to be around for a while, so suck it up," I'd grinned.

"I got something you can suck," Joel had shot back, and grabbed his crotch, but winced for the effort.

When McQuinn's army of jackwads had tried to take us down, we'd concocted a stupid plan that involved leading an army of Zs right at the other guys. Joel had made use of an ambulance, complete with flashing lights and a siren that told all of southern California we were still alive. The ambulance had crashed, and that's when he'd been shot. His armor had saved his life, but it hadn't saved him from looking like he'd been punched repeatedly by a gorilla.

"Get some rest, Joel," Roz had advised. He'd rolled his eyes at me, so I'd shrugged and gone back to staring out of the space between the curtain and the window. I'd expected a horde of undead to locate us at any moment and make our lives hell.

To be clear, I expect this from every moment of every day.

"I'm fine. Just got the wind knocked out of me," Joel had said.

"Fuck's sake, Joel. It's like you got kicked in the chest by a donkey. Just chill and stop being a jarhead for a day," I'd said.

"Yeah. You say that now. Wait till your ass is hanging in the wind and a bunch of ZULUs are about to take a bite," Joel had said.

"I'll keep that in mind, and I'll keep my ass pointed in your direction."

Joel hadn't said anything and instead, started to field-strip his assault rifle for what seemed like the twentieth time. Of all the weapons we'd had along the way, Joel had never abandoned the Rock River Arms AR-15 with its EOTech holographic sight. He loved it like it was his own rotten little kid. When he thought he'd lost it during a firefight, he'd made us go back a few days later and scour the area for the gun.

08:35 hours approximate
Location: Vista

THE NEXT FEW DAYS PASSED IN A BLUR. WE STAYED A TIGHT GROUP for the most part, but being a tight group meant that we were together too much and for too long. We laughed, bickered, fought, and had to keep more than one screaming match down to more of a hissing match so the Zs didn't hear us. Joel and I had been cooped up together for days at a time, but we'd developed a way to deal with it: just not talking to each other. With a teenage girl and two women in our group, it wasn't that easy.

I think it was a Thursday when we decided that we'd have to range out in a wider area to find a cache of supplies. I hated it, but we were going to have to hit some houses. That was dangerous. Open a door and there could be a Z waiting to pounce. Knock on a door and there could be a civilian waiting to shoot. And houses weren't our only worry. We hadn't seen a shuffler in days. Instead of being reassuring, it scared the shit out of me.

The shufflers were smart and cunning. They weren't like regular Zs, because they seemed to be able to think. Not only that, but they acted in groups and were able to hide in masses of Zs.

But that wasn't the real reason. Anna had a bullet in her arm, and as much as she'd played it off--and even though Roz had cleaned the wound and told us everything was okay--Anna was hot. She'd had a low-grade fever for a couple of days. We needed to get the bullet out, and Roz said she needed antibiotics.

So I counted rounds, readied gear, and then lay next to Anna for the night. She slept like a rock, but it was a long time before I dropped off.

06:10 hours approximate
Location: Vista

MORNING ARRIVED LIKE A BITCH WITH A HANGOVER. I ROLLED over, studied the light streaming in from the outside world, and thought about taking a siesta for the rest of the week. Let the others do supply runs. I was sick of it. Running, hiding, ducking, sneaking, and bashing in heads. Wears a guy down, you know?

After I quit feeling sorry for myself, I became aware that Anna had backed up against me in the night. I had one arm over her waist and she was snuggled right against my chest with her head resting on my arm. My hand had fallen asleep but I didn't care to move it. She smelled good. Feminine.

When it was time to do the supply run, I tried one last time to tell Joel to take it easy and take care of his wounds. Joel flatly responded that he and I were going out there. I nodded. Besides, if we had to spend another day holed up in this tiny camper, I was going to go fucking postal.

Joel said he was better and Roz seemed to agree.

"I'll take it any way I can get it," he said.

Roz looked like she wanted to punch him in the face.

Joel had gone over his IMTV tactical gear and made adjustments. He'd tossed out a shattered ceramic piece of armor that had saved his life, then twiddled with other pieces until his chest was protected. After the battle at the RV camp, we were dangerously low on ammo. I took Anna's Smith & Wesson R8 .357. She glowered at me but I promised to bring her boyfriend back.

"Don't lose him," she said.

"I meant me," I said and tried to pull off a cool smirk-wink thing. All I got in return was a flat look.

06:40 hours approximate
Location: Vista

We had an assortment of 9mm pistols, but barely enough ammo to fill all the magazines. Joel settled on the Beretta 92FS and stuffed a handful of extra rounds into his pockets. He had nearly a full magazine for AR-15. Joel slipped the mag into a pouch, snapped his assault rifle onto a two-point sling and draped it around his body.

During scouting missions, food runs, and house invasions we'd come up with so many different types of guns it was hard to keep track. I was happy with my Springfield XDM compact and always kept it close.

I hoped we had enough ammo to get us out of a scrape.

I took my trusty wrench and draped it over my shoulder. I'd found a piece of webbing that had been a guitar strap, and constructed a half-assed strap for the weapon. The wrench was conveniently left to swing under my arm, but it banged against my hip and side with every step. I had to figure out a better way to carry this thing, or leave it behind. But if there was one lesson I'd learned over the last three weeks, it was to never go unarmed. Never.

"Think we should bring Frosty?" I asked Joel.

"I don't know. What if we get stuck and have to hide out for a day or two? How we going to keep her from going stir crazy?"

"How am I going to keep *you* from going stir crazy? Put a jarhead in a box and shit gets busted and shot up," I said.

Joel snorted, but eyed Frosty.

"I don't know, man."

"Just leave her with Christy. She loves the girl more than me anyway."

"Because I'm cute and you smell like a sweaty guy," Christy said.

"You smell like sweat too. You just can't tell," I teased.

Christy looked at me like I'd slapped her.

"I do not stink! And it's not like I can take a bath unless you can bring back a barrel of water."

"I'm sorry, dude," I tried. "I was just teasing. You smell like roses and puppy dog farts."

"You're so gross, Creed," she said with a laugh.

Frosty nudged Christy's side, and got her head rubbed for the effort.

"We'll leave her here," I nodded at Frosty. "Hear that, dog? You're on guard duty."

Frosty didn't answer but she did loll her pink tongue out of the side of her mouth.

Roz said she'd stay behind and keep an eye on Anna and Christy. Better her than me. She handed me a list of usable antibiotics and told me to be on the lookout for them.

I'd been stuffed into this fucking sardine can for days and I needed a break. I needed fresh air, even if that air reeked of the Zs. With quick goodbyes that included me unsuccessfully trying to kiss Anna Sails on the cheek, we left.

We'd walked a few minutes when Joel broke the silence.

"Sails doesn't seem to like you much."

"What, that? She just doesn't like public displays of affection."

"She tell you that?" He raised his eyebrows.

"I figured it out."

"Lotta figuring with that girl," he said.

"Tell me about it."

09:00 hours approximate
Location: Vista

WE FOLLOWED A WELL-WORN PATH DOWN CONCRETE LANES littered with--you guessed it--more fucking trash, and the remains of whatever had been inside shops and houses. There was enough empty luggage to fill an abandoned Kohl's. Joel was not much of a conversationalist while we made the trek toward town.

Someone had painted a mural of zombies eating a couple of children. The piece of art was complete with heads smashed in and brains leaking onto the ground.

"Worst graffiti I've seen in my life," I muttered.

A shape flashed across an alley and faded into shadow. Joel followed it with his gun but didn't start blasting, so I didn't either. I'd learned a great rule from Marine Sergeant Joel "Cruze" Kelly, and that was not to start firing until after he started firing.

When he finally unlocked his gaze from the alley, I took a step and accidentally kicked over a can. It clattered across the ground and landed next to the sidewalk. Joel froze and swept his gun up. Luckily, a dozen Zs didn't descend on us.

"Fuck is wrong with you?"

"What? I didn't see it," I said.

"How could you miss a big empty can of Campbell's soup sitting right in the middle of the walkway, man?"

"Because I'm taller than you and that gun put together."

Something moved in the alley again so I took a step toward it. I crunched over someone's cheap bead jewelry and a pile of soggy trash. I couldn't tell who was moving around back there, and curiosity was getting the better of me. The shape faded into shadow after I caught a glimpse of someone dressed in black complete with a ski mask to up the creep factor.

I got the chills just seeing the guy. If someone was stalking us I'd prefer that me and Joel do our talking with guns or fists.

"Bad hombres. Let's move out," Joel said.

I agreed with him and followed.

It was 0900 hours and I hadn't seen a Z since the day before.

It felt fucking eerie.

GOLD MINE

09:40 hours approximate
Location: Vista

The Z hit me like a ton of bricks.

My partner in crime yelled for me to move out of the way, but I was slow on my feet. We'd come across a group of feisty assholes about fifteen minutes ago and ducked into the remains of an ampm. He and I huddled for a few minutes, but the sounds of something moving in the back of the convenience store finally got under my skin.

The Z had been hovering near a shelf, and no more than a few feet away. In the gloom I didn't even see him until his shuffling steps betrayed him. He moved fast, arms up, milky white gaze locked on my face like it was prime rib. I spun, and panic made me lose my cool. That's when the Z almost got a piece of my dumb ass.

I hit the wall hard enough to see stars. Breath whooshed out but I got my hands up, purely by instinct, and fought off the Z. He had about fifty pounds on me and slammed me right back into the wall. I pushed the Z away. Something clamped my wrist and I squealed like a six year old.

It wasn't teeth, it was his hand. Most of his fingers had been gnawed to the bone, and he had a hell of a death grip. I got my foot up and kicked the zombie in the chest. He fell away but his hand was still fastened to me. That's when I noticed he'd fallen away, all except his arm. I bounced around like I was in a one-man idiot dance-off as I tried to shake it loose.

Joel was fast on his feet, just like I'd expected. If a Marine wasn't shooting stuff, punching stuff, or just snarling at stuff, he was probably asleep while standing up, expecting an attack at any second.

He grabbed the zombie by the collar and knocked him to the ground. Joel lifted his boot and brought it down on the Z's head once, twice, and then a third time that left pulp leaking from the man's cracked skull. The Z didn't move again.

I leaned over and tried to catch my breath. Hands on knees, chest spasming as I sucked in air.

"Need a hand?" Joel nodded at the Z's appendage that was still stuck to my arm.

"Oh that's real funny," I said.

Fuck! It really was stuck on there. I flailed around, trying to shake it off.

"Looks like he had a strong grip," Joel deadpanned.

"Okay, that's enough," I said, and mostly meant it. I was worried that if I actually caught my breath I'd break into laughter.

The arm refused to let go and as I shook it, bits of blood and flesh flew. Joel moved out of the way of the little projectiles.

"You're giving shaking hands a new meaning, man."

"I hate this fucking place."

"Your ability to state the obvious is a real gift, Creed." Joel smacked my shoulder, lifted his assault rifle and moved toward the back of the store. I grabbed the remains of the arm and pulled it free, and left it next to the Z's battered body.

More movement in the rear of the store meant that my little break was over.

Joel held up a hand to motion me to stay put. I did just that, trusting that he was confident enough to take on whatever was creeping around. From the soft scraping, I hoped it was just a torso looking for a meal.

A few weeks ago that shit used to get to me. Seeing bodies or halves of bodies still crawling around used to freak me out so bad I wouldn't sleep for days. Now it was just another sun-up in Undead Central US of A. The Zs had lost their souls or whatever made them thinking and reasoning beings, leaving them as brainless meat bags capable of little more than piss-hate coupled with an appetite for human flesh.

I've learned, thanks to the walking Marine hard-on named Sergeant Kelly, to be more aware of my surroundings. Don't let the above Z attack fool you. I'm a lean (because I haven't had a proper meal in days), mean (because I haven't had a proper meal in days), killing machine (you get the goddamn picture).

I NOTICED THAT THE LITTLE STORE REEKED OF SPOILED FOOD, rotting flesh, and blood when we sniffed around the entrance, but give a squid a break for hoping for a bag of Doritos.

Turned out the shelves were bare and probably had been for days. Mom and Pop stores had been well-defended at the start of the damn apocalypse, but then the looters had gotten into it.

Guys like Frank McQuinn, who just over a week ago had led his merry band of jackholes against my group and a bunch of retirees who wanted to be left to their own meandering devices. We'd hurt McQuinn and his group and they'd scattered. The quick brains of Kelly and my girl, Anna Sails, had saved us. Now she was stuck in a camper with a bullet in her arm and I was out trying to find supplies to fix her up.

A pair of shapes slid behind a shelf. Joel motioned for me to take the other side. I moved away from him, head low, shoulders hunched, eyes on the floor as I sought out anything that might make noise like an errant Funyun or potato chip. If I saw one I would likely start drooling, then it would be a struggle to stop from eating it. Was there such a thing as "the three or four week rule"?

I met Joel's eyes. He nodded and we swung around the shelving from opposite sides.

My wrench was already in hand and I'd raised it, preparing to bash in at least one head, all the while hoping that Joel wouldn't shoot my ass off.

I nearly jumped out of my skin when the little figures dashed into view.

The kids were filthy and had to be a lot younger than Christy. A pair of boys, just little kids really, with faces covered in dirt, hair a rats-nest, clothes holed and hanging in strips. My first impulse was to swing the wrench, because they looked like Zs.

"We ain't like those things," one of the kids said.

"We're just looking for water or food," the other said.

Joel blew out a breath and pointed his gun toward the floor.

"You dudes got family?" I asked.

"Yeah. Right outside the door," one of them said.

They were on the move before I could ask who was waiting for them. The kids were fast and slipped away and out the front before I could get another word in.

"Well shit," Joel said.

"Hey! Come back!" I called and moved toward the door.

I poked my head out, but they were gone. I could probably pursue them, but the little rug rats were a lot faster than me. Besides, what was I going to do when I caught up with them? More than likely they did have someone around here watching after them. Someone with a big ass gun, and a bullet labeled "Jackson Creed".

I stopped scanning for them when I noticed a shape across the street. He was dressed in black from head to toe with only his eyes peering through some kind of ski-mask-looking thing. This had to be the guy I'd seen earlier in the day.

The person had a big assault rifle at the ready, so I slowly raised my hands to show I didn't feel like getting shot today. If that was one of McQuinn's guys, I was probably wasting my time and should plant my gut on the ground.

Another figure appeared next to the first and I could have sworn one of them nodded in my direction. Then they both faded from view.

10:10 hours approximate
Location: Vista

WE MOVED OUT A FEW MINUTES LATER. I KEPT MY EYES PEELED BUT I never saw the two figures again. I tried to convince myself that they'd been a figment of my imagination.

We came across decaying corpses, most unmoving. Whenever we did find a Z, we quickly assessed its threat level, and ended up leaving the majority of them behind. If any got too jumpy, a quick swing of my wrench put them down for good. They were a sorry bunch even for zombies. Most had taken damage of some kind and were no longer up and moving around.

A particularly enthusiastic female--in her fifties, if I had to guess, hard to tell with the crushed face and shattered eye socket--pursued us with one working arm and one working leg. Her other limbs had been shattered like someone had dropped her from twenty feet up.

After a while it was just pathetic, and so I also put her out of her misery.

A telephone pole had a hand-printed sign nailed to it. I moved closer and read. Joel covered for me while I shook my head. After considering the words, I pulled the sheet off and showed Joel.

"Think this is real?"

"Sounds no good to me, brother," Joel said while rubbing his chin with one hand.

"But what if it's true?"

"I'm not sure I want to find out."

I nodded and stuffed the flyer in my backpack.

Every store we came across had been picked over. We finally got lucky when we started to boldly bust in doors on houses. Risking noise, because I was a little out of my mind with worry over Anna, we ransacked three houses in a row, killed the undead inhabitants, and taken everything that wasn't nailed down. A three-quarters eaten box of stale Ritz crackers. Some beef jerky that didn't amount to much more than a taste for both of us. I found a can of chicken broth. I couldn't wait. I broke out my can opener and punched a pair of holes in the aluminum, then Joel and I took turns drinking like it was a fifteen-dollar bottle of whiskey.

"This won't last," Joel observed.

"What?"

"The houses with goods. As more and more get picked over we'll be coming up empty on our supply runs."

"These are mostly picked over *now*. Guess we better stock up while we can. We have the camper, it can hold a lot of food."

"Yeah, but five people can *eat* a lot of food. *You* eat enough for *three* people."

"I don't eat that much. Shit, man, I've lost enough weight to look like a college basketball player. Look at this trim and fit example of military bearing."

"You look like you should be going into rehab. Like a damn crackhead."

"Yeah, well *you* look like you should be on a milk carton."

"The fuck does that even mean?" Joel asked.

"I don't know. I'm tired, man. Brain ain't up to sparring with you today."

Joel looked me up and down. "You're alright. Let's get this shit over with so we can lounge around in robes and sip espresso while Roz and Anna feed us grapes."

"Anna's more likely to feed me the barrel of a gun."

Joel snorted and moved out.

We dashed across a street littered with all kinds of crap that had been left behind, or tossed aside as people realized they were more likely to live if they were mobile. Bodies lay here and there, but no biters rose to greet us.

We checked out a house that was missing its door, and after hearing an awful lot of banging around on the second floor, decided to try somewhere else.

We moved between a pair of apartment complexes and found a group of Zs milling around. They were lethargic and dressed in tatters. Joel and I backed up, but one of them got its eyes on us. It lurched toward me, but it was barely ambulatory. I took it out and then the one behind it. Joel used the stock of his gun to smack Zs down and I finished them off.

"Why are they so messed up?" I asked.

"Fucking zombies, man," Joel said.

"No shit, but they were a mess even for Zs."

"Maybe they been decaying. Old Zs," Joel said. "Give 'em another week and they might be crawling. A week after that they might just stop moving."

"What if they all get old and slow? Think the shufflers will slow down?"

"Don't know, brother. I'm too tired to worry about it right now."

10:50 hours approximate
Location: Vista

THE NEXT HOME WAS A GOLDMINE.

The house we'd picked was a single story with three bedrooms. The last door on the left was closed and I thought I'd heard something thumping around in there, so we didn't bother exploring that room.

There was a huge bloodstain on the carpet leading into the dining room, but we couldn't find a body to go with it. Didn't matter anyway. After a couple of weeks of this shitty new life, I was just about immune to the horrors. I might have been squeamish at one time. I might have looked away when a doctor cut into my finger to sew a tendon back together. Now it was different. A guy with his guts hanging out, half his face eaten away, and dragging a broken foot, was just another day in undead central.

I hit the bathroom while Joel tossed the kitchen. I needed to piss, and got lucky and didn't find a mess in the toilet. Sure, I can pick any corner of the world to take a leak in, but it didn't hurt to pretend to be civilized from time to time.

I opened drawers and came up with a bottle of Percocets that had expired a year ago. There was a bottle of TUMS, so I ate a few for the calcium. I found some birth control pills, considered them, and decided to leave the packet. It was better than getting slapped in the face by Anna Sails.

"Oh yay. Jackpot, baby," Joel called from the other room.

I followed his voice into the hallway. He was rifling through a pantry, and he wasn't being very organized about it. Open boxes were tossed to one side, while cans and closed supplies were put on the other side.

"What?" I asked.

"Found this," he said and held up a flat box.

"That looks like a pan or something," I said.

"Nah, man. It's a burner. Takes these little cans of butane. You can even use it inside and it won't kill ya."

"Nifty," I said.

"No more digging a fire pit and hoping we aren't sniffed out. As long as we have fuel we can cook inside." Joel grinned and pushed the box into his backpack along with a bunch of cans that looked like old-school hairspray.

I wasn't as excited as Joel. I'd gotten used to eating stuff right out of cans and cold. Chicken noodle soup wasn't half bad in a congealed form. It filled the gut and was easy to open and consume.

In the bedroom I tossed the contents of a nightstand and came across a half bottle of something with a name so long I wasn't about to try to pronounce it. I added it to the bag, along with a full bottle of antidepressants. Too bad there wasn't enough to keep us all medicated for a year. If I was going to spend all of my time shooting Zs, I'd love to do it with a smile on my face.

I also found a pair of fuzzy handcuffs.

"Kinky bastard," Joel said. I hadn't even heard him moving down the hallway.

"Antidepressants and handcuffs. Ain't that some shit," I laughed.

"Place must have belonged to white people," Joel said, and went to check out the last bedroom.

I went through a dresser and found enough silky lingerie to open a Victoria's Secret store. I held up a pair of flimsy, see-through panties and squinted. "Why not?" I muttered and stuffed a few items in the bottom of my backpack.

"Shit yeah." Joel said from the other room.

He'd put a dresser drawer on the bed and was busy sorting out ammo. Whoever had lived here had been ready for action. It made me wonder where they were now.

"Box of nine. Seven boxes of forty. Damn, we should check for that piece. And look at this. A few boxes of .45 rounds. Dude had a fucking armory. I love whoever lived here."

"You could tell him. He's probably the fucker thumping around in the last bedroom."

"If at all possible, let's avoid looking in that room. Could be another shuffler-kid, I'd rather just leave it a mystery."

"Good thing those smart Zs can't figure out the complexities of a doorknob," I said. "Reminds me of the aliens in that movie *Signs*. They traveled a million light years to conquer earth but couldn't open a damn door."

I pulled out more drawers and felt underneath clothing. I opened the closet and took down boxes and moved hangers around.

"I think some of this will fit your girlish figure," I said, and tossed a few button-down shirts at Joel.

"I always wanted to wear shirts decorated with little alligators," Joel said.

"No gun. We might have to open the last door."

"Check under the mattress," Joel said.

"Genius," I nodded.

I slid the mattress to the side and found something that made my eyes light up.

Underneath, we'd hit the jackpot.

The .40 was a Smith & Wesson sized for conceal and carry.

There was an extra magazine with an extended grip that would hold a few extra rounds. The gun was already loaded, and the second mag also contained a long row of rounds.

Next to the .40 was a weird-looking assault rifle. Joel went around to the other side of the mattress, and together we lifted it and put it against the wall.

"Holy fuckballs," I said.

"This isn't a bed, it's a damn armory."

There was a hunting rifle, a double barrel shotgun, and an assortment of knives. There was even a broad-bladed sword in a scabbard. I picked up the long weapon and pulled the blade out a few inches. Steel gleamed back at me.

"Look at this thing."

"You finally found a hand weapon more impressive than the wrench."

"I'll stick with my metal club," I said. I didn't know the first thing about wielding a sword and didn't want to learn while Zs were on the attack. I'd probably be just as dangerous to Joel as to the Zs if I started swinging the blade around.

Joel picked up the rifle and looked it over. He popped the magazine out and looked inside.

"That's wild."

"What?"

"Sig MPX. It fires .40 caliber rounds. That explains all the ammo."

"Is that weird?"

"Nah. Probably good for home defense. Stock slides in to make it a pistol. See that short barrel? You can make a burglar regret every syllable in 'breaking and entering'. I'll have to test it to see if it has any kind of range. Might not be too accurate."

I shrugged and started stuffing ammo into my backpack. We didn't find any shotgun ammo, which was a shame. I'd have loved to sling the double barrel over my back. I missed the Mossberg tactical shotgun I'd lost during the battle at the RV park.

We'd been in the house for longer than I liked. The first week of the event had seen us planning for fights and timing them. If it took more than thirty seconds to take down Zs, we'd just haul ass. That was before the shufflers had become so prevalent. Our raiding time had been two minutes: in and out, squeaky-clean. See some Zs? Just move out and find another home.

Now we were almost leisurely, and that was going to get dangerous. I thought about telling Joel that we needed to move with a purpose, but he'd been quiet about how badly he was hurt, so I didn't push him.

Joel ripped a case off a pillow and stuffed it with boxes of rounds. He didn't bother with the knives, and I tossed the sword back on the mattress. The next group of survivors could have them.

Joel moved into the hallway and I was right behind him. I paused to listen at the closed door. I pressed my ear right up against the particle board and listened.

"Nothing," I whispered.

Something hit the door so hard it rattled in its frame. I jumped back, barely covering a curse.

"Like a peeping Tom with your pants around your ankles. Okay, I'm calling it," Joel said.

I nodded sheepishly.

We stopped in the kitchen on our way out for a last look around.

Someone had cleaned before they left. I could almost picture a family moving around, thinking that the worst would be over soon, that they'd be back in their house in a day, maybe two.

We grabbed canned goods and even a box of crackers. I found an opened can of Easy Cheese in the back of a pantry.

"Know how bad I want to squirt half that can into my mouth?" I asked Joel. "Reminds me of a few months ago when supplies were more abundant. I think we found some of this gas inducing crap back then."

"I know about you squids and squirting stuff in your mouths," Joel said with a half-smile.

"We learn from the best." I winked at Joel and went back to stuffing goods into my beat-up backpack.

"Nasty ass Sailor."

I leaned my head back and squirted some of the cheese into my mouth anyway. Then I tossed the can at Joel. He laughed at the look on my face, which was probably something like a cross between food-ecstasy and an O face. Stuff tasted so good I wanted to take it on a date and ask it to move in.

Joel tossed the can back, so I went ahead and finished it off. I'd pay for it later as it hit my gut, but it was worth it for now.

With our packs full and our bellies no longer rumbling, Joel moved to the hallway and stared at the last door on the right.

"No, man."

"What if there's something in there that we can use? These assholes had a lot of food and guns. Maybe there's a bottle of Viagra in that room with your name on it," Joel said.

"Let's just go. They need us." I was trying to keep my head on, but we'd been away from the camper for a few hours and I was worried.

"Keep it cool. We're headed back to the rest of the crew."

"I know. I'm just worried about Anna. She's got a bullet in her arm and I'm worried that it may already be infected, for all I know."

Joel put his hand on my shoulder.

"We got this, brother."

I shrugged his hand off my shoulder and opened a few more cabinets. I found dishes and cups, but nothing to eat. On impulse I grabbed a shaker filled with meat seasoning and added it to my collection. Joel stalked down the hallway and listened at the door, and then when something thumped, he returned.

"Curiosity is killing me, Creed, but you're right. Let's call it and get back," he said.

First damn thing Joel had said today that actually made sense.

He moved toward the door.

"Joel, want me to take some of that gear?"

"I'm good."

"You don't look good. You look like you're in pain."

"Just weakness leaving the body, man," he said.

He opened the door and peeked outside.

I'd done my best to string anything that didn't fit in my backpack around my waist and over my back. The little home defense machine gun rode next to the wrench. We didn't have time to sit around and load it, and neither one of us wanted to contemplate leaving leave it behind.

Joel stepped into the street and then immediately ran back inside. A pair of figures pushed into the doorway after him.

I had my wrench raised, ready to bash heads, when one of them raised a hand.

"No. Wait," a voice with a strong eastern European accent said.

"Civilians, Creed, and we're about to have company."

"Many come," the man said.

The couple were probably in their mid to late thirties. He had a craggy face, with early frown lines and dark skin. She was slight, with a huge blast of curly black hair that surrounded her head like a big halo. She wore a pair of thick-rimmed glasses and a bright yellow rain slicker. I stared at the loud jacket.

"Keep zombie bites out," she said.

"Smart," I said.

"Fall back. We need to find another way out of this place," Joel said.

"How many?" I asked.

"Oh, about a hundred," Joel said, and stormed down the hallway.

"We help?" the man asked.

"I don't know, can you?" I asked.

Don't judge me. It's the zombie fucking apocalypse. I'm all for helping my fellow man, but they have to be able to help themselves first.

The woman unlimbered a lead pipe. There were bloodstains almost to the handle she'd made out of duct tape. I won't lie, I was nervous. My encounters with other survivors had been hit or miss, from the nice folks at the RV park to the army led by

McQuinn. I was about as trusting as a rat guarding the last piece of moldy cheddar on earth.

The man lifted his jacket and showed a pair of revolvers. He didn't make any other moves.

"Well shit, I guess we're friends now," I shrugged, and followed Joel, hoping the man wouldn't shoot me in the back.

"I'm Tomas, and this is Doroyeta."

"Dori, like the fish from *Finding Nemo*," she said, and smiled.

"Creed, Jackson Creed. And that guy is Joel Kelly."

Movement at the door. The first Z came in and sized us up. He actually looked surprised, but that could be because his mouth was stuck wide open, thanks to a broken jaw. Tomas reached into his jacket, drew his gun, and calmly shot the monstrosity in the face. The Z went down but was soon replaced by two more. To make matters worse, I thought I'd heard a shuffler out there.

"Shit, man. Windows got bars. I guess we check the room with the locked door."

I rolled my eyes and prepared for the worst.

SURVIVAL OF THE FASTEST

11:20 hours approximate
Location: Vista

I wanted to trust the couple, but it wasn't easy. This was a different world. Gone were the days of small talk, neighbors who helped each other out, and even passive-aggressive comments. What had become the norm--the social media-driven Facebook world--was toast, hell, the internet was deader than a zombie. Now it was down to survival of the fastest.

Joel listened at the door for a half second then muttered, "Fuck it."

He stepped back, lifted his foot, and smashed the door in. It splintered around the lock and flew open to crash against the wall. I fumbled for my wrench, fighting all of the gear and shit that was hanging from my pack. The strap caught in the stock of the little assault rifle, so I ripped it to the side, banging the stock against my elbow in the process.

The room was something out of a nightmare. The wall was liberally smeared with blood. Equal amounts of red stained the bedspread where it lay in a heap at the foot of the bed. The sheets were also a mishmash of gore and blood and the carpet, light brown, was splotched with blood stains.

A picture hung on the wall, at an angle. It was the famous

painting by Edvard Munch, called *The Scream*. Not that I was an art expert, but who didn't know this work? I also had owned a print of it when I was a kid. Mom thought it was something that would make me smile. It gave me nightmares for years, but I never had the heart to tell her.

The room contained a dresser with most of its drawers hanging open.

A pathetic looking Z lay on the ground. He'd been eaten almost to the bone around his abdomen, and most of a leg was gone. He lifted his head to look us over, then dropped it again, hitting the wall right next to the door. That explained the banging.

Another Z came at us. She'd been near the corner of the room, staring at nothing in particular. I didn't even see her at first, because she was garbed in a dark dress and standing next to even darker drapes. She tripped over the Z and fell, hands out, so she caught Joel and dragged him to the ground.

The couple moved in fast, taking her by the arms and hauling her off. The man pushed her against the wall and the woman bashed in her forehead with the lead pipe. She fell in a heap and her head lolled to the side. Sightless white eyes regarded me.

Dori then took mercy on the man on the floor, two strong blows leaving a pile of rotted brains.

I grasped Joel's hand and helped him up.

Joel moved toward the back of the room and peeked inside a door.

"Bathroom's empty," he said.

The door banged at the front of the house.

"Any way out?" I asked Joel as he eyed the bathroom.

He shook his head.

"Guess that means we're going to have company," I said. "We need to get the hell out of dodge, partner."

"Check the window," Joel said.

I moved the drapes aside.

Something crashed inside the house, rattling the walls. Moans and snarls came from the hallway.

"Bars!" I yelled for Joel. He joined me at the window but didn't say a word.

"Now what?" I shrugged.

The couple pushed the door shut but it wouldn't stay closed, because my Marine pal had destroyed the doorknob with his big Marine foot. Brilliant, Joel.

"This isn't good," he said.

———

HE LOOKED AROUND THE ROOM FOR SOME EGRESS POINT. HE DIDN'T need me to tell him that there wasn't one.

I unlatched the window and it slid open with a squeal. Joel joined me, and together we tested the bars. They had been constructed on a row so that they were welded together and set into the opening. Joel grabbed the windowsill and put his foot on the jamb. He tested the bars with a quick outward kick.

The couple grabbed the corners of a large dresser and grunted as they slid it across the floor toward the door.

"Wanna know how I know we're fucked?" I asked Joel.

"How?"

"Because that shit never works in the movies," I nodded toward the door-damming operation.

Joel snorted and kicked the bars again.

My pack was in the way so I shrugged it off and then fought all of the extra gear into a pile. My wrench stayed across my back.

I moved beside Joel and lifted my leg, hoping that my recently-healed sprain wasn't going to be a problem.

"On three," Joel said.

I nodded.

He counted and together we kicked the poles. It was like kicking a brick wall.

"Again," he said.

Again we got the same reaction.

"Watch out, Joel." I ripped the wrench off my shoulder and maneuvered it between a pair of bars.

Joel took this cue and moved aside. He grabbed the little home invasion rifle we'd dug up in the other room and examined it. He fiddled with a switch on the side, checked the magazine, inspected the trigger assembly, and then moved away to help the couple.

He dropped a box of shells on the ground, and with deft and well-practiced fingers, loaded the magazine.

"We can't hold for long," Tomas said.

"Got it," I replied.

I pulled the wrench and got a little give from the bars.

The Zs smashed against the door. I looked over my shoulder and caught the entrance budging. Joel motioned for the couple to move out of the way. He lifted the little SIG, aimed, and fired. Not for the first time, I wished I had some ear protection.

In the movies, the shots weren't this loud. Dudes shot each other and then had quiet conversation about drug dealers and the best way to break someone's knee. In this room, the gun might as well have been mortars going off around us.

The gun bucked under his arms, and something dropped on the other side of the doorway.

"I like this thing," Joel said.

I wedged the wrench a little tighter and pulled.

Christ, we did not have time for this!

Joel fired several more shots, but there was always an answer in the form of something banging against the entrance. The next time the door moved, a hand darted inside.

Dori pulled her knife and slammed it into the palm, pinning the Z to the doorway. Joel stuck the barrel of the gun into the gap and fired. When Dori yanked the knife free, the hand fell away from the doorframe, hopefully attached to a twice-dead fuck.

Tomas pushed her out of the way and pulled his guns. Dori fell back and shot him a dirty look. A smattering of a language I didn't understand ensued. He snarled an answer back at her. She turned away in disgust and moved to my side.

"I can help?" she said.

"I don't think so," I said, and jammed the wrench between a pair of bars.

Joel shot something. Tomas shot something. I wanted to look, but forced my attention to stay on the task at hand.

"Open the mouth," Dori looked up at me from under dark curls.

"Huh?"

"I show you," she said.

Dori took the wrench from me and gently pushed into the spot I'd occupied, shooing me out of the way. She propped the head against the window jamb and then loosened the teeth so the span opened a few inches.

"Help me. We put on bar, there, and we have leverage."

"Jesus," I said, suddenly seeing it.

"Jesus isn't here, only the dead," she said.

With the teeth of the wrench stuck against the wall and the other part against the bar, I suddenly had something to work with. I grabbed the handle up high so I would get the most control, and yanked, putting my body into it.

The bar popped off and the bolt hit the ground. I quickly worked at the next bar. One down, and too many more to go.

Joel fired off a few more rounds.

"How we looking?" I called.

"The bodies are making a nice blockade out there. Door's still not gonna hold," Joel called back.

Several somethings hit the door hard enough to rattle the dresser. Then they hit it again.

Joel took a step back and unleashed half a dozen shots at the door. The ensuing thump of a form hitting the ground answered.

I popped off the third bar and found the fourth to be a mother. Dori and I both worked at it for a minute, but it wasn't moving. She guided me to another one. It came off with a nice groan, leaving just two more bars.

Something pushed into the door again.

Hands reached for Tomas.

The window led to a backyard that was butted up against an

apartment building. There was a small chainlink fence that ran the perimeter but several sections had collapsed, while others sagged. A few Zs roamed the yard, but nothing we couldn't deal with. The trick, as always, was to take them out quietly. Cave in a few heads and avoid attracting a horde.

Another Z had managed to weasel its way inside the room.

Joel fired until the gun was empty, and set it down.

"Where'd you put those .40 rounds?" he asked me.

I wiped a line of sweat off my forehead and nodded toward my backpack. Joel unzipped the bag and dug around, pulling out boxes of ammo.

The door rattled again and this time, the dresser was partially bucked into the room. Tomas shot something in the face, but another Z was right there to take its place.

The last bar wasn't budging. I was pretty sure Dori would be able to squeeze out of the room and maybe Joel Kelly, too, but I was stuck. Tomas was portly, so he wasn't going, either. Maybe we could shoot out the wall and crash through. Maybe we could slither up into the ceiling after bashing a hole with my wrench.

Both options were pretty far-fetched. With my luck I'd get halfway into the ceiling only to be dragged back into the room while a pair of Zs ate my legs.

Dori looked over her shoulder, fear etched upon her face. She pressed the wrench head onto the last bar, but up high this time.

Joel had a few boxes on the ground and he was going through them, but a whole lot of cursing accompanied his actions.

"I'll hold. You kick," Dori said.

"What if I break your wrist or hand?"

"Take risk or we die," she nodded toward the door.

"Fuck it," I muttered.

"Exactly. Fuck it," she said.

Dori held the wrench low on the grip and then dropped down as far as she could. I lifted my leg and braced myself on the window frame. I put my foot up and pressed against the wrench. If I didn't get this right, she'd have some broken digits.

I pulled my foot back and then kicked the wrench handle, but I was so concerned about her hand that I barely tapped it.

The dresser got pushed halfway into the room; a pair of very determined and very freshly turned Zs pushed on the door until it gave.

Joel stumbled back, managed to load his handgun, snapped the magazine home, lifted, aimed, and blew one of the bastards' heads off. The guy had been dressed in a sky-blue running suit complete with a bright green headband. He had a mullet that didn't look any better covered in gore.

The second Z was just as fast and dressed in the same gear, but in a ridiculous orange.

What a pair of assholes.

It got a hold of Tomas and dragged him to the ground. There was a brief struggle, but Tomas was strong and didn't put up with any of the Z's crap. He knocked the guy to the side and then rolled over. He was on his feet with a snarl. The Z grabbed Tomas's leg and tried to get a piece. Tomas ripped free and kicked the dead guy in the face. I was really starting to like this scrappy fighter.

The Z fell away but Tomas wasn't done. He rolled over and drove his knife into the Z's face, yanked it out, and did it again.

The dresser moved again, and more Zs barged into the room.

I kicked the wrench again and the bar budged.

"Come on," Dori urged me on.

I pulled my boot back and slammed it into the wrench, catching the edge of Dori's finger. She didn't have time to pull back, because the bar snapped free.

"Out!" I yelled.

Tomas came to his feet and kicked another Z. It fell back into the crowd at the door, creating a temporary roadblock. Joel fired a pair of shots and then came at us. I moved aside, but he urged me to go ahead.

I helped Dori out the window and Tomas was right behind her.

Joel shot a pair of Zs while he jammed stuff back into my backpack. Boxes of rounds and empty magazines were stuffed in. He tried to zip it closed but I reached over, grabbed it, and tossed it out the window.

"Dude, let's go!"

Joel grinned, rose to his feet, and calmly shot a female Z in the forehead. She'd been covered in blood, her hair like some kind of nightmare of bright red dreads. She went down and then Joel was tossing our shit outside.

"Piece of cake," he said, and then lifted his foot and shrugged out the window like he was about to go for a leisurely Sunday walk around the city.

I was right behind him. A Z managed to grab hold of my shirt but I shook his hand off. When I was outside I picked up my wrench and crushed the Z's head that came at us. The next one crowded in, so I bashed it just as hard. The two bodies created a nice little dam that would buy us some time.

"Piece of cake, my ass," I muttered.

I grabbed my bag, shifted stuff around until it would close, and then worked it around my shoulders.

Dori and Tomas had advanced into the yard and taken out a pair of Zs, nice and quietly. He got a young guy's attention and backed away, and she shattered in the back of the Z's head. The last one was a guy who had to be in his seventies and weigh close to three hundred pounds. Tomas tripped him and Dori smashed his head to pulp. They nodded at each other and then turned to regard us.

"I like them. They're the model of killing efficiency we should all strive for," Joel said like a typical Marine.

"I like them too, because they're alive and they're not trying to kill us," I muttered back.

11:25 hours approximate

Location: Vista

THE LAWN WAS JUST AS DEAD AS OUR PURSUERS. ADOBE HAD BEEN set in a sidewalk of sorts and then outlined in fist-sized stones. Plants wilted in pots, except for three palm trees. They rose three or four feet and didn't look any worse for wear. A few more years and the owners had probably planned to plant them around the perimeter of the house. One thing that southern California didn't lack for was palm trees.

Someone had posted a sign: "Don't be a dope. Clean up your dog's poop." Someone else had scrawled "Brains" over the word "poop".

A pair of legs lay, unmoving from beneath some shrubs. I didn't bother investigating, because--zombies.

We'd only been in the house for fifteen or twenty minutes, but the sky had turned a nasty shade of grey. San Diego didn't really have a winter--it was seventy year-round--but this November had become dismal in the early weeks. I was convinced it was because the world currently sucked ass. More than likely, it was just a normal weather pattern. If rain broke out right now I'd be happy. That meant precipitation would pool up so we wouldn't have to rely on bottled water for the rest of our (presumably) short lives.

Joel motioned for us to drop. The Hungarians caught on and went into a crouch. We shuffled low until we were behind a planter box. A small horde of ten or fifteen dead meandered past our position. A straggler took an interest in the fence because Zs are stupid, and decided to hang out for a while.

Tomas pulled a gun, but Joel shook his head.

I snapped my fingers to get the Z's attention. It lifted its head and drooled blood.

The kid couldn't have been more than fifteen years old, and that made me think of Craig.

The Z didn't catch on, so I snapped my fingers again.

He walked into the fence and then fell over. His ass was in the air and his hands were on the ground. I maneuvered around the planter, wrench in a tight grip.

Something caught my eye at the corner of the yard where the fence met the back of the house. A shape came into view and then faded again.

I waited, hand lifted slightly to tell Joel to wait. When I didn't see the form again, I advanced on the kid.

He was dressed in the remains of a pair of tighty-whiteys. The only other thing that he wore was one red knee-length sock. His back and arms were a mess of wounds that were hard to look at. No one, especially not a kid, should have to go through that kind of trauma.

"What are you waiting for?" Joel hissed.

I stared at the kid. He was stuck, and his legs were kicking in slow motion. His hands scrabbled at the ground, but as much as he wanted to crawl toward me, he didn't have the motor skills to pull himself off the fence.

Thing about killing Zs is you get used to it. Sure, I've seen my share of the dead wanting to take a bite. I'd fought back, because that was survival. What I hated was all the necessary killing. This was no different.

11:50 hours approximate
Location: Vista

"WHERE TO, BOSS?" THE HUNGARIAN MAN ASKED.

"Tomas. I don't want to be rude but we don't exactly have room for more people in our little group."

"We help, then we and you go."

"Why?"

Tomas stared at me like I was an idiot.

"It is normal to help, yes?" Dori chimed in.

"Fine. Ya'll wanna help, that's great, but we're not far from our base of operations. When we get back, we're out of this city," Joel said.

He was being purposefully obtuse. No sense revealing too

much to folks we didn't know. It was like I had a psychic connection to my pal. Neither one of us had found a reason to trust another human, but I wasn't going to turn them away if they were going to help with my plan. The plan I hadn't told Joel about yet.

We hid behind the burned-out husk of a doublewide that had probably been a piece of shit even before it had been set on fire. The roof was bent the wrong way and hung inside the monstrosity, judging by the limited view I got from the kicked-in doorway. I was pretty sure one of the blackened husks on the floor had been a person.

The house next to the doublewide backed up to a sprawling trailer park that was littered with debris and bodies. One of the homes was at least intact, but something thumped against the walls and wasn't being quiet about it.

I motioned for Joel to join me, and we moved a few feet away.

"No, man. We can't bring them," Joel said before I could get a word in.

"I know that. I need to do something and I understand if you want to get back to our base."

"Stupid sailor. What half-assed plan are you about to get killed over?"

"So little faith, Joel. Have I steered us wrong yet?"

"Yeah. Many times."

I gave Joel a flat look.

"Alright. What is it? We can't keep tossing houses all day."

"I know, but I have to come back with antibiotics. Anna's wound can't wait."

Tomas and Dori kept watch. He spoke to her in Hungarian and she nodded. Both of them took pains to pretend like they weren't listening to us.

"Even if we found a pharmacy, place has probably been picked over twenty times."

"Remember the piece of paper?" I said, and lowered my backpack.

I moved aside cans, boxes of ammo and boxed food until I

found the sheet and pulled it out. One side had been a poster for a rock band from the eighties. The other held the message.

"Probably a trap," he said and handed it back.

"So we scout it out and get our new friends here to help."

"What's in it for them?"

"Maybe they have needs that can be met."

I motioned for Dori and Tomas to join us, and told them what I had in mind.

A shambler moved past the burned-out house, but didn't catch wind of us. We kept silent for a few minutes while its mindless legs carried it away from our position.

"We have needs too. We go," Tomas said.

Dori said something in Hungarian and he shook his head. They spoke together, her sounding pissed, him sounding like he didn't care.

"I apologize. We must leave you now," Dori waved her hand, indicating our location. "After we are clear of this place we go."

Tomas didn't look happy, but he nodded.

"It's cool, I understand," I said. "Maybe we'll run into each other again."

They probably didn't trust us either, but at least they were being civil and not trying to shoot us in the back and take our stuff. The only reason we'd joined up in the first place was because we didn't have a choice.

WE NODDED AT EACH OTHER AND TOGETHER MOVED OUT. JOEL and I scouted, while they followed and covered our backs. The two were smart and keep their eyes up and focused. They worked well as a team; I couldn't help but think about the value of adding them to our little group of misfits.

We made good time as we ducked into homes and buildings, constantly on the lookout for Zs. As much as I'd come to expect threats around every corner, under every car, inside every doorway, we only came across a few, and they went down quickly and best of all, quietly.

As we neared the center of town, I broke out the little map again and looked at street signs and landmarks.

Dori and Tomas made short farewells, and then they moved out. A minute later and they hunkered down between two homes, then ran to a road and stayed near a low line of shrubs.

"Shame they couldn't stick around," Joel said. "The little firecracker was growing on me."

"Me too," I nodded. "But I don't think any of us were ready to shake hands and become BFFs. Plus, how do we feed two new mouths? It's hard enough to keep *ourselves* fed, not to mention the shit machine known as Frosty."

"Maybe we'll get lucky and come across an overturned tortilla chip truck. I'd just about kill for a bag of Doritos."

"You had to mention chips. One of the greatest inventions in the world and we can't find a snack-size bag to save our lives."

I thought I was going to start drooling. Hell, I'd take a shower in Doritos and call it the perfect day.

12:15 hours approximate
Location: Vista

THE MAP HAD BEEN CRUDE BUT WELL DONE. A SIMPLE SKETCH WORK of lines representing streets as well as one landmark: that being a street roundabout that contained a fountain that was dry as a desert. There was a statue of some guy on top, and tied to him were the corpses of two of Zs who'd been executed. Their rotting husks hung over the fountain and had given it a rust color, thanks to all the blood. Whoever had shot these two hadn't been kind. Bullet holes riddled every body part.

A dog ran across the street, barking at the top of his lungs, but was gone before I could think to quiet him down.

We found the convenience store we'd raided an hour ago and then studied the street signs again. I pointed at one labeled

La Jolla and Joel nodded. The street was free of bodies, but cars had been pushed into an interesting pattern. Joel and I hunkered behind one while we studied the lay of the land.

"This shit is creepy."

"What do you mean?" I asked.

"It's been done up to slow us down."

"Or slow down Zs," I said.

Joel's assault rifle was pressed against his shoulder. He stared into the EOTech scope.

"Could be. Could be a trap."

"Agreed, but why a trap if they want to barter?"

"Shoot the folks coming in the gauntlet and take their shit. Drag the bodies off somewhere," Joel said.

I gulped.

"How about this. I'll go ahead in and you cover me."

"No shit, Sherlock. Think we're both gonna just wander into a death trap?" he said.

"Wouldn't be the first time," I said, and stood up.

"Keep your head down. If anyone starts shooting, I'll shoot back."

"I know, man. Just don't shoot me in the ass."

Joel nodded and I moved out.

12:30 hours approximate
Location: Vista

I FELT LIKE I WAS UNDER THE CROSSHAIRS THE ENTIRE TIME. THE gauntlet, as Joel had called it, was just that: trucks, cars, furniture--anything that could be used as an obstacle--had been dragged into the street to form a maze. Spikes made out of sticks and metal tubing had been driven into the sides of vehicles to catch unwary Zs. Bodies hung from some traps, but they were fresh kills.

I didn't see anything resembling a freshly-killed human.

Only rotted flesh, bald and balding heads, and a whole lot of blood and rot. Pretty typical stuff for the apocalypse.

I glanced back, expecting to see Joel, but I should have known better. He'd disappeared, however I didn't think for a minute that he'd abandoned me. Like a Marine hedgehog, he'd probably found some place to get nice and invisible and had the area I was waltzing into under his sights.

I didn't want to think about the alternative, that someone had him and me under *their* sights, especially since I was probably walking into a trap.

What I wouldn't give to have some kind of Bluetooth radio headset to talk to Joel as I walked toward my death.

But I had to do this for Anna. I needed to get her antibiotics, or the bullet extraction could go south real quick like. Assuming Roz could even get the damn bullet out, having Frosty lick the wound probably wouldn't do much good. I needed to get her the drugs Roz had listed.

I came across a crudely-drawn sign done up with a Sharpie.

"No ZEDs within. Advance to safety, state what you have to barter, then get the fuck out. Wrong move gets you erased."

What was the wrong move exactly? Was I supposed to leave my weapons here?

"Leave your weapons and come on in," a voice called from the shadow. Damn, that guy should have been on psychic hotline.

I dropped to a crouch and ducked next to a burned-out sedan. My wrench was in one hand and my pistol was in the other.

"If we wanted you dead we'd a shot you a while back. You're a big fella," a husky female voice said.

"I haven't exactly had the best luck with other people," I said lamely.

"I know. We're not animals. Just here to trade and get you back on the road to wherever the hell you're going. Oh, and we're not Reavers, because fuck those guys."

"Reavers?" I asked.

"Those wackos that want to see the world burn. We're businessmen, not bullies."

I shook my head. Reavers?

"I don't know anything about assholes burning the world. How about if I just turn around and go back the way I came right now?" I asked.

"Have a nice day, but feel free to come back when you need something. We got a whole shop fulla goods. Just ask. We probably got it. See ya," she said.

"Fuck," I whispered.

"Not my type," she said.

"So you're not going to steal my stuff?"

"Hell no. We need guys like you to bring back goodies. For the love of Pete, show yourself, Devon."

A person materialized a few feet from me. He'd been hiding in a dark doorway, and he was dressed all in black, including a ski mask. I guessed that he was one of the figures that had nodded at me earlier in the day. He had a sidearm, holstered, and some kind of assault rifle I'd never seen before but Joel could probably write a love poem about.

Anna needed this.

I put my pistol aside and dropped my wrench.

"Fine. I'm leaving my pistol and wrench here. I have backup, though, so don't do anything stupid."

"Black fella with a hard face? Yeah, we know about him. Just play it cool and no one gets holey. That's what happens when bullets start to fly. People drop to the ground and start praying to god. Plus there's the actual holes. Nasty business."

I lifted my hands and moved around the car. There was a low wooden door, and behind that stood a woman in her fifties or sixties. She was whip-thin and had a crazy mop of curly white hair. Thick glasses rode her nose. She smiled, though, and I wondered if I was going to take that as my last sight before I woke up in hell.

"You *are* a big one. Just keep a calm head and we'll do the same. Got guys coming and going all the time, but it's always the first-timers that are twitchy. We've been in business for a week and only one person's messed this up. He's out there, on the side of a car. Keeps the Zs away," she cackled.

"So how does this work?" I asked and lowered my hands. I tried to eye the man in black but he'd disappeared. Instead I lifted my hand in the air and did a little circle so Joel knew I wasn't in immediate danger.

"How do ya *think* it works? Ya come in here, tell me what ya need, and I tell you what *I* need. If we got stuff to trade then we smile, give each other our stuff, and part friends. Handshakes are optional."

"What if I don't have what you need?"

"I bet you could make an old woman feel good," she smiled and winked at me.

"Thought I wasn't your type," I said and thought about just leaving.

"Mom, leave him alone," a voice called from inside.

The woman broke into another cackle and gestured for me to join her.

"I'm just messing with ya. Name's Elda. Come on in, we got some hot beef stew. Ain't the best, 'cause it's from a can, but it's warm and fills ya up. Guy came in needing some bandages and left us a case. I'll share if it makes ya feel any better. You can even watch me sip it if it makes ya feel safer."

I was practically drooling at the mention of stew.

"Fine. Just make it quick if you're going to kill me," I muttered. "I don't want to die knowing I let my friends down."

"So melodramatic. Just barter and then go along your way. I won't hold it against ya if ya don't want stew or hospitality."

I considered the older woman. This might be an act. A really good act. A few weeks ago I probably would have trusted her. After McQuinn I wasn't in the mood to trust anyone. But I did my best to keep my wits about me.

She opened the wooden door and gestured, then turned and kept talking as she walked. I followed, wary of anyone that might jump out and try to plant a knife in my skull.

"We have some food, ammo, and meds. Most people want meds, but we're fresh out of Oxy. I guess the next best thing would be to go to L.A. and find someone that deals heroin, then stick a needle up your ass and say goodbye to this shitty world for a few hours."

"How's L.A.?" I couldn't help but ask.

"Still there, last I heard, but ya have to watch out for the Reavers. The city took a lot of damage, but I heard some mercenaries working with the military have cleared up part of the city and they're fighting the Reavers. There's talk of big walls, but I don't know--could just be talk. If you're heading up there I suggest you approach by daylight. Also heard they shoot anything that creeps around at night."

"That's the second time I've heard the term Reavers. Who are they?"

"You *are* wet behind the ears," she said with a half-smile. "We don't know much, but when they appear we disappear. They're some kind of wackos who think God brought on this plague and it's their job to convince unbelievers with fire or bullets. Rumor has it they took over some military bases or they were already *on* bases, inside job and such, can't say for sure. They're bad news. Look for the bloody skullcaps."

"Bloody skullcaps? The hell is wrong with people?" I shook my head.

"People got guns now and no one to tell 'em to put 'em away. All that shootin'. Figure they'd run out of ammo at some point. Then I guess stuff will get medieval. Swords and maces. Like that big ole wrench you carry. I heard about you from my boy Devon, out front."

I nodded as she kept talking.

"You just steer clear of Reaver camps, you'll be okay. Not sure I'd recommend going to L.A., but it's your skin. Now, what do ya need?"

She'd taken over an antique store. Old clothes and collectibles had been piled on shelves and counters. A typewriter that had seen better days fifty years ago sat in a corner with a fresh sheet of paper protruding from the roller. Plates, picture frames, and a chair that had a spin seat and a weird thick wicker back were all pushed aside. Boxes of MREs, bottled water, and cases of soup and vegetables were stacked in one corner.

"Antibiotics."

"Oh yeah? Someone sick?"

"Something like that. What do you have?"

"What do you need?"

I reached into my pocket and found the crumpled-up note that Roz had prepared. I tried to pronounce the first pill on the list, but after I'd butchered it for the second time, Elda grabbed the slip of paper.

"I got one of these. I think. I'll have to have my son take a look."

Someone slipped out of a corner of the room. He was dressed in the same shade of "don't fuck with me" black as the guy near the doorway outside. He wore a couple of guns, but one was under his arm and his right hand stayed close to the stock. This did nothing to make me feel safe.

"Hi," I said lamely.

"Yo," the guy nodded.

He took the list and disappeared into the back of the store. A lock clicked and he rummaged around.

"I don't have much. Some canned goods, a box of crackers. Half a can of Easy Cheese. Got a burner and some butane," I said, and hefted my bag.

"Not bad."

The guy returned with a couple of pill bottles and handed them to the woman. She squinted at the labels.

"I have ten Amoxicillin That's good for a few days. What kind of wound are we talking about?"

"Gunshot," I said, and didn't elaborate.

The itching feeling on the back of my neck, like someone had a gun pointed at my head, wouldn't depart.

"Let me see the burner."

I lowered my pack with a clank. The burner was stuffed in the top so that it barely closed. I had three bottles of fuel, which I also set out. The thing was, this was something we could really use, but Anna needed the meds. If she got infected there was no way to take her to a hospital or clinic. An infection could easily become a death sentence.

"I'll let ya have five pills for the burner and butane."

"Come on," I protested. "I need those pills."

"You and folks with a lot more to offer. What else ya got?"

I rolled my eyes and dug around in my bag, pushing aside the Percocets, TUMS, and the stuff I couldn't pronounce, until I found the last bottle of pills. I held them up to the light, and read the label out loud.

"Well, hell. Why didn't ya say so? Lotta folks living on anti-depressants now that the end of the world is here. Kinda ironic, don't you think? Everyone felt like their world was ending and took pills. Now the world *is* over and they really *need* the goddamn pills."

"So you want these?" I stared into the bottle and figured there were at least fifty.

"Oh yeah. Take the antibiotics."

"Works for me," I said, and started to stuff the burner back into my backpack.

"And the burner?"

"I don't think so. See I'm a Navy hole snipe and that means I'm not all that bright. But I can count, and fifty of my pills are worth a hell of a lot more than ten of your pills. All things being equal and all."

The woman's son choked back a chuckle from his vantage point.

"I can throw in a few more pills."

"Sounds like a winner. Toss in a case of that beef stew while you're at it and we're good. Oh, and you have any 5.56 ammo?"

"Half case and two boxes of shells," she said.

I tossed her the pill bottle.

13:00 hours approximate
Location: Vista

"Are you fucking nuts, man? How are we going to hike back to the RV with our packs and that big-ass box?"

"I'm going to carry it, Joel, and you're going to shoot anything that looks at me in the wrong tone of voice," I said. "It's a case of beef stew. We're eating like kings tonight."

The box wasn't that heavy, but with my pack, weapons, wrench, and the case of food, it was going to be a long walk.

"You kidding me? You get the drugs?"

"Yeah and I got some interesting news. There's some fringe group called Reavers operating near L.A. The store owner told me they're a bunch of idiots in bloody skullcaps and they have an agenda that involves guns and fire."

"Wait, what?" Joel asked.

"That's all I know, man. We can't worry about it now, I guess. California's a big place and hopefully we won't run into them."

"We'll steer clear, and good fucking deal on the supplies, brother," he said. "We're a day out from Pendleton, and if I know my brothers they won't put up with this Reaver bullshit. We'll be safe once we get to the base."

I grinned at Joel and hefted the pack. He moved out and I followed close behind.

I wish I could say that the Marine base was the start of our salvation. Turned out, we had a long way to go.

A PAIR OF EXTRACTIONS

13:15 hours approximate
Location: Vista

The trek back to the RV was just as wretched as you can imagine. We ran, ducked, hid, shot, and bludgeoned stuff. We took out enough Zs to fill a small classroom, and then we did it again. There comes a point when the bodies fall away and you just have to wonder if they will ever end.

Joel kept looking back over his shoulder.

"What are you expecting?" I asked.

"Just don't trust the dealers. Wanna make sure they aren't following us."

I hadn't even thought of that, so paranoia crept into me and soon I was looking over my shoulder before every turn. Thankfully the men dressed in black didn't make a reappearance.

A Z was, though. He came out of a doorway and made for me.

I had no choice but to back away and carefully set the case of beef stew on the ground. In the time it took me to stand up, lift the wrench, and swing, I also had time to miss. The bastard hit a curb and stumbled so I hit air. Joel was already moving down the alley, so he didn't know I was in trouble. I hissed and called

407

his name, but he didn't hear me, or maybe he was sick of saving my dumb ass and decided to leave me behind.

The Z was all rotting breath, yellow, and bloodstained teeth. One side of his head was torn away leaving muscle, sinew, and crusted blood. His other ear dangled by a strip of skin and flapped against the side of his head.

I pulled back but the Z was fresh, in that "I just got bit a few days ago and most of my limbs still work" kinda way that was real damn annoying.

I used one of my best weapons, my foot, and pushed the fool back. He grabbed my ankle and leaned over to bite me, so I swung the wrench again and connected with his shoulder. He took the blow and almost went down, but his grip on my ankle pulled me off-balance and I stumbled, striking my knee on the curb. Pain shot up my thigh, so hot and sharp I had to fight back a scream.

The dead fuck fell away as I managed to sit back on my ass and shake him lose. I rolled to the side and got a fresh shambler around my neck for the effort. Jesus Christ! Were they *breeding* back there?

I did the only thing I could think of: I lowered my chin to my chest and then snapped my head back hard, catching the Z right in the face. Cartilage broke and something cold and wet hit my neck. Fighting back nausea and an intense wish to find all of the Purell in the world to squirt down my shirt, I stood up, dragging the Z along with me.

It dropped in a pile of arms and legs, fighting to get to its feet. The first Z came at me, so I backed up a step, knee aching as it took my full weight. I shuddered but soldiered on.

"Joel," I called, but my voice was a ragged gasp.

The pair of Zs closed in on me from opposite sides, both eyeing my pale white flesh. They probably looked at me the same way I'd look at a rack of baby back ribs covered in BBQ sauce. The stupid thought invaded my mind and saliva actually shot into my mouth.

"Here, piggy," I said, and bashed the first Z in the head.

He went down in a lump, my wrench stuck in his head. I

had to let go or be dragged down to the ground, so that left me--with a full pack and assorted weapons clanking around my body--to stumble away as the zombie closed in.

She was about my age, and her wounds weren't as bad as those of the guy who had my weapon sticking out of his noggin. She was small but wiry, and fast. She moaned: that low rumble of greed for flesh that I'd heard endlessly since this shitstorm started.

I fell back and my leg went out from under me as pain made me grimace. One second I was on my feet, the next I was on my aching knees.

Her hair might have been a pale shade of red once, but now it was like knotted curtains around her head. When she spun around to track me, her dreads of gore spun with her, slapping against the side of her face. I never wanted to hear that noise again.

I managed to crawl a few feet, rip a can of beef stew off the pile and throw it at her. She took it in the chest, so I picked up another and pelted her in the neck. She snarled at me and staggered to her feet. Hands up, fingers mostly intact except for a few that were bent back at an angle that made me shudder, she crawled on her knees.

I smacked her with another can, but it hit her shoulder and the can sailed away.

I struggled to my feet, but the Z tripped on her shoelace and fell on me, taking me to the ground. I fought her as she went for my arms. She got a piece of fabric and ripped it in her greedy mouth. I punched her in the side of the head, feeling like a misogynistic asshole, and then hit her again. By the time I pounded her to the side I'd gotten over myself, stood up, and crushed her head.

Before I could breathe a sigh of relief, a fresh pair of Zs exited the building and stumbled toward me. I tried to get up, but my leg screamed in pain. It was the same leg I'd injured a few weeks ago, so my freshly-healed ankle now had company. That was just great.

"Fuck every one of you!" I said, realizing that I was about to join their ranks.

Joel's knife blurred out and took one of the Zs in the temple. He was like some ninja as he let go of the blade and then lashed out a foot to trip the other Z.

"You gonna sit there crying or help me out?"

"I got a choice?" I said.

My wrench was only a few feet away. I shuffled toward it and grabbed the haft. The weapon felt good, like an extended arm terminating in a fist of heavy metal. I lifted the piece and then spun as one of the zombies broke from the cover of the building.

I struck it at about knee height, a staggering blow that took its legs out. The Z wasn't even on the ground when I hit it in the head a couple of times.

Joel helped me to my feet.

"Wondered where you were, then come to find out you're back here playing with some new friends."

"Fuckers came out of nowhere, man. There was one and then two. After that I lost count."

"That's because they don't teach squids how to count. You good?"

I put my arm around him and tested my weight on my leg. It ached but took the pressure, so I took a half step away.

"Jesus. Look at this mess. Let's haul ass before more of them come out of that clown car of a building and try to finish us off."

Joel chuckled.

"Gather up the cans and let's hit it." Joel grabbed one of the precious cylinders of stew and put it back on the box.

I grabbed two more and dropped them onto the crate, trying to ignore the blood and gore that were pasted to the sides of the cans. Where'd the last one go?

A pair of snarls made me forget about it. I grabbed the box, shouldered it, and staggered after Joel.

We moved around the block, ducked around some wilting

hedges, and then stood and ran for it. Well, to be fair, Joel ran; I limped after.

Moans followed us.

After a pair of turns, we reached the block where we'd left the RV, came around the corner, and both stopped in our tracks.

The RV was gone.

But that wasn't the worst part. Sniffing around the ground the RV had occupied was a shuffler, and he was surrounded by a half dozen fresh Zs.

13:40 hours approximate
Location: Vista

THE BUILDING HAD BEEN A JUNKYARD, AND THE ZS WERE PROWLING around rusting hulks of cars and car parts. One of the bastards had taken an interest in a bumper and kept nudging it with his foot. That's not a person, you dumbass zombie.

We faded back behind the building. I held my breath and waited for the telltale sound of a shuffler's cry. If he'd spotted us we were going to have to either stand and fight--something I didn't relish--or run, something I wasn't going to be so good at.

Joel didn't say a word. He carefully lowered his pack and weapons. He leaned them against the house and gestured for me to do the same. I tried to keep the noise down and wasn't sure if I did a good job. The cans were first, then I had to maneuver a few of the weapons we'd snagged from the house onto the ground. My wrench was next, followed by my pack.

Joel touched my shoulder and motioned me close.

"The fuck we gonna do now?" I whispered next to his ear.

"It's gonna go down like the old days. You sneak around the back. I'll shoot a few, starting with that shuffler, in sixty seconds."

"Why the hell are we going to take on this bunch? Let's haul ass and regroup."

"There's a piece of paper taped to the side of the building. I think they left us a message. The girls wouldn't desert us unless they felt threatened. I think they left behind a clue."

"A clue? Been watching too much *CSI*?"

"I ain't seen a TV in months, ya dumbass," Joel said.

I rolled my eyes.

"So I'm bait and you're going to shoot them with what?"

"I have a few rounds for the AR. I can take out the shuffler, but after that it's going to get tough. You go in swinging and shooting once the shuffler's down."

"What if you miss?"

"When have I missed?"

"I don't know, about fifty times, give or take."

It was Joel's turn to roll his eyes.

"Fine. We go in shooting, we get eaten, should we leave a note while the shuffler's eating our brains?" Joel said.

"Our only other choice is to hide this stuff and then split up. We could each take a direction and try to find the RV. I'm betting they didn't go far."

A shot echoed to the east.

I looked at Joel, but he only shrugged.

"What, can't tell what kind of weapon from the sound? Could that be Anna's piece?"

"Man, I don't know what the fuck a gun sounds like unless it's an AK-47. Those things are distinct."

"It's like we speak two different languages, Joel. Okay, so the plan is like this: I flank 'em, go in swinging and shooting, and you kill the shuffler. It *is* like the old days."

The first week we'd been in San Diego, we'd become a tight fighting machine. Short, fast engagements resulting in twice-dead corpses, then we got scarce real fast, and hopefully with a few supplies for the effort. Things had changed as the shufflers had gotten smarter. I was also banged up pretty badly, and didn't even know if I'd be able to get around the building in time.

"We got this, man. It's going to be smooth as melted butter."

"Famous last words," I said, and looked at my watch.

"Sixty seconds," Joel said, and picked up his assault rifle. He looked it over, and then popped into a squat.

"Better make it seventy. I'm a mess."

"Getting slow in your old age?"

"No, man. Ankle's hurting like hell, shoulder's banged up, the feeling just came back to my knee and it's not a good kind of feeling."

"I'll give you a minute and a half to flank 'em. When I drop the shuffler, you go in swinging."

I dragged my pack to us and quietly unzipped it, then rummaged around inside for a few seconds.

Joel looked at me questioningly.

I found the small box of shells I'd picked up from the old woman and handed it to Joel. He smiled and slid the cover open.

"Merry early fucking Christmas," I said.

"Best gift ever," Joel said.

He popped the magazine out of his assault rifle and started loading it. I noticed there were only two rounds in the mag.

"Really, man? You were going to risk my life with two rounds."

"Gimme some credit. Two rounds equal two kills."

"Ninety seconds. You better not miss that damn shuffler."

Joel grunted, quietly slipped the full magazine back into the rifle and shot me a cool look. I nodded back, picked up my wrench and handgun, and moved out.

13:50 hours approximate
Location: Vista

I STARTED THIS JOURNAL A FEW MONTHS AGO. THE FIRST ENTRY WAS about a mission just like this one. We were in the process of finding supplies for "fortress," and that meant making runs into town. As we ranged farther and farther out, we ran into problems with Zs as they got hungrier. I took to calling it "The Fuckening".

I was ultra-cautious back then and took little risk, except for the day we had to get past a bunch of Zs, and one of the quick ones I later came to call shufflers. Since then, the shufflers had grown smarter and could, much to my horror, control a small army of their undead brothers. I didn't know how the mechanism for communicating with their little minions worked, and I really didn't care. All I wanted was to kill every shuffler I came across. I wanted to bash in heads and then take a minute to piss on their corpses.

Just like the first days, I was about to do something dumb. I was about to be bait.

The building had seen better days before the z-poc and was now what I'd call comfortably dilapidated. Some kind of vines clung to one side and sunlight shone through space where the walls had been kicked or just fallen in. Two windows faced out, but both were devoid of glass. If it came down to it, I guessed I could just *Die Hard* my way through a window and hide under a desk. The problem with that plan? I'm no Bruce Willis.

I ran into my first difficulty as soon as I tried to move to the backside of the building. A big fence was in the way. It was chain-link, sure, and it wasn't all that tall. But it was going to be noisy as hell. Plus there was a wreck parked right next to the fence, and there was no way I was risking tetanus today.

My internal clock was about to hit forty-five seconds, so I needed to move with a purpose.

I crept alongside the fence and found another building that was probably someone's house. The doors had been mostly boarded up, but a limp and half-devoured body lay near the remains of the wood planks that were scattered all over the busted-ass porch.

I skirted the building at a near sprint before rounding it and finding the path clear. Then it was just a matter of another thirty or so feet. I reached the edge of the building and peeked around. The Zs were still there, but the shuffler wasn't in sight. The fact that we had no way to communicate--like those cool little throat mics that the mercenaries had possessed when we were in the city of Vista--sucked.

There was no real plan, except that it was go time. My internal clock dinged at ninety seconds, so I strode out into the open.

The first Z saw me as soon as I saw it. I lifted the wrench in my right hand and pointed the gun with my left. Not that I was ever a good shot, and sure as shit not at all good with my off hand, but I had still learned a thing or two about shooting Zs.

"Hey, you godless fucks," I said.

Joel was not in sight, but I assumed he was low and at the corner of a building, covering me from a forty-five degree angle so I didn't accidentally shoot him.

The thing snarled at me. Three others turned their milky white gazes on me and staggered. I aimed, exhaled, and fired, expecting to miss the first time, because I'm sharp like that.

I fired and the Z took a round in the neck. It spun around and dropped to one knee.

The others didn't care about their buddy. They saw me and thought I was human steak.

A shot rang out, and one of them dropped.

Where the hell was that fucking shuffler?

I took a half-dozen steps, pulled the wrench back, and flattened the Z who was on his knees. His head turned inside out, and that was okay with me. Pulped brain matter exploded and hit the ground. He dropped without another sound and lay on his new pillow of squished and gnarly rot.

A pair broke from cover and came at me. Another shot and one of them fell over. His head snapped to the side like he'd just remembered something. Most of his face was gone. What in the hell kind of bullets had the old woman traded to me?

A pile of car parts that could use a bath in WD-40 provided a decent amount of cover as I dropped to a crouch and took cover.

An old man in golf shorts and the remains of a tank top looked around in a daze. In general, I don't recommend playing peek-a-boo with the dead. He was dark-skinned from time in the sun, time he'd spent before the change hit. If zombies got sunburned, I kind of felt bad for them.

Kind of.

I switched hands and used my much better right to aim. The gun bucked and the Z fell on its face with a neat hole in the side of its head. Damn, I was having a good day. Three shots and two kills. That was some Joel Kelly heroics right there.

The last Z was slow because he was dragging the remains of his foot. His ripped and shattered ankle hit the ground with each step, making a grinding noise. I gulped and aimed.

That's when a fresh wave broke from cover and came at me. There weren't just a few--there were at least ten or fifteen, and they were spry.

They'd been in the small alleyway across from our position. The sun had provided cover, and I wished I had a grenade to toss at the horde, because I was sure that's where the damn shuffler was holding court.

Joel broke from cover and came in shooting. I didn't wait around for him to accidentally shoot me; I headed for the side of a building. With my back against wood, I picked a target and shot him. He didn't drop, but I'd scored a hit, judging by the way he spun away.

A series of loud retorts echoed as Kelly moved in. He wasn't wasting time on theatrics; he was all badass Marine. His weapon was up and his eyes glued to targets. He dropped three in rapid succession as he strode onto the battlefield.

I took aim and shot another one, scoring a blast to the face. She probably hadn't been much to look at before death, and now she sprouted a third eye. Her legs went out from under her as she collapsed.

Something blurred across the ground and was in the air before I could fire. Joel dropped his aim and shifted to the side as the shuffler landed. He lashed out with his foot, but the shuffler was already moving. I wanted to rush to help, but there was an army of Zs to deal with.

I did my best to keep my cool as four of the bastards closed in on me. They weren't fast, not by a long shot, and each sported wounds. One was missing most of an arm, so I automatically labeled him as less of a threat. I went for the fastest one first, shooting him in the head. The chamber slammed back, waiting for me to reload, but I didn't have a fresh mag, so I dropped the gun back in its holster.

Taking up a slugger's stance, I knocked down one of the Zs, but there were still two to contend with, and they were already on me.

Out of the corner of my eye I caught sight of Joel. He slammed the shuffler in the side of the head with the butt of his rifle and then spun, dropped low, and took another one in the gut. His motions were timed and well-delivered.

I pushed one back into the other and swung, but missed and hit his arm. The Z didn't react to the blow--something that would have made a normal man scream in pain. The second Z was faster than I'd anticipated and moved on me. She was middle-aged, with grey-streaked hair that stuck up from a short haircut and a bunch of hair products consisting of blood and zombie goo.

She hit me hard, pushing my much larger frame into the wall. I levered myself forward by kicking back with my good leg. She fell back, but her arms came up in the classic zombie pose.

Joel was surrounded and fighting for his life. The shuffler had backed away, but I could tell he was preparing to leap.

I didn't have time for dealing with this Z. Instead of fighting her, I spun her around, picked her up, and barreled through the other zombie. The stinkbeast in my arms was so foul it made me want to projectile vomit for about an hour. Her arms were covered in wounds, and she leaked from pretty much everywhere.

The shuffler turned his rabid green eyes on me and snarled. I didn't give him a chance to leap, lifting the moaning zombie in my arms, and slamming into him.

He was skinny as a rail and his hair was long and lank. He'd been low to the ground, on all fours. The three of us rolled around--tussling, I guess you'd call it, although I also thought of it later as fighting for my life.

I drove my knee into the shuffler's stomach, but he was quick as a whip. His hands lashed out over and over, striking at me. I got my arms up to protect my face and batted his hands aside. The Z I'd used for a battering ram rolled over and struggled to get up.

I took a blow to the head, from the shuffler, but exchanged my protection for a strike. I threw from the shoulder, something I'd done many times, and smashed the shuffler in the face. His nose exploded from the blow and his head smashed into the ground. This gave me enough of a breather to strike him again, but he got his head to the side, so I only struck his ear.

The other Z managed to get to her feet and attack. Why she went after me when Joel was busy fighting off three Zs was weird. Was she holding a grudge, or was this stupid shuffler using some odd mental telepathy, or some kind of unspoken language?

Joel was surrounded, but went for his sidearm. He drew and fired and then clicked on empty. The Z he'd shot fell away but was still moving.

The woman I'd used as a battering ram got on her hands and feet and then lunged for me. I was bowled over, and away from the shuffler. I wasn't just mad that she hit me; I'd had the damn shuffler right under me, and a chance to kill him. Now he was free.

The breath rushed out of my body as I struck the ground. I tried to roll into it, but with my legs busted up it was a shock I wasn't knocked flat.

The Z grabbed me, so I grabbed her back and pushed her down. The shuffler hit me hard enough to make my head spin, and then leapt.

Joel backed up and tugged his knife. Jesus Christ! We were getting our asses kicked here.

I was just about out of gas. I managed to hold of the Z, but she was strong and managed to trip me up. She fell on me and her mouth snapped next to my exposed neck. I pushed her head away, but she leaned in and almost got part of my cheek.

Joel managed to slash the shuffler, but the other zombies were closing in on both of us. The largest tripped on part of a carburetor and almost bowled Joel over. He grabbed Joel's boot and tried to bite him.

I ripped my eyes away from Joel when a gunshot cracked. The Z on top of me slumped to the side. Her blood, cold and thick, hit my face and splashed over my forehead and into my hair. I pushed her off, letting her slump to the side, and looked at Joel to see if he was okay.

He kicked the biter in the face and trudged back from the shuffler. The shuffler came in fast. Joel slashed a Z across the face. Kicked back, making another Z drop. A rotter covered in rags reached for Joel.

Another loud shot, and one of the Zs that was after Joel went down in a heap.

A couple of shapes took form from the East. I looked, then did a double-take as they materialized, sun-high, blinding me. They strode like something out of a western.

Roz and Anna to the rescue.

Anna struggled to keep her arm crossed across her chest, but her good hand held a handgun. It boomed, and the shuffler that had been so persistent fell to the side like a wounded animal. It snarled, touched a wound on his leg, then skittered away on three limbs. Anna lifted the gun and aimed, but dropped the heavy barrel as the shuffler disappeared around the corner of a building.

I rolled over and found my feet. Then I found my wrench. Cleanup duty was almost fun.

———

14:30 hours approximate
Location: Vista

Turned out that the place had been surrounded by Zs. Anna and Roz decided to move a few blocks to the East, but Roz had been smart and left us a note: the flapping piece of paper I'd been trying to reach. When the shuffler had led his little army of dumbshits into our temporary Fortress, Roz had backed the camper up and moved down a few blocks.

Roz helped carry some of the supplies. I put the half-case of beef stew over my shoulder and ignored the rumbling in my gut.

We trudged back to the camper and found it under the overhang of a house that was long since ransacked, and partially burned-out. One of the walls had a hole big enough to drive a motorcycle through, and was surrounded by ash-covered belongings. Whoever had fled that place had come back to gather anything they could salvage, then left sans foreclosure sign.

We didn't have long before daylight was gone, and I planned for us to be on the road as soon as possible.

It was silent until we were close enough to see the drawn curtains covering the camper's small windows. Joel went first and inspected the site to make sure no one had taken an unwelcome interest while we were gone. He moved through the house, and then did a sweep of the camper.

When Christy and the dog appeared in the camper doorway, I finally breathed a sigh of relief.

14:50 hours approximate
Location: Vista

An hour later we'd pulled off a side road and parked under some trees. We warmed up a couple of cans of stew, and as much as I'd promised myself I'd eat slowly, I ended up wolfing down my portion. Some canned mixed vegetables got added to the mix. In a small pot, Roz had made a few cups of rice. It was the most filling meal I'd had in a week.

I wanted to take a nap, but we had business to take care of.

Anna tossed back a pair of painkillers, looked at the pills in the bottom of the little brown bottle, and added two more. She downed a bottle of water and then looked at us expectantly.

"Wish this was vodka or something," she said. "What will they do to me besides numb the pain?"

"Oh you're gonna feel really good in about half an hour. Those are Percocets, you've heard of Oxy, right?"

"Yeah."

"Same thing. Get ready to feel a little better about the apoca-lypse in about twenty minutes," Roz said.

"It'll be over soon, baby." I tried to sound reassuring.

"Call me baby again and I'll jam a pain pill up your ass just before I kick you up and down the camper."

"Damn, I like it when you talk dirty."

Anna looked away, but a half-smile curled her lips. She lay on the bed with her arm exposed. The wound was an angry red. Hot, puckered infection would kill her if we didn't get it under control. Roz thought that the best way to take care of Anna was to get the bullet out.

I took a few steps away and motioned for Roz to join me. I leaned over to talk to her, and kept my voice low.

"You know how to do this, right?" I asked.

"In theory, sure. I'll dig around and pull out the bullet. It's gonna hurt like a motherfucker."

"You've done something like this before?" I asked.

"No, Creed, I have never dug a fucking bullet out of some-one's arm. I've never taken a bullet out of anything. I saw a doctor take a lead pellet out of a dog's flank, but we had to put the little puppy out for the extraction. We can't do that with Anna--no drugs in our possession that can do that. Besides, there's no way to monitor her in case her blood pressure drops or she goes into shock."

"The Percocets should work, right?"

"It'll help put her in a haze. I don't know, it might work. It also depends on how much pain she can tolerate. She's pretty tough, so it might be a walk in the park. I really wish we had some kind of a local."

"Local?"

"Shot. Some Lidocaine, assuming I could get a hypodermic needle and put it deep enough into the wound."

I glanced over my shoulder at Anna, who turned white, which was about what I wanted to do.

"Just fucking get it over with," Anna groaned. "You're about as quiet as a cat in heat. Seriously, Jackson, your whisper is the way normal people talk."

"Hey, I'm trying to be sensitive to your needs."

"Jesus fucking Christ," Anna sighed.

We pulled chairs around Anna and talked about little things while we waited for the pills to kick in. Anna didn't have to tell me. I saw the glazed look come over her eyes pretty quickly.

"Okay. I kinda get it now," she said.

"Get what?" I asked.

"Why people get addicted to this shit."

Roz and I had found enough half-ass tools to do the deed. I'd found a pair of tweezers with a spring between the tines and managed to flatten the pointed ends with a rock and some oil.

Then Roz made me boil the shit out them.

The RV had turned up a number of useful goodies, like a bottle of rubbing alcohol, some peroxide, and small sewing kit. We found a small first aid kit in the RV, too, but the innards had been replaced with dice.

"Are you going to sew up the wound after the bullet's out?" I asked Roz.

"No, because if there's an infection we'll end up containing it. Better to just put a bandage on so I can irrigate the wound. Wish I had saline solution, but that water you boiled will be the next best thing."

"You're going to pour water in the hole?" I asked.

"Yeah," Roz said.

I got my degree in medical knowledge from watching TV, so I didn't argue.

"Can't you use some of the alcohol?" I asked.

"Don't you even think about pouring alcohol into my arm," Anna said, and then stared at the ceiling.

"We won't, because it could damage the tissue. Better to clean it, cover it, and feed her antibiotics."

Roz poured alcohol on her hands and then let them air dry.

"Should I do that?" I asked, nodding at the booze.

"Keep your hands away from her wound. No telling where they've been," Roz said.

"Yeah, Creed, you dirty bastard," Anna laughed. "No telling where they've been."

"Can you sit up, Anna? I need to be able to drain the area."

"Sure. Drain away," Anna said.

Roz used a small soda bottle with a hole punched in the cap to squeeze water into the hole. Yellowish fluid came out.

"Okay. I'm going to feel around the wound and try to locate the bullet, as well as any fragments. This will probably hurt."

"I don't really care right now. I'm high as a kite," she grinned.

Roz looked at me. "Hold her."

I leaned over and put a hand on her shoulder and then my arm across her chest. Roz moved beside me and pulled the bandage off of Anna's wound.

"I told you that I'm not into that stuff, Creed," Anna said, and then giggled. I didn't envy her when the high wore off. She was going to sleep and wake up hurting, but we didn't have painkillers to spare.

"Yeah, I'll keep that in mind," I said.

Roz started by probing the wound with her fingers. She didn't press hard but as she explored, Anna's body language changed.

"I can feel that but it's not too bad," Anna said and took a deep breath.

"It's going to get worse. Sorry," Roz said.

I had to look away when she stuck the tweezers in the wound.

"Motherfuck!" Anna said and nearly bolted up off the bed.

I held her down, but I didn't like it. Anna was slight but she was powerfully built, so I had to hold her none too gently.

"I'm sorry. I almost had it, try not to move."

I glanced over and then regretted it. Blood oozed out of the wound and ran down the back of Anna's arm. The hole was small, but it looked red and infected. I'd seen a lot of nasty stuff out in the z-poc world, but it was different when the damage was on someone I cared for.

"That can't get, like, *infected*, right?" I said to Roz and lifted my eyebrows for emphasis.

"Of course it can, Creed. It may be infected now."

"That's not what I…"

"He means can the zombie stuff get into my wound," Anna said between clenched teeth.

"I fucking hope not," Roz said.

Roz dug in the wound and then pulled the tweezers up. Anna bucked under me.

"Shit, I almost had it."

"Let me go, Creed," Anna said. "I'll do this myself."

I looked for confirmation from Roz.

"*Now*, goddamn it!" Anna swore.

Roz nodded.

I lifted the pressure off her body and stood up.

Anna reached across her body and grasped her upper arm.

The door rocked open and in stepped Joel Kelly. He took one look at the blood and his face dropped.

Anna grunted. She squeezed the skin around the wound, teeth clenched, lips in a snarl. She let out something like a growl and then pressed upward.

The bullet popped out of the wound and fell on the towels.

My mouth dropped open.

Roz grinned.

"Positively badass, Sails. Positively badass," Joel said.

I felt like passing out.

ALL HANDS ON DECK

nother day, another headache.

That's not a metaphor. For the last few days I'd woken up with a headache that started at the base of my skull, spread up my head, and then ended with a pounding sensation behind my eyes. I tried and tried to ignore the pain.

Today the thumping was bad enough to remind me of my epic drinking days: fun times that had ended just a couple of months ago, thanks to the zombie fucking apocalypse. It wasn't that there was a lack of booze--there was plenty, if you looked in enough houses. It was Joel Kelly, who ended up being my personal AA and sponsor all wrapped up into one.

"Get drunk, get dead," Kelly had said after I spun the top off a bottle of cheap whiskey.

I'd procured the drink from a rambler a few days before, and had been saving it.

"Not if I get whiskey dick."

"Gonna get dead is what you're gonna get. Can't stay frosty if you're drunk off your ass."

"A little sip or two isn't the end of the world," I'd argued.

"This *is* the end of the world, and there ain't no coming

back. No waking up in the brig cause you assaulted an officer. No waking up in your rack reaching for a half dozen aspirin. It's lights out like a mo' fucka."

I hated to admit it, but Joel had made a lot of sense. With very few exceptions I'd been clean and sober since then. Maybe not so much on the clean part. The last shower I'd had was one very cold one with Anna Sails the night we'd added Frosty to our crew. Since then it's been baby-wipe baths and splashing water under the pits from time to time.

But this headache. Damn. It was like someone was pounding nails into the back of my neck and skull.

It was time to be a baby.

07:45 hours approximate
Location: Just outside of Oceanside

"Roz. My head is killing me again," I said.

"Your face is killing me," Joel quipped.

"Man. If I wasn't in so much pain I'd have a comeback that would put you down for the count." I put my hands to the sides of my head, hoping to keep my head from bursting open.

"How much water have you been drinking?" Roz asked.

"I don't know. Enough, I guess," I said.

"Drink more," Roz said.

"Yeah. You can't get dehydrated," Christy said.

Christy had been walking Frosty and had just returned to the camper. She was dressed in jeans and a beat-up sweater. If I wasn't mistaken, the oversized and over-color-saturated top had been retrieved from the hotel we'd taken over with the mercenaries a few weeks ago.

"I'm not that thirsty."

"You need water. It's probably a headache from being dehydrated. You have to be careful, Creed," Christy cautioned.

Maybe she was right. While I ho-hummed, she unscrewed the lid on our water supply: a large, clear plastic container, and poured some into a sports bottle with a screw top. We had a bunch of those from raiding a store a few days ago. Most were pink, and that was the color she tossed me.

I sipped the tepid water and found it to be refreshing, even if it had a weird flavor--like silt and dirt--but it also tasted old, and had a plastic undercurrent. Not that I was a water connoisseur, but I wouldn't drink this stuff with my pinky up.

Thing is, you get used to hunting for something to drink, and when you find it you suck it down like there's no tomorrow. I hadn't been doing enough of that.

We'd need to filter more pretty soon, since we were down to a few gallons. That was tedious, but I'd taught Christy how to make a water filter out of a soda bottle, sand, and rocks. She'd made half a dozen of the devices, and used them on a daily basis.

"Drink," Christy commanded.

Roz and Joel had been conferring. As morning came on, they'd decided to move out. We were about ten miles from Pendleton, but those miles might as well have been walking distance for as slow as we were moving.

The confines of our portable house had become a breeding ground for arguments. Stick four and a half people together in a little space and they were bound to get grumpy with each other. I was ready for a place to stretch out.

We'd come to the agreement that we needed to rest up another day, because Anna, for all of her badassery, was still in pain. She was taking her antibiotics and painkillers, but she had also developed a low-grade fever.

"We're moving out," Joel said.

He moved to the door and pushed aside the shitty little rag of a curtain. Joel peered outside for a few seconds, then readied his gun. He cracked the door, and slid out like death with an assault rifle. He moved around the sides of the vehicle and then gestured. Roz slipped out, gun at the ready.

"Those two," I said fondly.

"What about them?" Christy asked.

"I don't know. I can't read them most of the time, but they have a thing and it's cool."

"Of course they have a thing. Everyone has a thing except me," Christy said.

"You don't want a boyfriend during this mess. Wait until we're settled in somewhere. You'll meet a nice boy who's good at head shots."

"I'm good at heads shots, dude," she smirked. "I don't need a boy to save me."

"You're right," I smiled. "You're a crack shot now. You'd probably scare the boys off."

Christy nodded and then went back to nursing the filters as they dripped water into cans.

The camper lurched forward and I was nearly thrown off my feet. Who the hell was driving up there?

I took a seat next to Anna and pressed a wet cloth to her head.

"You know that is really irritating, right?" she said.

"This is what they do in the movies when someone has a fever."

"Creed. The last thing I want is warm water dripping onto my pillow."

I lifted the wash cloth and wiped water off her forehead. I leaned over and kissed her in the same spot. Her features softened for a second, but then her mask returned.

"Sorry. I was just trying to be helpful."

"Help Christy with the water. There's a lot to filter, and you getting dehydrated is going to put a dent in what we have," she said, and closed her eyes.

"That's still up for debate. I'm calling this a normal headache, like your everyday variety, 'my head fucking hurts', headache. I'm drinking water. Jesus."

Anna opened her eyes. "What color was your pee this morning?"

"What?"

"Don't act like a twelve-year-old. We've seen each other. So what was your pee color: was it light or dark?"

"It was dark, why?"

"Because you're fucking dehydrated. Now go make some clean water and drink it while I lay here and try not to throw up. My skin itches, Creed. It's the painkillers. I hate this feeling."

"I'm sorry, baby," I said, unsure if I should touch her again.

"It's fine. I just need to be better. I need to stop the Percocets. But Roz is going to irrigate my wound later, and it's gonna hurt like a mother."

I nodded, touched the blanket that bunched up on her knee, and patted it gently.

"And stop calling me baby."

I rose with a sigh.

08:15 hours approximate
Location: Just outside of Oceanside

CHRISTY HAD BEEN BUSY GATHERING WATER FROM A NEARBY HOUSE. A week ago Joel and I had figured out that we could drain water from hot water tanks after the place we were raiding had already been picked clean. The water had been brackish and smelled none too clean, but our homemade filters made that shit taste like almost as good as low-rent Cristal.

We carefully poured the water into filters and waited while it seeped through the sand, charcoal, and fabric. They hung under the kitchen sink, and had tubes trailing into a large plastic container.

I poured out about sixteen ounces and drained it in a few long gulps--and then felt guilty for being such a hog.

Christy smiled at me and handed over another bottle. I sipped this one like a reasonably thirsty dude.

"Doing okay?" I asked her.

"Yeah. Just bored."

"We found some magazines in the last house. I put a stack near the door."

"I know, but it's all old news. Who cares which celebrity is getting married or which one has a baby bump? They're all gone now anyway."

"Maybe we should write a story together."

"I'm not that creative, Creed. You're the writer."

"Not much of one. I just write down our daily adventures, and I'm not very good at it," I said.

"You're really good. I read the first log book and thought it was great. Lots of misspellings, but it didn't bother me."

"I'll hire an editor when the world is restored," I chuckled. "You should ask before reading them."

"You and Kelly were gone for a while, so Anna and I looked at them. Anna said you exaggerated a lot."

I coughed.

"But she said you were kind of a badass." Christy leaned close. "She told me not to tell you that."

I looked over my shoulder and found Anna's eyes on mine. I winked, but her face was stone. Then she closed her eyes and rolled onto her side.

"I guess it doesn't matter. You can read them. I'll put this conversation in the new log book."

"Oh jeez."

The camper took a hard turn, then slowed.

Last night we'd been laying up in an open parking lot that was filled with ransacked cars. Our vehicle was as far away from the Walmart as possible while still leaving at least two exits. We didn't bother with the store, because the doors were shattered and carts and debris littered the entryway.

Someone had spray-painted obscenities over the front of the building. Others had even seen fit to crawl up on the roof and hack at the bright blue signs, leaving just a few letters intact so that it spelled out ALMA.

I was pretty sure people were camped on top of the building, but we didn't bother to investigate. If they stayed out of our shit, we'd stay out of theirs. Joel and I walked the perimeter of the camper, then ranged out to check for anything of interest, but as suspected, the few abandoned cars had long since been stripped of anything useful.

"That's a good idea: build a fort on top of a big-ass Walmart. It's easily defensible and you could hide out from Zs pretty easy," I said.

"Yeah, until the place is surrounded by five thousand fools looking for flesh. Remember when we fled our first Fortress?" Joel said, making sense as usual.

"They must know the trick, then, because whoever is up there isn't surrounded."

"One mistake, and it's undeadville, as you like to say. Like kicking over a soup can with those big feet of yours."

"Gimme a break, man," I said.

"Let's head out," Joel answered.

The truck rumbled to life and then lurched forward. I got a hand out to steady myself, and then stood with popping knee joints.

Christy grabbed a couple of old magazines and put them on the table, then hopped up to page through them. I grabbed one and joined her, but within a few minutes I was also bored, because Christy was right: these things didn't matter anymore.

Next chance we got, I was going to bring back a stack of paperbacks to help pass the time.

I laid out our weapons and inspected each and every one. If Joel had taught me one thing, it was that we needed to keep our guns ready for action. Christy was a quick study, and pitched in to help. Together we stripped guns, ran rags over the moving parts, and lubricated them from a can of motor oil.

Christy smiled more than once as we sat in companionable silence, so I smiled back. When we were done, I slipped the Springfield XDM 9mm into its holster.

The next few hours weren't so bad after all.

16:15 hours approximate
Location: Just outside of Oceanside

After bumping along back roads at a crawl for several hours, Joel brought the truck to a halt.

I'd been eyeing the world from inside the camper while we bounced along. It wasn't just the main roads; even the back alleys and paths had been littered with debris and abandoned cars. Bodies--always bodies, most unmoving--blocked us at points. I'd gotten used to jumping out of our vehicle and helping Joel move the dead out of the way, or bashing in the heads of rotters before dragging them off to the side.

Now that we'd stopped, I looked outside and found that we were near a housing development that was somewhat secluded, thanks to a tall line of cypress trees. The place looked like a country club in the making. Half-finished homes lay next to completed two-story stucco- and particle-board-sided buildings.

I stepped out of the camper and joined Joel and Roz.

"Nice place you found," I said.

"I think Oceanside is just a few miles west of our location. Tomorrow we should see Pendleton," Joel said.

"You think we're going to find the base operational?" I had to ask. We'd had this goal for weeks, and now that it was within reach, I wondered if we would find what we were even looking for. The camp could be a graveyard for all we knew.

"That's the hope, brother. That's the hope," Joel said.

"What now?"

"We need a place to sleep. Gonna take a look around. You two scout around but stay close. I'll get on top of the camper and cover you, but if you see Zs, you come back and we'll leave," Joel said.

"Aye aye, captain," I said with a smirk.

He clambered up the side of the camper to the roof. Joel stood up and scanned the area, hand shading his eyes as he took up lookout duty.

Roz and I explored but didn't find anything except homes with kicked in doors--assuming they had even been completed. I thought I saw a pair of eyes peeking out from one house, but decided not to investigate any further.

The largest problem was a pile of people who'd been dragged into the street and shot in their heads. From the state of decay--that was, rot and shredded clothing that might have been gnawed at by feral dogs--it was hard to tell if they'd been alive when they were killed or had already been Zs.

We found a heap of bodies with a row of decapitated heads next to it. They were stacked up in an obscene pyramid. Darkened and in some cases blood-filled eye sockets, from which dried-out and damned eyes stared back.

We dragged bodies off to the side, Joel with a stubborn look on his face, me with a red bandana wrapped around mine. It didn't really help to alleviate the smell, but it made me feel like I was making the effort.

A mini-horde of moaners found us just as we cleared the road, so we got back in the truck and drove on. No reason to stick around and try to slaughter them when they weren't a threat.

After we finished our sweep, Joel located a house with a carport and backed in, because with night falling, the development seemed the best place to call home for the night.

"Looks like Joel found us a pretty swanky place," I said to Anna.

I inspected her wound. It looked good, as far as my untrained eye could tell. It was hot around the entry point, but I suspected that was okay. I'd ask Roz later.

"We need another location to sleep that isn't this cramped camper, especially since Joel snores," I said.

"So do you, Creed. You snore like a goddamn train. Get me some fucking earplugs the next time you make a supply run."

"Earplugs? You wouldn't hear the Zs coming," I said, and made claws out of my hands, lifting them in my best approximation of a zombie.

"You're scarier when you snore," she said.

I rolled my eyes and lurched forward as the truck came to a stop. Joel cranked it to the right and then backed up again. Christy rose and looked out the window. She carried her snub-nosed revolver in one hand. I had to admire the kid. She'd gone from a sad and awkward teen to a tougher and still-awkward teen ready to pop a Z in the head if they got too close.

Anna pushed the sheet aside. She wasn't wearing much, and my eyes traveled up and down her legs. It'd been a week since we'd been intimate, and I missed looking at her.

Anna followed my eyes and blew out a breath. "Perv."

"I've been staring at walls for days. You're a sight, baby," I said.

Anna tugged her pants on and got to her feet. She leaned over and put her hand on my shoulder. I reached for her, but she shook her head.

"Sorry. Just a little dizzy. I'm okay now."

Joel opened the door. "We're here, kids. I hope you ain't been fighting back here."

Christy giggled and slipped past him. Anna wrapped her belt around her waist and slid the Smith & Wesson M&P R8 into the holster. She moved to the door, and Joel helped her down.

I grabbed my wrench and joined them.

16:30 hours approximate
Location: Just outside of Oceanside

THE HOUSE HAD TWO ENTRY POINTS, NOT INCLUDING THE WINDOWS. It was two stories, and the paint hadn't been applied on the inside or out. There was a For Sale sign driven into the ground outside. The lawn was dirt where grass would have been layered in long strips. A few shrubs had been planted, but most of them were now wilted.

Place like this was probably kept up until a potential buyer happened along. With the current drought conditions in California it wasn't a surprise. Should say *former* drought conditions. Without thirty-eight million people constantly showering, watering lawns, and filling pools, it stood to reason that there was now enough water to go around. All we had to do was find a mountain, and we'd have an unlimited supply.

"Pools," I said.

"Bars," Joel said.

"What?"

"Thought we were just saying random fucking words, Creed."

"I was just thinking--California is filled with pools. We should find one that isn't too stagnant and stick a hose in. Siphon up a bunch of water and filter or boil it."

"Damn, Skippy, you're pretty smart for a squid," Joel said.

I shot him the finger.

"That's a good idea. Maybe tomorrow we can scout some of the houses and look for water. It's been relatively cool. The problem is all the chlorine. I don't know if we can filter it out. Plus the pools have been sitting unattended for close to two months. I'm not even sure if we should risk it," Roz said.

Joel nodded. He slung his AR-15 around his neck on his two-point sling and double-checked his sidearm.

Joel and Roz walked the perimeter while Anna, Christy and I kept an eye out for Zs and moved our supplies near the back door. I tapped a few windows and then moved away. No faces--living or dead--appeared.

The backyard butted up to a small wooded area that made me think twice about this location.

"You sure that's safe?" I said and pointed at the trees.

"I figure it will be a last resort. We can move faster than Zs if we have to run. The trees'll slow them down. There's another house that's done and has a better view all around, but I saw something moving inside."

"I don't feel like a Z hunt tonight," I said.

About the worst thing in the world was going through a house, clearing it, and hoping we weren't surprised by some crafty rotter who'd shamble out of a closet while we had our backs turned.

When we reached the rear of the house I tried the door, but it was double-locked. I pushed, but Joel motioned for me to join him.

"See that window?" He pointed.

"Yeah, but how am I going to get up there? I don't see a ladder."

"I'm going, you weigh more than me."

"What's that got to do with anything?" I said.

"'Cause you're gonna give me a boost."

Joel put his assault rifle on the ground and motioned for me to cup my hands.

"You kidding? I'm not sure I can lift you with all that damn gear."

"One way to find out, sailor. I could climb up on your shoulders if that makes you feel better. Just stand there like a big-ass tree."

"Oh for Christ's sake," I said and cupped my hands.

Joel put his boot in my improvised sling and his hands on my shoulders.

"On three," he said.

We counted and he jumped. I felt like I was flinging him into the air, but he caught the edge of the roof. He nearly ripped the gutter off, but managed to pull himself up until his legs were dangling. He dragged himself over, then flipped around and motioned toward me. I handed Joel his assault rifle and backed away to watch.

Joel moved to the window and stared inside for a few seconds. He pressed the jamb and lifted. The portal opened without a sound.

Joel slipped inside and then was gone from sight.

16:45 hours approximate
Location: Just outside of Oceanside

I SLID OUT THE SPRINGFIELD XDM AND WAITED. THE GUN FELT good in my hand, but it wasn't my only weapon. I didn't go anywhere without my trusty eight-pound wrench, so it was hanging uncomfortably under my arm.

I half expected Joel's rifle to start barking out 5.56 rounds, but he reached the back door, unbolted it, and swung it open.

"Let's do a full sweep. I checked the bedroom I entered but the rest are waiting. The stairs and the entry to the kitchen are clear. I didn't go through all the closets yet. Stay frosty," he said.

Frosty lifted her head at the sound of her name.

"Get 'em, girl," I said and let her go.

Frosty dashed into the house and ran toward a back room.

I trailed behind Joel and followed his lead. One of the worst things about entering a new house is looking in all the rooms and doorways. We'd learned early on that folks couldn't kill a loved one. They preferred to lock them in a little space, presumably to wait for a cure or just so they didn't have to put up with the moans and biting.

Joel moved through the house, checking and clearing each area. When we entered rooms I kept my eyes on the corners and his back. The thing about the dead is: they might be hanging around, staring at a wall, and you wouldn't even know it until they were on you.

The floors weren't finished, but the concrete had a layer of padding. Carpet lay in huge rolls in the dining room and wood strips were stacked up in another corner. Fading sunlight lit the room from an abundance of windows, creating a space that was easy to inspect.

We hit every closet and room, looked in half-finished bathrooms and in cabinets and pantries. I expected the upstairs to have a few Zs, but the rooms were also clear and as bare as the downstairs.

We found some supplies and a surprise in a closet: paint, paint thinner, masking tape, a couple of rulers, some power tools, and other small contractor items. A toolbox revealed hand tools and a few boxes of screws, bolts, and nuts.

One of the tools--a cordless drill--was stuck in a man's head. His body was decayed and partially mummified. It was hard to tell if someone had killed him or if he'd done it himself. I considered what I'd do if I was bitten and all I had was a fucking power drill. Would I have the nerve to drive it into my own head?

Frosty growled at the body. I rubbed her head and got a lick for my efforts.

"Damn, that dude reeks," Joel said.

"Let's get the stuff we can use, and then leave him to his tomb. He's not going to bother us," I said.

"We're at that point, huh? Fucking corpse in the house and we're just gonna leave it?" Joel said.

"What else should we do, drag him outside and do a burial? Nah, man, I've seen enough corpses and body parts to last me three lifetimes."

"Let's not tell the ladies, eh?" Joel said.

"Sexist asshole," I laughed. "None of them is squeamish."

"I was thinking of Christy. Girl's seen enough bodies, rot, and Zs to last three lifetimes. No sense her worrying about a body in the house."

"Yeah, man. I get it. Well, looks like we got a home for a night," I said. "What do you think a place like this costs?"

"Before the Zs? Probably more money than you and I make in a few years. After the apocalypse? Shit's free."

We took out anything that might be useful and moved it into the kitchen.

One thing was for damn sure: I was looking forward to stretching out.

17:30 hours approximate
Location: Just outside of Oceanside

I BROUGHT FROSTY ALONG WHEN I MOVED THE TRUCK BEHIND THE house. She investigated the unfinished yard for a few minutes before finding the perfect place to take a dump. Christy stayed close to the dog, and praised her when she didn't run off. Frosty was loyal to us first, and teasing/chasing Zs second. Still, she paused a few times to sniff the air, and looked in the direction of the woods once or twice.

Joel and Roz moved food, the burner, and other gear inside the house. Anna picked up her bag and a couple of cans of food. I joined her and offered my arm, but she shook me off. She looked a bit dazed, but I suspected it was the drugs. Her short hair was frazzled and she looked like she needed a week off in a tropical vacation getaway. Her body language was tense--that was the best word for it. She ran her hands over the stock of the handgun at her side more than once.

"She spooked?" Anna nodded toward Frosty.

"Not sure. Maybe there's a maimed Z back in the woods somewhere."

Anna walked to the corner of the yard. She petted Frosty and waited, head moving back and forth as she scanned the copses.

The dog must have gotten bored, because she sat down and scratched her neck for a few seconds, and then galloped back to me. I rubbed her head and assured her she was a dyed in the wool killer.

We moved gear into the house, just enough for the night, and set up camp in the middle of the kitchen. The entryway was open, but there was only one window. Joel and I cut off a big chunk of carpet and wedged it over the portal. No sense in advertising that we had taken up occupancy.

I checked the faucet over the sink, but no water came out. I found the valves and twisted the cold lever all the way to the right. To my surprise, water gurgled up the tubes. It came out in a trickle, but Christy was quick and got a bucket under the stream until it ran out. We got about two gallons. I tasted it and found it stale, but grabbed a mug from our belongings and gulped it down.

"Don't want to clean it first?" Roz asked.

"It just tastes like pipes. Water's been sitting there but it's clean," I said.

Christy didn't look convinced, and told us she'd take it out to the camper and run it through our filtering system.

"Take Frosty," I said. She nodded and ducked out of the house.

"It's good to stretch out," Joel said.

"Yeah. Good to get some life back in our legs," Roz nodded.

Joel caught her looking at him and gave a small nod. He rose and together they went to "investigate" the house.

Anna pulled a sleeping bag out of her pack and rolled it out flat. She crawled inside and zipped it up.

"Room for me in there?" I winked.

"Sorry. I'm running a fever and everything makes my skin crawl right now. Nothing personal, Creed," she said.

I nodded and took out the burner and a couple of cans of stew. Might as well eat our precious supplies while we had the opportunity. Tomorrow we'd arrive at the Marine base, if we weren't ambushed by shufflers, devoured by fucking zombies, or killed by marauders--or if we didn't succumb to some stupid disease that was out to do us in. That's what our lives had come to: running from all of the things that wanted to do us harm.

"I'm going to see if there's enough water for a good flush in the bathroom," I said.

"Great, Creed. If not, nail the door shut when you're done," Anna said.

20:40 hours approximate
Location: Just outside of Oceanside

WE GATHERED IN THE TINY ROOM AND MADE A DECENT DINNER: stew, canned beans, a can of creamed corn, and a few crackers. Anna said she was feeling better, so I sat next to her and tried to cheer her up with dumb stories of being young and overseas. I got the occasional half-smile out of her, but she wasn't really paying attention to me.

Roz and Joel rolled out sleeping mats and piled on a few blankets. Christy wrote in a journal--something she'd seen me do every day, and something I'd encouraged.

Frosty rolled on her back and growled. Her tail swished back and forth while her tongue lolled out. She wanted to play, and nipped at my hand a few times while I rubbed her chest.

"Anyone want to play spades?" I asked.

Christy shook her head and went back to writing. Joel and Roz looked at each other, then shook their heads as well.

"Can't play with just two people," I said to myself.

"Play with yourself," Anna suggested.

I cracked a smile.

Christy and I played a few hands of high stakes five-card poker and I ended up owing her six million dollars. Just my luck. Last week she'd owed me fifteen million, give or take.

I know a lot of people probably love the quiet. I don't. I was used to the noise of the engine room, the hum of the pipes, steam, and the exhaust fans that blew air around the ship. I slept like a goddamn baby when I was out at sea. When I stayed in town I needed a fan cranked up to high just to doze off.

Out in Z land, I was lucky if I got more than four consecutive hours' worth of sleep. I was always on guard, and the quiet didn't help. Every time someone moved or sniffed or snored or burped or farted, it was like a bell rung next to my head. Exhaustion usually knocked me out, but today I was still on edge.

I tried relaxing and thinking of better times: times that involved beer and hookers in some overseas port. I thought of the night Anna and I had spent a few weeks ago. We'd taken an ice-cold shower together, and I for one had felt clean for the first time in ages.

Although she didn't want to share our sleeping bags, I'd laid mine out next to her.

I rolled over and looked at her. She looked peaceful for a change.

"What?" she whispered, opening one eye.

"Nothing. Just looking at you," I whispered back.

"Go to sleep, Creed. I'm beat," she said, and rolled over.

"Are you mad at me for something?"

"No, Jackson, I'm not mad at you. I just don't need a

boyfriend right now and that's all there is to it. Now get some sleep."

I blew out a breath and rolled onto my back. The view of the ceiling didn't help. It was white, unfinished, and boring.

An hour later I still tossed and turned. Joel snored, and Roz snored quietly next to him. The pair had curled into each other and looked rather goddamn cozy.

Christy had dragged her sleeping pad across the floor and was facing the door. Earlier we'd drawn cards to see who would take first watch. Even though we tried to coddle Christy when we could, she insisted on being treated like an adult. She wanted to take watch every night, and she was good. Christy never dozed off and she rarely ever bugged us, unless she sensed a genuine threat.

I'd had increasingly bad insomnia as the weeks fled past, and tonight looked like it would be no different. I rose as silently as I could and lifted my backpack. I moved across the room and leaned over to whisper to Christy.

"Get some rest. I can't sleep, so I'll keep watch for the next few hours and then I'll wake Roz."

Christy nodded and wiped at her eyes. I suspected she'd been crying, but she hit me with a hard look that would have made Anna proud.

"Okay. Thanks," she said and rolled over.

I took my pack into the living room and sat with my back to a wall. Then I took out my journal and wrote for an hour.

12:30 hours approximate
Location: Just outside of Oceanside

My eyes were heavy and the thought of sleep was getting more and more attractive. I'd spent the last few hours alternating between writing and staring outside.

A couple of creepers had wandered past the house and then into the woods. I let them be. The pair found something on the ground--the carcass of a small animal--and they fought over it. Not much of a battle, because one of the Zs was missing most of an arm.

I wondered, not for the first time, what their story had been. Had they been married, had kids, were they working-class, were they nice to their families? So many people gone now, and what was the world going to be like in a year? Would we all be mindless, wandering ghouls?

I closed my eyes a couple of times to let them rest, because they burned. I yawned and decided I could probably sleep.

Roz rose grumpy and took her place on watch. I curled up next to Anna as close as I could get without touching her sleeping bag, and closed my eyes. Within moments I drifted off.

IN THE CROSSHAIRS

08:35 hours Approximate
Location: Just outside of Oceanside

I woke to the sound of laughter.

Christy was playing in the living room with Frosty. I rubbed grit out of my eyes and rolled over to stare at the ceiling. I was the only one in the kitchen. The amount of sun streaming in through the window told me I'd done something I hadn't done in a long time: I'd slept in.

I peeked around the space that divided the two rooms and saw the source of Christy's laughter. She had the dog lying on the floor and was trying to teach her how to roll over. Frosty didn't seem to think too much of the game. She lay with her legs splayed in the air, her tail wagging across the floor while her tongue lolled out the side of her mouth.

The room had unfinished walls and a lack of carpeting. The floor was concrete, but Christy had broken into some of the padding and rolled it out for Frosty to sleep on.

I jumped when someone tapped at the front door, in a pattern consisting of three quick knocks and then two knocks spaced farther apart. Christy hopped up. Frosty scrambled to her side and got to her feet, her demeanor changed instantly from playful pup to "I'm going to rip someone a new one".

Christy peeked out the bay windows, then smiled and nodded. The door opened, and in strolled Joel Kelly and Roz. They carried a number of tools, some lumber, and a bag of screws or nails.

"Morning, sunshine," Roz said.

I nodded. Christy turned and shot me a smile, so I smiled back. Not hard to do when faced with her sunny disposition. We were safe for a while, and it had rubbed off on her.

Joel and Roz quietly placed their newly-acquired items around the living room. Roz removed a piece of paper from her pocket, and she and Joel studied the sheet.

"What's going on?" I asked.

"We're going to fortify this place and try to rest up for a few days. Tired of being on the run, bro," Joel said.

"What about Pendleton?"

"It'll still be there. Or maybe it's already gone. Rushing down there now while we're exhausted, Anna's hurt, and you're needing ten hours of sleep means that we are not an effective fighting unit," Joel said.

"So what, we're going to board up the windows and call this Fortress Mark III?"

"Something like that. This subdivision is half-finished, so a lot of families hadn't moved in yet. North of here a few homes that look occupied. We didn't bother investigating."

"So we're not getting a welcome to the neighborhood basket?" I deadpanned.

Roz chuckled.

"I'd love some cupcakes," Joel sighed.

"Don't talk about cupcakes. I haven't had fresh-baked *anything* in months, so you're making me drool," Christy said.

"Something bothers me about this place," I said.

"What, no store set up for bartering yet?" Joel said.

"It's the lack of people. This place isn't finished yet, sure, not a lot of families would be moved in, but why didn't other survivors take over and fortify? The place backs up to a small hill, the houses are close together, it seems like the perfect opportunity to build a community and keep it guarded."

446

"Thinking like a warrior, huh? I'll be honest, I had the same thought. What's missing is any kind of lawns. The backyards are barely in and who knows if anything can grow in that soil. If we stayed we'd need a garden at the very least. Grow potatoes and carrots. But California's been in a hell of a drought, so getting water in would be a bitch." Joel removed his ball cap and scratched his head.

"Maybe it's just been overlooked. Think about how many people the virus has taken. Think about how many are dead or roaming the streets. If only a percentage of the population is still alive, they have a lot of places to hide," Anna chimed in.

"Personally, if I wanted to become a warlord and rule a little kingdom I'd take over a fucking Costco. Big-ass brick building, lots of food, just need a few guys to keep it safe and sound," Joel said.

"And a bunch of scantily-clad women to call your harem?" Roz asked.

"If I'm a warlord of Costco, you bet your ass," Joel said.

Roz, characteristically, smacked his arm. "You keep thinking like that and I'll punch you into tomorrow, Joel Kelly."

I stifled a laugh.

"What, you asked," Joel said. "Peace, baby. I'm just playing."

Roz crossed her arms over her chest.

"Damn, Joel. That's like some stupid shit *I'd* say," I chuckled.

"Joel, Warlord of Costco. Has a certain ring," he said.

Frosty wandered to the back of the house and scratched at the door.

"Gotta take a dump?" I asked her.

Christy rolled her eyes and took Frosty into the backyard.

"Keep her quiet," I said.

"I don't think there are any zombies back there," Christy said as she stood in the doorway.

"How do you know?"

"Because they would have come if they heard your snoring," Christy said, and then closed the door as she stepped onto the back porch.

Anna strolled down the stairs. She wore camouflage pants and a t-shirt she'd picked out of one of our various bags. The shirt bore a grinning cat on a cartoon background.

She had a smile on her face.

"I don't even know what to say right now," I said to Anna.

Christy chased Frosty into the yard.

"Don't say a word," Anna said.

"But that shirt and that smile. Are you happy to see me?"

Anna sat next to me. She inspected a couple of scratches on my face and arms while I admired her sunny disposition. She'd either cleaned up in our small supply of water or she'd found some baby wipes along the way. She held her wounded arm next to her body, and when I reached out to inspect the injury she pulled away with an "I'm fine, Creed."

"So what's the plan for fortifying this place? Board up the doors?" I asked.

"If we board up everything, then someone may wonder what we're hoarding in here. We'll reinforce the door, but we need to keep the lights to a minimum. Avoid the windows if you can help it."

"What if no one bothers us?" I asked.

"What if monkeys fly out of my butt?" Roz said.

Joel snorted.

"The likelihood that we're going to be safe here for a few days is decent. The fact that Zs will find us is undeniable. Don't get too comfortable, folks," Joel said, looking between the members of our group.

"Is the truck prepped in case we need to make a quick getaway?"

"Yeah. Roz and I found a tarp to cover the truck, but if anyone gets too damn curious, they'll find the vehicle," Joel said.

"Good enough for Government work, I guess," I said.

Roz and Joel left on another scouting run. Anna stayed by my side but didn't say anything, so I leaned against the wall and enjoyed the companionable silence.

"I can't stay with you guys," she said, breaking the silence a few minutes later.

"What do you mean?"

"As soon as we find Bright Star I'm going to have to leave. I have responsibilities."

"To what? The world's gone now. Nothing but the dead and a few survivors scrounging for food. When it's all gone what are people going to do? Bright Star and the notion of any kind of functioning Government went out the window weeks ago."

"That's where you're wrong, Creed. There were contingency plans, and I believe we have a functioning Government, but they have been reduced. It's a matter of reestablishing bases and carving out our place in this new world. That's why they need me."

"Is this a paying job, this whole rebuilding-the-world thing?" I asked.

"I guess we're all owed some back pay. What are you going to do with a few months' worth of salary?" she asked.

"You're changing the subject."

"I'm turning it to something fun. You're so goddamn morose sometimes, Creed. You have this way of being a smartass and making everyone laugh, but half the time you're so depressed I wonder if you're going to slit your wrists," Anna said.

"Name one thing that doesn't suck now," I challenged her.

"Friends."

That got a half-smirk.

"The fact that you owe me seventeen million dollars from our last round of poker," she said.

"Any chance I can work that off another way?"

"We'll talk later tonight, Creed. I may have something you can do for me," she said, and hit me with a smile.

My day was starting to look better.

08:35 hours Approximate
Location: Just outside of Oceanside

After Anna and I had our talk, I rose and grumped around for a half an hour, wishing more than anything that I had an energy drink or a gallon of coffee. A couple of weeks ago we'd found some packs of instant Starbucks coffee, but I'd kept them tucked deep inside my backpack and managed to make them last for a few days.

Even mixed with cold water, tasting grainy and undissolved, I'd treated them like fucking gold. I'd even thought about snorting the damn stuff for a rush. Probably end up with a headache and brown-colored snot.

Christy had filtered about a liter of water so I drank down a cup, then greedily drank another. I'd make it up to her by helping her filter more water later in the day.

I moved to the rear door and watched Christy and Frosty play. They'd found a stick, and the dog was running around, alternating between playing fetch and playing 'try to catch me'. She had a devious look in her eye every couple of times she brought the twig to Christy. Christy would reach for the stick, and Frosty would dance back and shake her head while her tail flopped from side to side.

I opened the door and stepped onto the partially-finished porch.

I sat down and Frosty, seeing me, dropped the stick and dashed up the stairs. She puppy-attacked me for a few minutes of mock play that involved trying to grab my sleeve and pull me into the yard. I rubbed the dog's head, and when she tired of that she dropped to her side and rolled on her back.

Christy took a seat next to Frosty and rubbed her belly while I did the same.

"Are we going to stay here for a while?" Christy asked.

"I don't think so. It's not safe to hang out in one location for more than a day or two. When Joel and I first got to San Diego we managed to hold out for almost a week. The Zs were still fairly new, and we didn't have a lot of crazies out trying to steal our stuff."

"Do you think someone will bother us here?"

"Hard to say. It's not like we know the neighborhood. Joel's got a plan to reinforce the place. If we have to, we'll just bug out. The camper's ready and we have a quarter tank of gas."

"How far will that get us?"

"Not very far, but far enough for now," I said. "If we run out there's a lot of cars we can siphon from. Problem is, gas gets old when it sits around, and might not be useable in a few months."

"What else won't be useable? I'm worried about stuff like supplies. They won't last forever, and we can only break into so many houses before there are no more canned goods sitting around."

"I guess we learn how to garden, and hunt deer," I said.

"Is there a plan B?"

"Smartass."

Frosty stopped wagging her tail and shot to her feet. She stared into the woods that surrounded the backyard. She growled low in her throat, but then settled back down.

"Something back there?" Christy asked.

She stood and walked into the yard.

"Could be a Z that's stuck. We'll keep an eye out. If Frosty is on guard, I think that's a bad sign."

"Maybe we should just go," Christy said, looking back at me.

"Maybe we should, but I agree with Joel. We need a break. We've been on the run for weeks and I'd like to catch up on some sleep," I said.

Christy smiled tightly and went back to staring at the woods.

I put my back to the wall and took a minute to enjoy the afternoon sun. Frosty drifted over and put her head in my lap, so I closed my eyes and dozed for a while, content to enjoy a little quiet and companionship from the dog.

08:35 hours Approximate
Location: Just outside of Oceanside

VOICES FROM THE FRONT OF THE HOUSE WOKE ME.

I shook away the cobwebs and found that Christy and Frosty had left me. They'd left me to be devoured if a zombie wandered across my form.

I rose and entered through the backdoor. No one was in the kitchen. Thanks a lot. With friends like these, who needed the zombie fucking apocalypse? I found them in the living room. Anna had her hand on her piece. Joel stood in front of the door and Roz had her back to the wall so she could cover the bay window. Christy hovered in the back of the room, looking like she wanted to bolt.

"Let me guess, more Zs. Jesus, why'd you guys leave me out there to get devoured?" I called.

The kitchen was deserted, and that just added to the realization that my friends had left me alone.

Then Christy's head appeared around the corner. She looked at me with large eyes. "Jackson, someone's here," she whispered.

"Someone like a live person? Or someone like a dude drooling blood and looking for a free lunch?" I asked as I walked into the living room. "Can't believe you all left me outside and asleep. What if a Z…"

Joel shot me a flat look.

"We just heard this guy, jeez, Jackson. You were only alone for a few seconds," Christy said.

"Guard the back door, man. Something's up with this fool," Joel said.

"I was just back there and there's no one out there."

"Dude. This guy might be a decoy while others move on our six. Grab a big gun and get ready for the worst."

I nodded and complied. If Joel was right, we needed to keep all entry points covered.

Joel moved his AR to the high ready position and covered the front door while Anna slid around a corner. If someone came in blasting, they had the entryway covered from two positions.

"Come on, Jackson," Roz said, moving into the kitchen.

She drew her gun and double-checked the magazine. Roz was armed with one of the 9mms--the Sig, if I wasn't wrong.

I unholstered my Springfield XDM and followed her.

We dropped next to windows facing the backyard and peered outside.

"Hey man, I don't mean any harm," a man's voice called from outside. "Can you spare some food? Just a little bit, I got a wife and three kids. Please. We're all starving."

Joel didn't answer.

"I know you see me and I know you're there. There's at least four of you. I swear I don't want any trouble, just a little food. Anything you can spare. I've even got a few things I can share."

"Does he look dangerous?" I called from the kitchen.

"He looks like he's scared, but he also looks like he's wearing something under his shirt. My guess would be some kind of body armor. I can't see any weapons, but he hasn't turned either. Could be he's packing," Joel called back, just loud enough for us to hear him.

"Be careful," Roz said.

"Go away, man. I'm sorry to hear about your family but we don't have any extra food," Joel yelled.

"Please, just a few bites. We haven't had anything in days."

"We're well-armed, so just fuck off, okay? Go to town and raid just like the rest of us been doing," Joel tried to reason— like a Marine.

"You see anything?" I asked Roz.

"Nothing, but stay frosty."

The mutt heard her name and wandered over to see what we were up to. Frosty's wet nose on the back of my neck almost scared me out of my own skin.

I reached around and pulled her close. Frosty took a seat next to me and panted. The dog must have sensed our tension, because she cocked her head and stared in the direction of the door.

"What?" I asked her, like she could answer.

Frosty's ears perked up.

"Just give us a little bit and we'll leave you alone," the guy outside the house called.

"We? I thought it was just you," Joel called back.

"Shit," Roz said. "This guy's full of it."

Frosty stood and moved to the door. She bared her teeth growled deep in her throat.

"Make this easy on yourself, man. You're going to give up some food one way or another."

"He's moving," Joel called. "I'm going to drop him."

Joel's AR spoke in the house. Glass tinkled as he fired a couple of rounds.

Frosty got spooked by the gunfire and prowled around the living room before she went to Christy and sat next to her.

"You get him?" I called.

"He's behind a car. As soon as he shows his skull I'm putting one in it."

"I don't like this, Joel."

"Keep it together, Jackson," Roz said.

"Movement, there." I pointed toward the East. Someone was fucking around by some shrubs.

I caught a glimpse of something dark, but then it was gone.

"I didn't see it," Roz said. "Wait, I see something but it's at three o'clock."

"Someone's trying to flank us," I called to Joel.

"Then put them the fuck down," he said.

I pushed the window up and it gave without a screech-- thank goodness for the new house. All I needed was for it to give us away.

I lifted my pistol and aimed where I'd seen the shadow, but it didn't reappear.

"I got the other side, Jackson. You start shooting and be sure to call out targets. I'll do the same," Roz said.

Over the weeks we'd come under fire from a variety of bad guys. One thing I'd learned early on was that I'd rather face a horde of ravenous Zs than a bunch of dudes with guns. The mercenaries we'd been holed up with had shown me just how fast you could go down if someone had you in their sights. Now I felt like that again, like I was in the crosshairs.

A gun rang out and something struck the door. I dropped to all fours.

"Dumbass can't hit the side of a barn," Roz said.

She raised her head high enough to peek over the windowsill, then lowered herself back down.

Joel fired from the front of the house.

Frosty was smart and moved away from the door. She ran into the living room, hopefully to sit with Christy in a quiet corner. If someone got us and came through the door, they'd be in for a surprise when the dog took them down and Christy opened fire.

I took a quick look and saw a person moving across the line of shrubs near the woods. I poked my gun out the window and aimed, leading the target as it moved. I exhaled and squeezed the trigger. The gun bucked in my hand and the figure dropped to the ground, so I followed up with a couple more shots.

"I think I got him," I turned and said to Roz.

A bullet burst through the window overhead and made me kiss the floor.

"I don't think you got him," Roz said.

She lifted herself off the ground and aimed. She took a couple of seconds to zero in and fired a pair of rounds.

"I saw three of them back there but they don't look well-armed. Handguns, most likely," Roz said. "Hope one of them isn't toting a shotgun. I'd kill to have my Remington again."

I took a look, but no one moved back there.

"I'll cover from upstairs," Anna said, then she pounded up the stairs.

"Watch the backyard, Sails. I think a couple got around the house. I got this asshole," Joel said.

"Aye," she called.

Something rattled on the side of the house. I strained to see over the windowsill, but there was no way to spot them without opening the back door.

"I think they're trying to get into the camper," Roz said.

"Goddamn it. I'm going out there," Joel said.

"Joel, wait. We don't know how many there are. You might be walking into a trap," I said.

"That's why you're going to come up here and cover me. Roz, you got the back, Sails has the high ground, Jackson will cover me," he said.

I shook my head and moved into the living room. Christy was huddled up with Frosty, but she looked very determined. She held her revolver in a shaky hand, but I was pretty sure the kid would drop anyone who came through the door.

"Creed, lay down a few rounds near that burned-up Mustang. I got him bottled up. If he peeks out, pop him. Stay in the doorway, behind the wall, and make sure he doesn't shoot me in the back," Joel said, and put his hand on the doorknob.

"Dude, I don't know if I can do this," I said.

"Piece of cake, brother, just aim and shoot. That guy's probably more scared than you since I've been putting some heavy ammo on him. In a few minutes, all of these assholes are going to wish they'd stayed the hell away," Joel said.

I nodded and sucked in a few breaths. I took station at the bay window and sighted the car. No shape had presented itself yet.

Joel opened the door and dropped to his knees. His gun swept up to the ready as he studied the battlefield.

"When I move, pop two rounds at the car. I think he's behind the hood. Just spook him until I'm out of sight."

A gun spoke from upstairs--Anna's big .357, if I wasn't mistaken.

Joel moved, so I did as he'd instructed. I fired a round, and then another one. Both struck the top of the car.

The figure that had been hiding dove from cover and sprinted toward a house. I aimed, exhaled, and dropped him with a single round. His arms flew up and he fell face first into the unfinished lawn across the street. He didn't move again.

Joel was already gone, so I moved to the door to cover his exit.

08:35 hours Approximate
Location: Just outside of Oceanside

ANNA'S GUN BOOMED AGAIN FROM UPSTAIRS. THEN ROZ OPENED
fire. I held my handgun nice and high, ready to shoot anything
else that twitched. I tried hard not to think about the man I'd
just killed.

Jesus, but it had been him or us, and he hadn't exactly
wanted to sit around and sing campfire songs. This guy could
have been a Reaver and wanted to kill us and take our supplies.
Worse, what if he'd got a hold of Christy? I didn't want to
contemplate what crazy men might have done to her.

Joel fired a half dozen times. I ignored his advice and moved
out onto the porch so I could see what he was firing at, but his
form had disappeared. I backed up and kept myself in the little
bit of shadow the roof provided.

Anna fired again.

"One down," she called.

I studied the street, gun raised, looking for targets. The only
thing that stood out was the body of the bad guy I'd taken out. I
drifted to the other side of the unfinished porch and kept a
lookout.

I glanced over my shoulder repeatedly as I waited for one of
the attackers to come back.

Joel's gun sounded a few more times.

"Another one down. Anyone left back there, just throw your
gun out and run," Joel said.

Someone returned fire.

Roz shot back and there was a scream.

I decided that I'd had enough sitting there, and hopped
down off the porch. Then I hit the fucking ground as something
exploded near my head and took a chunk of wood out of where
I'd just been crouching. Had I not moved, I'd probably be dead.

A shape ran from the back yard. I managed to lift my gun

and fire once. The man spun to the side and dropped his gun. It clattered across the sidewalk.

More shots from outside, and rounds kicked up dirt near the fleeing man. He tucked his head and ran toward me, but hugged the side of the house.

I dropped to my belly hard enough to knock the wind out of me. The shot I'd gotten off had been nothing but luck. As the man came alongside me, ten feet away, I managed to struggle to my knees. He froze in place and lifted his hands in the air. One of them dripped blood from where I'd hit him.

"Please, man. I didn't even want to go, but they told me I had to or they'd kick me out," he said.

The man turned out to be a kid, no more than eighteen or nineteen. He had a scraggly beard that looked more like a bunch of pubes. Tears streamed down his face as he moved past me.

"Clear up," Anna called.

"Clear down," Joel said from the other side of the house.

"Please, just let me go. I swear you'll never see me again," the kid said. "It's bad out there and we didn't have a choice. You'd do the same thing, right?"

"Wrong," I said and shot him.

He looked surprised for a split second as a red hole appeared above his eyes. He fell back in a heap and didn't move.

I exhaled and put my back against the wall. The shakes kicked in, and that was how Joel found me.

08:35 hours Approximate
Location: Just outside of Oceanside

"Do I even need to say it?" Joel asked me later.

We'd dragged the bodies from the back of the house and placed them side by side in the front yard.

"I know, it was them or us."

"You did the right thing. For all we know the kid might have gone back for reinforcements and then burned us out."

"What makes you think there aren't more of them waiting to move on us?"

"I don't know, but we're entrenched now. I thought we could stay here a few days, but I think we need to get the fuck out of here in a few hours. We should rest up after we move the bodies," Joel said.

"Why move the bodies? There are enough corpses around as it is."

"Don't want someone seeing fresh dead and wondering what went down here," Joel said.

"Yeah, no sense in telling more raiders to keep away."

"I was thinking of shufflers," Joel said. "We don't want them to wonder if this is a house ripe for the picking."

"You make a lot of sense. Let's get them into another house," I said.

We tossed their backpacks into the middle of the yard. Joel and I went through pockets, but there wasn't much to find. A pocketknife, some coins; one guy had a wallet with a few dollars inside. He even had pictures of a family, but he wasn't in any of them. For all we knew, he might have lifted the wallet from someone else.

We came up with a few guns, including a .45 without any ammo. The man I'd shot across the street hadn't returned fire because he was out of rounds. The kid had even less on him, but we found two fifty-round boxes of 9mm in a backpack. Christy took the ammo and added it to our stash.

Roz and Anna kept watch while we took the bodies and dragged them into the house. Joel had torn off part of the tarp that was used to cover the truck. We rolled each body onto the heavy plastic, dragged them up the stairs, and tossed them in the living room. The house was much like ours: unfinished, with rolls of carpet, siding, and paint left in neat rows along the walls.

Once we had put the five in a row, Joel and I did the dirty

work and put a knife through each skull except for the kid I'd shot. The bullet hole above his eyes stared back at me rudely.

They were dead, but was it possible they'd rise if they'd been bitten by Zs? None of us wanted to find out.

"Remember that TV show about zombies?" I asked.

"Yeah, I never saw it," Joel said.

"It was all drama and zombie killing. I guess they got that part right."

"I never cared for all that shit. Give me a good Bruce Willis or Danny Glover action flick over some weekly drama about emotions and monsters of the week. I like it when bullets are flying," Joel replied.

"I'm getting too old for this shit," I said, and planted the knife in a dead guy's eyeball. It stuck, and I had to hold his face to pull the blade out. I half-expected the dude to open his good eye, unhinge his mouth, and bite off part of my hand, but he was well and truly dead.

Joel snorted. "Welcome to the party, pal."

His blade went in and out of a head a lot easier than mine.

"There's going to be a lot more of this, isn't there?"

"As supplies dwindle and the Zs increase, yeah, there's always going to be a bad guy looking to take what's ours. We need to always be vigilant."

"Goddamn shame. The death of humanity bringing out the worst in people. Wonder how long until someone gets the drop on us?" I thought out loud.

"Ain't no one taking us out unless we let 'em," Joel said.

"Right, because we're badass action heroes," I said.

"No, because I'm a Marine and we're a fighting unit. Look at these assholes. Five of them and none of us got hit. I like those odds."

"I guess I did alright," I said.

"Yeah you did, you dumb squid, but don't get cocky," Joel said.

"Sure, Han Solo. I'll keep that in mind," I said.

Joel chuckled.

We slit the plastic covering and ripped it off a roll of carpet.

Joel and I rolled it out and used it to cover the dead. As far as burials went it wasn't the best, but at least these guys were going to hell covered in light blue carpeting.

The rest of the evening was less eventful. We ate, played cards, and tried not to talk about the battle. I wanted to run for the hills, but Joel argued that we'd be better off after a night of sleep. I didn't draw first watch, and for a wonder, I was asleep in five minutes.

03:35 hours Approximate
Location: Just outside of Oceanside

"CREED," A SHUFFLER WHISPERED IN MY EAR.

I shot up and reached for my wrench with one hand; my other reached out to grab anything else I could get a hold of. I'd been dreaming of mountains of chocolate and ice cream, in that order. Then a Z rose out of the mess and I was stumbling back, and that was how I came awake.

Joel grabbed my wrist before I could swing my fist into his face. He was wiry but strong, I'll give him that. My heart pounded in my chest as I fought back panic.

"The fuck, man?" I said.

"Keep it down. We got company," Joel said, sounding like he was in an action movie.

"Like dinner company, or fucking Zs?"

"Dinner. They want to eat us."

I shook my head to clear away the fog, and wished I had about a gallon of coffee to slug back.

"Shit. Where?"

"Movement all around out there. It's goddamn eerie, man," Joel whispered.

Anna was on her feet and checking her weapons. Christy held onto Frosty and alternated between stroking her head and holding her mouth to show her that we needed silence. Roz sat next to a window and peered into the darkness. She'd moved the corner of our improvised carpet-curtain up so she had a viewport.

"Zs are eerie."

"They are, but these guys are being quiet. It's like they know we're here. I haven't seen anything like it before," Joel said.

Anna moved next to us and dropped to a crouch. "I count five or six near the back and another dozen at the front. They're standing around staring at the house."

"We're trapped," Joel said.

"Hold the fuck up," I said, finally shaking sleepiness from my head. "Are you saying they're out there waiting for us? Like they *planned* this?"

"Pretty much," Roz said as she joined us.

"We need to get the fuck out of this place and fast. Frontal assault. We go out shooting, get in the truck, and haul ass."

"There's more in the back. I saw them hanging around the outskirts of the yard," Roz said. "It's murky, so I couldn't see them very well."

Joel dug around in his backpack and came up with his old NVGs. He unwrapped them and pushed buttons, and slid them over his head.

"Batteries low. I'll do a fast sweep from inside. Stay here," he said and slipped the goggles over his head.

Joel left the kitchen and moved out. He stopped at a window facing into the backyard and stared.

We'd left most of our weapons out, having done an ammo check earlier. We'd depleted the majority of our rounds escaping the last few encounters. The few boxes I'd picked up from the old woman in town helped, but mainly Joel, since they were for his assault rifle.

Anna dug out a small stash of .357 rounds and she dumped a handful into her pocket. With an 8-round cylinder, she would be able to reload at least one more time.

Roz went over her weapons while I tucked the Springfield XDM into my belt. The wrench was always at hand and never ran out of ammo. I was likely to run out of juice swinging the damn thing before my partners ran out of bullets.

Joel returned. He put a pair of large cans down, then slid the NVGs off and tucked them into his backpack.

"Damn. Probably thirty or forty out there. I lost count."

"What's that?" I asked, pointing at the cans.

"Paint thinner. Time to light up the night so we can get the hell out of here."

"What, Molotovs?"

"Yep," Joel replied. "We don't have cans and bottles, so we'll improvise. Gather up the empty cans and fill them about half-way. Jam a piece of wadded up cloth inside so it's good and soaked. Be careful not to sop that shit all over the side. When we light 'em, you need a few seconds to throw."

"Is this going to work?" Roz asked.

"Better than sitting on our asses and waiting for them to wander away."

"Dude. How are we going to keep from getting burned? The thinner's gonna splash all over the place when we try to throw the stupid cans," I said. "Not to mention Frosty. If she sees fire she might freak the fuck out."

"Tape. Just a little over the top. Cover the can so the cloth hangs out, but not too tight. Frosty's too smart to run at the sight of fire. Dog's smarter than me," Joel said.

"She is a keeper," I said and rubbed her head.

We gathered half a dozen empty cans and put them near the back door. Roz ripped a shirt into big clumps while Joel poured.

"Why not wait?" Christy asked.

"What?" Joel said.

"Just wait. They're dumb Zs, so they'll wander off soon."

Joel scratched his head.

"She's right. Stay inside, chill. Wait," I said.

More than anything I wanted to lay down and sleep for a few more hours. I rubbed grit out of my eyes and looked at my sleeping mat.

"No. We need to get the fuck out of here. Something is up. I didn't see a shuffler, but something weird is happening. Zs don't just hang around in clumps like that."

Something hit the front door hard enough to shake the side

of the house. We went still and waited, wide eyes staring at each other.

The door shook again.

"Right. Plan A: get-the-fuck-out sounds like a winner to me," I said.

"You got that right, man. We get trapped in here and we're screwed, so as they say in your branch of the military, all hands on deck," Joel said.

"You heard the Sarge," I said, trying to sound badass.

"I'll crack a window and throw the first can. That should give us enough light to see what we're up against. After that, we move to the truck. Push any slow fuckers to the ground. Don't stand around trying to kill them all. We're interested in speed, people." Joel looked around our small party.

I nodded and lifted my wrench.

We assembled by the back door with gear stowed back in our packs. We'd have to leave some stuff behind, but I tossed out a few clothes and gave up my sleeping mat in favor of jamming all of our food supplies into my backpack.

Joel held his hand up for silence. I looked outside, but the moon was obscured by clouds, so making out Zs was practically impossible.

Something hit the roof. Then it happened again. A window shattered, and the sound of feet upstairs made my hair stand on end. Then more crashes, like the house was being broken into by a giant hammer.

"Fucking shufflers," I said.

"Don't waste ammo," Joel whispered. "When I start shooting, you all start tossing bombs at anything moving around back there. Move fast to the truck and get it started. Don't stop to kill. Like I said, speed is your friend."

"Is that really the best plan? To have a bunch of burning Zs running around out there?"

"It'll provide enough light to get out. Just don't let one of the flamers take you down," Joel said.

"This shit isn't going to work," Roz said.

"Better idea?" Joel asked.

464

"I got nothing," I said.

Roz just shook her head.

Joel slipped a pair of loaded mags into his kit and moved toward the stairs.

"Joel, what are you going to do?"

"What I do best, mutha fucka. Shoot the bad guys."

Then he was gone.

OVERRUN

03:30 hours approximate
Location: Just outside of Oceanside

J oel's departing form wasn't what I wanted to see. With his skills--not to mention his assault rifle--it was going to be up to us to secure the area and make it to the truck in one piece. There were only about fifty feet separating us from freedom, but it might as well have been fifty miles.

Our weapons were piled next to the window, so I grabbed the little hell-raiser we'd dug up in the abandoned house a few days ago. The Sig home defense assault rifle was loaded and ready for action. I had a spare mag filled with .45 ammo, so I shoved it into my pocket.

My backup was the Springfield XDM 9mm. I had one extra magazine, but it was only half-full—I guess I'm still an optimist after all this shit. I pulled it out of the holster, slipped the magazine out and made sure it was filled. After slamming it home, I racked back the slide and let it slam shut, loading a fresh round into the breach.

I didn't want to fight these things. I wanted to follow Joel's advice and make a run for it. At the same time I felt a sense of panic, because he was stuck in the house fighting shufflers without backup. As if to punctuate my thoughts, his rifle hammered away from upstairs a couple of times before going quiet. The ceiling creaked as figures moved around upstairs.

Frosty was on her feet and growling toward the back door. I patted her head and tried to reassure her.

Roz kept her cool, even if she did keep looking over her shoulder toward the stairs. No doubt she wanted to go as backup. She grabbed my upper arm and gave me a squeeze. I nodded to her, hoping she got my intention, which was to say "we got this". I didn't actually feel like we had anything but a slow death in our near future.

The ceiling rattled as things up there moved. Joel's gun sounded a couple of times, and one particularly loud crash probably meant something had just bit the dust. I hoped it wasn't my buddy.

Moans from the outside drew my attention to the window.

"Light me," Roz said.

Anna put a lighter to the flammable rag and it flared to life. Roz didn't waste any time and threw, but it fell short and splattered paint thinner a few feet short of the Zs. The yard lit up in a spooky glow, making the shadowy figures that approached look more like demons than the undead. I tried to count them, but gave up at twelve.

"Should we go?" asked Christy.

She knelt next to me, the snub-nosed .38 in one hand. She'd picked up a copper water pipe from somewhere in the house, and held it in her other hand. Christy's eyes were wide and nervous.

"We need more light," I said. "Christy, when we move, don't let go of Frosty if you can help it. She's gonna go batshit and we need to get her into the truck in one piece."

"Sorry about my short throw. I thought that stuff was going to splash all over my hand," Roz said.

I thought the same thing as I hefted one of the cans. It wasn't quite half-full, and the smell made me blink my eyes a couple of times. Anna held up the lighter.

The shufflers upstairs made a hell of a racket. Joel's gun

spoke a couple of times, and something hit the floor above hard enough to shake the glass light fixture. Then it was quiet.

Frosty wasn't too happy with all the noise. Her hackles rose and she bared her teeth. She alternated between growling in the direction Joel had disappeared and toward the noise in the front yard.

I moved next, and Roz slid out of the way. I wanted to throw right-handed, but was sure the damn thing was going to blaze up and burn my hand. We didn't have time to make these things very well. My can had held some of the stew we'd enjoyed the night before, and now it sloshed with flammable liquid.

The ceiling shook again under pounding feet. Joel's gun fired several times and then it was quiet again.

Anna lit the cloth. The fire flared immediately and just like Roz, I panicked and threw. The night came alive with more light, but I'd hit nothing.

"Oh Jesus," Anna exclaimed.

Anna picked up a can and shouldered me aside. She still cradled her injured arm, but managed to do a hell of a lot better than me or Roz. As soon as the cloth was lit, she held the can tilted slightly until she was sure it was aflame. Throwing from her fingertips, the can sailed through the air and plastered a Z in the chest.

Thinner exploded all over the man. He howled and fell back, knocking down another Z. The pair thrashed, and managed to make the flames even worse.

Joel pounded into the kitchen and nearly got a face full of wrench.

"*Dude.*"

"Gimme a can. I'm gonna light this place up. I took down a shuffler, injured another one, but one other fucker is still sneaking around up there, too scared to show his face. See how he likes *this* shit."

Joel snagged a can and Roz lit the rag. He moved fast, with the mini-torch lighting his way. A few seconds later there was a *whoosh* and something screamed: a tiny *whoof* of noise as the improvised bomb must have come to life.

Frosty nearly broke free. I grabbed her collar, and tried to reassure her with a few soft words.

"We're out of here," I said and grabbed another can. "Christy, take the lighter and fire us up as we go. Follow and get ready to pop anything that gets too close."

She nodded.

Roz, Anna, and I each took one of the last three improvised Molotovs. I pushed the back door open and was on the landing before I could acknowledge the fact that I was holding a can of flame that could light me up just as quickly as it could a Z. With the backyard now illuminated, it was easier to make out the Zs. I drew back and let the can sail. It splashed across a Z and turned it into a walking torch.

I had other issues.

In my excitement I'd managed to splash flammable liquid over my hand and shirt. When I threw I knew I was in trouble.

Flames roared to life on the Z's shirt. It stumbled back into another creeper and set his ass on fire. They actually looked like they were scared of the flames as they tripped, and ran into each other.

I flailed my arm around as fire and pain raced across the top of my hand.

Anna slapped at my burning appendage while Roz moved into position, lit her can, and tossed it.

As far as Molotovs went, I'd have to say these weren't the best idea. With the partially-exposed lids, a lot of fluid leaked out as they were jostled. Flames followed on a stream of paint thinner, further lighting the night, but also splashing fire over the partially-finished yard.

Zs by the dozens moved in on our position. They stumbled, flailed, shambled, and generally scared the ever-living *fuck* out of me. I moved in front of Anna as I slapped my hand into my armpit to extinguish the blaze.

"Move!" Anna said, and gave me a small push.

I did.

With the wrench in my off hand, I took the two steps to the yard and smashed a Z to the ground. Dude was reaching for me, his shirt on fire, flames eating at his face. His mouth was a horror of broken teeth, dried, copper-tinged blood, and something that might have been a nose. White and partially-desiccated eyes fixed on mine.

I hit him hard enough to cave in the side of his head. He dropped, but his body caught my legs, and I staggered into Anna.

Roz came to the rescue and shot a flailer between the eyes. The Z's head snapped back, and her body hit the ground.

They were all around us.

Frosty darted in and nipped at a Z, then danced around as it reached for her. The dog played it smart and kept out of the rotter's grasp.

Christy called to Frosty, so the dog shot between the legs of a Z, knocking it down.

In a panic I recovered, and did a little half-spin as I tried to decide which of the creepy crawlers to take on first.

There was a teenage kid who was taller than me and skinny as a rail. His clothes were rags, his once grey-and-black cammo shorts barely hanging onto his hips. An older couple dressed in the remains of hospital smocks. The woman still trailed an IV tube from one arm. The man wore a cast that immobilized his leg, but he shuffle-stepped like he was in a weird dance.

I shoved the couple aside, batted the kid's hands away with my wrench and kicked him into a flaming Z who shambled in circles.

Anna drew her big handgun and shot the kid as he sat up and reached for me.

Christy shot the woman with the IV and clipped the side of her neck. I swung up and caught her under her chin. Rotted teeth flew, and part of her head broke loose. The Z flew backward into another of the rotted things, and the pair fell in a heap.

With our way free and only a dozen or so feet from us to the truck, I thought we now had a straight shot.

Hands reached for me, so I slapped them aside.

Frosty barked at something, but I didn't have time to look.

I made out the truck in the murk and ran straight for it. I had the whole thing mapped out in my head. I'd beat down the Z that was in front of me. Reach the truck, make myself a big barricade while the others got to my location. They'd load and then we'd be inside. We'd be surrounded, but with any luck the big truck would shove the dead aside. That was, if the shufflers didn't hit us first.

I almost made it.

03:45 hours approximate
Location: Just outside of Oceanside

SURE ENOUGH, A SHUFFLER DROPPED FROM THE ROOF AND HIT ME from behind.

He was a snarling mess of wounds and open sores. His eyes glowed with hate and his mouth opened to reveal teeth filed to points. The smell was the worst: like someone had left a body covered in dead fish to rot in the sun.

He caught my leg and I nearly fell, but stumbled into the truck and recovered.

I gagged as I turned to confront him.

A Z had been closing in on me, but I had his number and kicked back, catching him in the groin. The decomposing little shit bent at the waist and collapsed.

The shuffler moved sinuous as a whip, and swung out a leg to catch Anna. She stumbled back and caught herself on the porch railing. Roz reached for her, but the shuffler spun and took her to the ground. She thrashed as it covered her and leaned in to rip at her face. I ignored a Z that almost got a hand on me, and rushed in.

I grabbed the rotting creature by a foot and with adrenaline roaring in my ears, ripped it off of Roz. The shuffler wasn't much more than flesh and bone, but it was strong and lashed a foot up, catching me in the shoulder.

My left arm went numb, but I didn't let go. I got my other hand on its ankle and used all of my strength to rip the bastard off of Roz and fling it at another Z. The shuffler didn't even hesitate; it scrambled to all fours and leapt.

Roz clambered back, legs kicking at the ground as she tried to get to the porch.

Anna lifted her gun and fired, but the shuffler was fast, and the shot whizzed past its head.

Frosty darted between Zs in the yard, avoiding the burning Zs, but harrying others.

The night took on a glow as flames rushed across the upper story.

In the wan light, I caught a female Z coming at me. I didn't want to take my eyes off Roz and the shuffler, but I couldn't ignore the arm that looped over my neck. Teeth went for my shoulder, so I whipped my elbow around and caught her in the side of the head.

Roz fell under the smart Z again. I howled in fury as I shook off the rotting Z and lifted my wrench, intent on cracking shuffler bones.

Roz got her handgun up to shoot the Z, but it batted her firearm aside.

Anna tried to get a good shot, but it was obvious that if she fired, she had every chance of hitting Roz as well.

I hit the shuffler's leg, and bones cracked. It hissed in fury, and its head spun to regard me. Eyes glowed with malevolent intelligence as they swept over me. It rose up and lashed at me with one claw-like hand. I drew back and turned so he didn't have a chance at my numb shoulder. Make that *kind of* numb. Feeling was returning, and it hurt like a bitch.

A Z was on me. I didn't have time for this Mickey Mouse bullshit, so I lifted my wrench and took off most of its head.

Anna drew her knife and slashed at the shuffler from behind. She tried to drive the blade into his neck, but the creature was fast, and got a sliced shoulder for his efforts. Take that, you bastard.

Roz choked and rolled onto her side.

The shuffler turned to take on Anna, so I swept the wrench around and hit him in the arm. I'd aimed higher, but my shoulder wasn't exactly responding to what my brain tried to tell it to do. Anna lashed at the thing again as it came up on its two feet. Driving forward, she cut him hard enough to sever fingers.

The shuffler shrieked and leapt.

Anna shifted to the side but he still bowled her over. He scrambled over her as she fought him off.

"No!" I screamed, and got hit by another Z as I moved to help.

Frosty grabbed the shuffler's pant leg and pulled. The bastard struck back, and Frosty whimpered as her snout took the blow. She backed up and shook her head. Christy grabbed Frosty's collar and tugged the dog away from the melee.

Joel appeared in the doorway. I caught sight of him out of the corner of my eye. He paused on the landing, lifted his gun, and calmly dropped a pair of Zs that were bearing down on me.

Anna was my priority. If not for him the two Zs probably would have taken me to the ground. Leave it to Joel Fucking Kelly to come to the rescue.

Anna kicked at the Z as it crawled over her.

Roz rolled onto her back, saw the shuffler as it attacked Anna, and didn't sit around waiting for help. She scissor-kicked from her side and caught the rotter in the thigh. A normal man would have howled with pain, but this just pissed off the shuffler.

"Fuck you, asshole," she said and kicked again.

The shuffler shrugged off the blows, and his mouth leapt at Anna.

Anna did a neat trick where she leveraged her body off the ground and twisted to dump the shuffler on his side. She tried to move away, but the thing scrambled to its knees and then went for her.

Christy dashed past Joel with a flaming can in one hand. She skipped the last step, hit the ground running, and only paused to slam the improvised Molotov onto the shuffler's head.

Anna crab-walked out of the way as fire streamed around them.

The shuffler screeched as his hair flared to life. He leapt off of Anna and fell, slapping at his head as the fire spread. Skin and stringy hair burned. The shuffler tried to bat at the fire, but as he came up into a kneeling position, Joel put an end to his struggles with a shot to the head. The 5.56 round passed through his skull and exited with an impressive amount of red and rotted brain matter.

The shuffler's head snapped back, and for a second he stared with hatred at us. Even *I* was fucking shocked at how long it took for the thing to slump to the side.

Joel and I helped the ladies to their feet, and he quickly took point. He kicked a Z out of the way and shot another at almost point-blank range, blowing half its head off in the process.

Anna limped, and warded her injured arm, holding it tight against her body. Her Smith & Wesson hung in her other hand. Roz clung to me, her arm draped around my waist. She stepped on something on the ground and almost fell. I lifted her back up, surprised at how weak she seemed.

Christy moved to my side, Frosty sticking close to her. Christy had her little snub-nosed revolver in hand and fired into the darkness. The round caught a shambling Z in the shoulder. He spun away and crashed into another rotting corpse, and the two went down in a heap of limbs.

Behind me, flames crept out of the second-story windows, casting an orange and yellow haze over the backyard. I didn't want to think about the things coming for us, but I looked anyway. I should have kept my damn eyes front and center, because there were more than enough to kill us.

"Joel, we're about to be overrun!"

"I know, fuck, we're here though. Get them in the back and I'll start the truck. Christy, shoot any fucker that gets close, and don't let Frosty run off. Get her in the front seat with you."

"Got it," she said. Christy opened the gun's cylinder and dropped spent shells on the lawn. With deft and practiced fingers, she reloaded from her jeans pocket.

I had to kick a Z out of the way. The shambler had been hanging out in the tiny space between the camper and the side of the house. He fell on his back, and when he looked up I met his gaze with a blow to the head. My wrench felt like a fifty-pound lead pipe, but I managed to lift it one more time.

Anna slid past me and hit the side of the truck. She peeked around the corner and held up a hand.

Joel hopped in the driver's seat and started the truck. In the movies this would be the part where the engine wouldn't turn over no matter how many times Joel cranked it. The first piece of good luck all night occurred when the engine roared to life.

Anna swung around the back of the truck and fired two measured shots.

"Clear!" she said.

Roz and I clutched at each other as Anna opened the back door. She watched our six as I helped Roz on board. I didn't need to be reminded that we were surrounded, so the Zs thumping at the sides and back of the truck were like hammer blows upside my now-aching head. I needed water, some aspirin, and about fifteen hours of fucking sleep.

Roz and I collapsed on the floor. Anna slammed the door shut and locked it. The truck's engine engaged and Joel backed up. Anna was thrown off her feet and hit the little dining table. She grabbed at the edge, but lost the battle and was tossed to the ground.

"Fuck *me*!" she said.

04:05 hours approximate
Location: Just outside of Oceanside

I STRUGGLED TO GET ON MY HANDS AND KNEES AS THE TRUCK rocked us. I managed to pull Roz to my chest when Joel hit the engine again. The truck accelerated while I struggled to get Roz to the bed. Her breathing was labored and she had gone almost completely limp in my hands.

"Come on Roz, we're just about out of here. Tell me what hurts, okay?" I said.

She shrugged and pointed at her mouth.

The interior of the camper was cold and dark, so Anna hit the overhead light.

I nearly dropped Roz.

Her mouth was covered in blood and gore. She struggled away from me, so I let her go.

Roz spit out a mass of blood and saliva, then furiously wiped at her mouth with her sleeve. She rolled to her side, curled up in a ball and vomited. The reek hit me and I almost threw up myself. That would have been an interesting chain reaction, because Anna might have joined the barf patrol.

"What's wrong with her?" Anna asked.

"Don't know," I said.

I stared at Roz in horror. If she'd been bitten, we needed to get rid of her, and soon. I liked Roz a lot. We'd even shared a moment in a garage a few months back. She'd been with us ever since. If we had to toss her, I didn't want to be the one to tell Joel.

The truck spun tires and swerved to the right, and I was thrown off my feet.

"Jesus, Joel!" I yelled.

I doubt Joel heard me, but the truck accelerated for a full twenty seconds before he slammed on the brakes again. This time I'd barely gotten to all fours when I face-planted onto the tile floor. My arm stretched out to stop my forward momentum, but my nose ended up taking the impact anyway.

Cursing, I pushed myself back up and got to my feet. I wedged myself between the floor and the low ceiling and held on for dear life, because sure enough, the truck roared forward again. This time I got to the little table and sat down before Joel could knock me down again.

Roz was curled up in a ball and shaking. Anna lay next to her, and shot pleading looks my way.

"Can you tell what's going on with Roz? Was she bit?" I asked.

I rubbed at my nose and didn't find blood, but it hurt like hell.

"She's wounded, but I can't tell how it happened," Anna said. Her eyes didn't meet mine.

Anna's body language changed. She tensed and her hand crept to her holster.

"Is she?" I couldn't finish.

"I said I don't know."

"Roz. You okay?" I asked.

She nodded but didn't reply. One of her arms wrapped around her head like it was about to explode.

"Fuck," Anna said, which seemed to sum up what I was thinking as well.

That was all she got out before we hit something. *Two* somethings. The truck swerved again, and then came to a shuddering stop.

Frosty was in the front with Joel and Christy, but something must have spooked her, because her bark carried into the camper.

Roz rolled across the floor and hit the little bed. Anna and I managed to hang onto the table. The truck moved again and came to a halt.

"He's playing fucking pinball up there," I muttered.

I moved to the window and slid the curtain aside. Anna didn't move, and kept an eye on Roz.

"What's going on out there?" Anna said.

I didn't even have the words to answer her.

The quiet neighborhood we'd found eight hours ago was filled with the dead. They were in the streets, streaming around houses, shambling corpses covered in rags and filth. White eyes fixed on nothing as they advanced.

The truck backed up a half block and came to a halt again as we hit a couple of Zs. They bounced under the bed and were chewed up by tires.

"We are so fucked," I finally said.

Anna moved to the window and looked outside. She turned to me, her lips a slit as her mind churned.

"Maybe he can find a way out," Anna said.

Joel's assault rifle spoke. It rattled off a few measured shots, and then the truck moved once again. It accelerated and swerved to the right. Anna grabbed at me as I reached up and wedged myself against the roof.

Another shot rang out. From the sounds, it was the little revolver that Christy carried. I didn't stop to let the surrounding horror consume me. I needed to assess the threat from up high, and there was only one way to do that and communicate with Joel.

The trapdoor was small, but I thought I could at least get my head out, and maybe an arm.

"Keep an eye on her," I nodded at Roz.

I pushed a chair in the middle of the floor and stooped as I stepped on it. The hatch popped up, but there was a bar that kept it from opening all of the way. I hit the little door, but it was bolted tightly. I grabbed the bar that held it in place and twisted until it popped loose. The screw that held it against the opening wasn't that strong, and the head hit the floor. It popped like a champagne cork and flew off. With any luck, it smacked a Z upside the head.

I grabbed my 9mm and pushed myself up into the opening. I wiggled my gun hand out and got my upper body wedged in the entry. With a little more twisting I managed to get my shoulder in along with my arm, so I hoisted myself up and on top of the roof, which wanted to buckle under me.

It was still dark, but morning was coming on, and with it, enough light to wish it was still pitch black. The things were all around us, and I understood now why Joel had been bouncing us all over the damn place: the Zs were an ocean in every direction, illuminated by the burning house we'd left behind. Sure enough, Joel's idea had turned into an inferno. That meant it wouldn't take long for the rest of the neighborhood to go up in flames.

Something rattled loudly in the distance, shaking the night. I twisted around, looking for the source of the sound, pretty sure I knew what it emanated from.

Hands hit the side of the camper as they reached for me, but I was far enough up that they weren't a threat.

Christy's head appeared as she slid out of her window and crawled on top of the cab. She shot a Z that would have grabbed her ankle, and slithered on top of the truck.

"Joel said we have to get inside and fortify."

"How were you planning to get in here?" I asked.

"You were going to open the little roof door, duh," Christy rolled her eyes.

I shot a Z that got a little too adventurous. The bullet passed above one eye and exited the back of his head with a fair amount of dead brain matter.

Joel leaned out of the window and shot a pair of Zs in rapid succession. The bodies fell away into the crowd.

"SITREP?" Joel turned and shouted at me.

"One word: fucked!"

"That's three words. How fucked?"

"We are so fucked, dude," I yelled back.

Joel nodded and ducked back into the truck. "Coming out the starboard side."

"When you use fancy navy terms I get all hot in my pants, Joel," I called back. "What about Frosty?"

"I hope you got that smart mouth ready when they close in on us and start eating us feet first. I'm going to leave her here for now until I come up with a better plan."

"A better plan? Better to let her go. Frosty's smart and quick. She'll get away," I said.

Gunfire again as he shot three or four Zs that were crowding around the passenger side window. Joel slithered out the side of the truck, and shot a Z in the process.

I leaned over and covered him, shooting a man with dreads.

Dude's head snapped back, and he was a twice-dead dread. "Joel, don't, man. You won't make it."

Joel shot another Z. "New plan," he yelled.

Joel disappeared and the truck jarred me against the roof. I grabbed the hatch and held on with a death grip as he shifted into reverse. The way behind us wasn't much clearer, but I understood what he was doing even as the truck backed up. With the weight of the camper we'd have more traction. Couple that with the fact that it was rear drive, and we'd buy ourselves a few more minutes, at the very least.

Christy got creative and used the camper's small side window to haul herself up. A Z reached for her, but she was quick to kick him in the head. He fell back and quickly stretched for her again. Christy grasped the edge of the camper's roof. I pushed through the portal and stuck my hand out for her, but she slipped away.

A Z roared and I just about went over the side.

Christy's hand reappeared, and this time I put a death grip on her wrist and pulled her up.

"Ouch, Creed. You're going to break my arm."

"I thought they got you, Christy, Jesus!" I said, and hugged her as I dragged her toward me.

She slithered around me and grabbed hold of the half-demolished hatch. I helped her turn around and got my arm around her waist.

"I'm going back in. You need to be right behind me, got it?"

She nodded, eyes wide.

I scrambled for purchase as we turned multiple Zs into speed bumps. The truck's rear lights lit up the faces of white-eyed ghouls before they were crushed to a pulp. Joel kept it at a steady fifteen or twenty miles an hour as he smashed the horde aside.

The hard part was getting my left arm back inside while I held onto Christy. She grasped the open hatch, slid around, and slipped her legs inside.

My feet hit the chair and I stumbled, falling the short distance, but managing to land with jarring impact.

"What in the fuck is going on out there?"

"It's bad, Anna."

Christy lowered her body into the camper. I got my hands around her and guided her to the floor.

"Roz?"

"Not any better, and all this goddamn bouncing around isn't helping. Do I need to go up there?" Anna asked.

"If you think it will help, sure."

Anna pushed me aside and stepped on the chair. It shifted beneath her, but she got her good arm up and pulled herself to her feet.

"Keep an eye on her," she said.

"I was kidding, I'll go back up there."

"Creed, I'm trained and I'm a better shot than you. Stay here and watch over Roz," she said, and then leaned close. "You know what to do if you have to."

"That's Roz," I whispered back.

"If she turns, she won't be anything except a danger. Do you really want a Z loose in the camper?"

Anna locked gazes with me, nodded once, and then climbed on the chair. She put her hand through the trapdoor and tugged her body into the spot I'd just occupied.

Anna's body didn't completely disappear from sight. She maneuvered around and got one hand inside the hatch. She pulled her gun and lay flat.

Christy dropped next to Roz to check on her. She'd taken a towel off the counter and used it to wipe Roz's face. The she grabbed a bottle of water and started to clean up the mess.

The truck came to a shuddering stop. I grabbed at the ceiling and managed to brace myself. Anna slid forward, but she quickly backed up until I could see her upper body again.

The truck moved forward, turned slightly, and then accelerated backward again. Hands pounded at the door, but the thumping of hands ceased after we moved, and was replaced by the thumping of bodies under the vehicle.

The truck once again slammed to a stop, and didn't move

again. Anna shot until her big revolver ran dry, then handed it down to me.

"Where's the ammo?"

"In the pile. Just hand me another gun."

"How many Zs are there?" I asked.

"More than we have rounds for." She gave me a flat look.

Christy had already dug into our supply and come up with a compact Ruger .40 we'd acquired somewhere along the way. I shifted stuff around and found the little house sweeper.

"Coming up," I said and got on the chair again.

Anna shimmied over as I popped out of the hatch.

The night was lit up by the house we'd set on fire. Flames roared as the house was engulfed. The orange glow was genuinely creepy, with flares casting shadows over the undead.

To the North there was a road that looked clear. To the South lay an army of dead.

Between us and a shot at the road were at least a hundred shamblers. It's great to feel wanted, except when a bunch of people want to eat your flesh and blood.

"Joel." I pounded on the roof. "About a block and a half North of here, the road is free."

Joel yelled back an acknowledgment. His assault rifle rattled a few times, clearing something of a path. He slowly backed the truck up, smooshing over bodies that reached for us even as he crushed them.

The truck roared ahead and I got my hand around Anna in case she lost her grip. She shimmied around so we had a good view of the front of the truck, and we both opened up, trying to drop as many of the Zs as possible.

The problem was that they just formed little speed bumps, but Joel wasn't deterred. He hit the high beams, bounced on a curb, tore over the sidewalk, and cut closely between two houses.

Our vehicle had enough blood and guts covering the hood and sides to make a horror movie fan stand up and shout for glee.

The yard was half-finished, and Joel had no choice but to drive over a couple of deep holes that had probably been dug for more trees. I got a glimpse of a Z rising out of one of the pits like a fresh-raised dead. The truck smacked him down and then bounced into the air. Anna hung onto me, and I held onto the hatch.

We were going to make it.

"Ow!" Christy called from inside.

"We see the road, Christy. Hang on."

What I'd taken for a low line of shrubs or trees turned out to have a different idea. As the truck bumped over the yard, the high beams told the tale: the road was indeed free, but Zs were closing in from every direction. Even this big-ass rig wouldn't be able to make it through that mess.

"I'll get us as far as I can," Joel called from inside the truck.

It was a great plan. Sadly, we didn't get very far.

I held on as Joel hit a fucking *wall* of zombies. Some were smashed aside, some were crushed underneath, and some exploded. Walking corpses, so I'd learned, tended to do that. Blood, guts, splattered brains, and body parts covered the front of the big truck, and with each impact, the body sustained more and more damage. There had to be a hundred of the things all around us, and instead of getting away from them, we came to a halt.

The truck died, and with it, the sound of the dead became the only thing I heard, until Anna took out a feisty, freshly-dead fuck who'd decided that he wanted to climb up the hood.

The engine turned over, caught with a weird noise that sounded like chains cracking together and then died again. Joel cranked a few more times, but the only answer was a grinding noise.

"Ah, shit!" he said.

I pushed myself up and shimmied through the little portal. My sides and arms felt like I'd been in a damn boxing ring with all of the scrapes and bruises.

Anna made room for me, but the roof bowed dangerously as we moved around.

Joel turned the key again and let it crank for a good ten

seconds, but nothing happened, except the truck groaned like it had given up. *That's right, fuck you people who abused the shit out of me. I can only take so much.*

The dead closed in all around us.

"What do we do now?" Anna looked me in the eye and I saw something that I had rarely seen from her.

She was just as scared as me.

UNCERTAINTY

05:20 hours approximate
Location: Just outside of Oceanside

Gunfire shattered the night.

The moans of the dead were the only noise that filled my ears. They also filled my soul with dread, because as many scrapes as we'd been in, this was the mother-fucker that topped them all. Not for the first time we were completely surrounded, but this time I didn't have a plan, and judging by the defeated look on Joel's face, neither did he.

I'd been staring at the mass as they surrounded us, and my thoughts had turned to how we were all going to off each other. Would one of us shoot the rest? Would we sit around in a circle jerk and watch each other blow their brains out? Maybe we could just have Joel machine gun us into oblivion, and then he could do himself.

The funny thing was that I worried about my body after we were dead, so I had been looking around for things to set the camper on fire with.

Then my mind raced as I thought about zombies eating our toasted bodies. Would they bring some Kansas City BBQ sauce to enjoy our ribs?

Joel managed to get out of the truck's window without being

pulled into the mess of Zs. Anna and I had provided cover while he shimmied up the side and onto the roof, kicking away grasping hands in the process.

There'd been one real moment where I thought he was being dumb. Joel had grabbed a couple of boxes of ammo and flung them at us, then he'd ducked in for more after batting aside a couple of grabby assholes. What was the use of all that ammo when we were completely stuck? It would take a thousand rounds to get out of this mess.

The basis of a plan formed in my head. We'd take turns sitting on the camper shooting all of these bastards until we were out of bullets. If that happened, we'd have a chance.

Or until a couple of shufflers appeared.

The three of us shimmied into the camper.

"This ain't good," Joel said. "And what the hell is that fucking smell?"

"Roz got sick after we got her in here. Not like we can open a window and air the place out," I said. "We've been in worse spots than this, Joel."

"Nah, man. This is the worst. Thing is, the truck is stuck. I don't know if I got too much zombie shit in the grill or if we just hit a Z wall. All I know is I couldn't move forward or back. Engine died and I couldn't get it to restart."

"Wait it out," Anna said.

"I saw at least three shufflers out there. Glowing green eyes and everything. I can try to take them out, but hitting moving targets isn't as easy as it looks, and we got limited ammo," Joel said.

"So much for my plan," I muttered.

"What was it?" Joel asked.

"It was stupid. Next plan?"

"We don't have a choice. We have to wait it out, and maybe we can keep them out of the camper long enough so that they lose interest and wander away. All we have to do is shoot the shufflers," Anna said.

"Works for me," I nodded. "Put Joel and his assault rifle up there and he can pick off the fast ones."

"Good plan, but I'm almost out of rounds."

Joel moved to Roz's side and brushed the hair out of her face. His fist clenched when he saw the damage.

"She needs help," I muttered.

Hands pounded at the back door.

"I tried to clean up the wound, but there's a lot of blood and I didn't want to hurt her," Christy said.

"How could you let this happen?" Joel said.

I shook my head. What the *hell*? We didn't *let* anything happen; a shuffler had dropped on us and taken us by surprise. Anna had been the one to get the bastard off Roz while I fought my way back to them.

"It was so fast, Joel, you were there. Oh, wait, you went upstairs to kill stuff, remember, that's what you do."

"Fuck you, man. I saved your ass and you let her get attacked."

"Don't blame me. Coulda happened to any of us," I tried to reason.

"But it didn't, it happened to her."

Christy sat on the floor next to Roz and held a bloodied towel. Tears left a clean line through grime as they trickled down her face.

"Stop arguing," she said.

"We aren't arguing, because I'm right," Joel said.

He looked around the tiny cabin and I saw something in his eyes I'd never seen before: despair. He was at the end of his rope, and I wasn't going to be much help, because I felt the same way.

More hands beat at the trailer. The truck actually tilted as too many of them pushed.

"Joel, we can't argue about this right now. We need to deal with that," I nodded at the door.

Joel pointed at Roz. "*That* is a *real* problem. *That* is what we need to fix. Tired of watching your ass all the time."

The side of the cabin bowed in and the trailer lifted a half foot off the ground. I reached for the sink and caught myself.

"Calm down, man. You're just upset."

"I'm not going to be calm until we're out of this. We gotta get some help for Roz. Get back to the city and see if that crazy bitch with the meds has something that can fix her up."

"Dude, you sound like a crazy person," I said.

"Fuck you, Creed. The only thing crazy is that we're stuck in this shitty mess," Joel fumed. "I'm going to thin the herd. Better than sitting here waiting to die."

"So you're going to go sit up there and shoot until you're empty and maybe, just maybe, we'll be able to get to safety. Sounds like we're going to have to run. Did you plan to leave Roz here? Because it's going to take more than one of us to carry her."

"No one's getting left behind. Hand me some ammo," Joel said.

Christy was quick, gathering up a couple of magazines and handing them to Joel. He shoved a few in his pockets and handed over his empties.

"I don't think we have enough to fill them," Christy said.

"Do your best," Joel nodded.

"What about us? What do we do while you're up there saving us?" I asked.

"What *can* we do, man? What the fuck can we do? Roz's hurt, we're completely surrounded, and we can't just sit around with our thumbs up our asses. We don't even know if she's going to turn into one of those fucking things. Give me a better plan or get the hell out of the way."

Joel shouldered me aside and stepped on the chair. He pushed his assault rifle out of the portal and then wedged himself in.

"We need something better than shooting them, come on Joel. Let's think this through."

"Like I said," Joel yelled back. "Come up with a plan or sit down and shut the fuck up."

"Don't be an asshole, Joel. Roz needs you now, and so do Anna and Christy," I said, because I couldn't think of anything better to say.

Joel was pissed, yeah, but he wasn't thinking straight. Even if he had unlimited ammo, could he really clear this entire area, kill the shufflers, and then get us out of here? The chances were nil. Fucking *nil*, and he knew it.

Joel dropped back into the cabin and got in my face.

"What do you have in mind, smartass?" Joel waited.

"Not having a fucking pity party, that's one plan. You want to go up there and waste all of our ammo, be my guest, but then what?"

The camper bowed in on both sides.

"Then we get the truck unstuck and get the hell out of here. Thin the herd, because it's worked before, so man up or sit down here and cry like a bitch," Joel said.

"Shut up," I said.

"Don't tell me the fuck to…"

"They're listening to us argue. Just shut up," I whispered.

Joel stared daggers but nodded. We stood in silence as the moans rose around us.

05:35 hours approximate
Location: Just outside of Oceanside

WE GAVE IT A FEW MINUTES AND SURE ENOUGH, THE POUNDING AT the camper died down a little bit. Joel and I sat on opposite sides, him with one arm crossed around his AR-15 and the other on Roz's shoulder, me holding my wrench and wishing I was out there swinging it, because I was fucking mad as hell.

Joel had every right to be a pain in the ass and he had every right to be angry at our situation, but taking it out on me was the wrong move. We'd seen a lot of shit, but I'd never seen him this close to losing it.

If we lost Joel, where would we all be? I'd like to say that the girls and I would be fine and dandy and live to fight another day. After all, Anna Sails was badass enough for both of us. The fact that she was a woman and smaller than me meant that I'd initially discounted her as needing to be protected. Turned out she was more than up for the challenge, and had been the one to protect me on many occasions.

Christy had latched onto us, me in particular, and I'd done my best to teach her everything I knew about surviving the zombie fucking apocalypse. She was good with a gun, but sometimes rattled easily. That was understandable, because she was a kid, but I'd seen her step up on more than one occasion.

Then there was Roz. She was always steady. When we'd met her she'd been outside of her house and intent on shooting her dad, who had already become a Z. Since then she and Joel had bonded. Now there was something wrong with her. The shuffler had done some damage, and unlike a zombie's bite, it wasn't turning her. But what did that mean?

After Roz had finished puking her guts out, Christy had been nice enough to slop the mess into a corner and out of the way, but the smell wasn't any better.

Frosty barked from the front of the truck, then quieted down.

Some of the Zs continued to pound on the walls, but some had given up and wandered off--or so I hoped. In an ideal world they'd all be gone, coast clear. As far as I was concerned, we needed to just stay put and hope the bastards found another bunch of people to terrorize.

It was another ten minutes before Joel decided he'd had enough. He rose to his feet and moved to the center of the camper, but didn't meet my eye. He looked back at Roz and then climbed onto the chair.

"Wait, Joel," I whispered.

He ignored me and pushed his head out of the portal.

"Shit," he said when he dropped back down.

"Told you to wait," I said.

"Wouldn't matter. Damn Zs are just hanging around out there like they know we're still here. I'm gonna go see if the engine will turn over. Maybe it's cooled..." He didn't finish his sentence, because something hit the camper hard enough to make it shake.

Green eyes peered in from the entryway, and another pair

appeared at the back door. I drew and shot before I'd thought it through. The sound of the 9mm in the tiny space was deafening, like I'd shoved cotton in my ears because a giant monkey playing cymbals had pounded my head.

Something hit the roof and Joel swung his assault rifle up. He dropped to one knee and aimed at the portal. When part of the ceiling buckled, he fired two rounds. There was a screech of pain, and then the roof buckled in another place.

I met the eyes of my companions and saw nothing but fear.

05:50 hours approximate
Location: Just outside of Oceanside

THE POUNDING BEGAN IN EARNEST. FISTS HAMMERED THE TRUCK and hands clawed at the windows.

The back of the camper flexed under the pressure. Joel pushed back.

A side window shattered and Zs reached inside. Anna pulled her knife and slashed at the hands that hunted for our flesh. A finger hit the ground and one of the Zs withdrew, but more hands appeared in its place.

I stood up and lifted my wrench. When they came through, I was going to be a wall capable of swinging heavy steel. I'd bash in every head I could reach before they took me down.

A blast from outside the camper scared the shit out of me.

Another blast and one of the creatures on top of the vehicle fell off with a thump. Several more gunshots, and the things above us departed. Joel and I looked at each other but he was the first one to say it. "Hit the deck!"

I got on my belly and hoped whoever was out there didn't spray our vehicle with lead. Joel was right next to me, and there was a glimmer of hope in his eyes. He rolled onto his back and pointed his gun at the ceiling.

More pops in the near distance. After a few seconds of silence, the blasts opened up with authority. Bullets whizzed through the air. The sound of rounds striking flesh and leaving mortal wounds answered.

After a thirty second barrage, it grew silent again.

"Anyone fucking alive in there?"

"Yeah we're fucking alive!" I yelled back.

"Stay put!" The man's voice was just about the best thing I'd ever heard in my life.

I hoped we were being rescued and not truck-jacked. Even if our would-be heroes wanted all of our shit, maybe they'd leave us alive. A brief moment of horror reminded me of McQuinn's army of jackholes. If they were outside, we were all going to die.

Christy crawled across the floor until she was right next to me. She grasped my hand and held on tightly.

Anna partially covered Roz's body with her own, because Roz kicked her legs up and down, striking the floor in pain. She gurgled something, and then coughed until it sounded like she was going to toss a lung. Anna held Roz's hands to her sides, and didn't let the other woman up.

There were a few more pops of small arms fire, and then someone knocked on the door.

"Don't fucking shoot. We're here to help."

"Yeah okay," I said.

"Don't get too excited, friend."

I smiled. "Sorry, man. We thought we were about to be lunch."

"More like breakfast, but why don't you come out nice and slow and do us a favor--don't show us any guns, if you know what I'm saying. You stay cool and we'll stay cool."

"We're cucumbers," Joel answered.

I looked at him and shook my head. Who says some shit like that?

I rose to my knees and shuffled forward, then stood and peered out, cautiously, at what awaited.

06:05 hours approximate
Location: Just outside of Oceanside

THE MAN WAS PROBABLY IN HIS MID-FORTIES, AND DRESSED IN battle fatigues. He had dusky skin, and brown eyes that were tight around the corners. He didn't wear any insignia that I could see, but he had a symbol on his collar that looked like a skull with a rifle behind it, and on either side were wings. His face was covered in streaks of dark camouflage. He nodded and I nodded back.

"You folks okay in there?" he asked.

"Mostly," I said.

"We were on patrol and saw the house on fire so we moved in to investigate. Sarge thought a bunch of jumpers on top of a camper meant they were up to nothing good. Not that jumpers need any excuse to be assholes."

I cracked the door open and took in our saviors.

"Thanks for coming along. I thought we were about to join the Zs," I said.

Although I was keeping it cool I was tense, and ready to jump if they made a wrong move.

It was like Kelly and I had a mental connection. I knew without looking that he was lying on the deck and had his AR trained on the door. I knew enough to hit the deck if he yelled "Down!" Not that it would do a lot of good; these guys had enough firepower to wipe us off the face of the earth.

"Name's Ramirez, and we're part of a delta patrol outta Fort Obstacle the third, on account a Fort Obstacle two being overrun a few nights ago," he continued.

I just stared, because a minute ago I'd thought we were all about to join the horde of undead, and now this guy was talking about having multiple fortresses.

"Ramirez, I could just about kiss you," I said.

"You're not my type, but I appreciate the sentiment, sir."

One of the men near him chuckled as he stood around looking like he was about to fall asleep. His weapon was a subcompact; probably an MP5, from the profile. I needed to smack Joel Kelly one of these days, for teaching me to recognize guns on sight.

Five other men who were dressed like our rescuer stood around in a semicircle. One of the guys hanging out to the side had a gun that made Joel's AR look like a toy.

He was on one knee and swinging the barrel around in a short sweep. His eye was pressed to a big scope. He lifted his right hand in the air and raised a digit. The others pointed guns in the direction of his barrel. He lowered his hand, got a finger on the trigger, and then fired. The boom sounded like the sniper rifle that Joel had used when the mercenaries had had us holed up in a hotel a few weeks back.

Behind our men lay several military transports. They idled, with diesel rumbles that were reassuring, to say the least.

"Shit. Jumper swerved, but I think I winged him."

I pressed my hands to the sides of my head as the echo faded into the distance.

"His arm still on?" one of the men in fatigues asked.

"Probably just nicked him. Arm's intact but it ain't gonna work right ever again."

The shooter had a slow Southern drawl. He yanked a soft pack of smokes out of his trouser pocket, shook one out and put it in his mouth before fishing out a lighter.

"That's Perkins. He's pretty good with the long rifle. Thinks he bagged a jumper. Couldn't tell for sure, 'cause the green-eyed asshole fell back into the crowd back there." Ramirez pointed toward the front of the camper.

Joel pushed past me and surveyed the damage.

"What branch are you guys?" he asked.

"Rangers, mostly. It's all mixed company these days. We got a few Marines and some dude from the Air Force who wanted to learn how to shoot."

I chuckled and thought about spilling my story. The difference was I was in the Navy, and didn't want to shoot a goddamn thing for the rest of my life.

"Rangers, eh? What are you guys doing in California?"

"Shooting stuff, mostly," Ramirez said, and wiped his nose. "About two months ago we were sitting around an airport waiting to take off for other parts of the world when the place went batshit. We ended up being a good team, 'cept for Park back there. He hates to change his socks. You can't miss him. He's the big Korean dude."

"Fuck you, I only have two pair," the guy I presumed was Park said.

"Anyway, what are you folks doing out in the middle of the road surrounded by a horde of zulu?"

"Didn't plan it that way," I said. "We were headed for Pendleton when we got stuck in a house. Seems like the shufflers had it in for us."

"Shufflers?"

"Those assholes with green eyes."

"That's pretty good. We call 'em jumpers, because that's what they like to do. Think those fuckers had springs in their feet," Ramirez said.

"We've seen them do some crazy shit," I said.

"So have we. Things are spooky," Ramirez said. "You have a problem, friends. Pendleton fell during the first few days."

Joel stared at the ground for a couple of seconds and didn't say a word.

"Sorry, Joel," I said, but it sounded lame. All of our plans had hinged on reaching Pendleton, reuniting with his Marine brothers, and then going from there. I didn't know what was supposed to happen after that; all I knew was that Joel Kelly had saved my ass and we were in this together.

"Before we start getting too friendly, you guys planning to take our shit?" Joel interrupted. He didn't exactly point his AR-15 at anyone, but he sure seemed like he was going to at any second.

"That wouldn't be very neighborly," Ramirez said. He removed his Kevlar helmet and pushed back his mop of black hair a few times.

"No it would not," Joel said.

I nodded, unsure of what to do. I'd back Joel, of course,

because he was generally smarter about these kinds of situations. After McQuinn, I tended to trust nobody.

"We're gathering survivors, and if you all can shoot, that's even more reason to join us. Jumpers are on the move, driving a horde on a couple of outposts, and we need all the help we can get," Ramirez said.

"One of ours is hurt. She was attacked by a shuff--I mean jumper--a half hour ago. Can you do anything for her at this base?" I asked.

Joel stiffened next to me.

"Probably. We have a medical team that stays pretty busy. If we get back before morning mess, we can get her seen. Means we gotta haul ass, though. Are you planning to follow in that piece a shit? No offense to anyone, but it's full a holes and covered in blood and guts," Ramirez said as he looked the vehicle over.

"This is too good to be true." Joel said what I was thinking.

"No sweat if you want to make your own way. We're not exactly in the habit of forcing people to join us. You want to move on, be my guest," Ramirez said. "Probably be in your best interest to take a trip to base. You ask me, we're about the best hope around these parts."

The others checked their weapons or moved around the vehicles, looking over the twice-dead. I couldn't help but feel like they were trying to surround us.

One of the guys took out a huge knife, leaned over, and stabbed a still-moving Z in the head. It took a pair of blows to crack the poor bastard's skull, but after a few seconds it stopped moving.

Anna dropped to the ground next to us and sized up Ramirez.

"Bright Star," she said, pointing at the skull pin on his collar.

"Involuntarily, but yeah," Ramirez nodded. "More like a joint task force. I got recruited a month ago. The rest of us fall under their purview, but for the most part we're peacekeepers." Ramirez shot her a tight smile.

"I'm Lieutenant Commander Sails," she nodded at Ramirez.

He popped a tight salute and then grinned at her. "You could say you're a captain for all I know, but it's good. We get you all back to base and get you sorted and you can start cracking orders. Until then, if you want our help, I'd appreciate it if you did what I asked and when I asked."

"He's okay," Anna said to us. "Unless he took that little symbol off a body. You in the business of looting and killing?"

"No ma'am. We're a little rough around the edges but we're good guys. 'Cept Park. He's real grumpy because he hasn't had kimchee in a few weeks. Personally I think the stuff is disgusting. Give me some crap bastardized Mexican food any day. Know what I miss most? You're gonna laugh. I miss Taco Time. Worst excuse for Mexican food in the entire world but it used to taste like fucking heaven."

I practically started to drool.

"Just like that?" Joel asked. "He comes in, says a few nice things, and we're going to trust these guys."

"Hey man, we just saved you," the guy with the big knife said. "A little gratitude would be appreciated."

"Not saying we're not grateful, just cautious. We've had problems," Joel said. "The worst shit in the world brings out the worst shit in people."

"We all got problems, brother. There's a bunch of quasi-dead fucks out there with a taste for meat and we're their main food source. We'll just leave you to your business. Have a good night, folks."

"Cook, that was some action hero line there, taste for meat, someone give this guy an Oscar," Ramirez chuckled.

"I'm just here to chew bubble gum and kick some ass. I'm all out of bubble gum," Cook said.

"Fucking shoot me now," Ramirez sighed.

06:25 hours approximate
Location: Just outside of Oceanside

RAMIREZ NODDED AT ONE OF HIS COMPANIONS AND TOGETHER THEY moved into formation.

"Wait," Anna said. "Tell us where we're going and we'll follow."

"Make up your frigging minds. We're about ten miles from base and it's a *long* ten with all those zulu and crap littering the roads. You want to follow us and we'll lead you to Obstacle Charlie. You check in and go about your business and we'll go about ours. But we don't know you all from Adam, so I'd appreciate it if you follow my lead. Sound good?"

I didn't know what to say. These guys had saved us, but we didn't know the first thing about them except that they seemed to operate out of some mythical base that was all puppy dogs and unicorn rainbows.

"Let's get the truck running and go with them," Joel said. "If Pendleton is toast then we don't have anywhere else to go, except to find a new home and wait for it to get overrun. Besides, these guys have enough firepower to take us out in a couple of seconds. If they wanted to kill us they would have done it already."

"Good point, I guess," I grumbled.

"Let's just get this rig moving and see where the day takes us," Anna said.

Roz thrashed once, then curled up in a ball. I moved to the door to check on her. She had her hands clenched to her stomach like they were holding in her guts. Her head whipped back so hard I thought she was going to snap her neck.

Ramirez poked his head inside the camper, then pushed past us. Anna reacted with a "Wait!" but he was already up the stairs. He slipped on a couple of spent shells, shoved aside a bag of canned goods, and dropped beside Roz.

Anna shoved herself into the space next to him and kept her hand on her sidearm. I moved into the camper as well, my wrench in hand.

"Tell me what happened to her again?" He pushed aside her hair and studied the wounds on her face.

"She got jumped by one of the green-eyes. I didn't see it bite her, but he was busy trying to rip her mouth open or something. The blood might not all be hers, and the wounds don't seem that bad."

He set a hand next to her, avoiding the glob of puke she'd spit up, and leaned in to peel back an eyelid. He slipped off a glove and felt her head.

"Did he put something in her mouth?"

"Dude. Why the fuck would a shuffler put something in her mouth?" I said.

He moved his hand down and pressed on her chest as she thrashed against his grip. She snarled and then her head snapped back again, hitting the floor hard enough to shake the camper.

"Don't know, but our mission just got more interesting. We need to get her back to the base as soon as possible."

"Damn straight," I said.

Ramirez triggered a mic near his neck and spoke a few commands. Men moved in and helped Roz and me down from the door. They weren't disrespectful, and when they got inside the camper they were very gentle with our friend.

A medic pushed aside one of the men and inspected the wounds on Roz's face. He ripped a Velcro closure and extracted a white package from a belt pouch. The medic took a pile of gauze and pressed it over Roz's wounds.

We were pushed out of the camper, and ended up huddling together. The clouds had been fat and grey, and I guess they'd decided they'd had enough of this day, because rain pissed down on us--sprinkles at first, before water fell in earnest.

"She's going to be okay, Joel," I said, and put a hand on his shoulder. I tried to forget his harsh words in the vehicle, but they still stung.

He shrugged me off, and moved to consult with one of the men who carried a submachine gun.

"Alright. We got our extract path cleared, now if this rig don't start, how do you feel about leaving it behind?"

Like most anything I'd gotten halfway attached to in this new world, I wasn't all that keen on leaving our home behind.

It wasn't even that I *liked* the piece of shit. It was just familiar, in what was about to become all-new and unfamiliar.

A mini-horde of Zs broke from cover and shambled toward us. The men around Ramirez were quick and dropped them one by one with timed shots. No one panicked; they just took care of business.

I shook my head to calm the ringing in my ears.

"We gotta call it, and soon. Many more Zs and we're just attracting attention with all of the shooting," one of Ramirez's men said.

"We have a lot of supplies in the truck," I said.

I moved to the front of the vehicle and inspected the damage. Blood, bits of clothing, and body parts were jammed into the grill. Most of the front end was crushed, and the bumper held on for dear life by a couple of bolts.

Frosty sat in the driver's seat like she was out for a Sunday drive. Her ears perked up when the new guys appeared next to me, and her lips rose. She issued a half-hearted growl.

I helped a guy pluck chunks out of the front of the truck. We both grimaced but took care of business. Another guy popped the hood and we looked at the engine. There was enough blood, guts, and chunks of stuff that resembled flesh to make a couple of horror movies.

"Cute dog," he said.

"Yeah she's cool. Likes to taunt Zs. Dog's been great on guard duty," I said.

I wasn't about to give them an excuse to leave her behind.

"Shit. I think that's half a hand stuck in the belt," I said, and grabbed a piece of clothing that had to have been a sleeve.

The sleeve *was* attached to a hand. The hand was jammed between a belt and a gear. Extracting the mess was an exercise I hoped to never repeat.

"Fire it up," my companion called.

The engine cranked, tried to turn over and died.

"We gotta call it," Ramirez yelled.

I looked around the side of the truck. His men were falling back into military transports that had appeared. They were drab shades of tan; they would have fit right in if we'd been engaged in Afghanistan.

More chunks, so I yanked them out as fast as I could. Bits of flesh were jammed in the radiator but there wasn't a whole lot I could do, short of hosing it down with a pressure washer.

They tried to start the engine again but it choked again.

"Fuck," I said in frustration.

"Hey man, we tried. Let's get the hell out of here before the main horde arrives," Cooper said.

"Main horde?"

"Yeah, be here in about an hour. We were scouting them when we came across the burning house. Good thing we came along. This bunch weren't nothing compared to the shitstorm's about to arrive."

I kicked the front of the truck a few times, hoping to loosen more crap. The man in the truck kept cranking, but it was no use.

"We're out of time. Delta squad, mount up," Ramirez called.

"Let's go, man." Cooper grabbed my sleeve and pulled.

A fresh batch of newly-undead broke from cover and came at us. I picked up my wrench, ready to bash heads to relieve some tension.

"That's just great," I muttered.

The men moved around me and then jogged toward the transports. I stared after them with contempt, because I was sure the truck would start if we took a few more minutes.

I kicked the grill again and then hit it with my wrench. The only thing that happened was the bumper gave up and hit the ground. I picked it up and lifted it over my head. "Screw you, Zs," I said, and flung it. The part fell well short and clattered across the pavement.

I stalked toward our new companions and wondered what we were in for.

REAVERS

06:55 hours approximate
Location: Just outside of Oceanside

The first order of business was to get Frosty out of the truck. She growled at the military guys, but they were flesh and living blood, so after a little coaxing she began to enjoy the attention. Most of the guys cautiously approached her and took turns patting her head. A few found treats in their pockets and bribed friendship.

Our new friends put Roz in the back of a military truck. When Joel tried to join her they politely, but firmly, pointed him in the direction of a HMMWV-looking beast of a truck. We piled in and I was reminded of our escape from the military hospital a month or so ago. We'd fled, Joel and I holding on for dear life while a gunner shot the Zs that pursued us.

When there was a break in the action, the warriors took turns inspecting weapons, reloading, and playing grab-ass. A woman with a scar across her face smacked a guy's hand away and then punched him in the chest, but she smiled and said something that made him laugh.

Joel and I took turns showing off our dog tags to Ramirez so we looked legit. One of the guys shook his head and looked away with a snort. Joel dug out a battered wallet and extracted his military ID. I had mine around here somewhere, but it was probably buried in the bottom of my bag. Ramirez looked Joel's over, looked at him a few times and then shook his hand.

"What's wrong with that guy who looked like someone pissed in his Cheerios?" I asked Joel after he and Ramirez were done with their little bonding moment.

"Could be we took the tags off a couple of dead bodies. He doesn't know us and we look like shit. When's the last time we tried to look like we belong in the military? That's why I dug out my ID."

"Who's got time for that Mickey Mouse bullshit? I'm glad to wake up every day. Shaving would be nice, sure, so would a shower, and a turkey and mashed potato dinner. None of that shit's gonna happen anytime soon."

Anna approached Ramirez and took him to the side. They spoke together for several minutes while she dug out a beat-up looking wallet and showed him the contents. Whatever she put in front of his face must have triggered something, because he nodded at her and then they both got very serious.

I drifted toward them, hoping to catch a hint of what the mysterious Anna Sails said, but she shot me a look and I gave up on learning her secrets.

Joel stowed his assault rifle in the back of a rig under the watchful eye of one of the men. I kept my wrench at my side and my gun in its holster. If they decided they needed to take our weapons, I was sure Anna and Joel would have a few choice words for them. Besides, we were outnumbered by a healthy margin, and we had a kid with us. As far as threats went, we were slightly above sad puppies.

Joel shook hands with a couple of men and crawled in the back of their vehicle. I tried to wave at him, to offer a half-assed flag of apology for our words earlier, but I didn't think he saw me.

Frosty stuck to Christy and followed her to our vehicle, licking every hand in sight as she passed soldiers. The woman with the scar on her face dropped to a crouch and cautiously pulled our dog into an embrace. Frosty looked at me with her big eyes, tongue lolling out as she waited patiently for the woman to let go.

Anna was done with her pep talk and joined us. She didn't meet my eye, but got into the back of the transport and settled in. She looked cool as she stared out the window. She had a look on her face I hadn't seen very often over the last few weeks: she was determined.

"I don't suppose you want to share your conversation with Ramirez?" I leaned over and whispered.

"I don't suppose you want to mind your own fucking business?" she shot back.

I bit off a retort when Christy crawled over Anna and sat between us. Frosty followed her and took up most of the floor space under Anna. Anna didn't mind, and told Frosty she was a good girl.

Christy looked very small and afraid. I dropped an arm around her shoulder and pulled her into me. She hugged me back.

"Are we going to be safe now?" Christy asked me.

"I hope so. I'm sick and tired of being on the run all the time."

"What if these guys aren't good and they want to, you know, *do* stuff to us?" Christy whispered.

"Then they'll have to go through me," I whispered back, trying to sound tough.

The rest of the crew piled into vehicles. Then someone gave a signal and we lurched into motion.

"What's the base like?" I asked our driver.

"Like a brick fucking fortress, brother. We got the Seabees to build the walls and they're about ten feet high. Got heavy equipment blocking some of the entrances. Talk about zulu-stoppers, this thing is meant to *sustain*. Regular choppers come in and drop supplies during the week. Then we got water coming in on the weekends. Sometimes we got us a surplus and you can even take a shower."

I didn't catch the guy's name, but he was sitting next to Ramirez. Ramirez, for his part, had stopped being Chatty Cathy.

If he had anything to interject about us or where we were going, he kept his mouth shut.

"How long has Obstacle, what was it, Echo, been there?"

"Outpost Obstacle Charlie. Been there for over a month now and we've repelled the best the goddamn jumpers threw at us, plus the Reavers. The worst assault was a week or so ago. We held our own and left a pile of bodies. Worst part was cleanup," he said.

"That's not the first time I've heard about the Reavers. Who are they?"

"Crazies, man. They want to run a cult or something--least, that's what I hear from up high. They fight the Zs, but they have a hard-on for those green-eyed bastards. I also heard they're working with the jumpers."

I shook my head. "So how'd the other bases go down?" I asked.

The man looked at Ramirez. The two exchanged a look, but the southerner didn't answer, and neither did Ramirez.

"Name's Cook, by the way. Freddy Cook."

We made our introductions. Sails did her thing where her voice changed as she announced she was a lieutenant commander.

"Well, ma'am. Sure is nice to have you all along for the ride," he said, and then went silent again.

We poked along roads, avoiding wrecks. Ramirez kept speaking into his microphone and advising which routes to avoid. We came across a mound of bodies, and everyone looked away. We passed a freeway entrance that was blocked by a semi that had crashed into the rail. Another car was wedged under the wreck.

The truck bumped over debris, and slowed when there was a pile-up ahead.

We moved away from the rural area and skirted a couple of shopping centers. Zs littered the roads and sidewalks--some moving, but most lying in heaps on the ground. There were a couple of times when I thought I saw green eyes regarding us, but I couldn't be sure in the light of day.

The driver found a back road and took to it at speed. We rolled past apartment buildings and gas stations, coffee stands, and convenience stores, all of which lay like wrecks of society. The few Zs we spotted kept to themselves.

We'd gone a few more miles when something in the distance caught my eye.

"What the hell is that?" Anna said, pointing out the disturbance.

Our ride slowed, because the vehicle ahead of us decelerated. Joel kept his eyes on the truck behind us, because Roz was in it. Ramirez said something into his microphone, and we all pulled over.

In the distance, something burned. We'd just left a fucking pile of ash behind us, and now there was a fire ahead.

Ramirez issued orders over his microphone. A couple of guys got out of the head vehicle and went to investigate.

"What's happening up there?" I asked.

"Might be civvies got stuck. Going to take a look," Ramirez said.

"What if it's Reavers?" I asked.

Anna snorted.

"What?" I argued. "Sounds like a bunch of wackos out there. Remember McQuinn?"

"I remember him well enough. I also remember that he got his ass kicked," Anna said.

"Bad stuff happens when the world goes to hell, man. People forget what it's like to be civilized. Luckily, part of the military survived and got organized. That's why we set up these bases and the battle lines. First month, it was all about survival. Now it's all about reestablishing order," Ramirez said.

Soldiers got out of trucks and set up a perimeter while a couple of them scouted ahead.

"What happened right after the outbreak? We've been on the run for a long time and we were on a ship when it all went down," I said.

"Not much to tell. World went to shit. Zulus became the enemy, as well as everyone's neighbor. When the power went out, that was the worst. You'd hear screaming and gunfire all night. Rapes, murders, it was like medi-fucking-eval times, brother. There were a lot more of us, but a lot of uniforms left and went looking for families. Some of us stayed and waited for order to be restored."

"Glad you all stuck it out. We've been playing hide and seek for weeks, and it sucked," I said.

"Yeah, man. I feel ya. Once we started establishing bases, there was an initiative put forward to clear the cities. Not easy, trust me on that one. We set up patrols that went out and made a lot of noise. They'd fall back, with a horde of the enemy in pursuit. Once they reached the line, we went to work and put them down. Set up big ditches and did the dirty deed. Thing was, we didn't have to shoot them all. Big old bulldozers moved in and pushed the bodies into the pits."

I shuddered.

"What happened to the Zs after that?" Joel said.

"We buried 'em under rocks and ten feet of dirt. Sometimes we demolished buildings and put the rubble in the tombs. Don't know how many we've put in the ground, but it's a lot."

Visions of Nazis stuffing graves with Jewish bodies filled my mind.

"That is fucked up," I said.

"The worst thing is that it's not even one percent of the dead. We have a long way to go."

It wasn't what I meant, but I let it go. No sense in arguing with our would-be rescuers.

The large truck that had been following maneuvered around us and then sped up the street.

I leaned forward and said, "Wait, Roz is in that truck."

"It's okay. Road's been cleared all the way back to base, and they need to get her into medical right away. We'll just take a look and then follow them," Ramirez answered.

"Will she be okay?" I asked.

He looked at me but didn't say a word.

"Any of you guys got .357 ammo?" Anna asked.

"I think Park has some, but he's in the other truck. We got a bunch of 5.56 and some .40. Thing is--and I'm not going to beat around the bush here, friends--we'd prefer if ya'll keep your weapons holstered. Now, I'm not saying you're bad people, but this is a bad world, and a bad world makes people do bad things."

He was right about that.

"We're not going to do anything stupid," Anna said.

"Didn't say you were, just stating that we all want to stay friends."

I sat back in my seat and stared out the window at the departing truck.

Ramirez got out, but Cook stayed in the running automobile. Anna was close behind Ramirez as he hit the ground. I sat for a few seconds, then decided that I didn't like the idea of sitting on my ass, so I followed them.

"Jackson?" Christy asked.

"Hang loose, dude. I'll be right back."

"What should I do?"

"Don't shoot anyone unless you have to, and keep an eye on that mongrel dog of ours," I added with a wink. Thing was, I wasn't leaving Christy alone in the vehicle with someone I didn't know. I stood near the door and kept an eye on Christy, but I also unlimbered my wrench.

Another transport came to a halt, and men popped out until there were five surrounding us. They moved crisply, and their gear and clothes, for the most part, were clean. Something I hadn't seen in a long time was military precision. These guys actually gave me hope.

07:10 hours approximate
Location: Just outside of Oceanside

RAMIREZ GATHERED HIS MEN UP INTO A SEMI-CIRCLE AND SAID A few words to them. He issued orders, checked on the status of his team, and asked questions about the fire. I found a free section of truck and leaned against it.

The respite was welcomed; we'd been running on pure adrenaline for the last few hours, and now my energy was fading. I wanted to sleep, so I took a deep breath, leaned back and closed my eyes for a few seconds.

Voices whispered around me as I drifted. Faces flashed, and memories of our flight from the house flooded my sleep-deprived mind.

Someone screamed in the distance, but I shook my head and fled from the horrors we'd seen over the last few days.

I closed my eyes again, but not for long.

Gunfire rattled me out half-sleep into full fucking alert. My heart hammered in my chest as more guns opened fire around us. Something clattered off the door, and that made me hit the deck.

Joel stood by the second transport, but when shots echoed, he moved into action. He reached into the back of the vehicle and tugged his assault rifle out of storage. Joel moved quickly toward the front of the car. The driver had already popped out of his seat and was looking for targets, gun at high ready.

A couple of guys took up station along the side of the road and pointed their guns. I stood around with my dick in my hands, wondering what to do. Gunfire? Check. Unknown assailants? Check.

I stayed next to the vehicle and tried to be small.

Rounds clattered across the back of the second vehicle. Joel lifted his rifle and aimed, but I couldn't tell what he was looking for. I risked a glance over the door, but all I saw were shadowy figures in the distance, moving away from the fire. They were armed, but I wasn't sure if they were friend or foe.

Ramirez yelled into his headset, looking for his team. He called to them several times.

"What's the word?" Joel yelled.

I decided that my word was "Get the fuck into the fight," and took out the XDM. Anna skirted the front of the vehicle until she reached my position.

Frosty growled from within the truck.

Men deployed from one of the other vehicles, dropping to the side of the road. They moved next to a low line of grass and took aim at the figures moving toward us.

A bullet whizzed overhead. I spun and tried to find the source, but I felt very much like a bug under a flyswatter I couldn't see coming.

Ramirez dropped to his knee, lifted his assault rifle, and fired in the direction of the houses along our side. Someone returned fire, so I hit the deck. Anna was right next to me. She pulled her Smith & Wesson and aimed.

"Who the hell is shooting at us?" I asked.

She shook her head.

"Suppressing fire there," Ramirez yelled and pointed at a house. "I want a line of fire on our six. Collins, and Mertz, don't shoot until you're sure, but when you're sure, make it count. I'm ready to call it but we need to hear back from our patrol."

"Got it, Sarge," one of the guys called back.

"Perkins, find me some targets and erase them. Park, set up the big gun."

I thought about hiding under the vehicle, but with my luck I'd probably get run over as soon as they decided to haul ass.

"I got movement at ten o'clock. I'm going to drop them unless it's our patrol," Joel said.

"We don't know yet," Ramirez said.

I hustled to the rear of the vehicle and put Joel between me and them. I'd taken out my 9mm, but no one had told me which direction to shoot in.

I held the 9mm next to my chest, hoping a target would present itself. Ramirez squatted next to me and screamed orders into his headset. It was all "Move here, bring in guys there, cover this, and cover that." He called for support and got a positive response, based on his tone. This was all very reassuring, because I didn't think I could clench my butt cheeks any tighter if I tried.

"Suppressive fire!" yelled Park and turned his gun on a house at our ten o'clock.

Joel Kelly joined in and ripped a few shots at windows. Glass shattered and holes appeared. I'd never in my entire life wanted to be hidden inside a tank until this moment.

One of the guys in the lead vehicle hit the ground and ran to an outcropping of rock. He slid behind cover and quickly popped up and fired. Another man was hot on his heels and slid next to him.

"Movement at three o'clock," someone yelled.

"Let 'em pass. That's Eakins and Ellis back from scouting the fire. When they get here we are going to evac. Cooper, lay down some smoke."

"You got it, boss," Cooper said.

"More movement on our twelve," one of the men called.

Ramirez did a quick scan of the area.

"Alright, gents, we have no more than ten hostiles. I want them put down. Ellis and Eakins, flank that low hill. You see anyone in black, you put 'em down. Park, I want you taking down targets in those houses. Cook, you and me are going to lead the assault."

"Assault?" I swallowed.

"Just stay here and try not to get shot," Ramirez said.

Joel tagged along with Ramirez and Cook as they moved out. The three moved quickly, assault rifles on shoulders as they ran.

A Reaver got brave, popped up and fired on the men, but he shot wildly. He didn't get a chance to fire another volley; he was blown off his feet when Joel Kelly put a pair of bullets through his chest.

A couple of figures fled the house and ran across the street. Park opened fire on their location and tagged one. He fell to the ground, his buddy dropping next to him, then fired a few rounds in our direction.

Park hit the ground, and before he could return fire, the pair had hobbled around the side of another house. Park didn't give up, and shot at the location for a few seconds. The men did not reappear.

The helicopter thumped overhead as it took up station. The

Reavers must have decided they'd had enough, because they turned and ran. More gunfire was exchanged.

Cooper pulled a pair of grenades from his pack and handed one to Joel. They nodded at each other and almost in unison pulled pins and tossed. A pair of pops echoed and then smoke rolled out and began to cover us from the houses.

"Second floor window, more movement," one of the men behind the rock called.

His partner, Park, turned his big-ass machine gun on the area and opened up. Whatever he was using to shoot with required the gun to have a bipod deployed from near the barrel of the gun. He grabbed it, and it looked like he was holding on for dear life as it rattled. His partner dropped to the side with his hands pressed to his ears as guns boomed.

The window and surrounding wall became shattered glass and shards of wood as rounds punched into the home. Someone screamed, but not for very long.

The gunner shifted his aim and lit up another section of the house.

"Fall back, Ellis and Eakins are here. We're moving out," Ramirez yelled.

His men moved fast, grabbing gear, slinging guns, keeping low, and moving to the vehicles. All told, it couldn't have taken more than ten seconds for them to get back into the trucks and prepare to drive us anywhere but here.

Anna stormed around the side of our truck, then paused to stare hard at something in the low outcropping of shrub near us. She lifted her revolver, and a pair of rounds snapped smartly.

"More shufflers, but they are so damn fast," she said as she got back in the truck.

"Shufflers?" I huffed as I got back in the truck and slid next to Christy.

Frosty kept her head down, ears down, and tail tucked. I didn't blame her one bit.

As we piled in, she shrunk into the seat and huddled next to me. The lead vehicle moved out with ours close behind before doors had been shut.

A helicopter buzzed overhead, passed us, and then came back. I half-expected that it would fire on us, but instead it swung to the side and a rattling filled the air. We were a good twenty-five feet away, and expended rounds clattered across the pavement as a machine gun opened up. The front of a house blew inward. The shooter paused and shot again, blowing part of the second house to smithereens.

We were already on the move, but figures in black garb popped up on one side of the road. They were armed with machine guns and rocket launchers. I thought it was amazing that a full task force had arrived to help us--until they started shooting.

BATTLE LINES

07:45 hours approximate
Location: Just outside of Oceanside

The men reminded me of the crew that had been guarding the old woman's shop back in town--garbed from head to toe in black. Their ski masks didn't do much except add to the fact that they looked like assholes.

One thing I noticed was that they were somewhat uncoordinated. Not that *I* was an expert of military strategy, but these guys sort of ran to the edge of a hill and dropped. One of the men was a little overweight and tripped, nearly dropping his gun.

I stifled a laugh when several assault rifles turned on us.

"Who the fuck..." I didn't get to finish my sentence before they fired on us.

"Down," Ramirez screamed.

The truck ahead of us swerved and was hit by machine gun fire. An RPG round roared, but missed them and sailed away on a tail of smoke. It impacted with an apartment building and exploded, raining debris on the ground. Chunks rattled across the roof of our ride.

No offense to whoever built our vehicle, but a round that size would send us to a fiery death.

The helicopter turned and swept toward our position.

Rounds punched into the side of our truck. Christy screamed, so I grabbed her and pushed her into Anna, making them sink lower into the seat. Frosty moaned, but there was nothing I could do for the dog except keep her from freaking the fuck out.

The driver turned his head to take in the threat. Glass shattered as a round shattered a window. The driver jerked and slumped to the side. Ramirez leaned over and grabbed the wheel to steady the truck.

"Cook, Cook, hit it, man," Ramirez said.

I thought the driver was dead, but he jammed his foot into the floor and the truck responded by leaping forward.

The helicopter opened up with a pair of rocket rounds that exploded into the ground around the guys assaulting us.

I ran my hand over my arm and side to make sure I wasn't hit, because the shockwave felt like it took a layer of skin off.

"Shoot back," Anna said and handed me her gun. She put an arm protectively around Christy and held her close.

I took the gun and sat up. Figures swarmed before me. I aimed and pulled the trigger, and regretted the blast that echoed around the interior. I clearly missed, so I guessed at the way the truck was darting and led my next target with the reticules. The gun boomed in my hands and a man slumped to the side, catching his friend and dragging him to the ground. I fired again and missed.

"I suck at this," I muttered.

"You did great, Creed," Anna said.

We'd moved past the line of shooters, most of whom were scattering now that we had air support. Another truck took a turn and came up behind us. I thought it was one of our guys, but when bullets peppered the back of the car, I realized they were also gunning for us.

Ramirez screamed more orders into his headset. I wished I could shoot back, but the rear of the vehicle was closed off and angled downward. The engineer part of my brain told me that it was probably designed to deflect shots, and the want-to-stay-alive part of my brain warned me that with enough power, a bunch of rounds would turn us into spaghetti.

The helicopter swung around again and opened fire on the pursuing truck. Thank the fuck Christ for the boys in that bird. If not for them, we'd have been toast.

Ramirez yanked the wheel hard to avoid an abandoned car. We swiped the truck's side, but managed to stay on the road.

Bullets hit the truck again, and we nearly went off the road when the driver overcorrected. Anna came out of the seat, still holding Christy. She slapped her hand against the roof and pushed them both back down.

I'd nearly dropped the gun as I reached for them both. Anna shot me a look of consternation, so I handed her pistol back. She took it, and then swiveled to her side and pressed her left arm against the door. She popped up out of the remains of the window, brushing aside safety glass on her way.

The helicopter skewed away from us and then spun hard. I caught the shadow as the blades cut into the sunlight, fuselage temporarily hiding the sun. The truck pursuing us took a small road that was covered with trees.

Something rocketed across the sky, trailing smoke. The chopper swerved, hard to port, and the missile flew by.

"What the fuck is going on out there?" I yelled.

The figure of Joel Kelly appeared in the truck ahead of us. He came out of the window and braced his upper body against the window. Anna on our left side, Joel on the lead vehicle's right, me holding onto a little girl. That pretty much summed up my life.

Joel must have taken issue with something ahead. He aimed, and fired rapidly. I knew that guy pretty well. He was usually calm, and reserved ammo whenever possible, so he must have been pissed.

Something slammed into the truck--*several* somethings. The driver held onto his side and groaned, but he and Ramirez kept the truck from running off the road.

The chopper faded back as another something whistled through the air. I hesitated to even call them missiles, because we were the *good* guys, right? We were the men and women fighting the hordes of Zs. This new world might suck, but it didn't have the right to throw *this* at us.

Ramirez cocked his head to the side. "Our air support is pulling back until they figure out who the hell is firing on them," he said over his shoulder.

"Then who's going to cover us?" I asked.

"You figure that out, I'll give you a gold fucking star."

"Great. Always wanted to be an admiral," I said, trying to sound like a smartass. Truth was, I was scared to death. We were in a high-speed tin can, being fired on by unknown assailants.

"No worries, we're close to the base now. Should be just over that rise," Ramirez said.

Joel emptied another magazine and then popped back into the truck.

Something took shape in the road. More guys in uniform? I strained to make out who they were, and realized there were a bunch of Zs with a couple of shufflers guiding them. The only good news was that they were facing away from us. So who were they after?

08:20 hours approximate
Location: Just outside of Oceanside

THE DAY WAS GRAY AND THE SKY WAS FAT WITH CLOUDS. LOOKED like it was about to piss rain on this part of the state. The landscape around us was a mess of dilapidated buildings that had probably been high-end stores a few months ago. Now they were battered and abused. Doors hung open, windows had been shattered, and mannequins, boxes, clothes, bags, and all kinds of crap were scattered among a host of roving Zs.

We'd pulled ahead of the battle and, I hoped, away from the guys shooting at us for good. After the battle at the house, I'd had enough of guys firing on me to get through the next six months.

A pair of pickups cut across the road and roared off to a side street. Joel aimed and fired. It wasn't until later that I thought to even ask if he knew who he was shooting at.

A third vehicle followed. It was a big Chevy Tahoe that had been spray-painted with green and gray. The windows were darkened, but the rear one cracked open, slid down, and revealed a guy with a machine gun. He leaned out and fired on the lead vehicle. Joel fired back and then popped back into the truck.

"Shoot back, Creed," Anna said.

The SUV roared away and followed the other trucks.

"They're gone," I said lamely.

The helicopter reappeared and squatted over our position. Ramirez shouted commands into his mic.

Our truck slowed to a crawl and the chopper kept pace over us. Then it must have gotten the green light to pursue, because it flew after the trucks.

"Why are they fucking around and shooting at us?" I asked.

"Million dollar question. Best we can figure, given reports at base, they're launching a full-scale assault on Fort Obstacle. We're to get back with a quickness and bring some thunder."

"Hooah," Cook said.

A pair of cars roared up on us, *Mad Max*-style. They were modified SUVs fitted with some kind of armor plating. They came parallel with us, and gunfire sounded. We got low in the backseat as rounds exploded around Joel's truck.

The HMMWV swerved onto the road and we followed, Cook fighting the wheel as he spun so hard I nearly turned Christy into a pancake.

More gunfire rattled around us, and that's when our salvation came into sight.

The base was just as they'd described it: walls had been set up in a semi-circle around a couple of buildings. Along the perimeter sat four taller lookout stations that couldn't have been more than thirty feet high. The walls were lined with razor wire and spikes. Along the wall lay piles of the dead.

A bulldozer sat near a curb, hulking and cold. Yellow paint had peeled in places, and the scoop was a dark red. I didn't need anyone to explain to me that it was dyed that color from blood.

Something in the distance caught my attention. I struggled to make out what I was seeing. Like a black wave, it shuddered as it strode the ground. "Massive" didn't even begin to describe it. I rubbed my eyes, shook my head, and squinted. Optical illusion brought on by smoke and adrenaline? An army of bad guys on the move?

I knew what it was, but my mind sank into the land of denial.

Something whistled five feet off the deck and exploded as it struck one of the walls. The East side was under assault, and entire sections had been blown away. A piece of heavy machinery moved into place and pushed the remains of the wall back into place. Then, it stopped. A couple of guys in green hopped out, firing into the distance as they hit the ground.

"Fucking Reavers," breathed Ramirez.

The helicopter flashed across the sky, having hopefully dealt with the trucks, and came to hover just over the base. It swept left and then paused so the gunner could concentrate fire on a location to the East.

Assault rifles hammered in the morning air.

"What the hell is going on?" was all I could manage. *Brilliant.*

"I'm scared, Jackson," Christy said.

I pulled her close and told her I was also scared, but that didn't help. She probably wanted me to go all Joel Kelly and figure out how to shoot the bad guys.

That's when the morning was shaken by an explosion that smashed into Joel's truck. The vehicle tilted a full three feet and then slammed to the ground. The force of the explosion pushed the truck off the road and into the gutter.

"IED!" Cook yelled.

They brought the truck to a fast halt, and Ramirez and Cook poured out. The truck behind us slammed on its brakes, and more men filled the street. They set up a perimeter while our driver and Ramirez ran to the truck.

Joel fell out, looking dazed and confused. He held his hand to his ear, but damn if that tough Marine still kept his AR in one hand. He sat down hard in the middle of the street and looked around. His eyes were unfocused and he shook his head. Blood dripped from his hands.

I was already out of the truck and on my way to help Joel. Something whistled over the ground and then roared past me. The RPG round smashed into the truck behind us and exploded. I hit the ground hard enough to see stars and the breath left my body. I rolled over, ears ringing, and stared at the sky.

Christy and Anna fell out of our truck, followed by Frosty, and made for me.

"Ambush, get off the street," Ramirez yelled.

A man near me dropped, and didn't move again. More gunfire rattled around me.

Anna was the last out. She helped me up, and together we stumbled to the side of the road, with Christy and Frosty hot on our heels. Anna held her pistol as we bolted for cover.

I felt dazed, like someone had punched me upside the head. My ears still rang and I got a case of vertigo so strong I dropped to my hands and knees.

"Get up, Creed. Get the fuck up and head for the trees," Anna yelled, but her voice sounded hollow, like she was yelling inside a room filled with mattresses.

Christy grabbed my arm and pulled. I looked up, and her face was frozen in shock. She yelled at me, but I couldn't understand her. Frosty nipped at Christy's arm, but she pushed the dog away.

I rolled over and struggled to breathe. Bullets rattled around me, so I hit the deck again. Always make yourself a small target: that was Joel's advice.

Ramirez turned and returned fire. He laid a line of fire on a building across from us. Rounds punched into walls and shattered windows. The roar of gunfire was a muddled mess in my head.

I got to my hands and knees again and decided that I didn't want to be a target, so I staggered--yeah, just like a Z--toward an apartment building that looked as if fire had taken it a few weeks ago. Christy stuck to me, and Frosty ran ahead.

We reached a caved-in doorway and dropped next to a set of concrete stairs. I reached for my gun, but it wasn't there. My backpack was in the rear of the truck, and with it, my backup weapon. The only things I had on me were a knife and my trusty wrench. I knew the heavy tool was still strapped under my arm, because I'd felt every bang as it repeatedly struck my ribs and side.

Christy pushed Frosty down and together we huddled while the air filled with bullets.

08:20 hours approximate
Location: Just outside of Oceanside

A ROUND KICKED UP DIRT NEAR ME, SO I GRABBED CHRISTY'S HAND and we dodged into the darkness the doorway offered. We stuck to walls, and stepped over debris and the remains of the door.

I poked my head around the corner and found that the military had set up a line of fire and were giving back as much as they'd taken. It was like a scene from a documentary on the battles in Afghanistan. They ducked and moved, found cover, and fired back.

The wave continued to advance. They weren't headed directly for us; more at an angle that might keep them off our path. The thing in *their* direct path, however, was Fort Obstacle.

I caught Joel's shape and noticed that he'd given up his AR in favor of the big rifle Park had carried, which didn't bode well for him. Joel dug in next to a tree, lifted the big weapon and fired. The boom echoed around the battlefield.

Perkins appeared next to Joel and yelled something in his ear. Joel nodded and fell back.

The thumping of a helicopter sounded, and a big one appeared. It was fat and had a flat bottom. A guy manned a machine gun and unleashed a few hundred rounds. A building fifty yards away took the brunt of the gunfire. Walls blew inward, and glass and wood fell.

The chopper hovered low, then nearly touched the ground.

Ramirez strode to the truck we'd arrived in. He yelled commands and waved hand gestures at his remaining men.

Something moaned in the darkness behind us.

"Creed, I think there's a Z in here," Christy said.

I made the mistake of lingering near the doorway, and a couple of bullets struck the wood above me. I grabbed Christy and we moved into the building. It was either face a Z or try to run back to the truck while we were shot at.

Anna and Joel wouldn't leave us behind. They were probably on the way now.

The first apartment door had been caved in. The room was filled with overturned furniture and a pair of rotting bodies.

"We need to find a way out the back. Keep Frosty close," I whispered.

Christy nodded.

A pair of doors on either side of us had also been broken in. We found more of the same: overturned rooms, clothes in heaps, dishes smashed on the floor, and blood.

The helicopter fired a few more times, and then the thump of blades faded as the chopper departed the area.

08:30 hours approximate
Location: Just outside of Oceanside

THE Z STUMBLED OUT OF A DOORWAY AND RIGHT SMACK INTO ME.

I managed to push him back, but he was a *hungry* fucker. His milky white eyes fixed on me. He wore a bathrobe that had probably been tan at one time. Now it was the same color as the shitty apartment he'd been hanging out in: blood and dirt.

He grabbed my arm and I swung him around and into the wall. He struck it, and then stumbled right back into me. Following the explosion I was still rattled; it was all I could do to keep him from getting his head in close.

Frosty was having none of this. The dog grabbed his robe, growled low in her throat, and thrashed her head from side to side as she pulled him off me.

Christy picked up a chunk of wood and pushed him back into the room.

He tripped over the remains of his door and fell over. Legs kicked, and feet scrambled for purchase. Frosty bit at his ankle and shook him again. I pulled her off, and then motioned for Christy to step back.

I unlimbered my wrench, and when the Z turned and started to crawl toward me, I swung hard and smashed his head to a pulp, but it took every ounce of energy. The entire morning was crashing in on me. Fleeing from the house, surrounded on all sides by Zs, shooting from moving vehicles, and the attack on our rescuers. It was too much. I wanted to find a little room, curl up in a ball, and sleep for about three days.

"We need to get out of here now," I told Christy.

"I know. I'm scared, Jackson. Can we please find Anna and Joel?"

"That's the order of business, but someone's shooting at us from the front of the building. We need to find a way out the back," I said, and grabbed her hand and tugged her behind me.

She nodded as we moved, and offered me her revolver. I looked at the little weapon.

"Hang onto it, dude. If things get hairy you know how to use it. I'll stick to my club," I said.

We ran down the hallway, past rooms filled with more debris and Zs. As we moved, they followed until they crowded the hallway behind us. Jesus Christ! The minute we ran into a dead end, we were going to be devoured.

A Z staggered out of the room ahead of me and I crushed him with the wrench. Christy turned and fired, hitting one in the chest. It didn't put him down, but it was enough to make a minor roadblock when he fell back into a mass.

Frosty nipped at a Z but kept well away. The dog was smarter than the two of us combined, with her little antics.

I grabbed a door that was lying in the hallway and wedged it between two entryways. Not a great barrier, but it would buy us a few seconds.

We rounded a corner and there were two brutes ahead. One of the Zs was probably Samoan, and his female partner was just as large.

"How many bullets?" I asked Christy.

"Two, but I have a few more in my pocket," she called back.

"Take the woman, I got the big guy."

Christy moved to my flank, set her feet and aimed. The first shot went wide.

I advanced on the guy and hoped we weren't swarmed from behind. He swung at me, so I swung back. The wrench connected with a fleshy arm and he shifted to the side. He came at me again, so I kicked at his knee and connected with a shin. It was like kicking a tree trunk.

The woman barreled into me and I hit the wall. Christy maneuvered behind me and I prayed she didn't accidentally shoot me.

I backed up a half step, swung the wrench around, and cracked it against the big guy's arm. The blow was answered by the sound of crushed bones, but it didn't even faze him.

Frosty growled and dashed between the pair. She moved down the hallway, turned and barked. The Zs turned to check out the noise.

I didn't have much left. The last swing had taken my energy reserves from around five percent to zero.

Christy shouldered me aside, stepped into a shooter's

stance, and shot the woman in the head. She fell back, slapped the gun open and started to reload.

The big Z stepped on the woman and fell forward. He grabbed me as he went down, and took me to the ground. He trapped my legs under his big body and crawled toward me. He reeked of rot and old blood. What little clothing he wore was ripped and covered in gore. His mouth, coming toward my face, was all broken teeth, blue-rimmed lips, and pale gums. When they got me, I was going to be one dead squid.

The wrench was a hundred-pound barbell. I could barely lift it, and my swing was weaker than a six-year-old's. The head hit the Z and pissed him off even more.

I wedged the wrench under his chin and pushed up with both hands.

The Zs behind us stumbled over the half-assed barricade and closed on our position.

I tried to get my leg under the Z and use the maneuver Anna had performed on the shuffler the night before, but he was too heavy.

Christy saved me.

She lifted the Z's head by a clump of hair, put her revolver to his temple, and blew his brains out.

It took me precious seconds to wiggle out from under the mass. When we both staggered around the corner with a horde of fresh Zs on our ass, it was only to find the back emergency door.

I ignored the "Warning: Alarm Will Sound" sign, took a running start, and hit the door hard enough to rattle the wall. Thankfully it gave, and I crashed through and hit the ground. Christy and Frosty followed close behind, the dog coming to my side, tail wagging like she was laughing at me.

Christy acted fast and slammed the door shut. She picked up a piece of splintered wood and jammed it between the door and the frame, then kicked it until it was wedged in there tight. The Zs moaned behind the barricade, but they were stuck for now. However, the barricade wouldn't last for long.

I got to my feet and poked my head around the corner, cautious for any gunshots.

What I saw made me utter a long and well-deserved "Fuck!"

The wrecked trucks were still there and burning, but that was all. The helicopter was a blip as it sped across the sky. Whoever had been shooting at the military guys was also gone.

The battle was over.

The shapeless mass that had been advancing on the base was a little more visible now, and it was just as I'd suspected: an army of the dead, at least as large as the one we'd fled from in San Diego was moving on the base. Gunshots sounded, but the inhabitants must have become spooked, because an exodus was underway. Trucks departed at high speed, with men and women pouring out from the walls.

The place was about to be completely overrun, and we'd been left behind.

THE FUCKENING

09:00 hours approximate
Location: Just outside of Oceanside

I dropped to the ground and leaned my back against the apartment building wall. Zs pounded on the door, but I didn't care. We'd fought, run, escaped the odds, and now our friends were gone. Joel and Anna had left us behind. I stared up at the sky and wondered what we were supposed to do now.

Not only that, but a flood of Zs was about to overrun this entire area.

Christy grabbed my arm and tugged, but I pulled back.

"Jackson, we need to move. That door's not going to hold for very long," she pleaded.

"I know."

She stared at me, but didn't say another word. Frosty panted and watched the doorway. She sat next to me and leaned over to lick my face. I pushed her away.

I took a deep breath and got to my feet. No sense in sitting around waiting to be devoured. If I'd learned anything, it was that finding a place to hole up--even if it was for a few hours-- was more important than just about anything.

Christy took my hand, and together we moved out.

Instinct kicked in, taking all of ten seconds. Bob and weave; that was the idea. Joel used to say that you had to think about every move, think about the layout of the ground you were about to traverse. Look for places to hide, and always keep your head up and on the lookout.

But Joel was gone.

We didn't have much, besides a few weapons and our wits.

I pulled it together, stood, and struck out with my companions at my side.

We traversed a four-lane road and moved West until we'd gone a few miles--hopefully far away from the horde. We found a burned-out Albertsons, but didn't bother to poke our heads inside the building.

A strip mall sat across a parking lot, so we made for a T-Mobile store that featured broken windows, a smashed-in front door, and displays that used to feature the best of current technology. Cell phones, what a convenience they'd been. I could have picked up my phone and called Anna to find out where they'd run off to. The way Joel had been talking, he might have just decided to abandon my ass.

The employees' room was small and had been tossed, but we found a chair and managed to wedge it against the door. I was hungry. Christy was grumpy, and Frosty had gas. Somehow we managed to settle into the little room and curl up together.

"Do you think they'll come back for us?"

"I don't know. I hope they do, but we're a few miles away from the battle and they won't even know where to start looking," I replied.

We chatted for a few minutes, but weariness was heavy and I found my eyes closing.

"Want me to take first watch?" Christy asked.

"If Zs wander in here, we're dead anyway. Just get some rest," I said.

Christy didn't answer, but tears welled up in her eyes.

"I'm sorry, Christy. I feel like I let us down and now we're all alone," I said.

"We have each other and we have Frosty. She's a badass dog, you know," Christy smiled.

I smiled back.

14:00 hours approximate
Location: Just outside of Oceanside

WE ROSE A HALF DOZEN HOURS LATER.

Night was in full swing, and my stomach grumbled about the lack of food. Christy didn't complain, but I could tell she was hungry because she kept going through the remains of an overturned desk, looking for a morsel.

I dragged the chair out of the way and opened the door in slow motion. When fifty Zs didn't fall on us, I moved into the room, my wrench held up high.

I felt a little better, rested, but every inch of my body hurt. I had bruises in crazy places, and my arms were so sore I thought I'd be good for one or two blows at most if we ran across any Zs.

We ranged out and poked around a couple of stores, but they were long since emptied. We managed to find a can of baby formula that had been left in a bag of diapers, and took it. With no water, we weren't sure how to consume it. Christy gave a half-laugh as I tried to eat a little bit, but my mouth was so dry that I coughed it back up.

We'd need to make some water filters and soon, if we wanted to survive. Rain had come and gone, leaving puddles, but we weren't about to drink anything out of a pothole.

As morning faded into afternoon, we were still on the lookout for anything resembling food or water. Christy and I found another apartment building, but it had been stripped clean a few times over, with the exception of some clothes and a couple of blankets, not to mention all the abandoned furniture, smashed glasses and broken dishes.

But Joel and I had become good at looking in weird places. I pulled a high shelf out of a closet and we found a small bag of chips that had expired a year ago.

We gathered a few more small items, consisting of a couple of mints, a Hostess Twinkie that we would have to fight to the death over, and a single Diet Coke. We kept to doorways and under the cover of strip malls as we made our way back to the T-Mobile store. After poking around and making sure that no Zs had wandered into the store during the day, I wedged the chair against the door.

Christy looked as dejected as I felt, but we passed the soda back and forth and tried to outdo each other with belches. Then Christy got a fearful look in her eyes, so we went into silent running mode again.

We ate the little bit of food, and then Christy spent an inordinate amount of time nibbling her half of the stale Twinkie, while I devoured mine in one bite.

After an hour of staring at the wall, I heard a noise in the store. Christy checked the load in her revolver, and I tried to act like I was prepared for the worst by checking my wrench.

I slid the chair aside and slowly opened the door.

It was late and night had set in. I stared into the darkness, but nothing moved. It was just as we'd seen it a few hours ago, with its overturned chairs and broken displays laying like giant skeletons. I was about to close the door when a woman's voice spoke.

"Easy, bud. No harm meant."

I stiffened. I'd heard that phrase one too many times. "No harm" usually meant that someone meant some very serious fucking harm.

Frosty growled low in her throat.

"I know that look, and I promise it's cool. We were on patrol when I noticed this place. Thought I might pick up an old cell phone, you know, like the old days. Sometimes you get one with some juice and a few tunes pre-loaded. I've gone through five or six now. The best is when you find one in someone's pocket or bag and it's filled with jams. I miss music, man. Cute dog, by the way. Hope she doesn't try to eat my face."

I didn't say a word but touched Frosty's head to reassure her.

She'd been squatting next to a pile of boxes--stuff we'd been through and tossed aside. She stood up on creaking knees and lowered her rifle. The gun looked like something Joel Kelly would have fallen in love with.

The woman was dressed in black and wore straps and a belt, from which a number of weapons hung: a sidearm, a pair of knives, a flashlight, multiple magazines, and what looked like a canister of pepper spray. She appeared to be a little younger than me, and had a pair of big brown eyes with arched eyebrows.

"You alone?" she asked.

"We don't want any trouble, truly. We've seen enough crazy shit over the last few weeks to last a lifetime," I said.

"We. Got it, so there's more than one. Listen, I know I look like I might be as dangerous as a flea, but I'm pretty fast with this gun. Plus, one whistle and this place will be swarming. Why don't you come out and join us? We're heading back to base, and we have hot food, water, and even a place to sleep," she said.

I swallowed back a curt "No," but my stomach grumbled loud enough to attract a couple of shufflers.

"Wait, base? You're from the military base?"

"Not those guys. Bunch of assholes trying to destroy the world, and we're trying to rebuild it. You'd think that the z-poc would bring people together, but it just made the divide even deeper. That's why we need some fresh blood. Just come on out and after we talk, I promise you that if you don't like me and my friends you can just fuck off on your way and go find a nice horde to party with."

Christy pushed past me into the room and studied the woman. She held her revolver in one hand, but it hung at her side. Frosty wandered into the room and sniffed the woman's leg.

She stayed still while the dog checked her out.

"I'm confused. We saw a battle earlier." I was careful not to show any complicity on either side. "We didn't want to get caught in the middle, so we've been in hiding. We lost our gear."

"That battle was a real fucking mess, friend. Didn't want any part of it, but they started shooting at us. We were scouting that massive horde when someone in a truck opened fire on one of our vehicles."

"Wow," I said, trying to play it cool. When we'd been heading back to base one of the military trucks had been blown half off the road. I clearly remember one of the men yelling "IED".

"It was a real clusterfuck," she said and reached down to let Frosty sniff her hand.

"So you got attacked, and then what?"

"Not much else. Returned fire, took a few losses, but that horde was closing in on the new Bright Star base, and we wanted nothing to do with a hundred thousand Zs." She slipped off a black cap and rubbed at her forehead.

"Jackson?" Christy asked.

I put my hand in hers and gripped it tight.

"I'm confused. Who are you with?"

"Easy enough, friend. They started calling us Reavers because it sounds more ominous than 'the others'. Sounds silly when you think about it, especially with us fighting to liberate cities while they are fighting to lock them down. Containment, they call it, but I call it a prison. Enough about all that stuff. Just understand that we're the good guys."

The ground rocked beneath us. I threw my hands out to grab for anything but ended up catching Christy. We both went to the ground in a heap. Frosty ran back into our little improvised room and cowered.

The woman sat down and looked, worried. No. She looked like she was about to shit bricks.

"That is not good. They're moving much faster than we'd anticipated," she said.

A roar built and passed over us taking more than a few

seconds to pass. The building shook so hard I thought it was going to fall apart.

"The fuck was that?" I realized I was yelling.

"They just nuked LA. The new plan is sterilization; build on what's left after the earth's been cleansed. Never mind that it's going to poison everything with radiation. Fuckers," she said.

I shook my head at the absurdity. I helped Christy off the ground and together we moved to the door. I stepped over shattered glass and poked our heads outside.

Much to my horror, I found that the woman hadn't lied because a mushroom cloud rose far to the North.

I nodded, unable to find words, because the entire world was nuts, and we were right in the middle of The Fuckening.

This is Machinist Mate First Class Jackson Creed, and I am still alive.

Check out the next 3 books in the Z-RISEN universe!

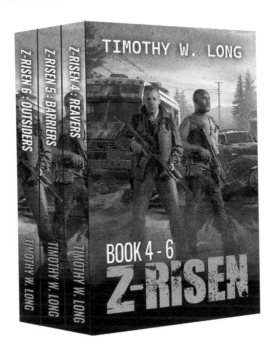

ABOUT THE AUTHOR

Timothy W. Long has been writing tales and stories since he could hold a crayon and has read enough books to choke a landfill. He has a fascination with all things zombies, a predilection for weird literature, and a deep-seated need to jot words on paper and thrust them at people.

Tim is the author of 25 novels. His works include The Bradley Adams series about a second civil war in America. The buddy zombie series Z-RISEN, as well as the seminal zombie classic Among the Living series.

Tim also co-wrote the post-apocalyptic novel The Apocalypse and Satan's Glory Hole with Sir Jonathan Moon. This book was recently named the preferred version of the end of the world by rapture survivors everywhere. True story.

Tim lives in the Seattle area with his wife constant inspiration Katie Cord. Four dogs of various sizes and dispositions share his home as well as a Bengal cat named LucyFurr

www.timothywlong.com
stupidzombies@gmail.com

BIBLIOGRAPHY

Z-Risen Series
Z-Risen 1: Outbreak
Z-Risen 2: Outcasts
Z-Risen 3: Poisoned Earth
Z-Risen 4: Reavers
Z-Risen 5: Barriers
Z-Risen 6: Outsiders
Z-Risen 7: Survivors (Forthcoming)
Z-Risen 8: Fortress (Forthcoming)
Beyond the Barriers (From the Z-Risen Universe)
Day of the Rage Apocalypse (From the Z-Risen Universe)

Bradley Adams Series
Drums of War
March to War
Casualties of War

Among the Living Series
Among the Living
Among the Dead

Other Works
Forged in the Fires of Heaven
Chicken Dinner
The Front: Screaming Eagles w/David Moody and Craig DiLouie
Impact Earth
Damaged w/Tim Marquitz
At the Behest of the Dead
The Zombie Wilson Diaries
The Apocalypse and Satan's Glory Hole w/Jonathan Moon

Enter the Realm
Dr. Spengle and the Unicorn Horror

58999627R00326